LAST TRAIN
FROM CUERNAVACA

Forge Books by Lucia St. Clair Robson

Ghost Warrior

Last Train from Cuernavaca

Shadow Patriots

The Tokaido Road

LAST TRAIN
FROM CUERNAVACA

LUCIA ST. CLAIR ROBSON

A TOM DOHERTY ASSOCIATES BOOK

NEW YORK

This is a work of fiction. All of the characters, organizations, and events portrayed in this novel are either products of the author's imagination or are used fictitiously.

LAST TRAIN FROM CUERNAVACA

A Forge Book
Published by Tom Doherty Associates, LLC
175 Fifth Avenue
New York, NY 10010

www.tor-forge.com

Forge® is a registered trademark of Tom Doherty Associates, LLC.

ISBN 978-0-7653-1335-5

First Edition: April 2010

Printed in the United States of America

0 9 8 7 6 5 4 3 2 1

This book is dedicated to the courageous souls who put themselves in harm's way to defend freedom and justice, but with a special measure of gratitude for the women who go to war.

ACKNOWLEDGMENTS

A work of historical fiction is impossible without help from a lot of people. My first debt of gratitude is to historians who chronicle events so they won't be forgotten by the rest of us. I especially admire Rosa King and Angelina Jimenez for their fortitude during extremely difficult and dangerous times and for leaving vivid accounts of their experiences.

Several people provided assistance during my stay in Cuernavaca. Special thanks go to William J. Cummins, creator, owner, host, and gourmet chef of the lovely Inn Cuernavaca, and to his grandson Nikita Andrew Schupbach. They were a mine of information about the city and its surroundings.

Lic. Rene Sanchez Beltran wrote the introduction to the Spanish edition of Rosa King's book, *Tempest over Mexico,* and he informed me of the whereabouts of the village so important to this story and to Rosa's. Without his knowledge I would not have known it still existed. His wife, Sra. Azalia Silva de Sanchez, manages Internet Siglo XXI, the cyber café in the building that was Rosa King's old Bella Vista hotel. Finding Sra. Sanchez and her husband was one of those serendipitous encounters that make research trips fun and fascinating.

Long-time residents James Sartin and Mel Puterbaugh shared with me a book of hundreds of photos taken in Cuernavaca from 1857 to 1930. Because of their generosity I could describe details that I would not have known about otherwise.

Sr. Onesimo Gonzalez, secretary of tourism and curator of the exhibit of old photographs in the Museo del Castillito, was also very informative.

I counted a great deal on the knowledge of friends. James Luceno provided insight into Mexican culture and customs and gave me obscure words and phrases that would have been in use a hundred years ago.

What David Eccles and Eric McCallister Smith know about guns continues to amaze me. If mistakes in weaponry appear here, it's because I neglected to clear the terminology with them.

Elaine Nash is an expert on horses. She set me straight on their behavior in general and on Andalusians in particular.

Dr. Terry DelBene, archaeologist, historian, and reenactor, knows a thing or six about dynamite and the niceties of blowing up a train. Always useful information in a revolution.

Inspiration for the book's title came from a story that appeared in *True West* magazine in 1986. The story, "Last Train from Cuernavaca," was coauthored by the late Dr. George Agogino and Lynda A. Sanchez. My thanks to Ms. Sanchez for graciously sharing the title with me.

I'm grateful to my erudite and patient editor, Bob Gleason, and to Tom Doherty of Tom Doherty Associates. Thanks also to my literary agent, Mel Berger, and to my former agent, Ginger Barber, who encouraged, inspired, and abetted me for twenty years.

As always, I'm indebted to Ginny Stibolt for her friendship, wise counsel, and Web site expertise.

Mid-November 1912

Why pay the peasant more when he will only drink away the extra money?
> —A hacienda owner in the state of Morelos

Hitch up your pants. The road we must follow is defiance.
> —General Emiliano Zapata

I

A CAKE WALK

Captain Federico Martín loved everything about women, but this was the first time he had fallen for a pair of pale English hands. Their owner sat so upright and Anglican on the piano bench that it could have been a church pew, but her long, supple fingers harbored no piety. They chased the syncopated lilt of the "Maple Leaf Rag" across the keys like sprites on a spree. Her fingers were so sure, so swift, they flouted assorted laws of classical mechanics, gravity, drag, and human fallibility.

A score of couples danced the Cake Walk and the One-Step under hundreds of tiny lights strung like stars across the 383-year-old ceiling beams of the Hotel Colonial's ballroom and restaurant. The Hotel Colonial was one of the few places where Cuernavaca's foreign community and its elite Mexican society mingled. Christmas of 1912 was six weeks away, but they could always find something to celebrate. Most of the dancers sported the latest fashions, but several men wore the dark blue dress uniforms of the Mexican Army.

Captain Martín wore the same uniform, and he thanked his own lucky stars that Colonel Rubio had chosen the Colonial as lodging for himself and his aides. The colonel was a difficult man, to say the least, but now Rico counted himself fortunate to be one of those aides. This was his first visit to the hotel where he would billet while in Cuernavaca, and he liked what he saw.

The glossy toe of his knee-high cavalry boot tapped in rhythm with the music. With arms and ankles crossed he leaned a shoulder against a tiled column next to the piano. He swirled a snifter of cognac in the palm of one hand, while his dark eyes followed those runaway fingers more closely than the dice in a game of hazard.

With her deft hands, the piano player would make a fine thimble-rigger. She could have held her own among the shell game experts he had seen fleecing suckers in Harvard Square. Federico imagined her shuffling the three walnut hulls with such speed that no poor sap could guess which one hid the dried pea.

What intrigued him most about her was the contrast of those devil-may-care hands with the ramrod line of her spine, the intensity of her concentration, and the gleam of two pearly teeth biting her lower lip. And such a voluptuous lower lip it was. Rico wouldn't have minded nibbling on it himself.

One of the waiters had referred to her as *la Inglesa,* so he assumed she was British, and aristocracy, too, by the refined air about her. She had hiked her long skirt up several inches, freeing her feet to work the piano pedals. Her slim ankles looked English enough, but a spatter of freckles across her nose and a mass of hair the dark amber of aged whiskey hinted at an Irishman somewhere in her family's woodpile. Her hair had probably started the day pinned in a fashionable heap on top of her head, but a gaggle of locks had slipped their tethers. They danced around her neck as she played.

He wondered if she was a guest here and if she was married. Not that the latter mattered. He had enjoyed the company of more than a few wives of careless husbands, but he had never laid siege to an *Inglesa* before.

Two years ago, against the wishes of his highborn family, Federico had joined the workers' rebellion ignited by Francisco Madero. Heaven knows, under the aging dictator Porfirio Díaz, Mexico's workers had much to rebel against. The insurgent forces had prevailed and sent Díaz into exile. Rico thought often about the day when, along with 100,000 of his cheering countrymen, he watched Madero installed as president.

Now, however, the prospect of peace gaped like a long yawn for him. Seducing *la Inglesa* would provide an amusing diversion. As easy as a cake walk.

Rico had no doubt about the outcome of his campaign. The high collar on his tunic framed a strong jaw, a sensuous mouth, and an aristocratic nose. He had a physique that didn't require a tailor for uniforms to fit perfectly. He didn't have to see his reflection in the piano's polished surface to know he was handsome. In his twenty-nine years, uncounted numbers of women had told him so, beginning with his Zapotec nurse when he was all of three minutes old.

The music brought him back to the present. *La Inglesa*'s right hand flickered through a long glissando before coming to rest, like a bird gliding in for a landing. The dancers applauded, then made their way back to the roast beef and parsleyed potatoes delivered by a bevy of white-coated waiters.

"Joplin was right," Rico said.

"I beg your pardon?" She looked up and Rico saw that her eyes were as deep blue as delft porcelain and just as cool.

His heart jilted her hands and fell boot heels-over-epaulets into infatuation with her eyes. He didn't realize yet that his plans for seduction had turned on him like an ungrateful cur. When *la Inglesa* stood up she could almost look straight into his own eyes. He noticed that most of her height was legs.

"Scott Joplin," Rico said. "He claimed he could 'shake de earth's foundations wid de "Maple Leaf Rag." ' "

He expected her to exclaim in surprise that a soldier in the Mexican army not only spoke English, but American Negro dialect as well.

Instead she gave him a smile that was cordial, but noncommital. "And you are? . . ."

"Captain Federico Martín at your service." Rico clicked his boot heels and bowed smartly.

"Pleased to make your acquaintance, Captain Martín. I'm Grace Knight."

Grace. *Gracia.* Perfect. God Himself must have named her.

She extended her hand in greeting, but instead of shaking it he raised it to his lips and kissed her fingertips. That didn't seem to surprise her either. Did men kiss her hand on a regular basis? If they did he had a sudden urge to floor them for it.

Charm had always worked for Rico. This woman's immunity to it caught him off guard. He was trying to think of his next move when a crash came from the Colonial's maze of back corridors. It sounded like breaking pottery, probably in the kitchen. Shouts followed, but not in any language Rico recognized, and he spoke six of them. The shouter's gender was also a mystery.

"Please make yourself at home here, Captain Martín," said Grace. "Now if you'll be so kind as to excuse me." She nodded and hurried off toward the commotion. The long curve of her skirt looked like water flowing.

Rico listened intently as he watched her go. He thought the distant shouting might be Chinese, but he still wouldn't wager serious money on whether the source was male or female. And Rico would wager serious money on just about anything.

"Rico! We've been waiting for you." Another blue uniform with captain's bars called to him in Spanish from the doorway of the Colonial's cantina. "Hurry up! They're ready to play." From the bar came the rarest, most beautiful sound in Mexico, the chime of ice in glasses.

Before he joined his friend, Juan, Rico glanced over his shoulder in hopes that Grace Knight would reappear. She didn't. The piano looked like it missed her, too.

Juan led him through the fog of tobacco smoke toward a table at the rear. On the way he gestured to Luís, the barman, to keep the cognac coming. Rico detoured to ask for a bottle of whiskey, a small glass, and a tumbler of ice.

"When did ice become available?" he asked Juan.

"Don't they have ice in El Norte?"

"Yes, but this isn't El Norte."

"We can't have the *chilangos* drinking warm whiskey." Juan used the less-than-affectionate term for people from Mexico City. "There's a new ice plant at the de Leon bridge. The flow of water produces electricity. Don't ask me how. Welcome to the twentieth century, my friend."

Juan turned his chair around, straddled it, and introduced Rico to the two lieutenants at the table. They would be today's lambs for the gaming slaughter.

While one of the lieutenants shuffled the cards, Juan said, "So, you've met *Mamacita*."

"The Englishwoman?"

"None other."

"Does she work at the Colonial?"

"She owns it."

"I don't remember a hotel here."

"*Señora* Knight came on the train from Mexico City with that piano lashed to a flatcar. She bought this place just after you left for El Norte five years ago." Juan leaned across the table to bring the lieutenants up to date. "My friend went to college in the United States and returned *agringado*."

The gist of what Juan had said about *la Inglesa* and the Colonial sank in. He looked around, startled. "Is this the pile of rubble that stood vacant for years?"

"The same."

Rico remembered the building's crumbling façade and broken windows. Its weed-grown courtyard had been visible from the street through a rotted gate. He had trouble reconciling that memory with what stood here now.

To reach the ballroom he had passed through a pair of intricately carved front gates and under a covered entryway to an open courtyard paved in a mosaic made of the local volcanic rock. Small wrought-iron tables and chairs lurked half-hidden in bowered nooks. A cascade of water flowed down one wall of blue tiles and splashed into a pool below. Darkness had since fallen, but when Rico arrived earlier birds still had been confabulating in the lush growth of trees and shrubbery. Hummingbirds had been attacking the tapestries of flowering vines like starving guests at a free steam table.

"Is she married?" Rico feigned interest in his cards.

"Who?"

"*La Inglesa.*"

"Widowed. Her husband was Carlos Mendoza."

"Of the Mendozas who administered the foreign mining concessions?"

"Exactly. What is it they say? 'The government, although a beggar, is the richest man in Mexico.'"

"Then why does she call herself Mrs. Knight?"

Juan shrugged. "Perhaps she is one of those modern women we hear about." He looked up. "If you're planning to woo the widow Knight, my friend, you're wasting your time. The word is that at least a brigade of men has tried to scale those ramparts."

"La señora es formidable," muttered one of the lieutenants.

Rico went back to studying his cards.

With only that local malcontent, Emiliano Zapata, left to stir up trouble, the next few months here in Cuernavaca were going to pass slowly. Rico had plenty of time to make the acquaintance of the formidable Mrs. Knight.

2

VERY DELECTABLE,
HIGHLY RESPECTABLE

Grace left the kitchen a quieter place than she had found it. Only the usual clatter of pots and the chatter of María and her scullery staff followed her out. The cook had gone back to basting the beef roast with his secret blend of herbs and oils. Now and then he poked it with an ivory chopstick to test its doneness.

His name was Wing Ang, although everyone called him Chinito, Little Chinaman. He was built like a wren and just as excitable, but Grace had learned not to take his flights of fury too seriously. As she strolled back toward the ballroom she hummed a tune from Gilbert and Sullivan.

Chinito's pidgen English had that affect on her. Conversations with him could set her to singing tunes from *The Mikado* for the rest of the day. Thanks to her music-hall parents, she knew by heart every song that Mr. Gilbert and Mr. Sullivan had written.

In the restaurant she found the waiters, their heavily laden trays held high, performing their nightly ballet collision-free. On the dance floor couples waltzed to the tunes of the musicians she recently had hired. Normally she would have checked with Luís, the *cantinero*, too, but tonight she passed by. That new captain was probably in there playing cards with friends. If she thought about it she could still feel a tingle in her fingers where he had kissed them. That flustered her, and Grace didn't like to be flustered.

In the past two years she had met plenty of young officers at the

Colonial. Most of them were from Mexico's bureaucratic or aristocratic classes, the upper middle class known as *los correctos*. The boys were gallant and full of fun and they had affectionately dubbed her *Mamacita*. But they had little on their minds except drinking, gambling, fast horses, pretty women, and outrageous pranks. Captain Martín might be more polished than most of them, but he didn't fool Grace. Besides, he must be at least six or seven years younger than she.

After talking with the night clerk at the front desk, she had one more task. She always made sure the pair of parrots had returned to their roost in the jacaranda tree. As she headed for the courtyard she softly sang a tune from the Gilbert and Sullivan opera, *Bunthorne's Bride*. "A very delectable, highly respectable, threepenny 'bus young man."

She jumped when someone started pounding on the Colonial's massive front gate. Whoever he was, he must have been using a sledgehammer to make such a racket. Grace didn't know much Spanish, but she recognized words that mule drivers employed when they passed the hotel on their way to the nearby market. Her chambermaids always advised her to cover her ears when mule drivers were in the vicinity.

Socrates hurried to open the gate. Grace would have been hard-put to define Socrates's position, other than do-all. If the Colonial had a mayor, Socrates would occupy the office. Grace wasn't sure she could manage the hotel without him and his wife María.

As the shouting crescendoed, Grace suspected that the culprit was Colonel Rubio. She had been expecting him to arrive tonight. Now that she heard him, she wished she had refused the governor's request to billet Rubio and his staff here, but saying "no" to the governor would have been foolish. Staying in his good graces was essential for her business.

"Our commanding officer has arrived."

Grace whirled and found Captain Martín standing behind her. Something about his stance gave her the notion he had come to protect her. She wondered if protection would be necessary.

"Is the colonel always this loud?"

"Only when he drinks."

"And how often does he drink?"

"Only when he is awake."

Rubio strode into the courtyard, but stopped short when he saw Grace.

"*Señora* Knight . . ." He bent into a bow that looked likely to end nose-down on the tile mosaic. To Grace's relief he hoisted himself vertical again. He was short and round and bald. He wore a uniform crusty with gold braid and brass buttons. His epaulets looked as big as the business ends of two push brooms. He had the air of a man with a high opinion of himself and a low opinion of everyone else.

He beckoned to Captain Martín for a conference.

"The colonel wants to know when breakfast will be served," the captain said.

Looking into Captain Martín's dark eyes, the words "very delectable" showed up in Grace's mind again. She elbowed them away.

"I take breakfast in the courtyard at eight o'clock, if the colonel would care to join me."

"He says it will be his pleasure. And he wonders if the plums that grow in Cuernavaca's orchards are available. He says his good friend, General Huerta, recommends the stewed plums you serve here."

"Yes, of course. And please ask the colonel to give my regards to General Huerta when next he speaks to him."

Huerta had billeted here last summer. *At least,* Grace thought, *Colonel Rubio won't be a patch on General Victoriano Huerta when it comes to a temper of the volcanic sort.*

Huerta looked like a bulldog wearing a monocle. He had always been polite to her, but some days Grace imagined she could see steam coming out of his ears and nostrils. The day President Madero called Huerta back to the capital Grace had celebrated with champagne.

General Huerta had served during former president Porfirio Díaz's regime, and President Madero retained him along with the rest of the federal army. Francisco Madero had come to the Colonial on several occasions. Grace admired him, but she could not understand why that genteel, intelligent little man had put his former enemy, Huerta, in charge of the military.

Colonel Rubio bowed again with the exaggerated aplomb of the inebriated. *"Entonces, hasta la mañanita, señora, y muy buenas noches."*

"Buenas noches, Coronel."

"May I ask which room is the colonel's, *Señora* Knight?" asked Captain Martín.

"Upstairs, room twenty on the left at the far end of the corridor."

Colonel Rubio started unsteadily up the curved sweep of marble steps to the gallery overlooking all four sides of the courtyard. Captain Martín followed.

On his way up, the colonel rapid-fired Spanish at the captain. The only word Grace recognized of it all was *garrapata,* louse. Rubio repeated it several times.

Dear God, she thought, *I pray the man is not infested.*

She did not notice the worried look on Captain Martín's face when he glanced back over his shoulder. She did not notice his relief when he realized she hadn't understood Rubio.

Drawn by the ruckus, the Colonial's day-manager, Lyda Austin, appeared. Her accent was distilled Texan. "I see Colonel Fatso found his way home. More's the pity."

"Now, Lyda."

"Gracie, the man has eyes like cold gravy."

Lyda and Grace watched Captain Martín climb the stairs behind Rubio. He looked ready to stop the colonel's momentum should he decide to topple backward.

"I see you've met Captain Martín," said Lyda.

"We spoke briefly."

"I registered him this evening. He'll be staying in the room next to Rubio's."

Captain Federico Martín would be living here. Grace's heart gave a desperate flutter, like a butterfly caught in a spider's web.

"He's a charmer, he is," said Lyda. "And you know what we say in Texas about charm."

"What do Texans say?"

Only when Captain Martín's muscular rear echelon had turned the corner at the top of the stairs did Lyda shift her gaze to Grace.

"Charm is as obvious as a barn fire." Lyda paused. "And Captain Federico Martín is a barn on fire with hay stacked to the rafters."

3

BRAT AND UGLY

Angela Sanchez ladled the beans onto a warm tortilla still bearing the imprints of her mother's fingers. As she rolled it up and shoved it into her mouth like cane into a sugar press, her father beamed at her. Well, he didn't exactly beam. He was a Spaniard. Pure Castilian, thin as a coach whip and twice as jovial. Beaming was foreign to him, but a spark of something like approval flickered in his obsidian eyes. The approval was not of Angela's manners, but of her motives.

"See how eager the child is to go to school. I told you she would like it once she became accustomed to it."

"I am not a child," Angela mumbled around the tortilla and beans. "I am almost sixteen years old." She was tall like her father, solidly built like her mother, and with a hauteur all her own.

"Daughter, have respect," Angela's mother murmured in Nahuatl.

Angela grabbed the satchel with her primer, slate, and lunch inside. She threw the satchel's strap over one shoulder, and bolted past her.

"Feed the chickens before you go," *Don* Miguel called after her.

"*Quin tepan, Tahtli*. Later, Father." Angela knew that answering in Nahuatl instead of Spanish annoyed him. Her mother and all the workers and servants on her family's small hacienda spoke Nahuatl. She couldn't help but be fluent in it, so annoying him was a bonus.

This was late October but a warm breeze riffled her hair as she hurried down the long corridor. She waded through pools of early morning sunlight where the high arched openings framed the exuberance of the

courtyard. Riots of bougainvillea vines and hibiscus bushes almost hid
the big stone cistern there.

Heavy beams and an iron crosspiece barred the oaken doors, but she
went out through the small portal cut into one of them. She found her
bay mare where the stable boy had left her. Like Angela, the mare was a
talker. She was small, chunky, and restless as a rat, but with good bones
and a fine lineage.

Angela looped her satchel over the pommel and tugged on the cinch
to make sure it was tight. She led the horse to the mounting block,
pulled her long skirts up, and vaulted onto the mare's back. With the
hem of her dress riding above her scarred brown knees, she urged the
mare into a canter under the canopy of eucalyptus trees lining the avenue to the house.

When she came within sight of the nine men and the yoked mule
teams she slowed to a walk. She didn't want them to think she had been
hurrying to catch up with them. At the sound of her mare's hoofbeats
they fell silent. Her father had always been fair and generous with his
workers. He even sympathized with General Emiliano Zapata's renewed
rebellion, but men will be human. Angela suspected they had been arguing about how they would divide her father's estate among themselves
when Zapata forced President Madero to make good on his promises of
land reform.

Angela didn't see what any of it had to do with her. The intrigues of
Mexico City might as well take place on the moon for all the difference
it made out here. She hiked her skirts higher and reined her mare alongside eighteen-year-old Antonio Perez.

"*Ujulé,* Ugly," she said in Nahuatl, "Is it true that God made the
mule to give the Indian a rest?"

"A mule like you gives no one rest, *Chamaca,* Brat." Antonio replied
in Spanish to make the point that Angela was his employer's daughter
and of a higher class, but he insulted her anyway. They had been doing
it since they were children.

"You are the tick in the mule's ear."

"Bold talk from one no bigger than the flea on a tick's butt."

All the workers except Antonio knew that Angela was infatuated with him; and everyone but Angela knew that Antonio had loved her since she was small. They also knew that nothing could ever come of it. A gentleman might take an Indian to wife, but the reverse did not happen. Ever. And even though Angela was half Indian, she was the *patrón's* daughter.

Arquímedes Guerra, the patriarch of the field crew, knew that. "We're all made of the same clay," he often said, "but a chamber pot can never be a vase. You, my child," he told her, "are a vase."

Arquímedes was no relation, but Angela called him *colli*, grandfather. When she wanted advice or sympathy she went to him rather than her father.

"Have you decided to go to school today, *mi hija*, my daughter?"

Angela grinned. "Maybe tomorrow I'll go." She had been saying that for months. Don Manuel's attempts to educate his daughter had been no more successful than his efforts to make a lady of her.

" '*Para pendejo no se necesita maestro,*' " Antonio observed. " 'To be a fool requires no teacher.' "

One of the men added his *centavo's* worth. "All a woman needs to know is how to cook beans, sew shirts, grow corn, and make babies."

There followed some discussion of the part about making babies. Antonio said he would rather stick a lighted firecracker in his pants than fall in love. Angela commented on how fortunate that was for the women of the world.

Arquímedes smiled at them both. "Men and women are two locked boxes," he said. "And in each one lies the key to open the other."

"There is no defense against love and a rash," Antonio grumbled.

Antonio led the mules onto the lane that followed the irrigation ditch to the cane fields. Before Arquímedes followed him, he put a hand on the mare's neck and looked up at Angela.

"You should listen to your father, *mi hija*. When Zapata's revolution comes we will need educated people of good heart to make sure everything is as it should be."

Angela shrugged. "The revolution came and went."

"Do you see any changes because of it? Have we poor farmers received back the land the *hacendados* stole from us?"

"No, but there's nothing I can do about that, educated or not." Angela reined her horse toward the river. *"Ma xipatinemi."* She called over her shoulder. It was the Nauhuatl form of good-bye. It meant, "May you be well."

She tethered her mare to graze beyond the bare dirt surrounding the roots of a banyan tree. The tree was as big around as the hacienda's blacksmith shop and its canopy spanned the river. Angela's great, great, great grandfather had brought it from Spain as a seedling.

In the 150 years since then it had sent down hundreds of aerial roots from its branches. They had reached the ground, taken hold, and thickened into trunks. As the trunks grew wider they crowded each other, forming a maze of nooks and crevices. As far back as Angela could remember the banyan had been her citadel, her kingdom, her refuge.

She kicked off her shoes. She tugged her blouse over her head and untied the drawstring on her skirt. She dropped it around her ankles and stepped out of it. She draped her clothes over a bush, then she took a running start onto a jutting rock and leaped off. She pulled her knees to her chest, wrapped her arms around her legs, and hit the river with a force that sent water up like a geyser.

She snorted and spouted and splashed, then she walked out of the river, dripping. She retrieved the bundle she had hidden among the banyan's roots. It contained the white cotton trousers, tunic, leather sandals, and wide-brimmed straw hat that all the farmers wore. She put them on and climbed the tree, finding footholds in the intricate fretwork of roots and branches.

She walked out on the broad limb that gave the best view of the men in the cane field and settled down where it forked. She reclined with her back against the upper branch, her legs draped along the lower one. Through the years the birds had gotten used to her presence. *Anoles* and chameleons commuted across her and an iguana as long as her arm dozed like a tabby cat nearby.

From here she could see Antonio guiding the plow. He had draped his shirt over the handle and Angela never tired of watching the glide of muscles in his bare back and arms. She wanted to tell him how she felt about him, but she was certain he would laugh at her.

Her eyelids were beginning to droop like the iguana's when the squad of soldiers galloped across the field. Their horses' hooves sent dirt flying from the newly plowed furrows. They herded the workers into a line along an old ditch, dry except for mud in the bottom.

Dread hardened into a canker in Angela's chest. Most of her father's men fell on their knees, but Antonio and Arquímedes remained on their feet. They were the first ones shot. Angela bit down on her knuckles to keep from screaming when the two of them pitched into the ditch.

The soldiers emptied their rifles into the rest, then dismounted to make sure they were dead before they kicked the bodies over the edge. They reined their horses around, and driving the mules ahead of them, they headed in a cloud of dust for the hacienda. Soon strands of vultures began weaving a wreath over the ditch.

Not until the sun was hovering above the horizon did Angela come down from the tree. As if to delay doing what she had to, she folded her skirt and blouse and put them and her shoes into her satchel. She rolled up her pants legs so they wouldn't get soaked with blood. She picked up the biggest stick she could find to beat off the vultures, and led the mare to the ditch.

The bodies sprawled in heaps above the muddy water. Somewhere under them lay Antonio and Arquímedes. Angela crossed herself before she slid down the steep sides of the trench. Flies, crows, and buzzards rose in a raucous black cloud when she hit the bottom. Ignoring the thunder claps of their wings, Angela grasped arms and feet and started hauling the corpses off the pile.

When three of them proved too heavy for her, she took the rope used to dislodge tree stumps and tied it to an ankle. She climbed up the embankment, looped the other end around the saddle pommel, and led the mare along the rim, dragging the body away. She repeated the operation for the second and third.

She uncovered Arquímedes lying face up in the shallow water. His lightless eyes stared at heaven. She knew he was dead, but she knelt next to him and put her ear to his heart anyway. He groaned.

"*¡Ay, Dios!*" She jumped back and realized that Arquímedes had not made the sound. Antonio had.

"Dream with the angels, *colli*." Angela made the sign of the cross over Arquímedes and rolled him away. Antonio lay on his side underneath, his body almost hidden by black sludge. His head was cradled on his arm as if asleep on his reed mat at home. It kept his nose barely above water.

Angela sat in the mud, lifted his head into her lap, put her arms around him, and sobbed. She was making God extravagant promises in exchange for Antonio's survival when he opened his eyes.

"Where did the bullet go in, Ugly?" she asked.

"I don't know, Brat."

"Where do you hurt?"

"Everywhere. What about the others?"

"They are with God."

"The old man, too?"

"Yes."

"The devil take the sons of whores."

"Why did they do it?"

"They wanted us to tell them where the men went."

"The ones who ran into the hills to join Zapata?"

"Yes. We told the sons of bitches to look in hell." He stared up at her face, covered with mud and blood. "Angelita, you are the most beautiful woman in the world." His eyes closed.

Angela shook him. "Do not die, my love." She was done with haggling with God. She looked up at a sunset sky so glorious that God must surely live there. "Do not let him die, or I will curse you. From the flames of damnation I will curse your name! Do you hear me?"

"We hear you, *Doña* Angela."

Angela looked around at a line of women standing along the ditch's rim, their faces shadowed by shawls. When they saw the bodies of their men, they pulled their shawls over their eyes and wailed. Angela should have been more understanding, but everyone had died and left her in charge. She hadn't time for her own grief much less anyone else's. The carnage was too horrific for her to absorb anyway. Her mind shut out emotions so she could do what had to be done.

"They are all dead but Antonio. We have to carry him out of here."

The women slid down the slope and helped her carry him back up it. They laid him on his back in the grass and Angela began scraping off the mud, trying to find the source of the flow of blood. When Angela probed Antonio's shoulder he winced.

Most of the women started wailing again, but one of them said, "*El gobierno* took your mother. No one knows what became of your father."

Angela knew anyone in uniform was *el gobierno* to them. She didn't bother to ask why the army of the revolution had turned on its own people. They wore the federal uniform now. They had become *el gobierno*. And anyway, men willing to murder were as easy to recruit as fleas.

One of the women ripped a strip of cloth from the bottom of her skirt so Angela could bind it around Antonio's shoulder. Antonio struggled to his feet and swayed.

"Careful, Ugly." Angela put an arm around his waist to steady him.

She and the women helped him into the mare's saddle and Angela mounted behind him. The women had brought a donkey cart to carry the bodies home. Angela gave the oldest of them the few *pesos* she had.

"Gracias, *Doña* Angela."

"God go with you, *mamacita. Ma xipatinemi.* May you be well."

Angela put her arms around Antonio and took up the reins. The mare headed for her feed trough, but stopped short at the charred, smoking rubble of the stable. The corncrib, blacksmith shop, and sugar press building had also been set on fire.

With her pulse pounding in her ears, Angela rode through the big doors now standing open. No chickens wandered the courtyard, which looked as if a bomb had gone off in it. It was littered with upturned flagstones and pitted with holes the soldiers had dug in search of silver the family might have buried.

Angela left Antonio by the cistern and ran through the house, calling for her father and Plinio, the family's *mayordomo*. Furniture lay overturned and smashed. Debris covered the floor, but the soldiers had taken everything of value that they could carry.

Angela went to her father's study and waded through the scattered books. *El gobierno* had not considered them worth stealing. She put a stool on a chair and set the chair on a big chest. She climbed onto the stool and pushed aside a panel in the ceiling. She stood on tiptoe and felt around until she found her father's Winchester 30-30 carbine, the 1894 model, and the box of ammunition for it. She knew how to use it. Riding and shooting were the only activities her father shared with her. She had practiced throwing knives and rocks on her own.

She replaced the panel and put the stool and chair back where she had found them. She pressed one of the carved wooden medallions at the edge of an ornate cupboard and slid out a narrow vertical drawer, invisible when closed. Inside was a wallet containing forty of the big silver *pesos* called *bolas.*

She put them into the bag around her neck and picked up the rifle and ammunition. She found a couple old shirts and two pair of her father's trousers that the soldiers had missed. She figured she could replace her filthy clothes with one set and give the other to Antonio.

She returned to the cistern, and in the last of the day's light she sluiced buckets of water over Antonio and herself until she'd rinsed off the worst of the dirt and blood. She took the skirt from her satchel and tore off material to change the bandage on Antonio's wound and make a sling for his arm.

"Where do you want to go?" she asked.

"Wherever you're going."

Shadowy figures darker than the gathering night slipped through the gate. Angela shoved a shell into the Winchester, levered the action, and rested the barrel on the rim of the cistern with the muzzle aimed at them.

"Who are you?" she called out.

"I am Plinio, princess." The family's *mayordomo* had always called her *cíhuapilli,* princess. "The women told us you had come here."

Plinio and five of *Don* Sanchez's employees lined up in front of her as if for military inspection. They had armed themselves with hoes, machetes, knives, and a few ancient rifles. They carried their belongings in satchels with the straps running diagonally across their chests.

"Do you know where my father is?"

"No, but we want to go with you to fight in General Zapata's army."

Angela hadn't yet decided where she would go, but now she realized that the choice was inevitable. "How do you know what I'm going to do?"

It was too dark to see the wry smile on Plinio's doleful, wrinkled face. "*Muchacha,* how many years have I known you?"

"All my life."

"Well then . . ."

Angela wore her hair in a braid that reached the small of her back. "Cut this off." She held it away from her body. "Hurry. The sons of dogs could return."

Plinio knew from experience that arguing with *Don* Miguel's daughter was a waste of time. He could barely see the braid, so he measured it with his hand before he sawed through it with his machete. Angela shook her head to let her hair fall in a parentheses around her face. She ran her hand through it, disoriented when her fingers came to the ends so soon.

She took a deep breath. She was glad night had come so her father's men could not see how frightened and distraught she was. She did not know where Zapata was and the mountainous countryside was perilous even in daylight.

Antonio must have guessed what she was thinking. "I know a cave nearby where we can spend the night. Tomorrow, we can go to San Miguel. My family will know where to hide us."

Angela mounted her mare with Antonio behind her. The men rode double on the three mules they had been able to muster. Angela raised her father's rifle over her head and started for the main gate.

"*Vámanos, muchachos,*" she said. "The devil himself cannot frighten us."

4

THE MAGICAL MARKET

Grace worried that she had caused the disappearance of Cuernavaca's central market two years ago. Lyda tried to persuade her that it wasn't her fault, but she hadn't been able to convince her. As Grace, Lyda, and Lyda's eleven-year-old daughter, Annie, crossed the new park where the market building once had stood, Grace started fretting again.

"I shouldn't have said anything."

"Gracie, the governor and his wife were dining in your hotel. The wind was blowing this way. Of course you would apologize for the smell."

"They didn't move it far," added Annie.

That was true. Cuernavaca's small plaza with its Victorian bandstand was across the street from the Colonial. The market had occupied an entire block just beyond the far corner of the plaza. Now it splayed out through the streets next to the hulking Governor's Palace on the other side of the park. Grace could see the canvas awnings of the market kiosks from her balcony.

"And anyway," said Lyda, "they started demolishing the old market within days of your conversation with the governor. Nothing happens that fast in Mexico. They must have planned it long before."

"They made that wacking great building vanish in a hurry," said Grace.

That was also true. However the official demolition crew had unofficial help. It seemed that everyone in the city wanted part of the former market.

The building had encompassed a city block, open to the elements in the center, with a large fountain there. Grace had looked out from her balcony one morning to see workmen swarming over it. A parade of mule-drawn wagons waited to haul away the debris. But after the workers left each night, more of the building disappeared like cake at a wedding. People dismantled it to use the tiles, wood, iron work, and stones on their personal construction projects.

Grace took consolation in the fact that most of the old market's parts now provided shelter for the poor. And the new park created where it once stood served a purpose possibly not intended by the city fathers.

To reach the market, many people walked for miles from the outlying villages. The new park, called Jardín Morelos, with its trees and shrubbery, walkways, fountain, and tiled benches, provided a lovely place for families to camp the night before laying out their wares. Smoke rose from their small cooking fires. The new streetlights illuminated their sleeping forms, curled up on the reed mats they had brought with them.

Grace imagined Cuernavaca's market as a rabbit pulled out of a magician's hat. Its brightly colored awnings and crowds of people appeared like abracadabra in the steep labyrinth of Cuernavaca's streets. Foot traffic and the passing of an occasional burro were possible in the press of people and goods, but nothing so large as a horse or motorcar.

Whenever Grace ventured there she wore her high-top laced boots and held her skirts up so the hems wouldn't trail through the offal and rotting produce. The stench was overpowering at times. She wanted to hold her nose, but that would have been undignified, and insulting besides.

Lyda solved the offal problem by hemming her skirts six inches above her ankles. Underneath she added a pair of white cotton trousers like those the Mexican farmers wore. It was an audacious departure from fashion, but Grace had come to expect audacity from Americans in general and Lyda in particular.

Lyda tossed a copper *centavo* to the Indian woman squatting under the tattered canvas of her awning, then scooped a handful of *chapalines,* fried grasshoppers, from the heap of them. They were about as long as a finger joint, just right for snacking. Lyda and Annie ate them as they strolled along, the insects crunching like popcorn. Annie was adept at tossing them into the air and catching them in her mouth. It was a feat that had won her a share of admirers among the market children. The children called out " 'Ello" to Annie as she passed and she always answered *"Hola."*

"Wish I'd known how tasty these are when I was coming up," Lyda said. "Lord knows we had locusts a-plenty in west Texas."

"I prefer my victuals with fewer appendages."

"They taste like chitlins." Lyda held out her hand, offering to share. Grace waved them away. "What are chitlins?"

"Fried pig intestines."

"That's disgusting."

Lyda laughed. "You're a fine one, you are, to talk about disgusting, what with all the kidney pies you Brits put away."

"I would never eat a kidney," observed Annie. "That's where pee is made."

"How do you know that?" asked Grace.

"Annie has her mind set on becoming a doctor," Lyda said.

In spite of the smell and the chaos, Grace loved the market. Foothills of roots, fruits, and vegetables, and festoons of gutted critters from goats to guinea pigs made wandering through it an adventure. The amount of food astonished Grace, although she couldn't identify a lot of it.

Los correctos called the Indians *brutos,* brutes, but Grace knew better. They were dark-eyed magicians to coax such abundance from the stony soil as if it were the fertile muck of Eden. They were artists, too, in the way they displayed their wares. Great waterfalls of colored hemp hung from lines. The pyramids of mangoes, plums, oranges, and guavas looked like Christmas ornaments. Candles were suspended by their wicks. Even a burro's burden of palm fronds were arranged in enormous green rosettes.

The place always had an air of fiesta about it, too. The Indians dressed in their best clothes embroidered in vibrant hues. Their blankets, shawls, and awnings shimmered with color, and so did the heaps of food, the toys, the piñatas, and the pottery. Children ran laughing among the stalls, and musicians performed for the coppers that people tossed to them. Grace encountered no hard sell here as she would have in English markets. Women called softly to Grace, *"¿Que va a llevar, señora?"* What will you take with you?

The market was Grace's main contact with Mexico's poor. Most of the Colonial's Mexican guests were *los correctos,* the upper crust on holiday from Mexico City. They and the Colonial's British, German, and American visitors, its European meals, clean sheets, and hot water, made it almost possible for Grace to forget that she lived in a foreign country. The redolent chaos here, however, reminded her that she wasn't in London anymore.

María and the kitchen staff shopped for the food served at the hotel, but Grace had come here often enough to learn that the market wasn't as chaotic as it seemed. The Indians paid a fee called a "floor tax" that assured them a spot to set up their awnings of canvas or striped blankets, and spread out their wares on the ground. Even though the market had moved, individuals sat in the same configuration that their ancestors had occupied for generations.

The folk of each village sat together and Grace was learning to distinguish them by the differences in the embroidery on their clothing. Grace, Lyda, and Annie headed for the side street where the potters of San Miguel displayed their goods. Their pottery was simple, made of undecorated red clay, but it was popular with the guests at the Colonial.

The problem was that San Miguel's potters were not used to anyone wanting so many pieces at one time. Weeks before, when Grace tried to buy all their stock they became indignant.

"You can't do that," they scolded. "What would we do the rest of the day with no goods to sell?"

So Grace accepted the fact that market day wasn't so much about commerce as that ineffable Mexican concept of *ver y ver-se,* to see and be seen. She bought a few vases from each potter, saving her favorite, José, for last. She couldn't have said what it was about José that affected her, but he had a presence that occupied more space than his short burly body, his voluminous mustache, and his impossibly large, hound-dog eyes. Grace realized that even though she had been buying goods here for her gift shop for a year, she didn't know anything about the artisans who made them.

Lyda was appalled when Grace paid the first price quoted. "You'll spoil them."

"They ask a pittance, and how can I give them less than a pittance?" Grace turned the rotund little pot over in her hands. Its design, she'd been told, had changed little from the ones the villagers were making when Hernán Cortés arrived in 1521. "Besides, my guests pay five times their asking price, and they buy all I can get. The problem is supply, really."

"Then go to the source."

"Go to San Miguel?"

"Why not?"

Grace was considering that suggestion when a ripple of consternation passed along the street. People covered their goods with shawls and blankets or moved to stand in front of them. A group of women, ragged and barefoot, with their babies strapped to their backs in their blue shawls, strode toward them.

"*Soldaderas,*" Lyda said. "The army's camp followers."

"*Galletas,*" Annie added.

"*Galletas?*" Grace asked. "Cookies?"

"People call the soldiers' women 'cookies.' "

"*Sopilotas en jupones.*" One of the potters spit into the dust. "*Robando hasta los muertos.*"

"Buzzards in petticoats," Annie translated. "They even steal things from dead soldiers."

But as the women passed, Grace wanted to weep for them. Their faces held no trace of joy. Even the *indios* here in the market laughed and smiled, though Grace had heard that their lives were hard. What misery had robbed these creatures of joy?

Besides, the rebellion had ended. The fighting had stopped. Why didn't they return to their homes? Why were they following an army that wasn't going anywhere?

5

THE OLD MAN

Rico sat stiff as a ramrod on the front edge of a velvet sofa in one of the three overcrowded parlors of his family's sprawling hacienda. He balanced his flat-topped, duck-brimmed officer's hat on his knees and tried not to tug at the itch under his high collar. He was here to ask a favor of his grandfather, whom everyone called *El Viejo,* The Old Man, although not in his hearing.

As *El Viejo* waved his glass of cognac around and held forth from the depths of his favorite overstuffed wingback chair, he reminded Rico of a bulldog straining at his leash. Chronic choler and an abundance of alcohol had turned his cheeks and nose red. They made a startling contrast with his unruly shock of white hair. Rico wondered if this would be the day the Old Man gave himself apoplexy and died. He felt bad that he didn't feel worse about the possibility.

The Old Man was why Rico rarely came home for visits. He wouldn't have been here now if Juan hadn't wagered a ridiculous sum of money that Rico's grandfather's big Andalusian stallion could outrun any horse put against him. Rico would have preferred to forfeit the bet rather than ask *El Viejo* for the loan of the horse, but Juan needed the money to pay off gambling debts.

Rico could have given Juan the money, but he knew from experience that was the fastest way to destroy a friendship. Rico and Juan were as different as beer and brandy. They had their disagreements, but they proved that while love may be blind, friendship closes its eyes.

Thanks to exiled president Porfirio Díaz's policies of modernizing the country, *los correctos,* the upper crust, had a mania for all things European. Rico's family was no exception. The musty smell of the horsehair stuffing in the sofas and chairs made Rico sneeze. The dusty, voluminous velvet drapes suffocated him. The hulking wardrobes, bureaus, and highboys, the curio cabinets, spindly French tables, and crystal chandeliers made him feel as though the walls were closing in on him.

His mother's collection of several hundred porcelain shepherdesses and celluloid Kewpie dolls made him uneasy. As a child he had liked to stare at the bright blue walls until the pink rosebuds and gilt scrollwork painted on them began to move. He no longer found that entertaining.

His grandfather's rantings were the worst. They were like a cylinder on one of those newfangled phonographs, playing the same song over and over. Maybe it was inspiration, maybe it was a hallucination of the sort a bad headache can cause, but suddenly the Old Man's voice became no more noticeable than background noise.

Phonograph. In his trancelike state, Rico thought of a way to get *la Inglesa's* attention. On his next assignment in the capital he would buy one of those newfangled phonographs for the Colonial. He imagined dancing with Grace Knight to the music. He even knew what music he would bring.

He almost smiled, but stopped himself in time. A smile would have alerted *El Viejo* to the fact that his grandson wasn't listening.

The Old Man finished his praise of Porfirio Díaz and launched into his favorite subject—the ingratitude of *los indios brutos* in general and the most brutish of all the Indians, Emiliano Zapata.

"He demands that we *hacendados* pay him a tax to support his mob of bandits. And if we don't, the dirty thieves will destroy our sugarcane crops and burn our estates. It's extortion. They should all be hanged from a thorn tree while buzzards eat their eyes and entrails." His anger propelled him out of the chair and set him to pacing. "General Huerta is right. Zapata and his rabble must be crushed like lice, and Rubio is the man for the job."

Rico had heard the same crush-them-like-lice speech from Rubio himself the night he met *la Inglesa*. He didn't bother to point out that Rubio would have a hard time persuading his men to turn on their own people. That would have made his grandfather angrier. Not making *El Viejo* angry was essential if Rico was to race the stallion. He had to get the horse or the afternoon would be a total waste of time, dignity, and forebearance.

Rico had heard his grandfather's oration often enough to know that he was coming to the personal part of it.

"When will you find a woman to marry, Rico? When will you produce offspring?"

"I am looking for the right woman, Grandfather."

"I know several young women who would marry you."

"Don't you mean you know several women who would marry me to get your money?"

"Don't be insolent. By the time you finish with your gambling and whoring there won't be any money left."

Rico knew he only had to sit through an assessment of his lack of ambition, and then he and the horse could leave.

"Thanks be to God that you did not continue that ridiculous pursuit of a career in medicine. Otherwise, you would be smearing salve over the rash on some peasant's buttocks and receiving chickens in payment. You should light a candle in gratitude that a word from your father into the ear of General Huerta obtained the position of Rubio's aide. You will be able to make important connections with influential people in the Capital."

The Old Man confirmed Rico's suspicions. His family was at the bottom of his promotion. Merit had nothing to do with it.

"How many years are left in your enlistment?"

"Two, sir."

"When your time is up you will take a law degree. Law and government service are where the power and prestige lie."

And the bribes, Rico thought. In Mexico, justice was a commodity to be bought and sold like any other.

Rico could have recited what his grandfather would say next. He had to concentrate on not letting his lips form the words silently. That too would have propelled the Old Man to a higher level of righteous outrage.

"With your army connections you can get a good job," *El Viejo* went on. "You're white enough to be elected president one day."

Rico coughed to keep from laughing. Laughing would never do.

When Rico finally stalked toward the front door he felt as though he were breaking out of prison. Or an insane asylum. He was too familiar with the ancient, elegant magnificence of his family's home to be awed by it. Cortés had built it as one of many sugar plantations, or rather his thousands of *indio* slaves had. Whatever one might say about Hernán Cortés, the man thought large.

The archways of the first floor corridors reached sixteen feet tall. The second and third floors had twelve-foot ceilings. Four hundred and eighty years of rain and wind had given the rough stucco walls the look of an Impressionist work of art. The goldfish in the fountains had grown to the size of Rico's forearms. The sinuous vines embracing the walls had had time to approximate saplings. Always the hacienda's background music was the grinding and clanking of the machinery in the sugar refinery behind the house.

Rico was headed for the stable when he encountered something that jolted him from his grandfather-induced brown study. Six men lounged under a huge *tabachine* tree. When they saw him they leaped up. They wore khaki uniforms with high, stiff collars. They hustled to form a line, as if preparing for inspection.

They looked somewhat like *indios,* with spiky black hair. They had the *indios'* golden brown skin and almond-shaped eyes, but they certainly weren't *indios.* They bowed. They bowed again. They were still bowing when Rico entered the redolent warmth of the stable. He waited a few heartbeats, then peeked out. They stood at attention as if waiting for his return.

The stableman was brushing the stallion, although his silver-gray coat already gleamed. Because of his color the Old Man had named him *Grullo,* Crane. Rico's grandfather claimed he was a descendant of the Andalusians ridden by Cortés and his men. If a creature existed more beautiful than this original Spanish bloodline, Rico had yet to see it. Even the stallions of the breed were less high-strung and more manageable. Rico could not look at Grullo and stay angry.

"Good afternoon, *Don* Federico."

"Good afternoon, Pablo." Rico did not want to ask information from the help, but his curiosity got the better of him. "Who are those men?"

"Japanese." Pablo had worked for the Martín family all his life. He knew that answer wasn't good enough. He also knew the young *patron* would be too proud to ask for an explanation, so he provided it. "Your grandfather hired them to protect the hacienda. They finished fighting the Russians a few years ago. Their commander is some Frenchman."

"The Russo-Japanese War." Rico knew about that. The world had gasped in astonishment when the diminutive Japanese warriors whipped the Russians, Cossack cavalry and all. "It ended seven years ago, in 1905."

Pablo grinned. "I suppose they missed fighting. So here they are."

"Please saddle Grullo. He's going with me."

Japanese? Rico had never studied that language. How could he have been so negligent? He had a lot of questions he would like to ask them.

The racetrack was laid out on the level ground behind the enlisted men's barracks near Cuernavaca's train station. Not until Rico rode the gray there did he discover how Rubio intended to make good on his promise to crush the local peasantry like lice.

New conscripts were being herded off cattle cars. They had on the same ragged clothes they'd been wearing when they were rounded up. Most of them were barefoot.

Juan's face lit up when he saw the stallion, but the horse race no longer mattered to Rico.

"Who are they?" he asked.

"Pochos." The word meant northerners, more specifically Yaqui Indians. It was not a compliment. "This is the second load of them in the past three days."

Rico shouldn't have been surprised that Rubio would bring in outsiders to do his brutal bidding. Madero's high-minded revolution had become a snake eating its own tail. Peace might be boring, but this was not the sort of warfare Rico had signed up for.

6

SWEEPING AWAY THE WINDS

The cave ended fifteen feet or so from the entrance, but Angela had a terror of being trapped in it. Lying on her side, curled up against the chill night air with the men sleeping around her, she imagined soldiers sneaking up and firing into it. When she did fall asleep she dreamed of trying to escape a hail of lead ricocheting off the cave's walls and low ceiling. She was relieved to see the early morning sunlight shining on her feet.

The gravel road from the Sanchez family's hacienda to the village of San Miguel was only five miles long, but Angela and her men could not travel it. They followed the paths made by burros and pack mules to reach tiny hamlets scattered through the foothills. The trails snaked down into deep canyons and out again. The main road wasn't laid out as straight as a *caracara* bird would fly, but Angela and Antonio's route stretched three times longer.

Angela had never used these paths, once trod by bare Aztec feet, but Antonio had. He had worked for a year as a muleteer, hauling a little bit of everything from one isolated mountain village to another.

Patrols of federal soldiers used the main road and so did the hated local police force called the *rurales*. The back trails through the thick growth of trees and bushes had their own peril, however. That was why Angela and the others had tied pepper tree branches to their saddles. The plumelike leaves of the pepper tree were the most effective for sweeping away *los aires,* the winds.

The Aztecs called the winds *yeyecatl.* They were tiny deities older, Angela liked to say, than the hated President Porfirio Díaz himself. They lived in caves and were likely to be found in wells and near water. They had brought rain to the Aztecs, but if offended they caused all sorts of trouble. Sicknesses brought on by evil winds included chills, rheumatism, paralysis, gout, and open sores. Whether they induced impotence or not became the subject of murmured discussion among the men as they rode behind Angela and Antonio.

Their route passed through tiny villages far from the main road. In each collection of ramshackle houses Angela asked if anyone had seen her mother. The answer was always "no." But the villagers greeted them like heroes in the dusty little plazas. A few barefoot youths in frayed white trousers and shirts insisted on joining them. Angela wasn't happy to take on responsibility for more souls, but at least they brought their own mules and weapons, machetes mostly.

As the little band left each village, the inhabitants called down blessings on them. Angela couldn't have said when last she had cried, but as she rode through the shower of goodwill, tears welled up. She didn't much like crying. The tears stung as though she had rubbed jalapeño juice in her eyes.

The only blessings she had ever received were the pious mumblings and tawdry groping of the local village priest. And that was before he absconded with the pittance in the poor box. The children had called him *camopotonilitzli,* bad breath. No one had come to replace him.

The Sanchezes' old field foreman, Arquímedes, had tried to bestow a blessing on her once. She had waved away the gesture and spit to one side to avert the evil eye. Now she knew, as deep as the salty marrow in her bones, that she needed all the help, divine or otherwise, she could recruit.

A river tumbled in a series of cascades through a small canyon near the last village. When Antonio told the men about it they spurred their mounts in a race for it. They pretended not to hear Angela call them back, and she galloped her mare ahead to cut them off. Two of the reasons they accepted her as their leader was that she had the fastest mount and the finest rifle.

"*¡Pendejos!* Idiots!" She stood in her stirrups so those in the rear could see her. "Are you muleteers rushing to the river before others muddy the water? No! You are soldiers in General Emiliano Zapata's Army of Liberation. You are the wolves for whose heads the *hacendados,* the rich landowners, offer a bounty." She paused for effect and got it. The men were hushed and attentive. They had been called a lot of things in their lives, but never soldiers. And certainly never wolves.

"Do you have lumps of clay between your ears? If I were setting an ambush I would choose a river."

Angela had never been known for her forethought. She couldn't have said why she knew to tell them this. More than that, she was astonished that they listened to her. With the exception of Arquímedes, no one had ever listened to her before.

Angela was even more surprised to discover she had been right. From an outcrop the men looked down at a patrol composed of at least two companies of *federales,* each led by a captain. The sun glinted on the brass bars on their shoulders. She knew these weren't the men who had attacked her home. Thanks to her father, she knew about equine blood-lines. She would have recognized the beautiful gray Andalusian now drinking at the river.

That these were different government soldiers didn't matter. They were *el gobierno,* the government. Before she could decide what orders to give her own men, they charged. Those without mounts raced down-hill on foot. Those with guns used them.

All Angela could do was gallop after them. As she rode, she shouted Zapata's slogan, "Land and liberty," although her family owned land, and she had enjoyed liberty all her life. One of her men, whose father's dead body had been kicked into the irrigation ditch, felt less idealistic.

"For my father, you feces of the devil!"

In the excitement, most of the men's shots went wild. Some of the rusty, ancient weapons refused to fire at all. The blue-jacketed soldiers took orderly cover and their return fire was more accurate. As lead pinged on rocks all around, Angela's band scattered for whatever shelter they could find.

Angela and Antonio crouched behind a large boulder. With her mare's reins clutched in one hand and her father's Winchester in the other, she made her first battlefield assessment. Taking the army-issue Mauser rifles from the *federales'* lifeless fingers and distributing them to her men would give her great pleasure. She even had a brief image of herself mounted on the big crane-colored stallion.

On the other hand, the soldiers outnumbered her band two to one and her men had little ammunition, which was just as well. They were terrible shots and were as likely to hit each other as *el gobierno*. Besides all that, Angela was scared.

Antonio didn't know she was scared, but he agreed with her about the other points. The two of them ran at a crouch from man to man.

"Scatter into the underbrush," they said. "We will meet under the big waterfall downstream from San Miguel."

As the attackers fled up the slope away from the river, Rico saw flashes of the white cotton shirts, trousers, and big straw hats, that all peasants wore. He could also tell there weren't many of them. He was content to let them go, but he knew Juan would feel differently. Anytime someone shot at Juan he took it personally.

"Don't lower yourself by chasing farmers."

"They tried to kill us." Juan vaulted onto his horse and raised his rifle to signal his men to follow him.

"They're armed with a few machetes and some rust that's shaped like rifles. Let them go."

Before Rico finished the sentence Juan had galloped off in pursuit with his company behind him. Rico mounted and led his men after them. When they all arrived at the end of a blind canyon with no quarry in sight, common sense prevailed. Keeping an eye out for the glint of a gun barrel in the rocks above them, they headed across country toward the main road.

As far as Rico and Juan were concerned, the cavalry was the only army unit to belong to, but Juan never looked at ease in the saddle. He was a city boy who had had almost no contact with the peasants in the countryside. Until two years ago he had rarely left Cuernavaca and had seemed intent on making a career of attending college and flirting with women on the plaza every evening.

His family belonged to the middle class that constituted ninety percent of Mexico's bloated bureaucracy. Like most lawyers, teachers, and intellectuals in the provinces, Juan saw little hope of advancement under Díaz's regime. He and his friends were eager for a change in their own lives, and Francisco Madero promised it. As a bonus, he had discovered the allure an army uniform held for women. He gave little thought to the exploited mine workers in Cananea or the impoverished farmers of Morelos.

"What do the *indios* want?" he asked.

"They want their land back."

"President Madero has said they can settle their claims in court."

Rico didn't bother to answer that. Everyone knew the judicial system was still packed with Díaz's appointees, all of whom were either big landowners or their friends. The two rode in silence for a while.

This inept little attack by a gaggle of farmers had convinced Rico that General Huerta was right about one thing. They had to stop Zapata. If he managed to restart the revolution the country would descend into chaos.

Uneducated idealists like Zapata could fight and they could rally followers, but they couldn't govern. Governing depended on intellect and compromise. Rico knew Zapata was angry that Madero had passed him over as governor of the state of Morelos. He hoped the president would come to his senses and give him something equally important to do. He owed him that much. Zapata had won the war for him in this state, and in spite of the current unrest, he was probably the only leader truly loyal to the president.

The closer they came to Cuernavaca the faster the pace Rico set. Juan noticed it.

"*La Inglesa* has put a spell on you."

"She has not."

"Then she has paid someone to put a spell on you. I know a curer who can blow a counterspell into your ear and clean you of it."

"You're an educated man, my friend. How can you believe such nonsense?"

"Books don't contain all the knowledge that exists. There remain some mysteries that scholars cannot explain."

Rico let it rest. He knew better than to try to talk anyone out of their superstitions. Even the sensible Mrs. Knight held séances in a corner of the ballroom from time to time. Although Rico was pretty sure Grace staged the table-tapping sessions only for the amusement of the hotel guests.

Rico had never retreated from anything in his life, except his grandfather and, as a child, his nurse. Now that he'd verified the futility of a frontal assault on Grace Knight, he preferred to think of his next strategy as a flanking movement rather than a retreat. Until he could obtain leave and take the train to the capital to order his secret weapon, the phonograph, he would play a cool hand where she was concerned.

In the meantime, he would make it his duty, his mission, his passion to create diversions that would keep Grace Knight from finding out how bad things were in the mountains and valley surrounding Cuernavaca.

He decided to start with a *burrada*. If that didn't distract her and melt her English reserve, nothing could. He smiled at the thought.

7

GENERATING ELECTRICITY

The clamor sent Grace hurrying through the Colonial's front gate. She found at least twenty-five burros gathered outside, along with most of the hotel's guests and staff. If Grace had tried to tell people back in London how much noise even one burro could make, they wouldn't have believed her. A Klaxon horn stuck in holiday traffic at Marble Arch had nothing on a burro expressing an opinion.

Grace wasn't surprised to find Federico Martín in the middle of the uproar. He held an army bugle under his right arm and a megaphone in his left hand. With the megaphone he directed the Colonial's two gardeners in decorating the saddled burros with bright garlands and tassels.

"Captain Martín, what's going on here?"

"A *burrada*, Mrs. Knight."

"I don't much fancy the sound of that."

Frau Hoffman, the wife of Cuernavaca's German brewer, tugged on Captain Martín's sleeve and shouted to him in her own language. He answered her in kind. Grace wondered how many languages Captain Martín spoke, but the matter of the burros took precedence.

Rico shouted into the megaphone. "The riders will race three laps around the plaza."

Now it was Grace's turn to pull on his sleeve. "What riders?"

He flashed her his ingenuous, barn-on-fire of a smile. "Your guests."

"Someone could fall off and be trampled." Grace planted her fists on her hips and stamped her foot. "I forbid it." But one of those guests was tugging on Rico's other sleeve and he didn't hear Grace.

The ladies wore long dresses of billowy lawn and big hats piled with silk flowers. The men sported serge suits and canvas hunting jackets, starched linen collars, and headgear that ran from bowlers to yachting caps.

Laughing and chattering in a variety of languages, the guests chose their mounts. The men selected burros at the back of the herd to give the women an advantage. Members of the Colonial's staff helped them all clamber aboard, then handed the women the reins and their parasols.

Rico shouted into the megaphone again. "No one may spur his or her burro faster then a walk. Anyone breaking into a trot will be disqualified. Remember, ladies and gentlemen, three laps around the zócalo. The winner will be able to put all food and drink at the Colonial on my bill for the rest of the weekend."

By now a crowd of passersby had gathered to watch. More people ran from every direction. Grace realized the affair was out of her control.

Rico strode across the street and climbed the stairs to the bandstand's stage. He put the bugle to his lips and blew "Call to the Post." He played it quite well, actually, clear and crisp and on key.

He replaced the bugle with the megaphone and shouted, "They're off!"

If Grace hadn't been so mortified she would have laughed at the spectacle. Everyone else did. The plaza had never witnessed so much hilarity.

Juan stood next to Grace while he waited for the mule-drawn trolley to rattle past on its tracks set in the cobblestone street. After it had gone by, with it passengers leaning out to watch the race, Juan winked at Grace.

"*Diez y siete* calls this the Mexican Ass-cot, *Mamacita*."

"Who's *Diez y siete*?"

"Rico."

Grace was about to ask Juan why he called Captain Martín "Seventeen," but the the riders came past in a clamor of brays and shouts and laughter. When they had completed their high-spirited second lap, Juan stretched a red ribbon across the street from a lamppost to a palm tree. He tied it with a slipknot to serve as a finish line.

Grace turned on her heel and stalked back inside. She didn't want to get Captain Martín into trouble with his superiors, but she really would have to speak to Colonel Rubio about him. With pranks like this, the man would ruin the Colonial's reputation for dignity and decorum.

As Grace headed for the upstairs balcony to watch the finish, Lyda hailed her from the front desk. She waved a fistful of yellow paper.

"Gracie, we're almost full and still we're getting telegrams from Em Cee." Mexico City had too many syllables for Lyda, so Em Cee it always was. "A station cab is on its way from the train with a load of customers. They should just about top us off."

"Top us off?"

"Fill us up." Lyda grinned. "I would say your dashing captain is good for business."

"He is not my captain."

Grace walked away and did not hear Lyda mutter, "Oh yes, he is."

Captain Martín's ability to organize frivolity was impressive but infuriating since he never bothered to clear his escapades with Grace. She would learn of it as guests set off in victoria cabs for the horse races and shooting matches he arranged at the army barracks near the rail station. She would have thought he was trying to annoy her, except that he hardly seemed aware of her existence.

In the evenings Grace always knew when Rico was in the cantina because of the laughter and song spilling out. She avoided the bar when Rico was there, but Lyda didn't. She reported that Rico must have seen the newsreels shown before the films at Cuernavaca's posh new theater. He did passable impressions of Theodore Roosevelt, Austria's archduke Ferdinand, and David Lloyd George, the British chancellor of the exchequer.

Lyda said her favorite was Rico's version of the late Queen Victoria eating taffy. Lyda didn't know where Rico might have seen film of her majesty, but Grace wouldn't have been surprised if he had had an audience with her. By this point, Grace wouldn't have been surprised to learn that Rico had actually shared taffy with the former queen of England.

That first night's hand-kissing episode had given Grace the impression Captain Martín was interested in her. Now a polite bow and a "Good day" were all she could expect from him. She told herself she didn't care, but she found reasons to stay downstairs later than she used to, on the chance she might see him.

One evening a trumpet playing "Tiger Rag" drew her to the cantina's doorway as if reeling in a fish on a line. Grace saw that Rico was the source of it. She added musician to the list of his accomplishments, and that was a title she did not grant frivolously.

He wore oxford shoes, gray flannel trousers, and a white linen shirt with a soft collar open at the neck. He sat atop the far end of the long mahogany bar with his lanky legs dangling. When he finished "Tiger Rag" he moved smoothly into "Ostrich Walk." He had everyone's rapt attention, yet he played as if he were alone.

In the fog of tobacco smoke, the dim electric light in the ceiling cast a diffuse glow around him. Grace felt a tingling in her fingers, as though from electricity. She backed out of the doorway, hoping he hadn't noticed her. The music trailed her up the stairs to her rooms.

"Tiger Rag" and "Ostrich Walk" were both jolly tunes. Grace wondered why they resonated with such melancholy when Captain Martín played them. The thought she might have something to do with his melancholy didn't occur to her.

Grace's home in the Colonial was a small, second-floor suite at the southeast end of the hotel. Her narrow balcony faced the zócalo, as the small plaza was called, with its small bandstand.

She often had trouble sleeping. So it was tonight with "Tiger Rag" echoing in her head, along with the memory of that tingling sensation. Electricity was a mystery to her and she wondered if it were leaking out somewhere in the cantina.

She put on a silk kimono the color of old ivory and went to the balcony. With her hands on the railing, she looked out over the tile roofs of the city sleeping in the moonlight. If she held on to the railing and leaned out she could see the shimmering snowcap of the volcano Popocatepetl. She had to lean far out, though, to look around the plaster gargoyle that shared the corner of the building with her. She had named the creature L.G., after Sir David Lloyd George. Years ago Grace had heard Sir David give one of his firebrand speeches in Hyde Park. The gargoyle, with its out-thrust jaw and pugnacious scowl, did resemble him.

The hour was late. The cantina must be closed. So why did she hear music playing? It grew louder as five musicians crossed the zócalo, passing through the moon shadow thrown by the bandstand. With guitars, guitaron, mandolin, and trumpet they played the rebels' anthem, "Valentina," with the trumpet carrying the melody. The song stirred the hair on the nape of Grace's neck.

She had stood on this balcony a year and a half ago, and watched the rebels' triumphant parade around the plaza with their women trailing behind them. Zapata's peasants had defeated the government's troops, but they could hardly be called an army. They wore rags and rode gaunt horses with primitive wooden saddles. Draped with bandoleers, and armed with knives, machetes, pistols, and rifles they looked like a convocation of bandits. "Valentina" was the song they sang.

If they're going to kill me tomorrow,
Let them kill me right away.

They had been so proud that day, Davids to the Mexican Army's Goliath.

But those singing now weren't an army. Some *señorita* will be waked from a sound sleep, Grace thought. And so will all her neighbors.

When the musicians set a course for the street under her balcony it became apparent that she would be that hapless *señorita*. Grace couldn't see their faces under their sombreros, but she knew with a certainty that Captain Martín was the one playing the trumpet.

She scurried off the balcony and stood with her back against the curtains framing the doorway. She pressed a hand over her heart to quiet the thumping, and pretended she wasn't here.

Then they began singing "Las Mañanitas." Rico's tenor led the tight, but barely controlled harmony that always, in Mexico, sounded as if it were about to jump the tracks and go off across country on its own. Grace had never heard Zulus harmonize, or South Sea Islanders, but Mexicans made the English music she did know sound halfhearted at best.

Grace's husband Carlos had waked her with this song on her birthday each year she had known him. She peeked around the curtain at the position of the full moon. A little after midnight. Did Captain Martín know she was born on this day, now only a few minutes old itself? She had a feeling he did.

Maybe the song triggered the remorse. It was never far below her surface. "I'm sorry, Carlos," she whispered. "I'm sorry I forsook your name."

While sipping oolong in Grace's former tea shop five years ago, the governor of Morelos had talked her into buying this old ruin of a building. He had convinced her she could turn it into a hotel. He had also persuaded her to use her father's name, Knight, instead of Mendoza, her husband's name. It would be better for business, the governor said. Foreigners who came here as guests would have more confidence in Knight.

Grace felt she had forsaken her dead husband's name, and now she was tempted to betray his memory.

"*Querido* Carlitos, what should I do about Federico Martín?"

Outside, the musicians came to the verse that had reached into her soul when Carlos sang it. Rico's voice poised on a high note as if balanced on a precipice, then slid down the scale like a waterfall.

"Wake up," the words said. "Wake up. A new day has dawned."

Grace clung to the heavy damask curtains and sobbed.

After an eternity of verses, the singers finished and dispersed into the night. Grace wiped her eyes and blew her nose, but she knew she couldn't sleep. She left her room and padded barefoot to the second-floor gallery. She leaned her hips against the half wall, braced her hands on the top of it and looked down into the courtyard and garden. The moonlight pouring into it lit the open corridors of the first floor.

She walked downstairs to prowl her creation, as she often did late at night. She liked to recall what this building had looked like the first time she saw it, filled with half a century of rubble and trash. It had devoured all her inheritance, but she never tired of seeing what she had made of it. Some day it might even turn a profit.

She savored the gloss of the terra-cotta tiles under the soles of her bare feet. She admired the columns topped with the plaster-cast lilies she had designed. She ran her hand along the colorful wall mosaics and remembered the soft-spoken *indio* artisans who had painted them, fired them, and set them in place.

Only at this time of night would she find the back courtyard quiet. She walked among the big cement washtubs, the gardening tools. She felt the warmth from the coals in the braziers where her employees cooked meals that didn't include roast beef, green beans, or parsleyed potatoes. In doorways and nooks she glimpsed bodies asleep on reed mats with handwoven cotton blankets over them.

The local members of the Colonial's staff walked to work each morning, but about half of Grace's people lived in distant villages. They shared rooms facing the back courtyard and the rooms had beds, although the country folk preferred the mats they called *petates*.

Grace knew how many people she had hired, but she had no idea how many worked for her. The number fluctuated as members of her staff's families showed up to pitch in. In Mexico a job was a gift to be shared. Standing there, Grace thought her heart too small to contain the affection she felt for all of them. Without them she could not have made her dream real. She knew this elegant old building was only stone and mortar and wood, but late at night she would have sworn it had a spirit.

On her way back she stepped into an arched niche on the north side. The wall was thinner there and Grace put her ear against it. She liked to listen to the hum from the transformer in the wooden shed just on the other side. It supplied electricity to the streetlights around the plaza, and to the buildings, including the Colonial. The steady hum reassured her that all was well.

As she headed for the stairs, she did not hear Leobardo, the night watchman, let Captain Martín in through the small door in the front gate. She did not see Rico standing still as a statue in the shadows of the banana trees in the courtyard. He watched her stride silently through the high white arches of the moonlit corridor, the pale kimono floating out in a nimbus around her.

8

LETHAL BEANS

Antonio's thirteen-year-old sister, Socorro, called softly at the cave entrance. She toted an old rectangular Standard Oil can with the top cut off and a rope handle attached. It held beans cooked with chilis and a stack of tortillas wrapped in banana leaves. Tied on her back was a blue cotton shawl containing twelve small pots made of the local red clay.

The pots all had arrived intact, which was remarkable, considering that she had had to descend a sheer cliff wall to reach her brother's hideout. A thread of a trail led from the village above down to the river, but if the dense growth of bushes hadn't provided handholds, Socorro wouldn't have been able to keep to it.

The cave's wide, low opening in the cliff face was twenty-five feet above the river tumbling along the bottom of the *barranca,* a deep, narrow canyon. The canyon began abruptly not too far upstream, which meant the river made a sudden drop over the edge of it, landing a hundred feet below in a cloud of mist. Dozens of swallows darted in and out of the spray. The cascade filled the cave with a low roar.

Angela divided the clay pots among them so they could practice making grenades. She did not want to arrive at General Zapata's headquarters looking unprepared for war. She had spent a fourth of her father's *pesos* to buy ingredients for the grenades—a mix of saltpeter, charcoal, and sulfur, plus cotton fuses, and ground-up dried beans for filler. She used a battered wooden kitchen ladle to scoop the gunpowder out of one small sack and the dried beans out of another. The potters of San Miguel supplied the vessels.

Plinio, to Angela's surprise, admitted that he had made grenades before. He knew what quantity of beans to add to make the powder stretch further, and still go "Boom!" Antonio was melting paraffin in a small tin can to seal the pots' mouths. The fuses protruded like tongues from the wax.

Socorro looked at yesterday's finished grenades stacked on a mat at the back of the cave. They had a rollicking, roly-poly look to them, like children waiting for school recess.

"*Papi* wants to know if you need more pots."

Angela hefted the half-empty sack. "Give your father our thanks, but we have only enough powder to fill these."

Antonio studied his sister through narrowed eyes. "Do you weigh more than when I saw you last?"

"No."

He lifted the hem of her skirt to expose another one underneath.

"Why are you wearing two sets of clothes?"

"I'm going with you."

"No, you're not."

"*Señorita* Angela rides with you. Why can't I?"

"Because I said so. Now go. And tell *Papá* to meet us at the old field with the mare and the mules."

Socorro glared at him before she went, but Angela knew what Antonio was thinking. His sister was very pretty. Some officer in the rebel army would try to recruit her as his concubine, and Antonio would have to kill him.

The men went outside with the rations Socorro had brought. They ate sitting along the narrow ledge by the cave's entrance. From here they had a bird's-eye view of the river and the swallows darting.

After they had eaten, the men unrolled their mats in the cave and took a siesta. When the wax had hardened, sealing the gunpowder in the pots, Angela prodded her troops with her foot.

"Gather your things. Pick up every piece of trash. We do not want to leave anything that might cause *el gobierno* to suspect Antonio's people of hiding us." She handed a bundle of brush to Ambrozio Nuñez, the last young man to join the group. She chose him because he looked the most likely to object. "When we've gone outside, sweep away all the footprints."

"That's woman's work," he said.

"Do you see women here?"

"I see one."

Plinio chuckled. The other men were familiar with Angela's temper. They swallowed their laughter so as not to attract her wrath. They all had seen her throw rocks with unerring accuracy and hit crows scavenging corn in a field. They could imagine the damage she might inflict at this close range.

"If you do not want to take orders from a woman, why did you join us?"

"I didn't know you were female." He used the word *hembra*. It described not a woman but a female animal.

The men backed away from him. When Angela whacked him with whatever came to hand they didn't want to get in the way.

Instead she said, "I understand, *pendejocito*. You have lost your courage. You want an excuse not to ride with us and fight for your countrymen."

He started to object, but she raised a hand and smiled. "Go in peace, *coño*. We will deliver your regrets to General Zapata. We will tell him that Ambrozio Nuñez of pueblo Azcatl went home with his tail between his legs. We will tell him that Ambrozio Nuñez is content to let the women fight for his people's land."

"I will fight alongside men, but not women." He picked up his bedroll, machete, and satchel and stalked out of the cave.

"May snakes and toads crawl out of your mouth," Angela called after him. "May your insignificant penis shrivel up like a chili pepper."

He looked back and crossed himself several times before he started up the trail to the top of the *barranca*. The perilous climb was not what worried him. His village lay not far from Miguel Sanchez's hacienda.

He had heard stories about the tricks she played. No one claimed she had supernatural powers, just a long memory and a strong shoulder for carrying a grudge.

Angela slung a pouch of grenades across her shoulder. She rolled her blanket inside her mat. She buckled the almost-empty cartridge belt at her waist. She put on her sombrero and retrieved her father's 30-30 from where it leaned against the cave wall.

As the men filed out past her she laid a hand on Plinio's arm to keep him with her.

"Grandfather," she murmured. "You should lead them."

"No, my daughter. God has chosen you."

"What if I can't do this?"

"God says you can. Who are we to question God?"

Angela sighed and followed her family's old *mayordomo* outside. The men waited on the ledge with their backs pressed against the cliff wall. Her band's mission now was to do what the government's soldiers couldn't. They had to find General Emiliano Zapata and the troops he called the Liberating Army of the South.

"*Adelante, mis guachos.* Forward, my foundlings," she said. "For land and liberty."

9

ALONG FOR THE RIDE

The first morning that Grace had found Rico sitting in the kitchen and holding a raw beef steak to his eye, she had become alarmed. "Are you badly hurt?" she had asked him. By now, she knew better.

When she saw him wearing a steak as an eye patch at seven-thirty this morning she only wondered if he had arisen early or if he hadn't gone to bed yet. She assumed the latter. He seemed alert enough, but his friend Juan looked like he'd slept in the middle of the trolley tracks while the mules pulled the *trencito,* the trolley, back and forth over him all night.

Rico leaped to his feet and gave a graceful but precise bow. He had made no mention of the serenade under her balcony a few nights ago, and Grace certainly wasn't going to bring it up.

"Good morning, gentlemen."

Grace could see that María had food preparations for today's excursion well in hand. Annie was helping her pack the picnic baskets. Lyda was fortifying herself with a cup of coffee almost strong enough to hold a pewter spoon upright.

"I trust you are not badly hurt, Captain," Grace said.

"A little accident, Mrs. Knight."

"He ran into a fist," mumbled Juan.

When Rico returned the steak to María, Grace saw that the area around his eye was swollen and bruised a deep purple with touches of red, umber, and olive green so subtle they would have made Claude Monet proud.

"Another late-night dustup in Cantina Lobo," said Lyda.

"There were five of them," Annie amplified. "Juan started the fight. Rico only evened the odds."

Evened the odds? Had these wastrels lured the child into gambling?

Lyda stood up. "Grace, would you check the 'whoop and holler' with me? It has an odd buzz to it."

Grace followed her toward the lobby where the telephone hung on the wall next to the front desk.

"What's wrong with the telephone?" Most people still sent telegrams, but more and more of the Colonial's business depended on the telephone line from Mexico City.

It generally worked well, but "whoop and holler" sometimes applied. In west Texas, where Lyda and Annie came from, folks strung uninsulated phone lines along the barbwire fences. Reception was uncertain at best. That was how the system came by its nickname.

They had barely rounded the corner when Lyda grabbed both Grace's arms in a blacksmith's grip and hissed, "Ask them to go with us."

"Whom?"

"Rico and Juan."

"They're Rico and Juan now?"

"Ask them, Gracie. The guests enjoy their company."

"They have other duties." Although to be honest, Grace couldn't see that those amounted to much, other than duty rotation to Tres Marías and occasional trips to Mexico City.

"Colonel Rubio will do anything you ask. Besides, it's Sunday. All Colonel Fatso plans to do is get drunk and visit the whorehouses on Gutemburg Street."

And a good thing, too, Grace thought. She had had to have only one standoff with the colonel when he tried to take a woman to his room. The outcome had never been in doubt for anyone but Rubio. Apparently he didn't want to risk another such loss of face. As for the junior officers, Grace had long ago intimidated them into gentlemanly behavior, at least as far as lady callers were concerned.

"Listen to me, Grace. Jake says there's been some trouble in the valley. We could use an escort."

"Who's Jake?"

"Just a fella."

"You're blushing, Lyda. Who is he?"

"Jake McGuire. A wildcatter for Standard Oil. And don't change the subject."

"What trouble? How can there be trouble? Rubio rides out with patrols all the time on the hunt for bandits. Besides," Grace added, "we're only taking the main highway for a picnic at the *barranca* bridge. That's not the tuley-weeds, as you call them."

Lyda cocked her head and gave her the Look.

"Very well then. I'll ask them. But don't think I don't know what you're really about."

Deciding what to wear to a picnic with Grace Knight and her hotel guests was not a trifling matter for Rico, and vanity had nothing to do with it. Well, maybe vanity had a little to do with it.

Lyda had taken him aside and said she would try to persuade Grace to go to San Miguel after lunch. The vases from that village were the most popular item in the Colonial's gift shop. Grace had to talk to José Perez and the other potters about providing a steady supply. Lyda asked Rico if he would be willing to escort Grace to the village. Of course he agreed, but the prospect of leaving the city's limits in her company complicated the wardrobe decision.

He could not wear his army uniform. If it didn't draw fire from disgruntled rebels-in-waiting, it would arouse fear and hostility in San Miguel. A suit with starched collar and pressed cuffs would label him as a government functionary come to demand a bribe or announce the latest legal loophole for stealing village land and water.

Rico drew the line at appearing in the pajamalike white trousers and shirt, and leather sandals of a farmer. He would look ridiculous, and he would have as much chance of fooling the villagers as if he wore a gorilla suit. In any case, he owned neither farmer's clothes nor a gorilla suit.

The only option left was his *charro* outfit—white linen shirt, waist-length embroidered jacket, tight trousers that flared below the knees to show the white pantaloons underneath, all finished off with black leather riding boots polished to a mirrorlike surface. If vanity had been Rico's prime consideration, he would have realized this was swoon-worthy attire.

Instead, he fretted about his bruised and swollen face. He considered putting a black patch over his eye, but decided that piratical was not the look he wanted either.

Rico buckled on his cartridge belt and his late father's pair of Colt Navy revolvers, Model 1851. If he had to name his most prized possessions, the Navys would be them. He collected his Mauser, grabbed his fancy black felt sombrero covered in embroidered flowers and birds, and left his small room in a rush. He wanted to go with Socrates, the Colonial's handyman, to put petrol in the Pierce's tank. Rico's grandfather kept a motor car at his house in the capital, but it was a Model T Ford and hardly counted.

If Rico had had his choice he would have owned a Thomas Flyer, model K6-70. That car had recently won the first and only around-the-world race ever held; but at $1,250, the Old Man refused to consider adding a Flyer to his inventory. Still, a Pierce, even a seven-year-old Motorette like Grace's, would do.

Rico's spurs jingled as he walked down the narrow back hallway used by the maids. He passed through the bubble of cool air that the maids claimed was the breath of a ghost. The stairs at the end led to the rear courtyard, which in turn gave access to the stable.

The Pierce sat in a former stall. Rico's grandfather's Andalusian stallion occupied one of the two remaining stalls. Grullo had struck up a friendship with the hotel mule in the other one. The Old Man had gone to Mexico City for a lengthy stay and Rico saw no sense in returning the horse to go unridden and turn restive at the hacienda.

Rico was supposed to keep his mount in the barracks corral near the train station. Even Colonel Rubio had to use the city's hostlery several blocks away. If he learned that one of his junior officers kept a horse within rock-chunking distance of his own quarters, he would be furious. Rico paid Socrates a few extra *pesos* each week to take care of Grullo and keep quiet about his presence. Socrates was awed by Grullo and probably would have done it for free.

Mrs. Knight called Socrates her *hace-todo,* do-everything. He oversaw the gardeners and artisans. He did repairs and kept things running smoothly. Juan called him the mayor of the Colonial.

Rico found him buffing the last square inch of the Pierce's lacquered red fender. Socrates made sure the car always gleamed. That was no easy feat since only the main streets were paved with cobblestones while the rest were dirt. Of course, the Pierce rarely strayed onto side streets.

The thought occurred to Rico that Socrates probably could answer some questions about his employer. Such as: Did she have any beaus? What was her favorite food? Did she ever cry? Did she know how to dance the newest craze, the tango? Those were questions a gentleman didn't ask, and he certainly did not make such inquiries of the help.

Socrates had brushed and saddled the gray, but Rico decided not to take him out yet. He wasn't going to pass up an opportunity to enjoy even a short ride in the Pierce. He stepped onto the small running board and climbed into the passenger side of the high seat. He waited while Socrates turned the starter crank near the right front wheel.

In a cloud of smoke, with the engine percolating industriously on both cylinders, the Pierce nosed out into the street and headed for the dilapidated automobile repair shop located behind the governor's palace. Inside it stood the only petrol pump in the city.

Rico looked up at the morning sun shining in a cloudless sky. Cuernavaca deserved its nickname, the City of Eternal Spring. Grace Knight would have a perfect day for her picnic and for a ride to San Miguel.

Rico folded his arms across his chest and settled back on the tufted velvet seat. Socrates, with one white-gloved hand gripping the steering lever, looked as proud as any king in Christendom. Rico knew how he felt.

He himself was going to spend the day with Grace Knight. He must have felt this happy at some time in his life, but he couldn't remember when.

10

PICNICKING ON THE PRECIPICE

Grace found it difficult not to stare at Rico. Those tight leather trousers were distracting, but to see them mounted on such a horse was hypnotic. The congestion of foot and burro traffic on the main road out of town meant that the cars could not travel very fast. Rico and the gray paced them the whole way, cantering just ahead and to the right of the Pierce. Lyda, who sat next to Grace, had two words to describe the view of him.

"Lordy, lordy." If Lyda knew the meaning of sotto voce she had no truck with it. "Doesn't *rico* also mean delicious?"

Grace was sure Captain Martín had heard that. The tinted driving goggles hid her eyes, but she wanted to sink down in the Motorette's seat anyway.

As Grace watched Jake McGuire help the women descend from the big Dodge town car, she wondered what it was about rogues that made them so irresistible. Lyda's new beau, in his tooled cowboy boots and battered Stetson hat, had rogue written all over him. No wonder Lyda giggled like a schoolgirl for no apparent reason these days.

Grace had had a run-in with McGuire the first evening he came into the Colonial and headed for the cantina. Grace had noticed the bulge of a shoulder holster under his jacket. Her job included noticing things like that.

"Mr. McGuire," she had said. "We will be happy to look after your weapon for you while you sojourn with us."

"What weapon?" He had looked confused, although Grace suspected the word "sojourn" was what had thrown him. He had pulled out a 32-caliber pistol and held it up close to his nose, as if its diminutive size made it difficult to see. "You mean this?"

"I do."

"Why ma'am, if someone were to shoot me with one of these, and I were to find out about it, I would surely be annoyed."

"All the same, Mr. McGuire . . ."

He had bowed and given in with good humor, but he didn't fool Grace. She could tell from those eyes set like pale sapphires in twin deltas of squint lines that giving in was not his usual response.

Jake McGuire drove the expedition's second motorcar, one he had borrowed from his boss. The Dodge was a town car with room for six passengers in the *tonneau*. Five more followed in a rented, horse-drawn station cab called a victoria. Jake, Rico, and Juan helped unload the picnic baskets and the passengers, the women in long, canvas dusters, the men in leather ones.

The guests took off their hats and driving goggles and trailed after Grace to the small park laid out along the top of the cliff. This was as close to Mexican wilderness as some of the women had ever ventured. A few of them fussed about that dreadful menace, Emiliano Zapata, creating problems in the countryside.

"Don't you worry about that little *indio,* ladies." Jake winked at them. "He's all hat and no cattle."

María and some of her kitchen staff had arrived ahead of time. While they finished setting out the lunch on linen tablecloths, Grace led the guests to the best place to take in the view. She doubted that any of them had noticed it no matter how often they drove across the bridge on their way to and from the railroad station.

She enjoyed hearing people's "oohs" and "aahs" at their first sight of the Barranca Almanaco. She liked to watch the looks on their faces as they stared into its green depths. Parrots soared among the trees below this overlook. Dozens of clear springs cascaded from the walls.

Grace asked them to note the bridge from down here, below the highway that crossed it. Porfirio Díaz had had it designed in the French style, and the graceful strength of its slender, eighty-foot-tall arches always awed her. She explained that like all monuments, public buildings, and the town's bandstand, the bridge was dedicated on September 15, Porfirio Díaz's birthday.

Grace left them clucking about how shabbily those ungrateful *indios* had treated President Díaz. They agreed he had been a brilliant, progressive, enlightened leader. More than a quorum of them thought he should return from exile and take control of a country that was obviously veering off into social and economic ruin.

Grace heard enough of politics in the Colonial's restaurant and lobby. This was not the place for it and she walked off on her own, following the rim of the *barranca*. Cuernavaca was built along the ridges separating seven parallel canyons, but she considered this one the most beautiful. It was a secret garden, wilder, lovelier, and more luxuriant than anything men could devise. She was listening so intently to the music of the springs and waterfalls that she jumped when Captain Martín spoke just behind her.

"Mrs. Knight, if you intend to go to San Miguel, we should leave now."

Grace turned to find Lyda with him. "Before lunch?"

"Jake and Annie and I can entertain the guests," Lyda said. "Rico says San Miguel isn't far, but the road is rough. You don't want to have to return after dark."

No, Grace thought. I definitely don't want that.

"Shall we take the motorcar then?"

"I understand a rock slide is blocking the road." Rico glanced at Grace's high-button patent leather shoes. "Can you ride a horse?"

"Impossible." Lyda laughed. "Grace says if God intended people to ride horses He would have equipped the beasts with an off-lever."

Grace was chagrined. "It's all those teeth, don't you know. And if only they weren't so big."

"The teeth or the horses?"

"Both."

"You can ride sidesaddle with me."

Grace took several deep breaths while she pondered the pros and cons of the invitation. The vases from San Miguel brought in steady revenue to the gift shop with little outlay of cash. She needed as much revenue as she could get. The rebellion of 1910 had broken out just as the hotel was becoming a paying proposition. All that shooting had frightened away tourists and driven her into debt to the bankers in Mexico City.

She shot a sideways look at Captain Martín. He stood with his hands clasped behind his back and stared at the tiny puffs of smoke from the train chugging up the distant mountain toward Tres Marías. He seemed to have little interest in her and hence, no ulterior motives for this excursion.

Then there was the debit side of the ledger, the gossip that an afternoon alone with Captain Martín would generate. Before she answered, Grace had to decide where on the horse she should sit. If she rode in front of Captain Martín his arms would be around her. If she rode behind him her chest would press against his back. Her face heated up at that prospect.

She realized that her worries about what people would think, or even what Captain Martín might think, didn't matter. She had to talk to José and the villagers about setting up a manufacturing facility for the vases.

Best to put a good face on it. This was, after all, the twentieth century. Grace headed back toward the car to retrieve her coat. At least it would insulate her somewhat from physical contact with the man.

"Tallyho, Captain." She flashed him a bright smile. "Let's be off then, shall we?"

II

A DEARTH OF EARTHENWARE

Rico was grateful Grace seemed unaware that people of his family's station considered it highly unseemly for a man and woman to touch unless they were married. Their prudery had always struck Rico as old-fashioned and silly, but now he understood it. The sun's tug on the planets, the earth's magnetic field, or a dozen strong men pulling on a stout rope couldn't compare with the irrational forces at work in Rico.

Grace sat sideways on the saddle in front of him. Rico's arms ached from trying to avoid contact with her, when what he wanted to do was encircle her waist with his hands, to see if it was really as small as it looked. He didn't know how he was going to make it to San Miguel without brushing away the tendrils of her dark red-gold hair and kissing the curve of her neck.

She also must have felt the tension because she kept up a steady flow of questions.

"Captain, why does your friend Juan call you *Diez y siete*? Doesn't that mean 'seventeen'?"

"It's nothing. A joke."

Then Rico thought of all the things Grace might assume it to mean. The number of women he had bedded. The number of illegitimate children he had fathered. The number of freckles on his backside. With Juan calling him that, seventeen could mean the number of venereal diseases Rico had contracted.

"Seventeen families own one-fourth of all the land in the state of Morelos."

"And your family is one of them?"

"Yes. Their original deed goes back to an *encomienda,* a grant from Hernán Cortés."

"And yet you joined Francisco Madero's army to fight for the rights of the poor."

"It is possible to have money in the bank and a conscience, too." He paused. "As for me, I keep my conscience safely locked in the bank's vault."

When Grace laughed she threw her head back and her hair tickled his nose. Her laughter was so carefree that it chased away his own cares.

"And yet your family had so much to lose with a change of government."

"As it turned out," Rico said, "they lost nothing." And that, oddly enough, was one of his cares. The cause for which he had fought seemed to have been forgotten once Francisco Madero became president.

"What do you think of Mr. Zapata?" Grace asked.

"He's an idealist, and you know what they say about those."

"What do they say?"

"An idealist observes that an orchid smells better than a potato, so he concludes that it will make a more savory stew."

"President Madero is an idealist and yet he governs."

Rico wanted to tell her that Francisco Madero had proven to be an educated fool, a coward, and a hypocrite. Instead he said, "President Madero is a logical man trying to run an illogical country."

"If the world were a logical place, Captain, men would ride sidesaddle, now wouldn't they?"

Rico laughed so hard he almost lost his balance, and the tension vanished. What had started as a strategy for seduction had become an outing with a friend, a beautiful, complex, desirable friend, but a friend nonetheless. He lowered his arms to a more natural position and he felt Grace's spine lose some of its starch.

As the horse struggled to find footing on the rocky trail, Grace asked, "Is this the only road?"

"The only one I know of."

"Then the villagers have to transport all their pottery on burros."

"Or on their backs. When the *indios* laid the railroad tracks they took the wheels off the barrows, loaded the sand and rocks into them, and carried all of it."

"You jest with me, Captain."

"I swear I do not. The Aztecs were clever people, but they left the invention of the wheel to the Europeans. Their descendants still regard it with suspicion."

"I trust someone in San Miguel will be able to speak English."

"Other than your acquaintance, José Perez, we'll be lucky to find someone who speaks Spanish."

"What if he's not there?"

"I can speak Nahuatl."

Grace turned to look at him, realized how little space separated them, and quickly faced forward. "When did you learn Nahuatl?"

"My grandmother was *pura india* and so was my nurse. I didn't speak much Spanish until I went to school. The teachers hit us with sticks if we answered in Mexican."

"Mexican?"

"We refer to Nahuatl as Mexican."

"Where did you learn French, Italian, German, and English?"

"Here and there."

"Your 'here and there' must encompass more of the world than most people's."

"I've traveled some and I tested the patience of the professors at Harvard for a time."

"Did you major in poker and pranks?"

"Those were electives."

"What was your course of study?"

"My family assumed I was studying law. They were displeased to discover I had enrolled in medicine."

"Why didn't you want to study the law? The search for justice is a noble profession."

"Not in this country. To succeed here a young lawyer must give up any principles and ideals he might have."

Rico realized that something was happening here subtler than he had experienced before. Grace Knight now knew a lot about him and he had learned almost nothing about her. Rico's conquests had always been younger women only too willing to tell him the mundane details of their lives whether he wanted to hear them or not. Was Mrs. Knight reticent because she was older and wiser or because she was British? Or did secrets lurk in the shadows of her past?

"Is the village much farther?" she asked.

Rico pointed ahead and up. "There."

"Where?"

"The houses follow the rim of the *barranca*."

"They look like a continuation of the cliff face."

"After a thousand years a village begins to resemble its surroundings. This one may be named in honor of Saint Michael, but don't be fooled. It was here long before Cortés came. It's divided into neighborhoods based on the Aztec kinship system. Each *barrio* has its ancient name, like *ayotl, azcatl, cueyatl.*"

"What do they mean?"

"*Ayotl,* means turtle. *Azcatl,* ant. *Cueyatl,* frog. They must sound silly to you."

"Those can't compare with names of English towns. Have you ever visited Slack Bottom or Bachelor's Bump?"

"I have not."

"My favorite place-name is Cockup. Big Cockup and Little Cockup, actually. In England's north country."

"What does 'cockup' mean?"

"A mess. A total disaster."

Rico could see where that would be a useful phrase to describe Mexico these days. They rode in a comfortable silence for a while. Comfortable silences were also something Rico had not experienced with women.

He had never been to San Miguel. He was surprised to find that it could be reached by a narrow concrete bridge across a river hustling along over rocks. Birds sang in the huge cedar trees whose drooping branches brushed the surface of the water.

Halfway across the bridge, Grace asked him to stop. On the downstream side of the bridge the shallow, boulder-strewn riverbed dropped away suddenly, sending a torrent of crystal clear water in a headlong plunge over a precipice.

"Just when I think I have seen all the beauty your country holds, Captain, it astonishes me again."

Beyond the bridge they had to dismount and lead Grullo up the steep climb to the aerie called San Miguel. Rico held Grace's hand to help her along. Grace was panting when she reached the top, but the village was worth the effort. Mango trees shaded the dusty main street. Drifts of purple, red, and orange bougainvillea flowers covered windowless houses made of the local volcanic rock. Many of the thatched roofs had been patched with flattened oil cans.

Visible through the open doorways were dirt floors, dented cooking pots, and the ever-present sleeping mats made of the reeds called *tule*. Set out to dry on boards in front of a few houses were examples of the earthenware that had brought Grace here.

"I expected to find more pottery," she said.

"Maybe they sold it all in the market yesterday."

The children wore rags or nothing, and they stopped their games to watch Rico and Grace ride past. Ladder-ribbed dogs barked or skulked away. The scrawny pigs and mangy chickens ignored them. Men sent oblique looks from under their sombreros. The women glanced up, but didn't break the cadence of patting out tortillas and grinding corn.

"The children are so thin," Grace murmured. "I didn't realize the village was this poor. At the market they all look so . . ." she searched for a word ". . . so spruce."

"They put on their Sunday best for market day. And San Miguel is better off than many." Rico called to one of the children, "*¿Mi hijo, donde vive José Perez?*" When he received a blank look, he repeated the question in Nahuatl.

The boy started off at a trot and Rico reined the horse around to follow.

Word traveled faster than they did. José was waiting for them at the gate of the adobe wall in front of his house. His stiff thatch of black hair was indented in a circle around his head, the impression left by the straw hat he held in his hand. Here in his home territory he looked very much the solid citizen.

He invited them to sit on a bench in the courtyard where laundry hung on a bamboo pole laid between the crotches of two papaya trees. Flowers rioted all around and heaps of drying cocoa beans made the air heavy with their aroma. José's wife, Serafina, and his beautiful daughter, Socorro, brought out small porcelain cups of hot chocolate. The cups were obviously prized possessions.

"Captain, please tell the Perez family how pleased I am to be able to visit them here in their home. And could you explain that I have business to discuss with *Maestro* Perez?"

Rico had assumed that Grace intended to negotiate a monopoly on the villagers' pottery output. He was surprised to learn that she had something else in mind. She went with José to inspect an open-sided, thatched shelter that might do for a factory.

Rico translated as Grace and José discussed quotas, delivery schedules, records-keeping systems, and the cost per pot. They estimated the price of ovens and drying racks, and even straw and rope for packing. Grace said she would like the Colonial to have priority as an outlet for their wares, but she also offered to speak to the owner of *Luz del Día,* the largest store in Cuernavaca. Perhaps he too would carry the pottery.

At the end of their discussion Grace asked José if he would accept the position of foreman, *jefe,* for a small monthly salary. She trusted him, she said, to choose not only the best potters but the ones most in need. He accepted. They shook hands.

When Rico and Grace rode out of San Miguel they left it a happier place than when they rode in. This enterprise was obviously about more than turning a profit in the Colonial's gift shop. In fact, Rico didn't see how Grace planned to make any profit at all after she bankrolled an entire village.

"You made a wise choice in José," he said. "He's the *mayordomo* of San Miguel."

"Like the village mayor?"

"More than that. The *mayordomo* is an Aztec tradition. José collects funds to maintain the chapel. That means people trust him with money. He organizes the annual fiestas for their patron saint. Also, every village has communal work days called *cuatequitl*. José tells people when their turn has come."

They reached Cuernavaca at sunset, with the sky pulsing as brilliant as fiesta fireworks over the mountains. A fiery, opalescent mist wrapped around the snowcaps on the two volcanoes. Rico dismounted at the Colonial's front gate. When he lifted Grace down from the horse his hands did indeed almost span her waist, even with her coat on. For a few moments they saw their reflections in each other's eyes.

Grace had eyes like *cenotes,* the pools of water trapped in limestone and as blue as the sky above them. *Cenotes* were also much, much deeper than they looked.

Grace thanked him, told him when dinner would be served, and hurried inside. She seemed all business again, but she began singing as she crossed the courtyard. Gilbert and Sullivan operas had been popular at Harvard, and Rico recognized "Bunthorne's Bride."

Maybe she would consent to harmonize with him on it sometime. In any case, he had to think of a way to hold her in his arms again because, as of today, he had become addicted to it.

He had known for several weeks that he loved her, but the situation had become much more serious. Now he liked her.

12

ANGEL IN DISGUISE

Two mules dragged the cast-iron safe out of the elegant old manor house. They crossed the courtyard with it, and hauled it through the hacienda's front gates. Hundreds of rebel soldiers and local farmers watched in silence while Emiliano Zapata set a charge of dynamite, lit the slow-fuse with his cigar, and retreated.

They cheered when the explosion left the heavy door hanging on one hinge. Zapata pulled out the singed land titles and other papers. He lit them with his cigar and held them up so everyone could see them burn. His cigar did what President Madero would not. It returned the land of this particular estate to the people who had lived on it and farmed it not for centuries, but for millennia.

Every hacienda owner maintained an arsenal. Zapata's officers handed out the knives, rifles, pistols, and ammunition to the *jefes*, the local leaders who had recruited their own troops. They would know how to distribute them to those who most needed them.

The farmers jostled forward, but not to receive weapons. They were eager to find out how the estate would be divided up. They wanted to know which parcels of land would be theirs and which would revert to the nearby village as communal property.

Angela stood on her mare's back so she could look over everyone's heads. She had never seen Emiliano Zapata before, but she had heard him described so often that she would have recognized him. He was smaller and darker than she had imagined, and much more handsome.

He looked ten years younger than his thirty-three years. He had delicate features and full red lips behind his drooping black mustache. His eyes reminded Angela of a spaniel she had loved as a child, if that spaniel had had a streak of zealotry in him. Zapata's eyes burned with the fire of conviction. No wonder men were willing to leave their homes and follow him into death if need be.

Zapata waved her forward and she looked around to see whom he had in mind.

"¡*Caray!*" muttered Antonio. "He means us."

Angel glanced over at her father's old friend, Colonel Fidencio Contreras. He had welcomed Angela and her men into his unit. Colonel Contreras nodded and Angela and the rest of the band rode forward.

People moved aside to form a passage with Zapata standing at the end of it. He waved them to within a horse-length of him, but Angela heard the clank of bolts being shot home and rounds chambered. Any suspicious move and she and the others would have more holes in them than a sieve.

Angela dismounted. She took off her hat, revealing dark touseled hair that looked like it had been cut with a machete because it had.

"The men of San Miguel are reporting for duty," she said in Nahuatl.

"Colonel Contreras says you came prepared to fight. He says you bring pomegranates that will give the *federales* a stomachache."

The troops and civilians laughed when Angela and the others held up their homemade grenades, the clay pots strung in bunches on cords. Because of the grenades' size and shape, the Spanish word for them was *granados,* pomegranates.

"We do not steal and we do not loot." Zapata ignored the flames rising from the house, the sugar mill, and fields. Zapata had figured out that burning the cane crop put the laborers out of work, which made them easier to recruit for his army. "We take land from the wealthy and give it back to the people they stole it from. If you are here only to make your fortunes, return to San Miguel."

"We came to fight for land and liberty, *mi general,* not trinkets and souvenirs," said Angela.

"Are you *xicolo?*" he asked. "*¿Ladino?*" *Xicolo* and *ladino* were Nahuatl and Spanish for an *indio* who spoke Spanish.

"Yes. And so are several of these men."

Zapata nodded approval. His army was made up mostly of Indians who understood only Nahuatl. He needed all the Spanish speakers he could recruit.

"What's your name, *muchacho?*"

Angela glanced at Colonel Contreras. His face was neutral, but she had a feeling he wouldn't betray her identity.

If she admitted she was female, Zapata might send her home. Worse he might order her to join the *soldaderas.* She had not ridden all this way to pat out tortillas by day and lie under some smelly, snoring weight of a man at night.

"My name is Angel. Angel Sanchez. This is Antonio Perez."

She glanced over her shoulder at Antonio, Plinio, and the rest of her father's men. Not one of them so much as blinked.

"Excellent!" When Zapata laughed his teeth flashed as white and tidy as twin ranks of hominy corn under his black mustache. "Our cause needs angels."

"What did the *comandante* say?" asked Antonio.

"Colonel Contreras doesn't know where my father is. He says he heard that he rode north to join Villa."

Angela said it with a nonchalant shrug, but she was aggrieved and furious. How could her father have deserted her and her mother? Why had he made no effort to contact her?

Then she spotted Ambrozio Nuñez among Contreras's troops and forgot about her father, as he apparently had forgotten about her. Ambrozio carried a shiny new bolt-action Mauser. He looked much more prosperous than when he had stalked out of the cave near San Miguel.

"What's that *chinche,* that bedbug, doing here? Where did he steal the new clothes? And is that a timepiece flashing sunlight off his wrist?"

Antonio shrugged. "A bad egg will float to the top."

"He's a thief." Angela spurred her mare forward.

"Where are you going?"

"Don't worry, Ugly. I have something to discuss with him. I won't make trouble."

"Brat, you don't know how to not make trouble."

Angela wove in among Contreras's troops as they prepared to ride. This would be the first time she and her father's men went on a raid with them. She didn't intend to delay them by making a scene.

She waited until Ambrozio went off to relieve himself before he saddled up. When he had unbuttoned his fly and gotten a good stream started she padded up behind him. She knocked his hat off, grabbed a handful of his hair, and pulled his head back. With her other hand she held the serious edge of the cold knife blade against his exposed throat. His stream canted upward in a steep, golden arc that spattered on a boulder.

"Remember the cave at San Miguel, *tzipitl,* crybaby?"

He rolled his eyes sideways trying to locate her in his periphery. "Angela Sanchez?"

"No, *chocho.* I am Angel Sanchez."

She pressed the knife harder against his jugular. He gurgled. If he hadn't already been peeing, he would have started now.

"Who am I?"

"Angel Sanchez."

"If you tell anyone anything different you will not sleep again, unless it's the sleep from which you never wake. No matter where you go, I will follow you. As soon as you close your eyes, I will cut your throat."

She let go of his hair, shoving him forward in the process. He tripped and fell face down into his own warm puddle. She walked away without looking back. She left her old name and identity behind, too.

From now on she was Angel.

13

AN AZTEC ANGEL

Mexicans made congregating in the town square a national pastime. The zócalo, the small plaza in front of the Colonial, was no exception. With Christmas only one week away it was even more crowded than usual. Young people flirted around the fountain. Old ones warmed the seats of the iron benches. Families picnicked under the *tabachine* trees. Strolling musicians serenaded and the occasional clown entertained. Birds seemed to sing more loudly in the plaza, as if trying to be heard over the noise below them.

In such a busy crowd the group of eleven women was hardly noticeable. They and their escort of soldiers walked across the plaza and turned north onto Guerrero Street. Grace saw them head in the direction of the train station.

She assumed they were *soldaderas,* the army's camp followers. Grace considered Francisco Madero a friend and he seemed a decent man. When he took over the presidency she expected him to forbid the practice of allowing women to follow the troops. But Madero had left General Huerta in charge of the army, and Huerta was everything Madero was not.

When Huerta billeted at the Colonial he had been more difficult to deal with than his replacement, Colonel Rubio. Grace had had three showdowns with Huerta before he stopped trying to use her hotel for his assignations. Grace knew only kitchen Spanish and a few polite phrases that didn't include, "You may not take prostitutes to your room." Fortunately, "No," was the same in both languages and bordello was close enough to the Spanish word, *burdel,* to get the message across, although her body language would have sufficed.

Grace knew that on any given night some of her hotel's guests were engaged in what Lyda called hanky-panky. Grace wished them joy while they were about it; but with so many officers quartering here, allowing their commander free rein would have opened a floodgate to hanky-panky. It would have ruined the Colonial's reputation as a respectable place to lodge.

Grace had to admit that General Victoriano Huerta possessed at least one virtue. He kept his word. Before he left for Mexio City eight months ago he made Grace a promise. Every evening, without fail, she would hear music from the bandshell on the zócalo. A military band provided the concerts and their repertoire was limited. By now Grace had memorized not only the songs, but the order in which they were played.

Each program began with "Jarabe Tapatío," the Hat Dance, then proceeded at a leisurely pace through a number of stirring marches. The national anthem always signaled the end of the concert with such tender sentiments as, "Take the national pennants and soak them in waves of blood."

Lyda remarked that the polka was all one could dance to a military march, but any music was better than none. The music had stopped during the darkest days of the 1910 rebellion. The lovely bandshell had become a roost for doves. Enterprising vendors had used it as a kiosk for the sale of food, balloons, and trinkets. The bandstand had been referred to as *el kiosco* ever since.

At the noon hour the bandstand stood empty. Most shops closed from eleven each morning until three in the afternoon. Grace's favorite form of inactivity then was to watch the plaza's drama from a steamship deck chair under the wide roof of the Colonial's front veranda. Today Lyda and Annie occupied two other deck chairs, and all three of them sipped tea.

The chairs had arrived by train, as had the bandstand's copper roof, and the zócalo's ironwork benches. Anything large came over the mountains and into Cuernavaca that way. Grace hoped that today the train would bring Rico back from Mexico City.

He had gone there on assignment with Colonel Rubio two weeks ago. The hotel, the cantina, and life itself were lifeless without him. All Grace wanted for Christmas was to see his smile in the hallways and hear his voice resonating from the bar. She even would have welcomed the sight of him in the kitchen with a beef steak over another black eye.

He had written her from Mexico City, witty letters detailing the pranks and pecadillos of his compatriots. They had arrived one each day, and sometimes two via the train's mail car. They were the sort of missives she would expect to receive from a brother. She treasured them, but they weren't as good as having him nearby.

"Gracie," said Lyda, "*Los correctos* claim that a Frog fella designed the bandshell. Do you believe them?"

"If you mean Alexandre-Gustave Eiffel, I think not. The building was a gift from England to President Díaz. My countrymen would not engage a Frenchman to design a horse trough, much less a concert hall."

"They call Mr. Eiffel the Magician of Iron, and that shebang doesn't look English to me. Not enough falderol and gewgaws."

She was right. Unlike British Victorian architecture, Cuernavaca's bandstand lacked falderol and gewgaws. Annie called its roof a fairy's hat, but its curve more resembled the bell of a flugel horn. Nevertheless, to Grace it represented England and home, even though both seemed as distant to her now as Outer Mongolia.

"There's José." Annie pointed to a burro coming toward them, with another following on a lead. "He's brought Cora with him." Annie waved and Socorro waved back. "Seems strange to see her outside the market."

"*Buenos días, Maestro* Perez," said Grace.

While her hotel was undergoing reconstruction, Grace had learned to call all the artisans who worked for her *maestro,* professor. It was the custom here to recognize a person's skill, no matter what his economic standing. It was a sign of respect that cost nothing yet was priceless in generating goodwill.

"*Buenos días, Señora* Knight."

After the usual inquiries about the health of the Perez family, Grace paid José in coins of small denominations to make dividing them up easier for him. She had discreetly enclosed the money twisted into a strip of cloth, knotted at each end.

Holding his hat against his chest, he accepted payment. "*Dios le bendiga, señora.* May God bless you."

The pots were each wrapped in straw, stowed in two grain sacks, and lashed to the burro with hand-twisted rope. Grace did not insult José by counting them. Nor did she doubt that he would divide the money fairly among the other potters.

She was becoming more proficient in Spanish, and Annie helped her when she faltered.

"Please take the wares to the entrance at the rear courtyard," Grace said. "María is expecting you in the kitchen. Will you and Socorro please eat something before you return home?"

He thanked her with the refined dignity that Old Money and Much-Older Poverty often had in common. Still he lingered, twisting the brim of his straw hat.

"What else may I do for you today?"

"Will you grant my family the favor of giving my daughter work?"

Grace looked at Socorro who, her hands clasped in front of her, stared at her own feet. Her sandals were brand-new, with no dust on them. Grace assumed José had bought them for her this morning from the clusters of them hanging in the market. Her blouse and long skirt were spotlessly white and embroidered in the style of her village. She carried the rest of her belongings tied in a faded blue shawl. And she exuded an aroma of new-mown hay, a sure indication that she slept on a *petate* each night, a mat woven of dried reeds. The maids joked about country bumpkins coming to the city and smelling of *petates*.

Socorro looked very young, thirteen at most. What could José be thinking? He didn't seem like the sort to hire out his child for the money.

"Of course I can find work for her, *maestro*, but are you sure you want her to leave home?"

"I know you will watch over her. She will be safe here."

Grace wanted to say, "Safer in this big city than in her own village?" But she didn't. José was no fool. He must know what he was doing.

Still, it grieved her to see the tears glistening in the child's dark eyes, innocent as a fawn's.

"I'll see that no harm comes to her. And you and your wife are always welcome to visit her. We can find a room for you in the rear courtyard."

"Thank you, Mrs. Knight." He settled his hat back onto the curved cradle it had indented in his hair and led the burros around the side of the hotel toward the delivery entrance.

"I'll show Cora where to sleep." Annie interlaced her fingers with Socorro's. "Then I'll take her to Consuelo to be fitted for a uniform."

As Annie led the way into the hotel, Socorro walked like a cat wearing socks. Grace assumed she was not used to having shoes on her feet. She would require training, but Grace had become adept at assessing people by the quality of the light in their eyes. This one took after her father. She would learn quickly.

She was darker-skinned than the other women in Grace's employ, and more exotic than any of them. She wore her hair pulled back and plaited into one thick braid that reached her waist. Her face in profile was a continuous curve from her high, backward-sloping forehead down the prominent ridgeline of her nose and bisecting her narrow chin. The curve was broken only by lips the color, shape, and fullness of rose petals.

It was a profile that could have stepped down from one of the friezes on the ancient ruins outside of town. Should God decide He wanted to create an Aztec angel, He could use Socorro as the mold.

14

TAKING THE TRAIN

Rico was heading for the switching yard at the station in Mexico City when he saw a group of women climb down from one of the freight cars. The train had just arrived from Cuernavaca and was scheduled to turn around and go back. The women must be transferring to another line. Rico did not know that before the day ended, he would exchange rifle fire with the daughter of one of them.

Soldiers used the points of their bayonets to prod the women along. They carried nothing with them and Rico knew their journey would be a long one. They were probably being transported to the labor camps in the jungles of Quintana Roo. Huerta had the idea that access to sex would reduce the number of mutinies among the male prisoners there. Huerta, Rico had long ago decided, was an idiot. But then, he thought the same of most of the men in power.

As Rico continued on toward where his men and their horses waited he felt a loathing for General Huerta like an ulcer in the pit of his stomach. Huerta's brutal policies were all the more reason to end this conflict before it went any further.

He had been elated at the prospect of returning to Cuernavaca and to the Colonial and its very proper proprietor. The sight of the women had made him melancholy. He knew his men wouldn't be happy about this trip either. He would have preferred to ride in the baggage car with the two large crates he had left there, but on this trip he wouldn't sit there or in the first class coach either. He wondered if convincing Colonel

Rubio to let the men stay with their horses in the stock cars had been a good idea.

The train would stop at each of the dozen or so mountain villages along the way. It would take on wood and water at the station at Tres Marías, the halfway point straddling the mountain pass. Then there would be the inevitable delays that seemed to have no reason.

All in all, Rico and his men might endure a miserable four to six hours for nothing. But if his instincts and a rumor he had heard were right, a cattle car was the best place to be. He waited until his men were aboard, then led Grullo up the wooden ramp. When the switchman slid the heavy wooden door shut with a bang, Rico took up a position next to it.

Rico's favorite place on a train was the angel's perch, the name for the cupola on top of a caboose. The angel's perch had windows on all sides so the brakeman could sight along the roofs of the cars. When Rico was a child his grandfather had arranged for him to ride up there. From that height the train had looked like an undulating river of metal.

He was happy anywhere on a train though, even in a smelly cattle car crowded with men and horses. Besides, if Rico was wrong and the journey proved uneventful, so much the better. The cattle car would arrive in Cuernavaca only a minute or so after the first class carriages. Rico would have to bathe before seeing Mrs. Knight, but see her he would. Tonight.

He reached inside his khaki field army tunic to make sure the letters were still there. Grace had written two of them while he was in Mexico City. He always carried them under his tunic and over his heart.

He looked out between the horizontal slats of the car's sides. The rhythmic percussion of the wheels hitting the joints in the rails had a hypnotic effect. Rico let his body sway with the motion of the train, and remembered his first railroad journey.

When he was twelve his grandfather took him along on the inaugural trip from the capital to Cuernavaca in 1897. He remembered the day and the month, but that wasn't surprising. During the thirty-four years of the Porfiriata presidency everything of importance was inaugurated on September 15, Porfirio Díaz's birthday.

The train had been packed with dignitaries dressed in cutaway frock coats, high collars, pince-nez, and bowler hats. President Díaz had patted Rico on the head and told him his country expected great things of him. Lines of black-bonneted carriages waited for them in Cuernavaca. A thousand people or more milled around. A band played. A breeze billowed the bunting draped on the front of the engine.

They all had reason to be proud. Nineteen thousand miles of track had been laid through some of the roughest country on the continent. Of course, none of the dignitaries had dangled over an abyss in a wicker basket nor dynamited tunnels through granite for twenty *centavos* a day. That, laughed *los correctos,* was why God had created *indios.* Thousands of *indios* had died in the undertaking, but even they would have agreed that their lives and their deaths were in God's hands.

Little did those starched shirts know, Rico thought, that their magnificent acomplishment would prove their ruin. The railroad had opened up markets for sugarcane far beyond the borders of the state of Morelos. That made land valuable for agriculture and the wealthy began taking it from the villagers. Now, the villagers seemed intent on taking it back.

Colonel Contreras had put an earnest young second lieutenant in charge of Angel's men. If the shavetail noticed that they all looked at Angel before obeying any of his orders, he didn't mention it. Before joining Zapata's army he had taught elementary school, so maybe he was used to being ignored.

Angel, Antonio, and the men of Contreras's battalion hid with their mounts among the welter of boulders on both sides of the railroad tracks. The rebels ranged in age from fourteen to seventy. They wore no official uniform, but they looked remarkably alike in their loose white shirts, white cotton trousers, and wide straw hats tied on with bandanas. Closer scrutiny revealed a gaudy assortment of vests, sashes, scarves, striped stockings, and satchels. Flowers, ribbons, and religious medals decorated their hats.

Angel carried her father's carbine on a strap across her back. Her knife rode in a sheath tied under her trouser leg. She wore one ammunition belt buckled around her waist, and two more crossed on her chest. She was looking forward to blowing the doors off a freight car with her homemade grenades, although Antonio was of the opinion that they might detach their own fingers in the process.

Angel used her new binoculars to sight north and south along the rails. Then she shifted in her saddle and surveyed the crags and cliffs around them. She turned to Antonio.

"Ugly, are you sure the *federales* won't be joining us?"

"They patrol this section of the track at dawn and dusk. My sister overheard the officers say so at their card game."

"At the gringo hotel on the zócalo?"

"Yes."

"The one the English owns?"

"Yes. Socorro says they're bringing arms and ammunition on the train from Mexico City today. And horses in the stock cars."

"Maybe they wanted to trick anyone who might be listening."

"My sister says the officers were emptying bottles of cognac as fast as she could bring more to the *cantinero*. She says they were so drunk they could hardly play their cards, much less make up lies about anything except the size of their cocks."

They saw the smoke from the train's stack before they heard the steam whistle, forlorn as a calf who knew he was destined to become veal. The engine rounded the curve. The engineer must have seen the tree trunk lying across the track and swung on the brake lever with all his weight. Sparks sprayed from the wheels like fiesta fireworks. The train stopped with the cowcatcher nudging the log.

Angel and the others spurred their horses into a gallop. Most of them headed for the freight cars where the ammunition and weapons would be stored. Grenade in hand, Angel rode toward the cattle car. The last thing she expected was for the doors to rumble open and ramps to rattle into place. A young captain, saber raised, led a troop of cavalry down them with bugle blaring and rifles blazing.

The surprise caused time to slow for Angel and she took a good look at the captain as he charged toward her. She had three rapid thoughts. One: he and his men weren't supposed to be in that cattle car. Two: he

was very handsome. Three: if she killed him, whom among her compatriots would she have to fight for possession of his magnificent horse.
Then she realized it was the same horse she had seen at her first skirmish
at the river a few weeks ago.

Even if she had had time to light the fuse and pitch the grenade at
him, she wouldn't have. She didn't mind blowing him up, but she
wouldn't risk injuring that horse. She fired off a few shots before she realized that breveted discretion now outranked valor. Most of her comrades had already scattered under a hard rain of federal lead. She held her
ground until the last of her men found cover. She emptied her carbine,
then reined the mare in a tight turn and fled with bullets zinging past her
ears.

She had almost reached shelter when she saw the company's flag lying
on the ground ahead. With the mare at full gallop she took her right foot
out of the stirrup and slid toward the left. She hooked her foot on the
pommel, leaned down, and snatched the flag as the horse thundered by.
She held it high, shouting "Land and liberty" as she spurred the mare up
the rocky slope.

Antonio knew the bottomless nooks and craggy crannies of these
mountains better than anyone and Angel followed him. She expected
the *federales* to give up the chase quickly. They always had before. But
the pretty captain on the big Andalusian stayed close behind and Angel
resented him for it. Why wasn't he flirting with the simpering *señoritas*
in some small-town plaza instead of bothering her?

She and Antonio hauled their mounts up perpendicular slopes and
slid down the other sides. They finally ducked through a narrow opening not visible from the path and lost the captain. They rode until they
were certain no one followed them. When they dismounted Angel put
both hands on Antonio's chest and shoved him.

"*¡Chinga!*" She shoved him again. "Your sister said this train would
carry horses and supplies with only a small guard."

"*Cálma-te,* Brat. Maybe Colonel Fatso changed his plans and forgot
to mention it to the kitchen help."

Antonio reached out and took off Angel's hat. He put a finger through the bullet hole in the brim, snug up against the base of the crown. He wiggled the finger at her.

"God watched over you today, my love."

Angel stared at the finger. Half an inch to the right and she would be buzzard bait. Still clutching her company's colors to her chest, she began to shake. Antonio put his arms around her and pulled her close. He stroked her hair and then he did something strange. He lifted her chin and brushed her lips with his own. She pulled away and wiped her mouth.

"What are you doing?"

"It's called kissing. Gringos do it. I saw it in a movie."

"It's disgusting."

But Angel was curious. She moved close and tilted her head back. Antonio kissed her again and shivers went through her. She kissed him back, tentively, awkwardly, then enthusiastically. This was one of the gringos' better ideas.

15

ALL'S FAIR IN WAR AND TANGO

Grace pulled her long skirt aside and slid onto the piano bench. She began to play, her fingers hitting the keys lightly.

Lyda drifted in from the front desk. She set her elbows on the piano, put her chin in her hands, and crossed her ankles. Her latest outfit included a midnight-blue coolie shirt, pale green harem pants, and leather sandals from the market.

"Isn't that a song María sings?"

"Yes. It's called 'Curses on the Kitchen.'" Grace sang her English version.

> *Curses on the kitchen, curses on the smoke,*
> *Curses on the woman who loves any bloke.*
> *Because men, because men,*
> *When they know they're loved,*
> *Ay caramba! They treat you like a moke.*

"A moke?"

"Slang for donkey."

"Your choice of music wouldn't have anything to do with an absent army captain, would it?"

"Of course not." Grace launched into a vigorous rendition of her favorite: "'I'm Henery the Eighth, I am.'"

"Where did a proper English dame like you learn to play honky-tonk music?"

"My mother and father performed in music halls."

"Like vaudeville? Do tell! I would have placed you among the Ascot swells."

"Rather unlikely. I grew up backstage. I spent so much time watching the acts through the curtain, it's a wonder I didn't bloom into a Peeping Thomas."

"Where are they now, your parents?"

"They expired in a theater fire when I was thirteen. Socorro's age, now that I think on it. Quite a scene, really. A great deal of shouting and running about. I escaped through a sewer pipe." Grace sighed. "The smell of smoke and sewage still gives me the shakes."

"Then you must be terrified all the time in this country."

Grace didn't elaborate on why that wasn't so. Mexico had been her salvation. Various performers had taken her in after her parents died, but they could hardly feed themselves. She had lived in London slums worse than anything here. If she hadn't met Carlos while she was performing in Hyde Park one Sunday afternoon . . . well, she didn't want to think about it.

Socrates arrived in what was for him an agitated state. "A delivery just came."

"For whom?"

"For you, *señora*."

"I'll bet I know who it's from," Lyda said.

Two big crates and several smaller ones sat in the courtyard like visiting dignitaries and entourage.

"Rico must have sent them," said Lyda.

"Not necessarily."

"You know he did. Listen, darlin', the man is smitten with you, and you're fighting off love like it was a case of the influenza."

"I doubt his intentions are genuine."

"So enjoy the fling. You know what they say, '*Amor lejos es para pendejos.*' Love at a distance is for fools."

"I have to maintain decorum. What sort of example would I set for the staff?"

"Your people want you to be happy, Gracie. They all know that God does not intend for a woman to sleep alone. And they like Rico."

Socrates cleared his throat. "*Señora,* the drayman who delivered the boxes said rebels attacked the train at Tres Marías."

"Did he say if anyone was hurt?"

"He doesn't know."

Grace wondered if Captain Martín was on the train with the boxes.

Annie showed up and soon most of the guests and staff had gathered to stare at the crates. Everyone but Grace speculated as to what they contained. She could only wonder if the sender was alive.

"They're addressed to you, Gracie," said Lyda. "Open them."

"We should wait for Captain Martín."

The sun went behind the mountains and darkness began gathering. On the zócalo the band finished its evening concert with a flourish and only one trombone out of tune. Grace was about to ask Socrates to drive her to the station to inquire about the attack when Rico sauntered through the front gate.

He looked surprised to see so many people assembled. He obviously had bathed quite recently, maybe at the barracks. He was freshly shaven. His hair was still wet and slicked back. He wore his dress blues with gaiters as white as egret feathers and the green collar piping and trouser stripes of the cavalry. From ten feet away, Grace could smell cologne.

She wanted to shout at him, "We have a telephone! Why didn't you call to tell us you were safe?"

Instead she said, "We heard there was an attack on the train."

"Just a few young hotheads taking potshots. Nothing to worry about."

Then Grace stated the obvious and felt like a walloping great fool afterward.

"Your parcels arrived, Captain Martín."

"They're your parcels, Mrs. Knight. Why haven't you opened them?"

"She said we had to wait for you," said Annie.

"Then let's not waste any more time."

Socrates and the gardener helped him pry off the lids. Rico unwrapped a gleaming brass horn as long as his arm. Its flared bell was large enough to accommodate a curious cat. He handed it to Socrates to hold while he took the wrappings off the mahogany case adorned with nickel plating.

Annie squealed. Lyda clapped her hands. "It's a phonograph!"

"Edison's Opera phonograph." Rico screwed the horn and the crank in place and began opening packages of celluloid circles, bamboo needles, and a device that would sharpen them. "1911 model. You'll notice it plays disks instead of cylinders. Each one contains two minutes of music."

Lyda murmured in Grace's ear, "Those contraptions cost fifty dollars in the States."

"I can't accept this, Captain Martín."

"Must you give it back?" Annie seemed about to cry. Even Lyda looked crestfallen.

"You're very kind, but really, it's too expensive."

Rico leaned close and spoke softly so only Grace could hear. "As Wordsworth once said, 'High Heaven rejects the lore of nicely calculated less and more.'"

"Even so, Captain . . ."

"Very well. I'll give it to someone else here because it is not leaving the Colonial."

Lyda spoke up. "Gracie, why not accept Captain Martín's kindness on behalf of the hotel? You can be in charge of it, but everyone can enjoy it."

Socrates had already brought a table from the kitchen and placed it just inside the archway leading to the lobby. Rico set the phonograph on it. He placed a disk on the turntable and cranked the handle. With the delicacy of an eye surgeon he lowered the arm until the tip of the needle kissed the grooves. The reedy notes of "Fig Leaf Rag" drew Grace like a cat to cream.

When the music ended everyone applauded.

Rico put on another disk. "The next song is called 'La Morocha,' 'The Brunette.'"

This music was nothing like ragtime.

"Do you dance tango, Mrs. Knight?"

"I don't know how." Grace had heard that tango originated in Argentinian brothels. Now she could believe it.

"It's all the go in Paris these days," said Lyda. Then she whispered in Grace's ear, "In the States women wear devices like railway car bumpers when they dance it. You can imagine why."

That didn't inspire confidence in Grace.

"It's easy." Rico held out a hand.

Grace looked for an escape, but Lyda and Annie hemmed her in.

Even María, wiping her plump hands on her apron, called from the archway, "*Baile, señora.* Dance."

"Follow my lead." Rico slid his right arm so far around her that she could feel the strength of his fingers pressing between her shoulder blades.

She gasped when he pulled her to him. In all those boxes there was not one bumper for her to strap on. She thought she would faint with the shock of his lean muscular body pressed against her, a line of contact from the knees, up the thighs, the hips, and chest. Even his cheek pressed against hers. He definitely had shaved before coming here and the cologne was intoxicating.

She wanted to pull away, but she couldn't bring herself to create a scene. Hotel guests watched from the downstairs corridors and the upstairs gallery. Drawn by the music, passersby crowded into the entryway.

She moved like a fence post and she stepped on his foot in the process.

"So sorry. Really Captain, we should stop before I make a cripple of you."

When the song ended, Lyda cranked the machine again and set the needle back at the beginning. Grace glared at her, but she didn't look in the least repentant.

Rico shook Grace gently to loosen her vertebrae. "Imagine that you're a rag doll."

Grace didn't so much relax as surrender, and he began to move slowly. He counted for her as he went, his cheek against hers, his breath tickling her ear.

"It's no wonder they banned this dance in Boston," she murmured.

"Don't forget Cleveland," he said. "They banned it there, too."

He moved her forward and back, his legs scissoring between hers, tautening her skirt against her legs. He whirled her until the walls began to revolve and she threw her head back and laughed. Lyda set a chair next to the phonograph and kept the music playing while Rico and Grace circled the courtyard under the starlit sky.

Grace didn't notice that the spectators had drifted away. She didn't even notice that the music stopped two minutes after Lyda reset the needle one last time, yawned, stretched, and left with Annie for home. By then the rhythm had soaked into Grace's muscles, bones, and viscera.

When Grace and Rico stopped dancing they stood as remote from the world as if on a cay in the middle of the ocean. A breeze rustled the palm fronds and the banana leaves. The water sang in the fountain. Rico slid his fingers along Grace's temples and into the waves of her hair.

"Captain, I can't."

"One of your countrymen said a very wise thing." Rico laid his palms along the sides of her face and tilted it up to look at him. "Francis Bacon said, 'Begin doing what you want now. We are not living in eternity. We have only this moment, sparkling like a star in our hand, and melting like a snowflake.'"

He tugged loose the pins and set her hair free to cascade down her back. He kissed her. Her first thought was that people didn't kiss in Mexico. She wondered if he had learned that at Harvard, too.

Then she stopped thinking. She kissed him in return and the world revolved like a carousel. When he picked her up she rested her cheek in the hollow where his shoulder met his neck. She had not been with a man since Carlos died seven years ago. She wondered if she would remember what to do, but she decided she could depend on him. He had taught her to tango, hadn't he?

He carried her effortlessly up the wide marble stairs.

16

GHOSTS

In honor of the birth of Christ, revelers were setting off firecrackers in the midnight city outside Grace's balcony. They crackled like gunfire in the distance. The reports invaded Rico's sleep. They filled it with horsemen chasing starved farmers across burning cornfields. Then the dream worsened. Rico became one of the soldiers firing into a group of women. They were the same ones he had seen getting off the train in Mexico City, except now some of them carried babies. One by one they fell into the smoldering stubble, cut down by his bullets.

He didn't know if the horror of the image woke him, or if the largest of the fireworks, booming like heavy artillery, did. Probably both of them caused his heart to race as he lay drenched in cold sweat next to Grace. He silently recited "Hail, Mary, full of grace." By the time he finished "Pray for us sinners, now and at the hour of our death" for the fifth time his heart had slowed to its normal cadence.

He rolled onto his side so he could look at Grace. The street lamps were tall enough to cast a dim light through the open door to the balcony. Earlier he and Grace had thrown off the covers, unwilling to allow so much as linen cloth separate them. Now she lay naked, as natural as if shame and embarrassment had never been thought of. Her hair was spread out on the pillow, her eyes were closed, mouth at peace. In the faint glow from the street her body was as pale and smooth as the silk kimono hanging on a peg nearby.

Rico could have spent the rest of his life studying every line and hollow of her, but the air had turned chill. He pulled the sheet and blanket over her, tucking it around her shoulders. Her breathing continued deep and steady. Rico could see no sign of the insomnia that her people said plagued her.

The upstairs maids and the kitchen help had confided in him that *Mamacita* didn't sleep well. The night watchman had told them so and they themselves had seen it. Sometimes when one of them got up to relieve herself she would see *la señora* wandering the corridors and the rear courtyard. At first those who saw her in her pale kimono thought she was a ghost. They said she had given Socorro such *susto,* fright, that María had had to call a *curandero,* a healer, to get rid of it. Of course, they hadn't told *Mamacita* about that.

Rico understood how the maids could mistake Grace for a spirit. The night he had seen her gliding along in a nimbus of pale silk was the most memorable of his life. Or it had been, until this night.

Still asleep, she sighed and turned toward him. He slipped an arm under her until the nape of her neck fit perfectly into the cradle of his elbow. Her hand rested on his waist and when he drew closer, it slid down to the small of his back and cupped into the hollow at the base of his spine. He put his other arm around her and gently pulled her against him.

She stirred, and with eyes still closed she murmured, "Federico Martín, I will love you always."

"My heaven, I have waited my whole life for you." He kissed her mouth, her eyes, the hollows at the base of her ears, her throat, the valley between her breasts.

Rico finally understood the lyrics of every maudlin ballad he had sung under countless balconies. When he was much younger they had meant nothing at all to him. Then he had wondered if he would recognize love should it happen along. A few years later he worried that it never would happen. And until six weeks ago, he had resigned himself to the probability that he would settle for something masquerading as love.

Now, here it was, serene and soft, lovely, tough, and talented in his arms. Love's warm breath tickled his throat. The beat of love's heart resonated against his chest.

Rico's nightmare became just another ghost. He could not imagine a better Christmas.

The maids' rebellion did not meet the standards of a mutiny. It was more of a sit-down strike or a group sulk.

When Grace left her room she found them sitting at the bottom of the stairway. She thought they had assembled to congratulate her, and a blush spread like sunrise across her cheeks. Congratulations were in order though.

Rico had waked her a couple hours earlier for an encore of the night's performance. Grace had still been floating blissfully between two ceiling beams when he kissed her on the forehead and slipped out into the dark hallway with his boots in his hand.

Grace danced down the stairs, singing softly.

> *A most intense young man,*
> *A soulful-eyed young man,*
> *An ultra-poetical, super-aesthetical,*
> *Out-of-the-way young man.*

Had Mr. Gilbert and Mr. Sullivan met Federico Martín?

There sat the maids on the steps, waiting for her. They had enlisted María in their cause. The maids were shy. María wasn't, and she wasn't sitting down.

She planted her feet a shoulders' width apart, and María had broad shoulders. She rested her hands on her formidable hips.

"*Señora* Knight, *tiene que echar la fantasma.*"

Grace's brain, still entwined with Rico, tried to back up and turn around. Did they want her to evict a ghost?

"*¿Como?* What?"

"*La Llorona, allá arriba.*" María pointed up the stairs behind her.

"Good morning, Grace." Annie arrived with Socorro close behind her. Socorro had filled her in on the crisis. "They want you to exorcize the haunt who lives upstairs. Or hire someone to do it. They call her *la Llorona,* the One Who Weeps. Socorro has heard her crying."

The maids gave a collective sigh of relief. The cavalry had arrived and she spoke English.

"They want you to get rid of the ghost before *susto* turns into *espanto.*"

"*Susto? Espanto?*"

"*Susto* means fright. *Espanto* means terror. María knows a witch who can perform a *limpieza,* a cleaning."

"I see."

But Annie wasn't sure she did. "*Susto* and *espanto* are serious. They can frighten the soul out of a body and cause it to wander off."

Grace had heard whispers about the cold spot in the rear upstairs hallway. She had felt it herself, but she blamed a draft from an airshaft in the ceiling.

She sorted through the options. An exorcism by a local witch would amuse the guests, but Grace could imagine them commenting in loud whispers during the ritual. The maids considered this serious and Grace had to do the same.

"Do they have any idea who the Weeper might be?"

Annie and the maids put their heads together. After much discussion Annie reported. "They say that one of Hernán Cortés's men got an Indian woman with child. When the baby was born the mother brought him here to ask the *gachupín,* the Spaniard, to give her money to buy food. He grabbed the baby's feet and dashed its head against a column. The mother ran away, but he chased her and ran his sword through her."

"Good lord!"

"She's been crying for her child ever since."

"All right." Grace turned and headed upstairs. Fortunately, the back corridor was where the army officers stayed and they had left early.

Annie followed. "What are you going to do?"

"I'll have a talk with her."

Grace retrieved a stool from her room and the Bible she had never read. She placed the stool under the air vent and sat on it. The Bible was a prop to impress the maids, so she opened it at random and laid it on her lap. Behind her she could hear the women rustling like mice, jostling for a view from where the stairs made a turn at the first landing.

Grace cleared her throat and for want of anything better, she said, "Good morning." That wasn't the Weeper's language, but if the maids wanted this done in Nahuatl they would have to do it themselves.

A faint moaning came from overhead. Grace knew it was the wind blowing across the air vent on the roof, but the hair stirred on her arms anyway. She glanced down at the Bible. The first words she saw were in 1 Samuel, verse one. "I am a woman of a sorrowful spirit."

Maybe the line was coincidence or maybe not, but Grace realized that nothing she could say about Satan or demons or evil spirits would be appropriate. She took a deep breath and began a heart-to-heart talk, as if the grieving young mother were sitting in front of her. When she finished she made an awkward sign of the cross and said, "Go in peace, dear girl. Your child waits for you in Heaven."

She returned the stool and the Bible to her room. She would ask Socrates to block up the vent on the roof immediately. The maids made way for her to pass, then closed in behind her, laughing and chatting, happy that the matter had been settled. When they reached the ground floor they scampered off down the wide corridor, playing tag on their way to the linen pantry.

One of her guests watched them go with disapproval stamped all over her. She was one of those English dowagers who would travel halfway around the world, only to demand that everything be exactly as she had left it in Kensington. Her idea of exotic cuisine was roast beef with a hint of pink in the middle.

She had a new complaint this morning. "Mrs. Knight, why does the chambermaid insist on turning my shoes upside down?"

"Some Mexicans believe that leaving shoes upside down overnight empties out the day's accumulation of evil. It also relieves pain in the feet and legs." Grace didn't mention that she stored her own shoes upside down to keep insects, spiders, and scorpions from setting up house in them.

"What rubbish! That's the most ridiculous thing I've ever heard."

"I'll instruct them to leave your shoes with soles on the floor in the future. But please do bear in mind, Mrs. Fitz-Goring, that they believed they were helping you."

Grace found Socrates and told him about the vent. She was headed for breakfast in the courtyard when Leobardo, the night watchman, appeared with his hat in his hand. He launched into his request, talking so fast that Grace called Lyda to help with the translation.

"Word spreads fast," said Lyda. "He claims his wife hired a *nagual,* a witch, to tie a knot in the drawstrings of his unmentionables so he wouldn't, you know . . ."

"Wouldn't what? Use the toilet?"

"No, Gracie, so he wouldn't fool around with other women."

Grace maintained a poker face. "Tell him I don't exorcise underwear."

Lyda managed to keep from smiling while she explained that to Leobardo. After he headed, crestfallen, for his hammock in the rear courtyard she said, "I should ask him for the name of that witch. Jake is going to Chihuahua on business for a month. I should engage someone to tie a knot in his nappies."

"Well, I'm not qualified."

Grace was glad Rico hadn't witnessed all this. She was pretty sure he would tease her. On the other hand, only a couple hours had passed since she saw him and already his absence was causing an ache in the vicinity of her heart.

After breakfast she climbed the stairs from the second floor to the Colonial's flat roof. Her excuse was to make sure the cisterns of rainwater were clean and to see if Socrates had closed off the air vent. She knew there was no need. Socrates always kept the cisterns clean and he had taken care of the vent immediately. She had another reason for going.

Grace was proud of the roof. Three years ago she had had workmen cover it with the latest in building material, something called tar-paper. She had not been up here since it was first installed, and it stretched around her like a desert of black lava.

She walked to the northeast corner. On her right rose the two volcanoes, Popocatepetl and Iztaccihuatl, the one called Sleeping Lady. To the left of the volcanoes were the three peaks known as Tres Marías. They rose only a little above the mountain chain. The three peaks and the range that encircled the valley reminded Grace of a tiara. Puffs of white smoke rose in a line above the dense stand of trees on the steep slope leading up to them.

The puffs of smoke were what she had come up here to see. Rico and his men were on that train. They were headed for the small railroad depot in the village of Tres Marías at the pass. When Rico left her this morning he told her that his company would be joining General Huerta. It was a routine patrol, he said, to make sure no troublemakers interfered with the operation of the railroad, but he might be gone for a week or more.

Why would the army's commander-in-chief come to Morelos for a routine patrol?

For all his scapegracery, honor counted with Rico. Grace could imagine him lying to her for only one reason, to protect her from an unpleasant truth. She stared at the smoke unreeling as the train chugged up the slope, and she wondered what the truth was.

17

SUMMONED

Angel believed she would not live to see the sun set. She wondered if there was anything she could say to make peace with the God she had taunted and spurned all her life. She decided to trust that if He were as all-knowing as everyone claimed, He would have a sense of humor where she was concerned.

She and the rest of Zapata's army had found what cover they could, but General Huerta's troops had them surrounded and outnumbered three to one. The train that brought the *federales* soldiers from Mexico City to Tres Marías had also carried a battery of 75-millimeter artillery lashed to flatcars.

Angel tried not to flinch when the big guns boomed and shells exploded in front of her, splintering trees and throwing up dirt and fragments. She had smelled burning powder from rifles before, but the odor that permeated this little valley was acrid and ominous.

Plinio glanced over at her and smiled sadly. "You are not a soldier until you have smelled cannon fire."

When the lull came Angel knew what it meant. General Huerta's mangy curs were preparing a final assault. From the rocks and trees around her she heard men screaming in pain. She could see one of the fallen, her company's young lieutenant. She had butted heads with him on a daily basis, but the sight of him, lightless brown eyes staring at infinity, made her as sad as if he had been her beloved brother.

She was almost out of ammunition and she knew her comrades must

be, too. They usually only had enough for *tiroteos,* skirmishes with patrols. Even if Zapata could raise enough money to buy munitions
from El Norte, the United States, he would have to find a way to transport it 1,500 miles from the border, mostly on the backs of mules.

Angel stood in her stirrups and shouted to the men she had always
thought of as hers. "If we are to go to hell today anyway, let's take these
chingados with us."

She didn't expect them to agree with her, much less follow her, but she
didn't care. She faced the mare toward the wall of rocks that hid the
nearest artillery battery and prepared to charge it by herself.

"Wait, Brat." Antonio rode to where the lieutenant's body had fallen
in a sitting position with his back against a rock. He made the sign of the
cross over him and took the company's guidon from the dead man's
hand.

When he held it out to Angel she hesitated. To carry the flag into
battle was an honor she didn't think she deserved. Besides, she couldn't
shoot her rifle and hold on to the flag, too. And she really wanted to shoot
someone. There was also the fact that the *federales* always tried to kill
the standard-bearer first.

"*De la suerte y de la muerte no hay huída,*'" Plinio said. "'From fate
and death there is no flight.' Carry it, *chamaco,* and we will follow you."

"Then I will arrive in hell first," Angel muttered. She took the reins in
one hand and held the flag's staff high with the other. "Come, *muchachos,* let's make ghosts of *el gobierno.*"

She urged the mare into a gallop across ground pitted with craters.
She didn't have to look back. She heard the sound of hoofbeats behind her.

They had to dismount, leave their horses at the base of the escarp-
ment, and labor up the steep slope to the battery emplacement. Angel expected an artillery shell to take her head off at any moment, but silence
prevailed. The stillness frightened her more than gunfire. What were they
waiting for?

Shouting at full volume, Angel and her men reached the rocks the ar-
tillerymen had piled up as a breastwork and scrambled over them. She
wedged the flagstaff upright between two stones so her hands would be

free to use her knife, but the emplacement was empty. She stared at the scuffed, scoured ground, the tracks of the artillery carriage wheels plainly visible in the dirt.

A cloud of dust rose in the distance. As best Angel could make out with her binoculars, it was raised by retreating cavalry, infantry, and the gun carriages bumping along behind the artillery mules. Angel's men cheered, shouted insults, and fired a few shots after them.

"Save your bullets," she said.

As she watched the dust cloud grow smaller she felt a churning in the pit of her stomach. What could have summoned General Victoriano Huerta away? From what she had heard about Huerta, he would not retreat from a sure victory. She tried to guess what evil he had planned for them.

Angel led her men at a brisk walk up the dusty main street of another village perched among boulders and outcrops. She came to the plaza, shaded by palms and banana trees and dismounted in front of the small, whitewashed church. The members of the welcoming committee looked as if they had been dug up from the local cemetery, but Angel wasn't surprised to find only old folks. The younger men had either fled or were hiding to avoid execution, exile, or conscription into the federal army.

With their frayed trousers and torn shirts, their knives, machetes, bandoleers, and pistols, Angel's band looked menacing. Only their rifles distinguished them from bandits, and these days, a lot of bandits carried those. But as far as the villagers were concerned, anyone in either Zapata's army or Huerta's was *el gobierno*.

Angel didn't blame them for thinking so. It was often difficult to tell them apart. Two of the men in her group still wore federal uniforms. They and a lot of others had surrendered to Zapata after Huerta pulled out. The deserters were conscripts from the north, as ragged and hungry as the rebels. Angel's men claimed that their enemy's abrupt withdrawal was a miracle. Angel wished that God, while in the miracle mood, had persuaded the *federales* to leave all their guns and rations behind. Especially the rations.

Any group of armed men sent village women and children into hiding. Children indicated mothers, and both sides had a habit of stealing
women to provide certain services for their troops. The difference was
the rebels usually borrowed them at night and returned them in the
morning. If the *federales* took them, they disappeared forever.

A barefoot antique with an armful of flowers approached Angel. Her
black skirt, blouse, and shawl had faded to gray from half a lifetime spent
in mourning. Her deformed spine bent her double at the waist. She held
out the flowers and swiveled her chin sideways to peer up at Angel.

"For you, my son."

Angel thanked her in Nahuatl. She stuck a dahlia into her hatband
beside the medallion of the brown-skinned Virgin of Guadalupe, and
passed the rest along. People had mistaken her for a young man everywhere she went, which was what she wanted.

The mountain folk may not have recognized that Angel was a woman,
but they sensed who was in charge. That was partly because she rode a
fine mare, but something more elusive was at work. Angel's Castilian
ancestors had passed to her an unspoken aura of command. In centuries of Spanish domination, *los indios* had become adept at recogniz-
ing it.

The village women distributed tortillas and beans and Angel's men
wolfed them down. An old man handed her the lead line with a gaunt
mule on the other end. His clothes were ragged. He wore no badge of
office, but he had the bearing of a *jefe,* a leader.

"*Colli,* grandfather, do you know any young men willing to join us?
We fight for land and liberty alongside General Zapata."

No front teeth impeded the *mayordomo*'s smile. He crossed himself,
an indication that Zapata had gained admittance to the pantheon of
Catholic saints, along with some much more ancient ones of whom the
priests wouldn't approve. He turned toward the small adobe jail and
beckoned.

The carved oak door creaked open and two men eased out. One kept
his rifle. The other threw his weapon to one side, raised his hands above
his head, and approached slowly. He wore the gray uniform of the local
police, the *rurales.*

When Porfirio Díaz had formed the *rurales,* his instructions had been succinct. "Catch in the act. Shoot to kill." Even though Díaz had gone into exile, his rural police force remained as hated as ever.

"Why do you want to come with us?" Angel asked him.

He shrugged. "I have had enough of being cursed, spat upon, and shot at by my own people."

"Pick up your gun." Angel handed him the mule's lead line. She turned to the second man. "And what is your story?"

He held up a ring of keys, each one as long as his middle finger. "My name is Jesus. I am the jailer." He nodded toward his companion. "I locked him up for being drunk and disorderly."

"Welcome to General Zapata's Liberation Army." Angel sighed. General Zapata needed fighters, but more men to fight meant more mouths to feed.

When Angel's band reached the rebel army's main encampment, she expected to relax after three days on patrol in the mountains. Antonio spread his blanket and, using his saddle as a pillow, settled in for a siesta. Angel kicked off the instruments of torture called shoes and rubbed grease on her blisters. She put a small tin pot on the cookfire and looked forward to enjoying a less than luxurious meal of the parched corn and beans she and her men had received from the villagers.

Later, when darkness had settled securely in for the night, she intended to lure Antonio away from camp for a repeat of that first kiss. Warfare, she had found, honed all the senses to a shiny, eager edge, yet limited opportunities to express the more tender of them.

She glowered at the barefoot boy who arrived as the beans were starting to simmer. She knew he hadn't come to pass the time of day.

"The general wants to see you at once."

"What general?"

"Zapata."

Antonio said, without opening his eyes, "What have you done now, Brat?"

"Nothing."

Angel winced as she put her shoes on over the blisters on her feet. She brushed off the seat of her trousers, slung her carbine over her shoulder,

and followed the messenger to the abandoned house where Zapata had
his headquarters. The boy ushered her into a room that was bare but for
a large desk, a crucifix, and some maps on the wall. General Zapata sat
behind the desk. Colonel Contreras stood next to him. Angel was relieved to see Contreras, then she had doubts. Had he revealed her identity?

She came to attention and saluted.

"Private Sanchez," Zapata said. "Colonel Contreras tells me you are
not who you seem."

"I am a good soldier, sir."

"He told me that, too." He held out a small satchel.

Angel opened it and found a woman's skirt, blouse, and shawl. Her
cheeks grew hot. Suddenly she didn't care if everyone thought Emiliano Zapata was a saint and the greatest leader her people had ever produced. She had admired him almost as a god, but she was disappointed
to find he was just like other men. She tossed the satchel onto the desk,
and turned to leave without being dismissed.

"Where are you going?"

"I am not a *galleta,* a cookie." She spun on her heel and spat the
words. "I am not a whore."

Angel never expected Zapata to smile at insubordination, but his teeth
dazzled under his heavy black mustache. This close, without the distraction of the dozens of men who usually gathered around him, his eyes were
the most compelling she had ever seen. Eyes like that could stare into a
person's soul and notice if it had been swept and dusted lately.

"I didn't say you were."

"*Cálma-te, chamaco,*" said Contreras. "Take it easy, lad. The general
has a mission for you."

Angel narrowed her eyes in a wait-and-listen attitude. "What sort of
mission requires a woman's clothes?"

"I want you to deliver a message to Cuauhnáhuac."

Cuauhnáhuac. It was the ancient Aztec name for Cuernavaca.

18

MESSAGES FROM ELSEWHERE

Victoriano Huerta pushed open the Colonial's heavy front gates with such force that they slammed against the walls alongside them. He charged through them like a gorilla headed for a grudge match. Grace was feeding stale bread crumbs to the goldfish in the fountain. She snapped erect when he came stomping through the covered entryway and into the courtyard.

With one hand on the butt of his revolver, Rico followed close behind Huerta. He was determined to shoot his commander-in-chief in the back of the head if he lifted a hand against Grace, and to hell with the consequences. His resolve was admirable, but it proved that he didn't really know Grace yet.

She advanced straight into the general's trajectory, her hand out in welcome. "General Huerta, what a surprise to see you."

She didn't say "Pleased to see you," Rico noticed, nor "Honored to have you back." He was impressed by how fast she could act, and with tact and honesty to boot. He was astonished by Huerta's reaction.

The smile that broke out on the general's havoc of a face was genuine. Grace's hand disappeared in both of his, then he threw his arms around her in a hug.

When Huerta let go of Grace he was beaming. "Ay, Mrs. Knight, I have missed the Colonial's stewed plums. My digestion has not been right since I left here."

"And shall you be needing a room, General?"

"Yes, my dear Mrs. Knight."

Lyda appeared in the archway leading to the lobby and announced, "A whoop-and-holler from Em Cee for the general."

When Huerta stalked off to answer the telephone, Rico took Grace's arm and guided her into the small room she used as an office. He held her face in both hands and kissed her for a long time. She kissed him back, then wound her arms around his waist and laid her head on his chest.

"I have missed you," she murmured to the first brass button on his tunic.

"*Mi cielo,* every moment away from you is an eternity."

When Grace looked up at him, Rico could see the anxiety in her eyes. Huerta had made the Colonial his home a year ago and Rico could well imagine the tense scenes he had caused.

"Will the general be quartering with us?" she asked.

"He's supposed to be on his way to the capital right now."

"Then why is he here?"

"The general is used to giving orders, not taking them."

The telephone hung on the wall just outside the office door. Huerta's rapid-fire Spanish carried across the lobby and echoed up the stairwell.

"To whom is he speaking?"

"The president, I assume."

"Madero?"

"Yes. We had surrounded a few of Zapata's troublemakers and were about to capture them when a message arrived. Madero called Huerta back to the capital."

"Huerta brought an army to Morelos for a few troublemakers?"

"It's nothing to concern yourself about."

Grace pulled out of his embrace. Placing the palms of her hands against his chest, she held him at arm's length.

"I am not a child, Federico Martín, to be shielded from the truth. This is my country, too."

In a long exhale Rico set his illusions free. He had thought he could avoid discussing politics with Grace. He had not been acquainted with her for long, but he had observed her closely enough to know better. He kept his voice low even though his commander-in-chief was still up-holding the holler part of the whoop-and-holler. Huerta didn't under-stand much English, but he assumed any hushed conversation was about him. Caution was the wisest course anywhere in Huerta's vicinity.

Rico explained the situation, in brief.

"President Madero has not moved fast enough to return land to the farmers. Many of them have joined Zapata. To finance their campaign they're demanding money from the *hacendados.* They've burned sugar-cane fields, lured away the workers, and fired on the trains. I don't agree with Huerta's methods, but if Zapata is not stopped, war will break out again and this time it will destroy the country."

"Zapata laid down his arms right here in Cuernavaca a year and a half ago. He disbanded his army. Do you think he plans to start another rebellion?"

"I don't know what he plans. Madero may be too slow with land reforms, but he is our best hope. Even Zapata knows that."

"General Huerta is a very dangerous man, Federico. Do you think the president is safe?"

"Madero's too popular for anything bad to happen to him." Which was half the truth. The people loved him, but many of the old Porfiris-tas, men who still wielded influence, did not.

Rico stroked her hair. How he had missed the wiry wilderness of it.

"Two good things have come from this," he said.

"What would those be?"

"Madero must realize that allowing Huerta to . . ." he searched for an English word ". . . to destroy those who disagree with government poli-cies is wrong. Maybe he intends to compromise with Zapata. And . . ." This was the best part. "He knows that keeping soldiers garrisoned in Cuernavaca is essential for the safety of the capital."

"Does that mean you'll stay here?"

"It does, my heaven."

As Rico breathed in the perfume of her hair he had an insight, like a telegram from the cosmos. He realized that his duty to his country su-perceded other obligations. If he had not enlisted in the army his grand-father would require him, as the only son and heir, to accompany the

family wherever they went. Where they went could be anyplace from
Mexico City to El Paso to Manhattan to Paris.

Rico might not have guessed how Grace would react to an irate tyrant,
but he did know one thing for certain. He could not ask her to choose between him and her beloved hotel. He was a gambler, but he did not bet
on losing propositions. Anywhere his family lit other than Cuernavaca
would lack Grace.

He would stay on with President Madero's army, flawed as it was.
He would fight and die if need be, to reunite his country and to protect
the woman he loved more than life itself.

When the president of Mexico came to the Colonial for dinner in Jan-
uary of 1913, he brought his own Ouija board. It was a beauty, made
of wood laminate with a bird's-eye maple veneer, but that wasn't why
Francisco Madero treasured it.

When he stayed at the Colonial before his election in November of
1911, he had confided to Grace that this particular talking board had
foretold he would be president. At the time, Grace didn't think it much
of a prediction. After all, the day he entered Mexico City 100,000 people
had thronged the streets to greet the man his followers called The Apos-
tle. Behind him rode a revolutionary army with the likes of Emiliano Zapata, Pancho Villa, and Venustiano Carranza leading them. Grace had
seen it all from a third-floor balcony of her late husband's family home.
It was a day she would never forget. It was the day she knew she could return to her beloved hotel and resume her life there.

Now she had another thought on the subject of Francisco Madero's
presidency. Be careful what you wish for.

Grace liked Madero. She respected him. But Mexicans must think
him an unusual man. He not only had stated the day his revolution
would begin, but had fixed the hour: November 20, 1910, at six in the
evening. Six in the evening. Why not seven? Or five past ten in the
morning?

Grace imagined him telling his compatriots to calibrate their watches.
The revolution will start promptly at 6 P.M. Did he equate overturning

a government, plummeting his countrymen into a civil war, and defying the world's most powerful nations with attending a theater performance?

Madero didn't seem a rebel. His voice sounded like it should come fluting from a canary cage. He belonged to a very wealthy family, members of Mexico's elite. He had studied in Paris and at the University of California in Los Angeles. He was an intellectual and a vegetarian. He had helped organize the first Spiritist Congress in Mexico City in 1906. He had formed a federation of Mexican spiritist societies and established a center for the study of the supernatural.

Grace wondered where he had found the time to foment revolution. Maybe that was why he had been so precise. The revolution had to start at a certain hour to fit into his hectic schedule.

He barely topped out at five feet in height. Grace could imagine Jake McGuire saying of him, "If he were to hit me and I were to find out about it . . ." Grace was glad Jake was not here to say anything. He made no secret of how unhappy he was with the increase in workers' wages that Madero's rebellion had cost his bosses at Standard Oil.

By the time Grace and the Maderos finished dinner, the restaurant had emptied. Maybe the bodyguard of half a dozen armed soldiers made the diners nervous. Grace would have felt safer if Rico and Juan were here, but they had been called for duty at the rail depot at Tres Marías. It wouldn't do to have disgruntled peasants blow up the president's train.

As the waiters cleared away the remains of a meatless meal, President Madero sent his compliments to Wing Ang in the kitchen. When he picked up the leather case sitting by his chair, Mrs. Madero excused herself. Perhaps she didn't want to know what the spook in the Ouija board would say tonight. Or maybe she was tired of her husband's trysts with spirits.

Socrates was waiting to drive her to the home of friends.

"Mr. President," Grace said, "please allow me to apologize again for asking that you and Mrs. Madero keep elsewhere."

"I perfectly understand, Mrs. Knight. This is a large building with more than one entrance. Our safety would be difficult to ensure, and our presence would put your other guests at risk."

Grace lit candles and turned out the lights while Madero took a dark green velvet drawstring bag from the leather case. He slid the board out of it and set it on the table with the pointer on top.

"Do you know what Mr. Fuld says about the talking board?" Madero asked.

"Mr. Fuld is the manufacturer of your Ouija?"

"Yes. He said 'It surpasses, in its unique results, mind reading, clairvoyance, and second sight. As unexplainable as Hindu magic—Ouija is unquestionably the most fascinating entertainment for modern people and modern life.' "

In her youth, Grace had seen too many sleight-of-hand stunts from behind stage curtains to be anything but skeptical about the Ouija's "unique results." But she could agree with Mr. Fuld that his board was entertaining.

The alphabet was painted in black in two concentric arcs on the face of it, with numbers from one to ten in a horizontal line below them. "Yes" was printed in the top left hand corner and "No" in the right. From the scratched and worn condition of the letters and numbers it was obvious that the board had had a lot of use.

Madero ran an affectionate hand over the surface of it. "The interesting thing about this board is that it seems to have several spirits willing to speak through it. Let us see which one we can summon tonight."

Skeptic or not, whenever Grace put her hands on the wooden pointer a tingling sensation started in her fingertips and ran up her arms. As the planchette moved under her hands and Madero's, the rest of the world dissolved. Grace's attention narrowed to the print on the Ouija. When the pointer stopped at a letter Grace wrote it down.

She was concentrating so hard that a loud rapping startled her into overturning the board. She looked around and saw a figure silhouetted in the doorway. The light was behind the stranger and a shawl threw a deep shadow across her face. She knocked on the door frame again.

For several thundrous heartbeats, Grace thought she and Francisco really had summoned up one of the Ouija board's resident spirits. Then Leobardo, the nightwatchman, appeared behind the mysterious figure.

Grace relaxed. Leobardo had hard and fast rules about consorting with ghosts.

Grace had made an exception to her no-firearms policy for the members of Madero's bodyguard. All of them drew their pistols at the first rap. If the intruder was a ghost, they were ready to kill her again.

"I told her to go to the rear entrance, *Mamacita*," Leobardo said, "but she claims she has a letter for the president. She says it's very important. She says she was told to wait for an answer."

Grace couldn't see the messenger's face, but she guessed she was young and pretty. Leobardo's wife probably had her reasons for paying a witch to tie knots in the drawstrings of his underwear. This woman had no doubt sweet-talked him into letting her in.

"Tell her to give the letter to Captain Salazar," said Madero.

Salazar brought it to Madero. He read it slowly, then looked up at the messenger.

"Tell Mr. Zapata that I thank him for his offer, but my own guard is protection enough."

When the woman left, Madero translated the letter for Grace.

"Emiliano Zapata thinks my life is in danger. He has offered to provide men as protection. He says he will come with them to assure my safety."

"You were right to turn Zapata down, Francisco. You can't trust him, after the trouble he has caused."

Madero's face, lit by the flickering candles, was a study in weariness, disillusionment, and grief.

"Ah, Mrs. Knight, I do trust him, more than any of the men who surround me. He alone has stayed true to his principles. Is not irony the most tantalizing of life's conceits?" His smile had little humor in it. "If Emiliano Zapata comes to the capital, I am certain someone will assassinate him. And then . . . how do the Americans put it? All hell will break loose. It is best that he stay here, in Morelos."

Madero and his guard left with Socrates. The Motorette wouldn't accommodate them all, so Grace had arranged for a horse-drawn station taxi to wait out front.

Grace blew out the candles. She had cause to worry about Madero's safety. His old nemesis, General Huerta, had eaten his breakfast of steak and eggs and plums in this room two weeks ago. When he left for the train station afterward, the look in his eyes could not be interpreted as anything short of murderous.

She had been relieved when he left, but now she would rather he were here than in Mexico City. There he could cause a lot more trouble for the friend she called Panchito Madero than he could here in Cuernavaca.

19

THE FOOL-SWAP

Lyda once said that the best place to think, sleep, or make whoopee was on a train. Then she had to explain to Grace what whoopee meant. Grace had never made whoopee on a train, but she was thinking about it.

The rhythmic clack of the iron wheels across the riveted joints in the rails provided a metronome for those thoughts. Maybe when the hotheads, soreheads, and knuckleheads in the capital sorted out their political differences, she and Federico could book a sleeping compartment on the night train to Veracruz and take in the sea air.

Even though she staged séances for her guests, Grace never claimed to have psychic abilities. But now she could not shake a nagging concern for the safety of President Madero and his wife. The memory of the look in General Huerta's eyes as he stepped into the victoria cab and headed for Cuernavaca's train station haunted her.

In spite of her uneasiness about the situation in the capital she felt guilty leaving Cuernavaca for even these few days. But if she were going to desert the Colonial, February was a good time. The flurry of Christmas pageants and 1913's New Year's celebrations had ended. Lyda, Socrates, María, and the rest of the staff could handle the hotel's daily operation.

Grace used the need for supplies as an excuse to go to Mexico City, but Lyda knew the real reason. Grace wanted to see Federico Martín at Tres Marías. If Lyda knew that Rico had been spending the late-night hours in Grace's room, she never let on.

Grace could have sent a telegram to tell Rico she was coming, but she knew that the telegraph machine sat on a table in the adjutant's office. A major source of entertainment for Colonel Rubio and his staff was reading telegrams as they came in. Rico's comrades-in-arms almost certainly would see any message before he did. Grace was acquainted with many of Rico's comrades-in-arms so she paid a muleteer to deliver a letter instead.

Now she wished she had hitched a ride with the mules, and to hell with her fear of the beasts. The most wayward mule could move faster than this train. Was it her imagination, or had the clacking, creaking, swaying, and rattling become more alarming since the last time she rode it?

Mexicans never ceased to mystify Grace. They had blasted through mountains, spanned chasms, and cantilevered trackbeds out into very thin air to construct 19,000 miles of rails in unforgiving terrain. Maintaining their feat, however, seemed beyond them. She suspected their fatalistic attitude toward death had something to do with it. After all, what sort of people buy skulls made of spun sugar as treats for their children on All Souls' Day?

To be fair, the engine had cause to slow down. The pass at Tres Marías was ten thousand feet in the air. The train had left the valley and had passed through the villages of bougainvillea-covered huts scattered among the foothills. Now it was chugging up a grade that, in Grace's opinion, put it in dereliction of the law of gravity. This was the part of the journey she dreaded. The railbed made sharp switchback turns and as the air grew thinner, her queasiness turned to nausea.

She knew that fretting wouldn't bring her to Rico any faster or make her feel better. The slant of the coach already had her tilted back. She laid her head against the threadbare velvet of the first-class seat and let her thoughts wander.

This little narrow-gauge train with its balloon-shaped smokestack reminded Grace of Annie's favorite story in the *Kindergarten Review* magazine. "The Pony Engine" was about a small locomotive that set out to haul a long line of freight cars over a steep hill after the bigger engines refused. When asked to do something, Annie usually gave the Pony Engine's reply. "I think I can."

As this train strained to make it up the slope, Grace could hear the pistons chanting, "I think I can. I think I can. I think I can."

Kind, rambunctious Annie. By the time Grace met Annie the child had few artifacts from her former life. She had brought along the *Kindergarten Review* magazine when her father took a job with the American Smelting and Refining Company in Sonora, Mexico. A few months later he ran off with, as Lyda put in, the part-time stenographer and full-time tart in the company's main office. He hadn't been heard from since. When anyone was tactless enough to ask if she had received word from him, Lyda said she had not, probably because hell did not have telegraph service.

Lyda and Annie had ended up in Cuernavaca, carried 1,200 miles on the fickle tide of choices and circumstances that arrange everyone's fate. Lyda had walked into the Colonial fourteen months ago and asked Grace for a job. She was strong evidence for one of Grace's favorite theories: some people must have been acquainted in a former life, because on first meeting they feel as if they always have known each other.

Grace pushed up the bottom half of the soot-smeared window and leaned out into the resin-scented breeze. She narrowed her eyes against flying ash and cinders, but the fresh air and the view were worth it. She noticed more stumps among the tall pines though, cut for firewood to keep the train running.

She saw Rico and Grullo waiting on an outcrop. She waved and he spurred the silver-gray stallion down the slope and alongside the tracks. The train labored along so slowly that Grullo easily kept pace. If any sight was more beautiful than Rico on that horse Grace couldn't imagine it.

When the train chugged to a stop in the tiny stone station, Rico was waiting to help her down the steps. She said, "Excuse me," turned away, and threw up on the rail. Evidence alleged that she hadn't been the first to do that.

Rico had seen a lot of passengers do the same thing and he was prepared. He dampened his big linen handkerchief with the cold spring water in his canteen. He gave her the handkerchief and then the canteen to rinse the taste away. Finally he handed her a bottle of Coca-Cola, also chilled, probably in the same spring from which the water came. The makers of the beverage claimed it cured morphine addiction, dyspepsia, headaches, neurasthenia, and impotence. It should do to calm an unsettled stomach.

Juan waved from the far end of the small platform. *"Hola, Mamacita."* Then he went back to flirting with the prettiest of the young women who sold food and trinkets to the train's passengers.

While one worker lowered the spout on the water tank, others threw wood into the tender. Rico led Grace up a well-worn path to an overlook. Below them the valley spread out in a patchwork of fields, villages, sugar refineries, and haciendas. Cuernavaca's roofs clustered in the middle of it with the two volcanoes standing watch.

Rico pointed to a mosaic of fields fanned out around the rambling terra-cotta tile roof of a house, and the chimneys of a sugar refinery.

"That's my family's hacienda. It's called *Las Delicias.* The Delights."

Grace was impressed. *Las Delicias* was bigger than any of the estates surrounding it. And its fields were still green. Rico had to be relieved by that. Grace was surprised by how much of the valley's area was charred. The rumors about the Zapatistas' depredations must be true.

Railroad workers weren't noted for their speed or efficiency, but Grace was sure only a few minutes had passed before the train's whistle blew.

"The fool-swap is about to leave," said Rico.

"Fool-swap?"

"One of your English poets wrote, " 'You enterprised a railroad, you blasted the rocks away . . . and now every fool in Buxton can be in Bakewell in half an hour, and every fool in Bakewell can be in Buxton.' "

"It doesn't rhyme."

"Don't blame me. I didn't write it. But thanks to the railroad the *chilangos,* the fools, in the capital can easily reach Cuernavaca and vice versa."

Grace had received hardly any formal education and the breadth of Rico's astounded her. "How do you know about British writers?"

"A course in English literature."

"At Harvard?"

"Yes."

LAST TRAIN FROM CUERNAVACA

"How broad-minded of the Yanks to include us in their curriculum."

"The Yanks have forgotten all about that tea party in Boston harbor."

"We haven't." Grace smiled when she said it.

Rico handed her back up the steps to the first-class coach. She told him where she would be in hopes he could take leave and join her. He waved from the platform as the train pulled away.

The downhill leg of the journey was much faster, but more terrifying. Grace kept her eyes closed for most of it.

She was never prepared for the clamor at Mexico City's rail station. Passengers hung out the windows and called to their friends. Porters yelled. Hotel touts burst into the car, each trying to out-shout the other. Police whistles shrilled and horns blared in the streets beyond.

Her late husband's cousin, Calisto Mendoza, was waiting for her. He loaded her bags into his Nike roadster and headed out into the busy street as if his were the only car on it. As he wove in and out of traffic Grace gripped the door frame so tightly the blood drained from her knuckles. The number of vehicles seemed to have increased exponentially since her last visit, and every other one was a trolley or bus. Every inch of wall space not plastered with advertising posters was covered with admonitions not to post them.

No wonder the Capital's residents, the *chilangos,* had a reputation for being high-strung and irritable. Grace felt grateful again for the mountain range that encircled Cuernavaca. No matter what that English poet wrote about the railroad making it easier for fools to travel, the mountains kept the *chilangos* from creating this sort of bedlam in her beloved City of Eternal Spring.

Calisto Mendoza drove past parks, monuments, and the magnificent opera house. Besides the big department store, *El Centro Mercantil,* there were German beer halls, English banks, Italian restaurants, French lingerie stores, and at least one Japanese curio shop. Once the car turned onto the tree-lined *Paseo de la Reforma* in the heart of the city Grace relaxed. The embassies and handsome homes that lined the boulevard had not changed. Nor had the Mendoza family's three-story house that fronted on it.

The drab façade gave no hint of the elegance waiting on the other side of the twelve-foot-high, carved oak doors. Calisto honked as he approached them, and the doors swung open to reveal a tropical paradise. Parrots and toucans flew among flowering trees and exotic plants. Vines almost hid the moss-covered stone walls and wrought-iron balconies of the house itself.

Calisto eased the Nike into the roofed entryway, but he hit the brake halfway into the tree-shaded courtyard beyond. Grumbling about useless modern gadgets, he got out and moved a velocipede and at least a dozen roller skates scattered next to the Minerva touring car, which was painted bright red to match the Nike. Grace never did know how many people lived here, but from the number of skates she assumed more children had been added.

The family was waiting for her in the parlor where a cheerful fire burned in the corner hearth. Tears stung Grace's eyes as her husband's kin embraced her. She and Carlos had been married only two years, yet they treated her as if she had always been a member of their family.

Carlos had never said what positions his relatives held in Porfirio Díaz's government, and Grace had not asked. In spite of the high regard that many of the Colonial's foreign guests had for Díaz, Rico had educated her about the dark side of his regime. Grace liked the Mendozas. She did not want to learn anything about them that might affect her affection for them.

Calisto translated as his family tried to tell Grace everything that had happened in the past six months. She learned that the newcomers in the house were distant relatives from Morelos. Zapata's *indios brutos,* they said, had burned their hacienda.

That night Grace shared a bed with the family's aged aunt. The aunt snored, but Grace was so tired she heard only eight or ten of the honks and whiffles before she fell asleep. Grace intended to take Calisto's wife, Rafaela, aside in the morning and tell her about Rico, but finding anyone alone in the Mendoza house was next to impossible.

For the next two days, a chauffeur drove the Minerva so Grace, Rafaela, and two female relatives could shop. When Grace finished buying the supplies she needed for the Colonial, they made the rounds of Rafaela's favorite stores. She insisted that Grace have the latest in French undergarments. She held it up by a strap for Grace's inspection. She said it was called a brassiere and she and the cousins offered suggestions while Grace tried to figure out where the hooks and laces went.

At dinner Saturday night, Calisto invited Grace to attend early Mass with the family at the cathedral on the city's central plaza. After that they could rent boats in the floating gardens of Xochimilco, then attend the Sunday afternoon band concert in Chapultepec Park.

It sounded like a perfect way to spend the day. Grace looked forward to relaxing on Sunday. On Monday she could visit President and Mrs. Madero and set her mind at ease about their welfare.

February 1913

No Mexican general could withstand a cannonball of 50,000 pesos.

—President Álvaro Obregón

Those bastards! The moment they sense an opportunity, they want to get their fingers in the pie, and off they go to where the sun shines brightest.

—General Emiliano Zapata

20

FIESTA OF BULLETS

When the women gathered in the courtyard Sunday morning, Grace wore the dress she had bought the day before. It was the latest fashion and looser and shorter than what she was used to. Even with lisle stockings and a long duster coat, she felt a draft on her ankles.

Rafaela and the other young women had dressed in white with bright shawls around their shoulders and high tortoiseshell combs in their hair. Each had sleeked back her glossy black mane and pinned it in a knot at the base of her neck. As they gathered in the courtyard they reminded Grace of a flock of swans.

The capital's main plaza was not like most in Mexico. Although the cathedral fronted one side and a large fountain spouted water in the middle, it was not graced with trees, benches, or a bandstand. White-gloved policemen directed traffic that formed massive snarls in spite of their shrill whistles and energetic efforts.

The Mendoza family occupied two of the cathedral's hundreds of pews. Grace had not ever spent much time in church. She closed her eyes and let the music and the Latin liturgy wash over her.

After the service, Grace and the Mendozas joined the hundreds of other worshipers fanning out across the plaza. Grace noticed the company of soldiers crossing the plaza toward the National Palace, but she thought nothing of it.

The soldiers had hardly disappeared inside when the shooting started. One volley originated at the National Palace, but other shots came from the far side of the plaza. Caught in the crossfire, people screamed and ran. Someone knocked Grace sprawling, but he probably saved her life. He hadn't gone far when machine-gun fire mowed him down.

The smallest of the Mendoza children stood crying in the middle of it all. Grace scooped him up and ran to the fountain in the center of the plaza. Shielding him, she crouched against the fountain's concrete side and peered over it, looking for the sources of the gunfire.

At first she thought the rebels had managed to bring their fight into the capital itself. Then she saw that the combatants all wore the uniform of the Federal Army. It made no sense to her, but she hadn't time to ponder politics.

Once she saw which streets gunfire wasn't coming from, she picked up the boy and raced for the nearest one. Just as she reached it, stray bullets hit the corner of the building close by, showering her with debris. She kept running, turning down one street then another until the crackling sound of the battle faded. She collapsed on a bench in a little park and realized she was lost. When she'd caught her breath, she took the child's hand and set off walking, asking directions as she went.

An hour later Grace and the boy made it to the Mendoza's neighborhood. The last few blocks to their front gate were the most dangerous. She was back in the heart of the city, and bullets were flying from all directions. Grace had lived through one revolution. She knew what heavy artillery sounded like. Someone had brought in a big gun. When it went off she pulled the child into a doorway.

While the howitzer was being reloaded, she sprinted along the front wall of the Mendoza's house, already pitted with bullet holes. Grace pounded on the door and shouted. After what seemed half an eternity Calisto let her in.

Everyone had thought the child was dead and the women screamed with joy. The rest of the family had made it home safely. The men dragged all the mattresses into the center of the house as a defense against stray bullets. Grace helped them build ramparts of them, but she had little faith that they would stop cannonballs or artillery shells.

The men gathered what few weapons they had—one musket, two rifles, three pistols of varying vintage, and a dozen machetes. All night the family huddled together, women and children in the center, while sporadic shooting continued. Grace thought the battle would stop the next morning, but it didn't. By midday the faint odor of decay drifted over the wall.

The adults held a conference and decided to flee to the hacienda of relatives in Xalpa, seven miles southeast of town. When night came they began loading the women and sleepy children into the Minerva. The Nike only had two seats, so one of the men rode as guard next to the driver.

By tripling up, the Minerva could accommodate all the women and children, but with no room for personal belongings. The men would return for Calisto and those who remained.

Rafaela beckoned to Grace to get into the car.

"I'll come later."

Rafaela tried to reason with her, but Grace kept shaking her head. She knew that as soon as Rico heard about the fighting he would come for her. When he did, she would be here. Still, fear sent a chill through her when the two cars drove away.

Just after sunrise, Rico did arrive. He was hollow-eyed and unshaven. He had a long, bloody wound on his cheek, and a bullet hole in the upper sleeve of his uniform jacket. Grace started to sob and he put his arms around her.

The introductions were brief. No one asked for an explanation of Rico's connection with Grace. They had more important questions.

"What's happening?" asked Calisto.

"Porfirio Díaz's cousin Felíz and about fifteen hundred followers have taken over the armory. Madero has put Huerta in charge of defeating them."

"Huerta?" Grace blurted out. "He's counting on General Huerta?"

Rico's glance let her know he had the same misgivings.

No one had to ask why Felíz Díaz had assembled an army. They all assumed he intended to take the country back for his cousin Porfirio.

Rico continued. "The insurgents have freed two thousand criminals from Belen prison. And a lot of electrical wires are down."

As if on cue, the lights went out. Calisto lit candles and oil lamps.

"What about Cuernavaca?" asked Grace.

"As far as I know, the trouble hasn't spread outside the capital."

They heard engines and Calisto opened the gate to let in the Nike and the Minerva.

He turned to Grace and Rico. "Come with us."

"I have to return to Tres Marías," said Rico. "A train will leave the capital tomorrow with troops to protect Cuernavaca."

"And I have to go home," said Grace.

"God go with you then."

As the men distributed themselves in the two cars, Calisto took Rico aside and gave him something. He embraced Grace, shook Rico's hand, and made the sign of the cross over all of them. He slid into the passenger seat of the roadster and rested the butt of his Mauser on his thigh.

Grace knew that "Be careful," was a stupid thing to say, but she said it anyway.

Calisto smiled. "No man dies before his time." He waved and the little caravan pulled out.

Rico closed the gates after them and shot the big iron bolt home.

They went into the house. Rico lifted the straps of his canvas satchel over his head and gave it to Grace.

"I thought you might be hungry, *querida*. I brought some tamales from Tres Marías." To head off the question she was bound to ask, he added, "They do not contain iguana meat."

He stretched out in a big overstuffed arm chair while Grace dampened a rag and cleaned the blood from his cheek.

"Did you take the train here?" she asked.

"I walked."

"It's more than thirty miles over that terrible cobblestone road."

"No one wanted to risk bringing the train in today." He pulled her onto his lap, put his arms around her waist, and kissed her. "I couldn't bring Grullo into the city to be killed by a stray bullet from one of those Judases."

"What about your family?"

"I don't know."

"You should find them."

"My grandfather doesn't need my help. I would rather be with you here, now, than anywhere else."

"What did Calisto say to you just before he left?"

"Nothing, my love."

"Tell me, Federico."

Rico sighed. When she called him Federico she expected answers.

"He gave me this." Rico held up a small pistol. "And these." He opened his palm to show her a pair of 32-caliber bullets.

She stared at the pistol. "That won't stop anyone."

"It's deadly at very close range."

The silence lengthened as Grace realized that the bullets were for her and Rico, should insurgents or marauders get inside the house

"I see."

"Don't worry, *mi cielo*. It won't come to that."

Grace could tell that exhaustion was about to overcome him.

Before he drifted off he mumbled, "They're calling it the 'fiesta of bullets.'"

"Who is calling it that?"

But he had already fallen asleep in her arms.

21

UNDER COVER

Maintaining two personas, one male and one female, required planning. No one who had known Angel as a scabby-kneed hoyden would have described her as a planner, yet she had worked out the logistics of a double life.

Every so often she put on a flowered blouse and a long skirt with a flounce around the hem and went to Tres Marías. Her mission was to beguile information from the soldiers quartered there. She was good at it.

On her first foray she had met Berta, who sold tamarind candy to the soldiers and the passengers. Berta was seventeen. She was small, dark, and delicate, with a soft laugh. Angel trusted her with the secret of her real identity. Berta shared her candy so Angel could pose as one of the women who walked alongside the passenger cars, calling softly, "What will you take?"

Today, Angel had learned about the battles raging in the capital. Not even the soldiers at Tres Marías' barracks knew what to make of it, but they thought maybe the troops arriving on tomorrow's train could tell them more. Angel left with Berta to retrieve the trappings of her other life.

The folk of Berta's village had been relatively well off until nine years ago. When the local hacienda owner moved the boundary post for water rights, the communal irrigation ditches dried up. Local officials, even under Francisco Madero's post-Revolution government, continued to ignore pleas for justice. Angel found sympathy there.

For a silver ten-*centavo* piece the size of a shirt button, Berta's widowed mother let Angel leave her trousers, shirt, sombrero, saddle, and weapons in her one-room hut on the outskirts of the village. Angel's belongings took up more of the dirt-floor space in the tiny house than the family's did. Berta's younger brother pastured her mare, since a poor Indian woman riding such a fine animal would rouse suspicions among the soldiers of *el gobierno*.

Whenever Angel returned from Tres Marías, Berta's mother insisted she share their evening meal. While Angel ate, the widow mended whatever rips had appeared in her clothes since the last visit. Berta had already reinforced the threadbare seat and knees of Angel's trousers with scraps of canvas. Like most of the Zapatistas, Angel called herself *guacho*, orphan. For her, these simple kindnesses were gifts beyond price.

As for the spying, Angel enjoyed fooling men into divulging information, but she preferred trousers to a skirt. She felt safer as a soldier than as a woman, and not because of the Winchester 30-30 slung across her back. As a soldier she faced threats from *federales* in battle. As a woman, men of both armies, and civilians, too, might menace her on any given day.

Angel had just changed into her shirt and trousers when she heard a stifled cry behind the house. She grabbed her carbine and ran outside, scattering the small flock of chickens scratching in the dust. She rounded the corner and saw that a man had pinned Berta against the back wall of the compound. He held one hand over her mouth and tore at her clothes with the other.

Angel could smell the rotten stench of *pulque*. She wasn't surprised to see that Berta's attacker was Ambrozio Nuñez. She was no stranger to coincidence where he was concerned. God must have a grudge against either Nuñez or her to keep inserting him into her life to plague her.

The thought also occurred to her that he had come here to cause trouble for her while her men weren't around. If that had been his plan, the lovely Berta had distracted him from it.

"Let her loose, *cabrón*."

He gave her hardly a glance. "Go to the devil, *coño*."

That he didn't seem surprised to see her made Angel think that neither God nor coincidence had anything to do with his presence here. His original plan might even have been to rape her.

Angel didn't consider him worth the waste of a cartridge. She grasped the carbine by the barrel and swung it with both hands. Ambrozio Nuñez was extraordinarily stupid as well as drunk, but even he must have expected her to attack. He dodged, but the walnut stock glanced off his skull with enough force to knock him out. He pitched backward onto the cone-shaped corncrib, crashing through its cornstalk and mud-plaster wall.

Angel dragged him out of the wreckage by his heels.

"Berta, help me carry him."

Angel picked him up under his arms and Berta grabbed his ankles. They hauled him to the public fountain where Berta's mother and several other women were gossiping while they filled their water jars. Angel didn't have to say anything. Berta's torn clothes told the story.

Ambrozio was beginning to stir as Angel finished stripping off his clothes and shoes. She left him naked to the women's tender mercies. They went at him with whatever hard objects came to hand. The last she saw of him were his bare soles and blanched backside and women in noisy pursuit.

Angel retrieved her saddle and belongings from the house. On the way to the forest clearing to get her mare, she threw Ambrozio's flea-infested clothes into a ravine. She hummed "Valentina" as she rode away. She looked forward to sharing this story with her comrades. Then she would play cards for cartridges until nightfall when she had plans that included Antonio.

First she had news to deliver.

She called out greetings and traded insults as she rode among the men squatting in small groups around their cookfires. Colonel Contreras had found a good bivouack site for his hundred or so troops. This mountain glen wasn't far from Zapata's temporary headquarters in Ajusco. It was densely wooded and could be reached only by an easily guarded defile.

Contreras's men didn't even have to worry about the smoke from their fires, although they weren't in the habit of worrying anyway. Two companies of *federales* were garrisoned at Tres Marías, only enough to patrol the tracks. They didn't stray far into the countryside. Since Madero had called Huerta back to Mexico City, the rebels and the government troops had operated on an unspoken agreement. As long as Zapata's people left the train alone the *federales* didn't go looking for them.

Angel brought information that would change everything. As she approached the farmhouse where Contreras stayed, she rehearsed what she would say about the battle raging in Mexico City. The squabbles in the Capital meant nothing to her, but she understood that the consequences could affect them all.

Many of the men in Contreras's units neither knew nor cared who occupied the president's seat in Mexico City. They pinned their loyalty on General Zapata and Colonel Contreras, and trusted them to tell them whom to fight. Like the other local chiefs, Contreras led by consensus. He was also the one who gave Angel and the rest their *chivo,* their pay, although not much and not often.

To be honest, while Angel waited to see Contreras, she was thinking about how she would torment Antonio when she finished here. He fretted whenever she left to mingle with the *federales* soldiers. She planned to tease him about her flirtation with the soldier called Juan.

Antonio said he was worried that *el gobierno* would discover who she was and hang her, but he also suffered a chronic case of jealousy. She knew how to reassure him on that second concern.

Wherever Angel's band camped, she and Antonio looked for a place they could be alone. Here they had found the vine-covered ruin of a one-room stone cottage whose thatched roof had long since rotted away. It wasn't far from camp, but it had a reputation for an infestation of snakes so people avoided it. Angel and Antonio took stout sticks to beat the vines and walls thoroughly to evict the reptiles, scorpions, and spiders lurking there.

They had progressed well into the exploration phase of love. Angel shook her head in an attempt to stop thinking about the warm, hard contours of Antonio's bare body, and the feel of his strong, calloused hands stroking her.

Tonight might be their last chance for days to come to lay out their blankets and entwine among the vines. Government troop trains carried guns, ammunition, and food. Angel knew that when she told the colonel about the train leaving Mexico City tomorrow, he would decide to attack it.

No matter what the outcome, Angel and her people would have to go on the run again. She hoped they would be better armed and fed when they did.

22

BONE FIRES

The gunfire stopped. Rico opened the front gate a crack and looked out. The sun wouldn't rise for another hour. The city lay dark and it stank of decay. The boulevard in front of the house was empty of vehicles and people.

He gave Grace the white flag to carry so he could hold one of his Colts half-cocked and pointed down at his side. He took Grace's hand. No matter what happened, he would not become separated from her. The two of them kept close to the fronts of the houses as they headed for the train station.

Rico had gone scouting the night before and he knew where some of the machine gun emplacements were. He had mapped out various routes, but the best way to reach the station meant skirting the main plaza. He saw flickering light from that direction and wondered who might be warming their hands at a fire.

The closer he and Grace came to the center of town the more electrical wires draped across their path. Rubble obstructed the sidewalks, forcing them to walk in the deserted streets. The buildings' dark silhouettes against the pre-dawn sky had large chunks taken out of them. The smell of gasoline and decay became stronger.

Grace stepped on the bloated hand of a corpse lying in deep shadow. She screamed and ran, dragging Rico after her. He held her in his arms until she stopped shaking

When they reached the plaza they saw the source of the illumina-
tion. Burning bodies lit the area. When carrying off the dead proved
dangerous, a few courageous souls must have waved white flags, darted
out, and poured kerosene over the corpses. They tossed lighted matches
and sprinted for cover.

The night sky was fading to dawn's dove gray when Rico pulled Grace
into a doorway. He studied the open ground between them and the train
station. A few soldiers milled around outside.

"On whose side are they?" Grace asked.

"I don't know."

"We have no choice, do we?"

"No."

From the center of the city behind them, gunshots resumed. Grace
hiked up her skirts, ready to race to the station. Rico held her back.

"Running might draw more fire than walking."

Rico had feared the train had already left, but white smoke from the
engine's stack rose above the station roof. All Rico had to worry about
now was convincing whomever was in charge to let Grace board a troop
transport while a battle was going on.

When he left Tres Marías he brought all the cash he had on hand.
He had even been desperate enough to borrow from Juan. He hoped
it would be enough for a bribe.

Hand in hand, he and Grace walked across the small park. Usually,
twenty-five or thirty of the horse-drawn taxis lined up. Today only one
brave soul had parked there.

The empty expanse in front of the station gave no indication of the
chaos inside. As Rico and Grace entered the big front door the din rever-
berated off the high ceiling and stone walls. A lot of the noise came from
the pigs, sheep, and chickens the soldiers were loading aboard. The soldiers might belong to the federal army, but they knew better than to
expect their government to feed them.

Most of them were conscripts from a thousand miles to the north.
They were as poor and shoeless as the rebels they were supposed to
fight. They knew their lives counted for little with those who had transported them here. They brought with them everything that might be

of value, and many things that had no worth beyond sentiment. Some carried pet crows or parrots on their shoulders. Others held aloft bamboo birdcages. Their dogs milled around, growling at each other.

They filled the five second-class coaches. Then they piled into the box cars and sat on crates of guns and ammunition. Their women and children climbed the metal rungs to the roofs. A few of the camp followers slung hammocks between the truss rods under the train. Rico assumed that many of the women only wanted to flee the capital and weren't connected with the army. Given the proclivities of human nature, they probably would be by the time they reached Cuernavaca.

Hundreds of upper-class civilians were having a more difficult time than the conscripts and their entourage. Even if the colonel in charge had allowed them to ride on the roof or between the wheels, they would have declined.

Women in silk stockings sobbed and pleaded for a seat. Their men shoved, threatened, and shouted. In the fray they lost their bowler hats and dislodged the gold stickpins anchoring wide silk ties to their starched shirt fronts. The soldiers guarding the train's doors fixed their bayonets and stood their ground.

Rico went looking for the colonel in charge. He turned out to be an old colleague of the Martín family. That didn't mean he would do a favor for free, but at least bribing him cost less than if Rico hadn't known him at all. The challenge was to spirit Grace aboard without causing a riot among the stickpins and silk stockings.

Rico needed a diversion. For a hundred more *pesos* the colonel agreed to play along. Rico told Grace to stand near the doorway of the first-class car while he walked back along the platform. When he reached the boxcars he took two handfuls of small change out of his pocket and heaved it straight up. The coins chimed against the ceiling, then fell in a silver and copper shower. The soldiers and their women and children made a rush for them. Even *los correctos* craned to see what the ruckus was about.

The colonel gave the sentry a wave of the hand and he stood aside so Grace could hurry up the steps. Rico found her standing in the crowded aisle. She knew to stay at the front of the car. The front seats swayed less and were farther from the stench of the overflowing lavatories at the rear.

The officers who occupied those seats knew it, too. Rico used the last of his funds to persuade them to move. Rico nodded an apology to Grace and brushed past her to take the window seat. He wedged his Mauser between the seat and the side of the car and offered a hand to help her settle in.

Anyone occupying an aisle seat in a car this crowded was bound to be jostled, but it was safer than the window.

"Do you think the rebels will attack us?" she asked.

"I doubt it, but it's best to be prepared."

"Will Colonel Rubio have you courtmartialed for desertion?"

"Rubio is on a spree in Cuernavaca and Juan is telling convincing lies as to my whereabouts."

"Juan is good at that."

Rico could tell Grace was keeping a stiff upper lip, as she would put it. He wished she would cry rather than bottling up the horror of what she had seen this morning.

"Do you know what the original term for 'bonfire' was?" she asked.

"No."

"It's a contraction of 'bone fire.' The Celts used to burn animal bones to ward off evil spirits." She paused. "Do you think the fires in the plaza will burn those poor people's bones, too?"

"I doubt it."

"I saw their faces as we passed them. Some of those bodies were women."

"Try to sleep, *querida.*"

Rico put an arm around her so her head rested in the hollow below his shoulder. He wasn't surprised that the train didn't leave for another hour. Grace was asleep when it finally started to move. She looked peaceful. Rico prayed to God that nothing would disturb that peace on this journey.

He knew God hadn't granted his request when the shriek of brakes woke him. The sudden stop threw him and Grace headfirst against the seats in front of them. That was fortuitous.

Whichever rebel fired the opening rounds knew that the officers rode in the first-class car. He was either an ace shot or very lucky. Two bullets broke the window. They whined past at head-height and two inches from the seat-back on which Rico and Grace had been leaning. They were the first lead snowflakes in a blizzard.

Rico threw Grace to the floor, which was none too clean. She landed on her back and he covered her with his body. Their faces were very close.

"Dab hand," she said.

Rico could hardly hear her over the yelling and the gunfire reverberating inside the coach and out.

"What?"

"Dab," she repeated. "Adept. Good shot. As in, 'Dab,' quoth Dawkins when he hit his wife in the arse with a pound of butter."

It was a ridiculous thing to say. Maybe he should have wondered if she'd lost her mind, but he assumed she was just being Grace. He laughed and kissed her. Then he got to his knees and looked out the window.

The first grenade sailed past farther down the line and the shape of its container looked familiar. Rico realized he had seen similar ones in the Colonial's gift shop. Clay pots were ubiquitous though. That one could have come from anywhere. Surely Grace's friend José had nothing to do with any of this.

Rico knocked out the rest of the window glass with the butt of his rifle. He braced the barrel on the sill and began picking his targets. From overhead came the jaw-jarring pulse of machine-gun fire.

Rico had to admit that the colonel in charge of the troop train had more brains than the average field-grade officer. He had ordered two machine guns mounted onto the roofs and covered with canvas. Thanks to them, the rebels decided to retreat and allow the train to limp on to Tres Marías with its cargo intact. And they would keep the train safe for the rest of its run.

Rico wanted to go on to Cuernavaca with Grace, but he knew he shouldn't. Not yet.

If Mexico City's troubles headed for Cuernavaca the news would reach this telegraph office first. If rogue federal soldiers intended to take Cuernavaca, they would pass through here. All he had to do was tell

Grace that she would have to leave without him. He gave her the news as they stood on the platform with the engine's steam swirling around their legs.

"Juan says Cuernavaca is calm. Rubio is on his way here, but he left Colonel Rodriguez in charge of enough troops to keep peace in the city."

"You're staying in Tres Marías?" She blinked back tears.

"Rubio will arrive this afternoon. I'll request to be assigned to Cuernavaca. If the situation has calmed in the capital, I'll see you tomorrow night."

If Rubio doesn't grant the request, Rico thought, I'll see you anyway.

Grace couldn't sleep, but she wouldn't want to if she could. Her dreams were populated with bodies enveloped in flames, and not all of them were dead. She turned on the lamp on the nightstand by her bed. Its steady glow made her appreciate an aspect of her electric light that hadn't occurred to her before. It couldn't be used to ignite anyone.

It illuminated the chubby clock whose hands registered almost two in the morning. Grace propped herself up on the pillows and looked around at the bedroom, parlor, and bath she called the Snuggery. Her rooms had an eclectic flair some might call bohemian. Wool rugs from Oaxaca adorned the wide-plank oak floor. A Persian rug hung on the wall.

Grace had found the slender-legged Queen Anne dressing table that had come from England at the Bank of Pity, the national pawnshop in Mexico City. One of *los correctos* must have fallen on hard times, a common enough occurrence in Porfirio Díaz's regime. In a way, the pawned dressing table symbolized why Francisco Madero's revolution had succeeded. It had not begun as a struggle to right the injustices done to Mexico's poor. What started it was middle class discontent with rising prices, limited career options, and a stagnating economy.

Grace's husband had been a diplomat. They had lived in official residences for most of their short time together. These three small rooms were the only real home Grace had ever known. She had thought them perfectly suited to her until Rico carried her through the door that night of tango. He added love and laughter. Without him even the furniture seemed dispirited.

Three gilt frames sat on her bureau. One held a daguerreotype of Grace's mother and father in their stage costumes. It was the only likeness of them she had. The second was a portrait of Rico, with the blue of his dress uniform hand-tinted. From the third frame smiled Rico and Grace, arm-in-arm in front of the bandstand.

In a rosewood box Grace kept Rico's letters, each in its envelope. Often, when he was gone and she couldn't sleep, she read some of them. What she loved about them were the turns of phrase written in English but Mexican through and through. "Against love and fate there is no defense," he wrote. And her favorite: "Love and a canteloupe cannot be hidden."

She was reading one of his letters when she heard the faint notes of a trumpet. She put on her kimono and ran barefoot down the stairs and along the open corridor to the ballroom. A gas-lamp sconce illuminated the far corner where the piano stood. Rico sat sideways on its bench, his face in profile. He had put a mute in the bell of his trumpet and was playing "La Paloma."

Of the infinite number of songs about love's lethal effect, this had to be the saddest. Grace knew the words. Everyone in Mexico did, with the possible exception of the redoubtable Mrs. Fitz-Goring.

> *How he suffered for her.*
> *Even after death he called to her.*
> *They swear that the dove,*
> *Is his very soul*
> *Awaiting the return of his love.*

> Cucurrucucú, paloma, ya no llores.
> *Little dove, don't cry anymore.*

Rico rested his elbows on his knees, dangled the trumpet by two fingers hooked through the back loop of the tuning slide, and turned his head sideways to look up at her.

"Panchito is dead." He said it softly, as if to avoid disturbing Francisco Madero's eternal rest.

"Oh, that poor little man." Grace wanted to ask if Huerta had killed him, but she couldn't bring herself speak the man's name. "And his wife?"

"They say she's been spirited out of the country. Francisco's brother and the vice president also have been shot. I don't know any details."

Grace sat next to him and he put an arm around her. She leaned against his shoulder. His face was dirty and his clothes were dusty. He had about him the earthy perfume of his horse's sweat. His indifference to his appearance showed how deeply ran his distress.

"The Maderos were your friends," he said. "I came to tell you myself. I didn't want you to read it in the newspaper."

Grace sensed there was more to his midnight ride from Tres Marías than that, but if so he would tell her in time. They sat in silence for a while. When Rico finally spoke he recited a verse, written no doubt by one of those British poets he so admired.

> God; I will pack and take a train,
> And get me to England once again,
> For England's the one land I know
> Where men of splendid hearts may go.

"There are men of splendid hearts in Mexico, too," said Grace.

"And the women? What of one woman of splendid heart?"

"She will stay where her beloved is."

So that was it. The fear that Grace would leave Mexico had brought Rico here in the middle of the night.

"Cuernavaca is my home. England holds nothing for me." Grace kissed him on the cheek. "Come upstairs. I'll run a bath for you." The best features of Grace's bathroom were the big tiled tub and the noisy, kerosene-fueled water heater.

"*Mi cielo,* what will become of my poor country?"

"Whatever happens, my love, we will face it together."

As they walked up the stairs Grace knew she would sleep peacefully in his arms tonight. Come hell or high water, as Lyda would say, they had each other. Swirl around them as it might, the storm could not hurt them.

23

THE CAROUSEL OF FOLLY

Neither Angel, Antonio, nor the twenty men riding to Tepotzlan with them gave any thought to the ironies of Lent. The Catholic Church declared the six weeks before Easter Sunday a time of sacrifice and fasting, but what do people forgo when they have nothing? How do they fast when they're hungry every day of the year?

On the other hand, Lent symbolized Christ's forty solitary days in a desolate area the Jews called The Devastation. Angel and her comrades understood what that was like. As for the temptations Jesus faced in the wilderness, they were eager to yield to as many of those as possible in the next few days. Unavoidable privation was one thing, but what better reason for a spree than the prospect of priest-imposed abstinence?

Tepotzlan's fiesta lasted through the four days leading up to Ash Wednesday. Everyone agreed it was the best celebration in the state of Morelos. The festivities offered a savory selection of temptations that included all seven of the sins the Catholic Church denounced as deadly—pride, covetousness, envy, anger, sloth, lust, and gluttony. Angel's comrades favored lust and gluttony. The Church considered all seven sins deadly because they led to even worse behavior. The boys hoped the priests were right, and that lust would result in fornication.

Since gluttony included drunkenness, it was the sin most likely to lead to trouble. Alcohol was the all-purpose lubricant for any wild slide into iniquity. Angel's comrades drank whatever they could afford, but they preferred mescal. Mescal, they agreed, was good for joy and sadness.

They had had enough of sadness in the past months. They were primed for joy.

Before they left camp, Colonel Contreras's adjutant had handed each of them sixty *pesos*. It was a full month's pay, and they felt as wealthy as kings. They didn't ask where Contreras got the money. Most of the *jefes* who raised their own companies of men were fairly well off. If Contreras had come to the bottom of his personal funds, he could persuade some rich landowner to support Zapata's cause or have his cane fields burned.

Plinio waved a slender brown bottle and shouted. "Today I will get as drunk as four hundred rabbits."

Antonio glanced at Angel and rolled his eyes toward heaven. He and Angel had no need to look beyond each other for lust. The question was, should they stay sober enough to come to the rescue when their compatriots got into trouble? For they surely would get into trouble.

Angel didn't intend to stay sober or rescue anyone. She leaned closer so Antonio could hear her over the ambient clamor of the pilgrims' burros and roosters, each proclaiming the road his exclusive domain.

"Better to get drunk than to have to deal with a drunk," she said. Besides, Angel knew she could count on Antonio to keep his wits about him. He would rescue her should the need arise.

Angel had the devil-may-care nature found in good lieutenants. She was the cheerfully reckless sort whom men would follow into battle the way a puppy will chase a stick. Antonio, on the other hand, was colonel material. He thought beyond whatever skirmish had Angel's blood up, and he tempered courage with caution.

Between swigs of mescal, the troop debated whether alcohol in a dead man's veins caused his beard to grow. Manuel swore that after an old toper in his village died, his beard grew until it filled his coffin

"How do you know that?" Antonio called back over his shoulder. "Did you dig up the coffin and open it?"

The men crossed themselves at the very idea, and changed the subject. Conversation was becoming difficult anyway. The nearer they came to Tepotzlan the more crowded the road. Indians streamed down from the mountains as they had since long before festivals had anything to do with

Christianity. Many of them had walked for days to get here, with their white wool jackets clutched close, ground fog swirling around their bare brown legs, and ribbons fluttering from their straw hats,

On their backs they toted sacks of corn, pottery precariously stacked, bundles of produce, rolls of straw mats, live chickens, and sheafs of sugarcane stalks. Penitents shouldered crosses of heavy timbers. Groups of musicians provided a discordant score on homemade guitars and harps, flutes, and drums. Woodcarvers carried painted statues, some almost life-sized. Most of the effigies were of St. Jude, patron of desperate causes.

Before the Church demanded forty days of self-denial from the faithful, it allowed them the most abundance they would see all year. Carnival was a mix of religious fervor and wild abandon. It featured saints that were Catholic in name, but purebred Aztec under their halos. What Maxmilian's wife, the Empress Carlota, said almost fifty years earlier still applied: "We are working to make this country Catholic," she once wrote to a friend, "for it is not now, nor has it ever been so."

One trait the Catholics and the Aztecs shared was a zest for pageantry and ritual. Tepotzlan had dressed for the occasion. Even the outlying streets flaunted paper streamers in bright colors. The closer Angel rode to the center of town the louder were the fireworks, firearms, church bells, music, whistles, and noisemakers. Hundreds of booths displayed a dizzying array of food. The maelstrom of color, noise, and aromas had a more intoxicating effect than mescal.

Angel and the others had existed on rations of beans and parched corn, and not much of those. For days she had thought about a tender hen cooked in spicy chocolate sauce. It was tasty, but she was impatient to finish it so she could try something else. She grinned at Antonio.

"By tonight I'll be too drunk to stay on my horse. By tomorrow I'll be too fat to climb into the saddle."

Antonio sighed. Sometimes he felt as though Angel were a jaguar in a house cat's skin. He didn't want to try to tame her, but he was always wary of being scratched.

The fiesta crescendoed around the church. From several blocks away

Angel heard the hypnotic music of the *Chinelo* dancers. Thirty men danced in a circle. They wore robes heavy with embroidery, and huge, plumed headresses festooned with strings of beads and baubles. Their masks featured thick eyebrows and pointed, up-tilted beards designed to ridicule the early Spanish conquerors.

The dance was simple. Each man took two shuffling steps, then leading with his shoulders, gave a hop to the left or to the right. They repeated the hypnotic pattern hour after hour.

When Angel and Antonio tired of it they headed for the main plaza. At its center stood the bandstand where the town's orchestra was valiantly attempting a brassy version of Verdi's opening march from *Aida*. Plinio and Manuel had settled down on one of the iron benches to drink mescal, wax philosophical, and enjoy the passing scene.

The younger men were testing the core Catholic doctrine of transubstantiation. Priests defined that as the transformation of bread and wine into the flesh and blood of Christ. For Angel's comrades it meant turning intangible lust into fleshly pleasures. The young women strolled arm-in-arm clockwise around the plaza just as their mothers, their grandmothers, and generations of great-grandmothers had done. The young men sauntered in a larger ring in the opposite direction.

Conversation between them was carried on in the language of glances. When a woman's eyes sent an invitation, the man pivoted around and walked beside her. Somehow the species replenished itself as a result.

Plinio called it *el tiovivo de tontería,* the carousel of folly. And what, he asked, was more entertaining than watching people commit folly? He waved his bottle at the parade and winked at Angel. "Men and women, always going in opposite directions."

Mezcal had turned the bulbous tip of Plinio's long beak redder than usual. The men called him tomato nose, but he didn't care. "I have a bird dog's nose," he would say. "I can smell trouble before you can see it."

Angel was enjoying the music and her men's attempts at love's folly when Plinio's nose sniffed trouble. He leapt up as though the iron bench had burned through the seat of his pants and hustled over to her.

"*Gobierno,*" he said.

He was right. The khaki uniforms were scattered through the crowd. They stood out among the white trousers and shirts of the *indios*.

"*¡Mierda!*" Angel muttered.

She and Antonio signaled their comrades. One by one they dropped out of the promenade and headed for the corral where they had left their horses. The men were grumpy as they rode away, but at least none of them had been drunk enough to refuse to leave.

When they stopped to water their horses at a public fountain, a young woman darted from behind a ruin of an adobe wall and sprinted to intercept Angel's mare. She grabbed a stirrup and hung on. Angel pried off her fingers, but the woman clutched her wrist with both hands. She trotted to keep pace while Angel tried to shake her loose. Her grip was strong.

"Take me with you, *Capitán*. I will cook. I will warm you at night."

"I'm not a captain." Angel broke free and reined her mare in circles to avoid those desperate hands. "Go back to your village."

"They burned my village, *Capitán*." The woman was determined to promote Angel in rank. "They killed my parents. I have not eaten in two days." The young woman sank to her knees in the dust and held her hands up in supplication. Tears streamed down her cheeks. "Please take me with you."

"Go with Manuel." Angel nodded toward the former member of the *rurales*. "He has no one to warm his blankets, and he won't mistreat you."

The woman didn't have to look higher than Angel's beautifully tooled saddle to see that the handsome young rebel was closer to aristocracy than anyone else. She must have assessed every traveler who stopped at the fountain. Angel wasn't flattered to have been selected.

"I want to be your woman, *Capitán*."

"If Manuel accepts you, you may accompany us."

"I don't want to go with him. I want to go with you."

Plinio leaned forward in his saddle. "One who disdains a gift insults God, my daughter."

Angel left the woman to work out an arrangement with Manuel. She reminded Angel of a younger version of her mother. Angel hadn't prayed since the day she found her father's workers dead in the dried up irrigation ditch. She prayed now that her mother would return from wherever *el gobierno* had sent her. She prayed that people had been kind to her, but she didn't think it likely.

24

THE EYE OF THE STORM

Rico knew that Mexico City's main newspaper, *El Imparcial, The Impartial,* was laughably misnamed. Porfirio Díaz had backed *El Imparcial* for the thirty years he held power and it still occupied a comfortable position in the back pocket of big business. But Rico's grandfather had received it by courier every week and Rico had learned to read with it.

He wasn't surprised that *El Imparcial* claimed Victoriano Huerta had nothing to do with the deaths of Francisco Madero, his brother, and the vice president. The president himself had entrusted the general with quelling the coup attempt, *El Imparcial* said. And besides, General Huerta was visiting with the Dutch ambassador when President Madero was shot.

Rico wanted to believe that Victoriano Huerta hadn't ordered Francisco Madero's assassination. Almost everyone of influence seemed to believe him. When Huerta took over as president pro tem, diplomats of every embassy came calling to congratulate him. Foreign investors expressed their pleasure at having a forceful leader in control again. The military hierarchy hadn't protested. The only government leader who refused to recognize Huerta's authority was Venustiano Carranza, governor of the northern state of Coahuila. And he lived too far away to matter.

Rico had taken a weekend pass to the capital to see how it fared. The charred corpses had disappeared from the streets, along with the cartridge casings and unexploded artillery shells. Workmen were repairing the damage done to the buildings. Electricity had been restored.

Rico shouldn't have been surprised by how quickly his people seemed to have erased from their memories the image of the dead bodies of men, women, and children, slaughtered by their own government. Maybe their history of thousands of years of violence had habituated them to it.

Only in Mexico, Rico thought, could such a senseless bloodbath be nicknamed a Fiesta of Bullets.

Before Rico returned to duty at Tres Marías a week ago, he suggested that Grace throw a fiesta of her own to celebrate the coming of Lent. He figured it would cheer her up and take her mind off the uncertainty in the capital. He had not experienced one of Grace's full-throttle extravaganzas, so he could not have imagined she and her friends among the officers' wives would organize something like this. The crowd of officers gathered in front of Cuernavaca's elegant theater should have tipped him off.

When Rico and Juan entered the theater, a flock of young women surrounded them and jostled to break eggs on their heads. Fortunately María and the Colonial's kitchen maids had poked holes in each end of the eggs and had blown out the original contents, leaving only the shells. Unfortunately they had filled the shells with cheap cologne and bits of gold and silver paper.

Being pelted with eggs was customary at pre-Lent celebrations, so Rico and Juan had worn their oldest dress uniforms. They both bowed and moved away from the door to give the ladies a clear shot at the next guests.

Juan stopped to stare around the room. *"¡Que maravilloso!"* And Juan wasn't one to use words like "marvelous."

The theater was another of Porfirio Díaz's monuments to progress and to himself. It would have looked at ease in Paris or Rome. Frescoes crusted its domed ceiling. Red velvet swags decorated the curved tiers of balconies and loge seats. It looked posh enough as it was, but Grace and her staff and her friends had turned it into a fairyland.

The seats formed a line against the walls to make room for dancing. A long buffet and smaller tables sat in a jungle of potted palms a-twinkle with small lights. A soft glow from Japanese lanterns illuminated the room. The parquet floor glittered with the gold and silver confetti that had fallen off the guests. Baskets contained brightly colored paper fans and parasols as gifts. Women were already using them to flirt with the men.

Luís, the Colonial's *cantinero,* presided at a bar set up in a side room. Rico was pleased to see him. The success of the surprise he had planned would depend on people drinking enough to lose their inhibitions.

Cuernavaca's social set was not large. Everyone knew each other so conversation was lively. They all wanted to forget, at least for tonight, the troubles in the capital. Besides, during Carnival they all had a duty to enjoy themselves.

Rico found Grace and whirled her around. He gave her a feather-down kiss that was more satisfying than a buss and a bear hug. It was a kiss of friendship and comfort. It was an optimistic kiss. It implied they would have the rest of their lives to enjoy more passionate embraces.

It also transferred confetti from Rico's lips to hers. He brushed it off with the tips of his fingers, then gathered her into his arms. She leaned against him as if coming home.

The band started with the usual Mexican *danzas* and two-steps. As the barrel in the bar filled with empty bottles, the laughter grew louder and the music livelier. By midnight Rico and Grace and all the other couples were dancing the tango. Rico gauged that the time had come for him to introduce his surprise.

He didn't doubt that people would like the Turkey Trot. The Vatican had denounced it with indignation. That alone would assure its popularity.

Rico had mailed a musical arrangement to the bandmaster a few days before. As the musicians launched into an exuberant rendition of "Stop-time Rag," Rico grabbed Grace by the waist and pulled her close to demonstrate the "hugging" that had so offended the Pope.

Rico and Grace had danced together so often to the phonograph that she caught on quickly to the basic moves. Four alternating hops—left, right, left, right—with feet wide apart. Up on the ball of the foot, and landing on the heel. Once Grace had the rhythm, Rico added fast kicks between her legs and the sudden stops and turns that made the dance fun and alarming.

Before Rico and Grace finished the first circuit of the floor, the whole company took off at a gallop that was more free-for-all than dance. As Rico steered Grace through the happy mêlée, she threw her head back and laughed.

Rico wanted to believe that as long as they were dancing, nothing bad could happen. Tomorrow he would have to tell Grace he had been assigned to Veracruz for six weeks. Rumor had it that Huerta intended to install Rubio, a general now, as governor of Morelos. The good news was that Rubio liked Grace and would make sure nothing happened to the Colonial. But Rico wondered if Rubio was sending him away because he planned a campaign he knew Rico would protest.

Much as Rico disliked Rubio, he hated Emiliano Zapata more. He remembered the view from the high ridge at Tres Marías, the blight of black patches that once had been productive fields and lovely old houses. Rico knew the names of every one of those haciendas—El Rosario, Los Arboles, Santa Fe. He knew the families who had lived behind their vine-covered walls. Zapata had to be stopped before he destroyed not only Morelos's economy, but its history and tradition. Huerta was a brute, but maybe Mexico needed him.

Still, Rico couldn't shake the feeling that the country was holding its breath, waiting for the rest of the tempest to arrive with a roar.

25

RAINS OF TERROR

"*El gobierno* attacked before dawn." José's hands shook as he reached for the canteen Angel held out. He took a long drink from it before he went on with his story. "They went from one house to another, shooting whatever moved."

"How did you escape, *Papá*?" asked Antonio.

José glanced at his wife, Serafina, sitting nearby with a blanket draped around her shoulders. She rocked back and forth, crying silently. "Your mother and I have not slept inside the house since General Fatso returned to Morelos."

"General?"

"Rubio is a general now." José continued his account. "Every night we unroll our mats in *el corral*, the courtyard. When we heard the shooting, we ran out the back gate and hid like mice in the cornfield. We saw black smoke rising from the village."

"Did they take the women?" Angel asked.

José stared at the ground. His answer was barely audible. "I don't know."

It was a question none of the men would have bothered to ask because they knew the answer. Of course, the *federales* took the women. When the army was through with them they would send them to labor camps in a jungle so far away the forest canopy might as well shade the muck of another continent. The only way to save all the women was to drive *los federales* out of Morelos and General Huerta from the President's Palace.

Angel had a more immediate plan, although "plan" might be too ambitious a name for it.

"We will hunt down the curs and free the women."

Angel could tell by the looks on their faces that no one liked the idea. Even Antonio shook his head.

Angel couldn't believe it. "*¡Carajo!* You let them defile our women and yet you pretend to be men?"

"If we attack the *federales* they will shoot the captives," said Antonio. "And Colonel Contreras would not approve such a raid."

At least the men looked chagrined as they skulked back to their off-duty pastimes. Angel spat in their direction, then stalked away to perch on a boulder and brood. She stared at the dark clouds massing over the mountains in the direction of the Capital. She was so preoccupied she didn't remember that the rains weren't supposed to come for two more weeks.

She gave a start at the sound of Plinio's voice behind her.

"Trying to rescue those captives will not return your mother to you, my child."

"*Quien de los suyos se aleja, Dios lo deja,*" said Angel. "He who leaves his family is forsaken by God."

"Then God has forsaken most of us, for we are truly orphans."

"Mexico is our mother. These mountains are our *casitas,* our little houses." Angel scooped up a fistful of dry, rocky soil and shook it at him. "This dirt is our soul."

"I pray you are right, my daughter. I pray God has not forsaken the handfuls of dirt that are our souls." When he walked away, his shoulders slumped as if still bearing the eighty pounds of sugarcane he had carried on his back most of his life.

Angel decided to ride to San Miguel and track the *federales* to wherever they were keeping the women. Then maybe she could convince her comrades to rescue them. Her plan involved leaving camp without permission, but she would take that up with Contreras when she returned. She had never tried to take advantage of the fact that her commanding officer was her father's old friend, but she would this time.

Even if she couldn't locate the captives, a trip to San Miguel could be useful. Maybe the soldiers' ravening horde of *galletas,* the camp followers, had overlooked some caches of corn or beans. And if *el gobierno* had burned the houses and corn cribs, Fatso's troops would not likely return there. The caves in the cliff face below the village would be safe. They would provide shelter from the rains.

In the distance, thunder rumbled approval of her plan.

From the balcony above the Colonial's wide entryway Grace watched lightning flick like snakes' tongues at the mountain peaks near Tres Marías. She could count on two facts of life in Mexico. The *tabachine* trees would adorn themselves with flame-red flowers in March and the annual rains would arrive in May. So why was an escort of dark clouds mustering in mid-April?

Their color, like tarnished gunmetal, matched Grace's mood. Two factors fueled her gloom. One was Rico's absence. The other was Rubio's presence.

Rubio had arrived in Cuernavaca much puffed up over his double promotion to general and governor. General Huerta must have learned an important lesson from his former boss, Porfirio Díaz: promote incompetents. Bumblers rarely staged successful coup attempts. Porfirio's cousin Felix had recently proven that.

Rubio spent a lot of time with his troops in the field, for which Grace was grateful. But when he came to town he passed more of his waking hours at the Colonial than in the pink stone hulk called the Governor's Palace. He claimed he came here for María's spicey stewed plums and the piano music, but Grace had seen him staring at José's daughter, Socorro. She kept the girl busy in the kitchen whenever his brass-bedizened bulk darkened the hotel's doorway.

Grace had nicknamed José's daughter Cora, but the child was so silent and sylph-like that Lyda called her The Wraith. The only time

Grace heard her laugh or speak above a murmur was when she and Annie had their heads together. Because of her friendship with Cora, Annie was becoming fluent in Nahuatl.

Grace envied Annie's ease with languages. She considered Nahuatl, and not the digestive distress known as the trots, to be Moctezuma's real revenge. She suspected the Aztecs had designed their talk to trip up the tongue, not trip off it, but she loved to hear her employees converse, their voices as soft and mysterious as black velvet.

Mrs. Fitz-Goring's voice was neither soft nor mysterious. It erupted from the dining hall below the balcony.

"Stupid girl!"

"Bollocks," Grace muttered. Rubio, the spring rains, and now Fitz-Goring. What vengeful Aztec deity had she offended to bring all this down on her head?

Grace headed for the dining hall at her emergency gait. She had had the seamstress sew gored panels into her skirts to allow more movement. An unfashionably long hemline hid the walk that to casual observers looked regal. Each stride, however, swallowed two stair steps or covered a meter of the Colonial's tile-paved corridors.

She found Mrs. Fitz-Goring standing like a monument to umbrage in the middle of the crowded dining room. Socorro stared up at her, as wide-eyed as a rabbit hypnotized by a cobra. Grace gently grasped the girl's shoulders and turned her toward the kitchen.

She reassured her with one of the few phrases she knew in Nahuatl, "*Ca ye cualli.* It's all right," and gave her a nudge to set her in motion. Then she faced the wrath of the dowager du jour.

"Good evening, Mrs. Fitz-Goring. What seems to be the problem?"

"It's not what *seems* to be the problem, Mrs. Knight. It's what *is* the problem." The dewlaps on each side of Mrs. Fitz-Goring's jaw quivered with indignation. They quivered so often that Wattles had become her nickname in the kitchen and back hallways.

"That clumsy girl spilled hot tea on me. She scalded me and ruined my gown."

Try as she might, Grace could see no evidence of tea on the dress, but saying so wouldn't help matters. "Bring the frock to Lyda tomorrow and she will see that it is laundered. And of course your dinner this evening will be complimentary."

"Your girls won't be scrubbing my new charmeuse on a rock in some filthy river, will they?"

"I assure you we have a proper laundry."

Wattles looked unconvinced. "Spigs are so lazy, it's a wonder you coax any work at all from them, Mrs. Knight."

Grace lowered her voice so as not to create more of a scene by chastising a guest. She also had discovered that in situations like these the more quietly she spoke the more closely people listened. It was as if she were sharing a secret rather than delivering an ultimatum.

"What you say in the privacy of your room is your concern, Mrs. Fitz-Goring, but we do not allow the word 'spig' in the public areas of the Colonial."

"What harm in it?" Wattles looked genuinely surprised that Grace would find offense. "It is merely short for 'No spigga da Eenglis,' is it not?"

"Nevertheless, I must ask you to help us maintain standards of decorum."

Grace had found that the word "decorum" worked like a charm for most British patrons, at least when they were sober. She waited until Mrs. Fitz-Goring had sat back down on her chair and wedged herself between its sturdy arms, then she left to comfort Cora. Behind her, she could hear Wattles soliciting sympathy from the other diners for the shabby treatment she had received at the hands of help and management. She did not, however, repeat the word "spig." And Wattles wasn't likely to get much sympathy anyway. These days, most of the hotel guests were grateful to have a roof over their heads, three meals a day, and no one shooting at them.

Because Fitz-Goring occupied a room here, Lyda had to turn someone away today. The Mexicans might be able to view coups with a fatalistic fortitude, but not so outsiders. Wattles was one of thousands of foreigners who had come to Cuernavaca to escape the ominous uncertainty in Mexico City. As a result, the Colonial was full to capacity.

And then there was the army. In the upstairs wing, officers slept on cots, eight to a room. Grace was grateful for the business, but she felt as frayed as the hems of José Perez's white cotton trousers.

That reminded her. José was supposed to have brought more pottery two days ago. He never missed a delivery. She would ask Cora about him in the morning. In the meantime, she had to convince the poor child that she had done nothing wrong and Grace was not angry with her in the least.

Socorro was always quiet, but these days Grace detected fright in her eyes, like a deer facing a shotgun. Maybe Annie could find out what was troubling her.

26

When Grace tried to talk to Socorro, the girl cowered like a cornered rabbit. Annie had difficulty convincing her that *Mamacita* wasn't angry with her. Grace suspected that Annie included some choice words in Nahuatl to describe Mrs. Fitz-Goring, because Socorro smiled, ever so slightly. Grace beamed back at her, trying to coax a bolder smile out into the open. A smile in Socorro's luminous eyes and on the succulent curves of her lips could brighten the darkest day.

Socorro claimed she didn't know why her father hadn't come. Grace believed her, but she detected a fear that went beyond the prospect of being sent home in disgrace.

She decided to go to the market, talk to José, and get to the bottom of his absence. She tucked twenty *pesos* and some small change into the hidden pocket in her wide leather belt. She put on her long canvas duster over her everyday skirt and bodice. She laced up her oldest shoes and pinned her new straw sailor hat onto the upswept heap of her dark copper hair.

In case the storm clouds made good on their promise of rain, she took an umbrella from the bouquet of them in the tall vase by her office door. It was of navy blue cotton with a cover of the same material and it had a stout ebony handle. It was the serviceable sort carried by a country doctor or a parson.

As she passed the front desk she told Lyda she was going to the market to look for José. She waited for the mule-drawn trolley to pass by the front of the hotel, then crossed the tracks and set out on foot diagonally across the plaza.

The market's vendors and shoppers filled the narrow streets near the Governor's Palace. They jammed in until it seemed as though the addition of one more person would make any movement, forward, backward, or sideways, impossible.

When Grace finally reached the area on the side street where the folk of San Miguel usually sat, she was astonished to find it unoccupied. She stared at the hard-packed dirt, bare except for the market's usual assortment of rotten produce and anonymous animal parts.

José and his neighbors always came to Cuernavaca on Tuesday. Grace's annoyance turned to alarm. She didn't notice people jostling her as they passed. She asked the hard-scrabble entrepreneurs on either side what had become of the San Migueleños. They shrugged and swore they didn't know.

Grace didn't think of herself as impulsive, which showed how little she knew. That going alone to San Miguel might not be a good idea didn't occur to her. She had visited the village often in the past months and she felt as safe there as in Cuernavaca. Socrates had taken the Pierce to Tepotzlan early that morning on an errand, so Grace walked to the side of the plaza where the horse-drawn cabs gathered.

The driver who had made the trip with her before demanded three times the usual rate.

She cocked her head and narrowed her eyes, a signal of displeasure in any language. "Why?"

"Zapata." He crossed himself. "The road is very dangerous." He glanced up at the sky. "And maybe the rains will come."

"Bollocks," Grace muttered.

He probably preferred the easier run to the train station and had settled on Zapata as a bogeyman. But she had made up her mind to go and the Devil himself couldn't turn her around.

"I will pay you half the fare now, and half when we return to Cuernavaca."

He nodded, pocketed the *pesos,* and helped her aboard.

The road had deteriorated since the last time Grace traveled it, but the carriage made it almost as far as the river. The sky had clouded over and thunder growled along the horizon when the driver pulled onto a level stretch of ground and looped the reins around the brake handle. He climbed down and trotted around to unfold the rickety steps. He held out a hand to steady Grace's descent.

She straightened her hat, pinned it back in place, and surveyed the rough trail ahead.

"*Vámanos, señor.* Let's go."

"I'm very sorry, but I cannot accompany you, *señora.*"

"Why not?"

With a look of regret almost genuine, he patted the battered side of the old victoria. "I must guard the coach. You know what they say. 'Temptation makes the thief.' "

" 'It takes a thief to know one,' " Grace muttered in English.

She hiked up her skirts and set out for the bridge. She stopped in the middle of it and looked over the side. The river was higher than she had ever seen it, swollen by the runoff of the rains in the mountains. She took a deep breath and started up the tree-covered slope to the village perched along the canyon's rim.

Thirsty and dusty, she trudged the last few meters to the top of the cliff. She leaned on her umbrella to wait for her breath to catch up with her. The many fruit trees and the bougainvillea flowers cascading over the courtyard walls disguised the destruction. The impact of what Grace saw took several heartbeats to register.

Many of the houses had blackened walls. Broken roof tiles and burnt thatch lay on the ground around them. The charred ends of ceiling beams jutted like splintered bones from collapsed roofs.

The narrow streets were empty of people, but littered with evidence of them—torn baskets and sleeping mats, broken crockery, a baby's hammock. Gardens had been trampled, adobe ovens smashed, grain cribs torn apart. A dead chicken floated in the village fountain.

Grace wanted to make haste back to where the victoria waited, but she would not leave without trying to locate José and Serafina. Her heart pounded as she walked down the center of the main street. She was afraid to shatter the fragile silence by calling out, as if doing so would summon back whatever evil had visited here.

She was relieved to reach the Perez house without incident and to find it intact. She pushed open the gate. Serafina swept the bare earth of the courtyard every day, but now leaves littered it. Grace called out to them. No one answered.

Lightning flared. Grace jumped when a crash of thunder followed it. The first large drops of rain landed on her hat and shoulders like big wet kisses. She took cover inside.

The two small rooms were empty. She held her palm close to the ashes of the open hearth. They were cold, but otherwise the house looked as if José and Serafina had just left and would return soon.

She tried to think of an explanation for the attack. The most likely culprits were bandits. Rebels burned haciendas now and then, but she couldn't believe Zapata would turn on his own people. If federal troops had done this by mistake, a few words with Rubio would clear it up. Maybe his soldiers would help repair the houses. Maybe the government would issue an apology.

Grace heard voices outside and went to the door. "José!" she called. "What happened here?"

But neither of the men who came through the gate was José. They both had on the grimy, ill-fitting khakis of the federal army. They wore no shoes and looked malnourished. They had the mahogany-brown faces and opaque eyes of *indios*. Over their shoulders they carried coarse hempen satchels. Grace pegged them as foragers.

She doubted they understood Spanish but that was all she had to work with. "Where is your captain?"

Neither of them responded with so much as the rise of an eyebrow. One of them carried a shovel. He began digging in the dirt of the floor.

Not foragers, Grace thought. Looters. She couldn't imagine what treasure they expected to find here, but then, when one was as poor as an alley cat, treasure was a relative concept.

The digger's comrade got Grace's attention by leveling his bayonet at her. She stood as tall as possible under the low ceiling, and brandished her umbrella. She felt as much foolish as frightened. Where was his commanding officer? Where were the troops?

She switched to English. "Don't be a bloody ass. General Rubio is a friend of mine. Harm me and he will hang you." She put one hand on her throat and pantomimed choking.

He kept advancing, crowding her toward the doorway to the inner room. Grace could smell months' accumulation of sweat and the stench of *pulque*. She tasted bile in the back of her throat.

Now would be a good time to call for help, but when she tried her voice had deserted her. By now hailstones were drumming so loudly on the terra-cotta tiles of the roof that no one would hear her anyway. Rico. She screamed it silently. Rico.

The drunken soldier seemed to exist at the other end of a telescope. Grace could see the coarse weave of his tunic and the crude eagles engraved on the pot-metal buttons. She noticed the crumbs in his bushy mustache and the black crescents of dirt under his long fingernails.

Time stopped. Grace couldn't move. She couldn't speak. She couldn't believe any of this.

What flushed her out of the briar patch of her bewilderment was a sonorous clang. As the soldier pitched forward the look of surprise that crossed his face was probably the most emotion he had shown in his life. Grace stepped aside to give him a clear trajectory to earth. He was so thin he made landfall with only a modest thud. Grace could tell from the caved-in back of his skull and the blood beginning to pool under his face that he wouldn't get up.

A teenaged boy stood in the patch of air he had just vacated. A faded serape covered all of him except for the bottoms of a pair of canvas trousers tied with hemp cords at the ankles. The serape filled the room with the aroma of wet wool. His big sombrero hung at his back. The shovel with which he had dispatched Grace's assailant was the same one the other soldier had been using in his hunt for buried treasure. He threw it aside

"*Tlazocamati*. Thank you." Grace knew that much Nahuatl.

The boy ignored her as he rifled the dead man's pockets. He stripped off the bandolier and picked up the army-issue bolt-action Mauser and bayonet. The other soldier had had his throat neatly cut. The boy stopped to collect that man's weapons, too, and roll them in a sleeping mat. He shouldered the mat, stepped over the second body, pulled on his hat, and headed outside where the hail had become a steady downpour. He turned in the doorway and gestured for Grace to follow him.

Grace didn't want to seem ungrateful, but she had no intention of going with him. She edged around the bodies, opened her umbrella and slid it sideways through the narrow door frame.

The boy turned left at the front gate. Grace turned right. On wobbly legs, she headed back the way she had come. She glanced over her shoulder and saw, with relief, that her rescuer wasn't inclined to chase after her.

27

SAVING GRACE . . . AGAIN

Angel rode along the rim of the canyon looking for a vantage point and shelter from the rain. She found both under two flat boulders taller than cathedral doors and leaning against each other like an affectionate pair of drunks. She reined her mare to a halt in the triangular opening between them.

Water had collected behind the upturned edge of her sombrero's broad brim and formed a moat around the conical crown. She tilted her head to the side to pour it off like rain from an eave.

She knew she should keep riding and not look back, but her curiosity about the *gringa* got the better of her. The woman had come to San Miguel alone at a time when merely wandering into the bushes to relieve oneself exposed a person to the risk of getting shot at. Either *la Inglesa* lacked the brains of a burro or she possessed her own pair of mule-sized *cojones*.

Angel surveyed the area with her binoculars.

"*¡Chinga!*" she muttered.

Centuries of foot and animal traffic had eroded the road below the surrounding land. Rainwater cascading from the rocky surfaces of the high ground channeled onto it and raced toward Cuernavaca in a muddy torrent. Anyone intending to travel it would need a boat. Angel was pretty sure the *gringa* didn't have a boat.

The top of *Inglesa*'s dark blue umbrella descended the path from the village. The umbrella vanished, then appeared again beneath the patchy canopy of cedar trees. It bobbed across the bridge and headed for the road.

Inglesa must have arrived here in a carriage, but none was visible now. Had she been fool enough to think the driver would wait for her in this storm? If he had stayed he would have been a bigger idiot than she. His coach would mire to the axles.

When *Inglesa* chose not to come with her, Angel thought she was rid of her. Her conscience had been serene. José's daughter worked at the *gringa's* hotel so Angel knew he would hear of the fray in San Miguel sooner or later. When he did, he would have to agree that Angel had saved *Inglesa's* honor and probably her life, too. That was more than Angel's comrades were willing to do for their own women.

It was a bitter thought.

Angel could still ride away. She could pretend she didn't know what happened to *Inglesa* after she refused the offer of protection. No one would be the wiser.

She watched the umbrella stop at the edge of the road. It turned one way and then another, as if considering its predicament. Behind it, the river spilled over its bank and rushed to meet the gully-washer in the roadway. The umbrella sought safety on a small rise of ground while the tide rose around it.

Normally Angel wouldn't have cared if a foreigner got her feet wet. Foreigners didn't care what happened to Angel's people. They came here to steal land, timber, oil, iron ore, and sugarcane. The only attention they paid to the *indios* was to work them to death.

But this wasn't just any foreigner. *Inglesa* had helped Antonio's family. She had provided income to their impoverished village. She had given Antonio's sister a safe haven. The Perez family referred to her as *"Mamacita."*

Angel loved Antonio Perez with such passion that the thought of him made her heart lurch in her chest as if tipsy on tequila. His family was her family. Their debt of gratitude was hers, but that didn't mean she had to be gracious about repaying it.

After seeing the devastation *el gobierno* had caused in San Miguel, no synonym for angry would suffice to describe what Angel was feeling. She was also cold and wet and in no mood for conversation. And though she wouldn't admit it, she resented the affection and respect the Perez family had for the *gringa*. She decided to let *Inglesa* go on thinking she couldn't understand Spanish.

She dismounted, wrapped her serape more tightly around her, and led the mare down the muddy slope. They both ended up sliding most of the way and arrived filthy at the bottom. That hardly improved Angel's mood, the color of tarnished gunmetal and stormy as the weather.

She would take *Inglesa* back to camp. Once there, the woman would be José's problem. Angel was certain she wouldn't refuse an offer of help this time. That notion proved she didn't know Grace.

Grace recognized where she was, but she couldn't remember how she got here. The day's events had sent her into shock. The road was her link to home and the transformation of it into a river deepened her confusion. She stared at the tumbling, umber-colored water as if it had nothing to do with her. For that matter, she now occupied a never-never land where nothing had anything to do with her.

Someone else had walked down San Miguel's desolate street. Someone else had been attacked by a rogue soldier. Someone else had seen a man's skull caved in with a shovel. Someone else had skirted a pair of corpses as if they had been logs fallen across her path.

The trees and rocks around her blurred. Her mind escaped its bone box and drifted above her body. From a height she looked down at a sodden stranger standing alone in the rain, holding an umbrella as if waiting to hail a taxi on a London street corner.

"Get a hold on yourself, Gracie old girl."

Her voice echoed hollow in her head, but it called back her wandering self. She took a deep breath. She flexed her toes and fingers to reestablish relations with her body. Then she got down to the task of figuring out what to do.

This was when Rico should come splashing up the road on his big gray horse. She looked toward Cuernavaca, more than half expecting to see him. It wasn't a completely foolish expectation. He had rescued her before.

The rain's tattoo on the taut hump of her umbrella provided rhythm for her thoughts. Being stranded on foot ten miles from the Colonial had one advantage. Her everyday pack of petty problems had been reduced to one: find a way to reach home.

The downpour stopped as suddenly as it had started. For the first time since she had stared at the bare patch of the San Migueleños's ground in Cuernavaca's market, Grace felt relieved. She knew one fact about rain in Mexico. The water would soak into the thirsty soil and evaporate so fast it would seem like magic.

Sunset was only a few hours away and she couldn't wait for the tide in the road to ebb. She collapsed her umbrella, slid it into its case, and put the handle's looped strap around her wrist. She hiked up her skirts and stepped off the mound.

Using the tip of the umbrella for balance she set out along the road's margin. The water was the color and consistency of lentil puree, and she felt her way where it was shallowest. Even so, it filled her shoes and soaked her skirts halfway to her knees.

She didn't hear the splashing of hoofs until the horse was almost close enough to nibble the brim of her straw boater. She whirled and saw the same boy who had killed the two soldiers. Had he decided to rob her? She had learned fencing as a teenager, as many theater people did. She took a firmer grip on the handle of the umbrella and extended it like a foil. She knew the posture was ridiculous, but it was all she had. She made a mental note to buy a pistol when she got home.

He sat forward in the saddle and beckoned for her to mount behind him.

Grace retracted the umbrella to her side and shook her head. *"No, gracias."* Surely he understood what those words meant. Even Mrs. Fitz-Goring knew that much Spanish.

She set out again, probing ahead of her with the tip of the brolly.

"Venga." The boy said. Come.

Aha! He did speak a little Spanish. Grace decided that if he intended to rob her, he would have to do it here where her body would be found. She wasn't going to ride off with him to be violated and murdered at his convenience.

She said again. *"No, gracias."* She gave a small wave, signaling that she could take care of herself, and he should go on about his business.

She put down another foot, feeling for level ground under the mud. Was it her imagination, or had the water already gone down a bit? She should be able to reach the outskirts of Cuernavaca before total darkness. She could find some sort of transportation there. Arriving at the Colonial after nightfall would be best anyway. She wanted as few people as possible to see her in this filthy and disheveled state.

The boy loosed what had to be a string of Zapotec oaths. He had reined his horse around, ready to ride away, when the report of a rifle sounded from the direction of San Miguel.

"Bugger all," Grace muttered.

Had the rest of the army patrol found the bodies of the two soldiers? And if so would they assume she and the boy were responsible? A spate of shots accompanied by shouts indicated that they had and they did. The shouts grew louder.

"Venga, idiota." The boy waved her toward him.

Grace assessed her predicament like the debits and credits in the Colonial's ledger, except that here every option required red ink. In one column were a lot of men more interested in shooting than asking questions. In the other glowered one surly young assassin smelling of sweat, horses, gunpowder, woodsmoke, and rancor.

"Cuernavaca?" Grace pointed at herself, then toward town. "Will you carry me to Cuernavaca?"

He gave an abrupt nod and Grace took the hand he held out to her. She was surprised by his strength as he lifted her off her feet. Using both hands, he hauled her across the horse's rump. He deposited her there like a sack of cornmeal with her hind end cocked in the air.

Without waiting for her to arrange herself into a more dignified position, he kicked the horse into motion. Grace grabbed the saddle and saddle blanket to keep from sliding off the other side and landing on her head. Hampered by her long skirt, she flailed and twisted until she was sitting sideways with both feet dangling off the horse's left side.

The ride was bumpy. She gripped a fistful of the boy's serape with one hand. With the other she tried to tug the hem of her skirt to within a decent distance of her ankles. When she had leisure to take note of her surroundings she realized two facts.

One: she had lost her umbrella and hat.

Two: this horse was not headed for Cuernavaca.

Only a coin toss could have decided whether Angel was happier to see her comrades or to be rid of *Inglesa*. The moon cast an opalescent glow over the trees and rocks when she reached camp. As usual, the men lay cocooned in their tattered blankets with the bare soles of their feet close to the fire. Their bodies radiated outward from the warmth like spokes from a hub. Once the rains began in earnest they would have to sleep in the nearby caves so they were taking advantage of fresh air and moonlight.

Angel roused them with a pistol shot. They swarmed to their feet, rifles in hand, but only Ambrozio Nuñez fired before realizing Angel wasn't *el gobierno*. Or maybe he did recognize her. Angel knew he would rather shoot at her than *federales*, but his bullet didn't come close.

She grinned at him. She had called him many names over the past months, but her current favorite was *cochi*, pig.

"Better luck next time, *Cochi*." Then she gave him no further thought.

Angel tried to see her comrades as they must have appeared to *Inglesa*. She had to admit they were a menacing-looking lot. Each man carried enough weaponry to wipe out a platoon. The moon's light illuminated wolfish grins that exposed ranks of tobacco-stained teeth behind shaggy black mustaches. They must look terrifying to someone used to balls and picnics and tea parties.

Angel found some small satisfaction in that thought until the woman slid off the mare's rump and strode up to the men. As they surrounded her she asked, very politely in Spanish, if any of them knew José Perez.

Angel made an adjustment in her assessment of *Inglesa*. She sat a horse like her arse was eggshell, but either she had nerve or the arrogant sense of superiority that defined gringos. Or both.

Angel was glad to see José and Antonio weave through the crowd. José would take *Inglesa* off her hands, and she could spend time alone with Antonio. The prospect of seeing him had been the one sunny ray in this long, dreary day.

He must have felt the same. When Angel beckoned with a sideways nod, he left his father listening to *Mamacita* and went with her. He reached for her but she held up a hand to stop him.

She also wanted to get right to the kissing part of her homecoming, but she had business to take care of first. She glanced back at the camp. Someone had thrown brush on the fires and by their light Angel could see *Inglesa* deep in conversation with José. She was no doubt demanding to be returned to Cuauhnáhuac. For once Angel and English were in accord.

Angel turned back to Antonio. "We can leave her at the train station in Ajusco tomorrow." Angel had given this some thought. The village of Ajusco was the most remote of the eleven stops the train made on its way to Cuernavaca.

Antonio sneaked a quick kiss before answering. "Fatso has set up barricades everywhere. We were afraid they had caught you." He didn't have to tell her what misery that thought had given him. "The *federales* pigs are watching the train stations closely, and they're stopping everyone on the roads."

"We have to get rid of her, Tonio. She doesn't know one end of a horse from another. She'll slow us down. And when Rubio finds out we have her, he'll send the entire army to take her back."

" '*Del dicho al hecho hay un gran trecho.*' " It's a long way between saying and doing.

Antonio pushed Angel's sombrero off onto her back. He twined his fingers into her short hair and kissed her. Bewitched by each other they did not realize they were silhouetted against the starlit sky. They did not notice Grace glance their way. They did not see her eyes widen for a split second before she went back to explaining her plight to José and the others.

28

RICO TO THE RESCUE

The gaggle of policemen in front of the Colonial should have alerted Rico that something was wrong, but he was a man on a mission. He leaped out of the station cab before it came to a stop. His plan was to sneak up on Grace, corral her with his arms, and plant a kiss of such ardor that a team of strong men would be required to pull him away from her.

Lyda screamed at the sight of him. "Thank God, you're here!"

She threw her arms around his waist, leaned her head against his chest, and started sobbing. The maids ran from every corner of the hotel. They all cried and talked at once and he couldn't make sense of any of it. Attentive guests clustered in the doorways.

"Where's Grace?"

Annie was the only coherent one. "We don't know."

"You don't know?"

"She's disappeared." Lyda retreated behind the front desk and blew her nose on a bandana that was thoroughly damp already.

"When?"

"Five days ago. She told me she was going to the market to talk to José and she never came back. We've looked everywhere for her."

"Have you seen José?"

"No."

"Has anyone gone to San Miguel to ask him about her?"

"Rubio says his men searched the village. He says that José and his family have gone. No one knows where."

Rico was starting to get a very bad feeling, lodged like a sharp stick just under his heart. "What does Socorro say?"

"She doesn't know anything," said Annie. "She's terrified that something terrible has happened to her family and to Grace."

"What about the police?"

Lyda waved the bandana, as if to dismiss the police. "They've asked all over town. No one knows anything."

Someone knows something, Rico thought. But he won't be fool enough to admit it to the police.

"Jake assigned two of his company's Pinks to work on it." Lyda seemed to think that was a good idea, but Rico knew better.

The men of the Pinkerton National Detective Agency specialized in putting down labor unrest. Under Porfirio Díaz's regime American companies had hired them to do plenty of that and their methods were brutal. It had earned them the hatred of the common folk in Mexico. They would have less success than the police at getting information.

"What was Grace wearing?"

"Her white sailor blouse and long blue twill skirt, the canvas duster, and her new straw hat with the red band."

Women's preoccupation with clothes had always seemed silly to Rico, but he was grateful for it now. The average man would not have noticed what Grace wore, much less remembered it days later.

"Did she carry anything with her?"

Lyda thought for a moment. "An umbrella, a dark blue one. It rained later that day."

Rico wanted to go straight to the market and start demanding answers, but he knew better than to question people while wearing the uniform of an officer in the federal army. He borrowed a plain brown suit and vest and scuffed brown shoes from a comrade staying at the Colonial. Even dressed as a dry-goods clerk he received only wary shakes of the head from the market's shoppers and sellers alike.

He walked to the plaza and caught the eye of Chucho, his favorite bootblack. Chucho always had a big smile for Rico because he tipped generously and his shoes never needed much work to make them gleam. If he was surprised to see the captain literally down-at-heels his round, good-natured face betrayed no hint of surprise or judgment.

Chucho was a thorough professional. For ten *centavos* he would deliver fifty cents worth of dash and patter while he worked his magic on Rico's borrowed footwear. Like all the boys shining shoes or selling chicle gum on the plaza, Chucho would know the comings, the goings, and the gossip within a ten-block radius.

He unloaded his tin of brown polish and his rags from his box. Then he set the box where Rico could prop his foot up on the wooden handle. He dug the polish out with his fingers and worked it into the leather. While the right shoe was drying, he started on the left. The grand finale was the buffing. Chucho snapped the rag with a syncopated rhythm, his elbows pumping hard enough to run a small turbine.

As he was repacking his equipment Rico leaned down and held a *peso* so only he could see it.

"Did you see the English woman from the Colonial here last Tuesday?"

"Yes, Captain." Chucho grinned up at him. "She hired a *coche* and driver."

"Which driver?"

"The one they call Chivo." He pointed his chin at a thick-set man smoking a cigar on a bench nearby.

Rico handed the boy the *peso* and twenty *centavos* instead of ten. Then he strolled over to sit next to Chivo. He extended his long legs in front of him and tilted his fedora forward so he could interlock his fingers at the base of his skull. He leaned back onto his palms as though relaxing in the sunshine.

He glanced over at the taxi driver, whose melon-shaped head was wreathed in cigar smoke. In a conversational tone Rico said, "Where did you take the Englishwoman last Tuesday?"

Chivo's heavily lidded eyes went goggly, as though a snake had just crawled up his baggy pant leg.

"I didn't see any Englishwoman last Tuesday."

Rico's silence held more menace than threats.

"I swear on my mother's grave." Chivo obviously wanted to run, and he just as obviously knew it would be futile.

"Tell me where you took her or I will break every one of your fingers. And then I will seriously hurt you."

Rico waited while Chivo tried to think of a plausible lie. His intellect wasn't up to the challenge. "She wanted to go to San Miguel."

"Why didn't you bring her back?"

That had to be the question the driver dreaded most. That was why he had claimed ignorance when the police questioned him. Why had he abandoned the *gringa*?

"I had to stay with the *coche*. When she didn't return I went looking for her, but she had disappeared. The rebels must have kidnapped her."

"And you couldn't find her?"

"No, *señor*. She had vanished."

Rico assumed he was lying about going to look for her, but he asked anyway. "What did the people of San Miguel tell you when you went looking for her?" He could imagine the gears of prevarication spinning between Chivo's ears like wheels in deep mud.

"They said the rebels kidnapped her so they could demand a ransom."

Rico stood up. He grabbed Chivo by the front of his shirt and lifted him half off the seat.

"If anything bad has happened to her, you will pay. There is no place on earth you can go where I won't find you."

He threw him down with such force the bench tipped over backward, taking Chivo with it in a tangle of hairy arms and ankles.

Rico was a shaken man when he left the ruins of San Miguel. Maybe Rubio would know what had happened here. The general harbored the delusion that Grace was his dear friend. Had he ordered his men to destroy the place in retaliation for her disappearance?

Rico led Grullo slowly down the steep path from the village, searching the bushes for any trace of her. He found the umbrella in a tall clump of grass near the road. Swinging between hope and despair he mounted and rode in expanding circles, looking for other evidence. The straw boater lay in plain sight beside a trail leading up into rough country. Last night's rain had washed away all tracks, but Rico could guess what had happened.

He scanned the surrounding mountains. He would ask to be reassigned to Rubio's command here in Morelos. If necessary, he would ask his grandfather to use his influence to make the transfer happen.

He would find Grace. If Zapata's people had harmed her he would not rest until he had killed them all.

May 1913

Poor things. With two centavos-worth of lard, I could fry them. (A rich man's comment on viewing the rebels from his balcony.)
    —From *Pedro Martinez: A Mexican Peasant and His Family* by Oscar Lewis

The Zapatistas were not an army: they were a people in arms.

    —Rosa King, *Tempest over Mexico*

29

MOSES IN THE WILDERNESS

The sinuous roots of a fig tree clung to the rock face around the cave's entrance and formed a lattice in front of it. Strong, graceful, and tenacious, it was able to draw life from stone. It made Grace think of José's people.

The cave was just big enough for the women and children and its entrance was hard to see even from close by. After a week traveling with Lieutenant Angel's band, Grace knew she was lucky to have it as shelter from May's nightly rains. Usually the men slept in the caves. The women dug burrows into the high riverbanks for themselves and their children.

Grace dreaded spending another night shivering between a flea-infested mat and an even livelier cotton blanket. She wanted to feel the clean, cool, polished tiles of the Colonial's corridors under her bare feet. She wanted to hear the parrots chattering in the courtyard. She wondered if Lyda had gotten word of her disappearance to Rico in Veracruz, or if the letters he wrote to her twice a day were still piling up in her office.

Most of all, she worried that she would find the hotel deserted when she finally returned. Nature took over quickly here when civilization was negligent. Grace imagined her beloved home sliding into the sort of ruin it had been when she bought it.

This little band of Zapatistas had been moving higher and deeper into the mountains. They had been dodging federal troops and patrols, but José's wife, Serafina, said that soon they would join Zapata's main army. The thought of being caught in a battle between the rebels and the officers who had billeted at the Colonial made Grace's stomach churn. So the next morning, when José introduced her to the mule, she recoiled, but she didn't flee.

José beamed and held out the lead rope. "I've named him Moses because he will lead you to the Promised Land."

Moses raised his grizzled muzzle, curled his purple lips back from his stumpy yellow teeth, and greeted Grace with a bray. She jumped and retreated several steps. José led the mule toward her and she backed up again. For Grace, approaching a sharp-hooved, snaggle-toothed creature the size of Moses was like trying to make friends with an animated threshing machine.

"*Mamacita,* Cuernavaca lies far from here. If you want to reach it you will have to ride him."

"May I go to Cuernavaca on him today?"

"*Quizás mañana.*"

Maybe tomorrow. That was the answer he gave her every day. "Then I'll get on him tomorrow."

"He won't hurt you, *Mamacita.*"

Grace didn't believe that for a second.

José handed her a banana. "Give him this."

Grace stood as far away from him as she could and extended the fruit. Moses folded up his prehensile lips again and grasped the end of it in his teeth. He eased it out of her hand with surprising delicacy and chewed it up, peel and all.

From then on he followed Grace wherever she went. She remembered one of Lyda's observations: "Feed a man or a dog and you'll never get rid of 'em." Obviously that also held true for a mule.

She asked José to tie him up, but he brayed incessantly. When that didn't bring freedom he chewed through the hemp line and set out to look for her. If any man came near her he would flatten his ears against his head, lower his muzzle, and swing it from side to side like a snake preparing to strike.

With the rain beating down on him, he stood guard all night outside the cave where Grace and the women slept. In the morning Grace decided that if he was indeed her means of going home, she should make her peace with him.

If he intended to kick her or take a chunk out of her arm with those teeth, now was the time to find it out. Serafina had given her an old straw sombrero and a large red bandana to hold it in place. Grace folded the bandana diagonally and tied it around his neck. She adjusted it to hang the way the rebel soldiers wore theirs, then stepped back to admire him.

"Don't you look the swell, though."

The expression in Moses's eyes could only have been adoration. He lifted his whiskery chin, expanded his bony chest, and affected a swagger.

Lieutenant Angel's band was on the move again. Serafina said lookouts had spotted a patrol of *federales* only a few miles from the camp.

Antonio gave Grace an old pair of khaki trousers to wear under her skirt and a piece of twine to hold them up. She used Serafina's knife to rip the skirt up the front as far as her knees so she could ride astraddle. The clumsy wooden saddle rubbed her in all the wrong places, but it was better than walking. She shared Moses's broad back with Serafina.

Grace didn't recognize the villages they passed through, but that was to be expected. When she took the train across these mountains she had caught only glimpses of distant rooftops among the trees. The view from up close was unsettling. This was not the picturesque, tranquil Mexico she knew. Angel's men usually sang to pass the hours as they rode, but not now.

Houses and fields were burned or abandoned. The old people were left to starve in the ruins. Angel's men shared with them what little food they had.

Grace didn't know where they had gotten any food at all since their own rations were scant. They probably had plundered it from haciendas.

Grace should have disapproved of that, but she didn't. The more she saw of the destruction, the more Lieutenant Angel and her comrades began to resemble Robin Hood and his men.

Many of Morelos's landed elite frequented the Colonial's restaurant, cantina, and ballroom. Grace was friendly with them and enjoyed their company, but she was certain that if the army had commited these atrocities, the *hacendados* were the cause of it. She was relieved that Rico had been assigned to Veracruz. At least he could not have been involved.

"Where are all the people?" Grace asked Serafina.

"*El gobierno* is sending the *indios* far away."

"But why?" Grace asked.

"God knows. I do not."

Then Grace noticed small yellow flags hanging on some of the doors. They reminded her of lithographs she had seen of English villages beseiged by the plague. A body abandoned at the side of the road increased her sense of foreboding. It was wrapped like a tamale in a palm leaf mat with the bare feet sticking out. Serafina crossed herself and tied her bandana over her nose and mouth.

"*Tifus.*" She whispered it, as though to avoid attracting the notice of the disease.

"*Tee'foos?*" Grace asked.

"*Sí. Tifus.*"

Grace repeated it until the answer came to her. She had heard typhus called many names—"jail fever," "famine fever," "putrid fever," "hospital fever," "camp fever," and "ship fever." By any name it was lethal as often as not. She knew that lice spread it. The itching on her skin suddenly seemed more than merely bothersome.

Angel, Antonio, and José rode stone-faced through the ravaged countryside. No one felt like singing today.

"I am going to Cuernavaca," José said. "I'll meet you at Yautepec."

Angel didn't argue with him. She knew he was worried about his daughter.

"Take the *gringa* with you."

José shook his head.

"Why not?"

"Fatso's men have put up roadblocks everywhere. I will have to travel at night over dangerous trails. If *los federales* find her with me they might throw her in jail. Or worse."

From the rear of the column came Grace's husky alto. She was singing the women's favorite song from her reportoire. "The Dreadful Wind and Rain" was about subjects dear to their hearts—passion, betrayal, murder, and a ghost. Antonio had helped her translate it into a haunting mix of Spanish and Nahuatl.

It told the story of the young woman drowned by her lover. A fiddler found her body and put it to good use. He made a bow of her long yellow hair and pegs of her finger bones. But the part the women loved best, and the men too, was this verse:

And he made a little fiddle of her breast bone,
Oh the wind and rain.
The sound could melt a heart of stone,
Cryin', oh the dreadful wind and rain.

The more popular *Inglesa* became, the less Angel liked her. But though she wouldn't admit it, she liked that song. She was surprised that *Inglesa* made the effort to sing it in Spanish, much less Nahuatl. Most gringos, especially those who spoke English, believed communication was impossible in any language but their own. Americans were particularly convinced that if they spoke English loudly enough, foreigners would understand them.

Inglesa, however, was a prime mimic. Every day she added to her stock of Spanish and Nahuatl words, what she called "Kitchen-Injun." And her accent was almost perfect. She had learned the words and the harmony to "Valentina" and other favorites.

"You have to admit," said José, "that *Mamacita* has spiced up our little corner of the revolution"

"The women like her," added Antonio.

"No they don't," muttered Angel. "Everyone's afraid that if they annoy her she'll curse them with warts or a pig's snout. They're afraid she'll make the women barren and the men impotent."

Angel was right about that. Socorro had told her father about the séances at the Colonial and Grace's heart-to-soul talk with *La Llorona*, the Weeping Woman on the second floor. News of *Inglesa* speaking with the dead could hardly be kept secret.

Angel turned in the saddle and scowled back at Moses and Grace, leading the flock of women and children.

"Nahualli," she muttered. "Witch."

30

ON THE BRINK

In daylight, even the most sympathetic observer would feel obliged to call the rebel camp squalid. Misshapen shelters of rags, brush, and flattened oil cans blighted the landscape. The daily debris of people on the move lay scattered among the spring flowers.

Nightfall, however, transformed it into something magical, as if fairies, or angels, had moved in and redecorated. As twilight deepened, candles flickered in the dozens of altar niches the women had dug into the dirt walls of the arroyo. Each one contained family portraits, images of saints, and bouquets of wildflowers in clay pots. The portraits were the most poignant since many of the faces were of loved ones dead or missing.

The candlelight shimmered in ribbons along the curves of the bowed heads and shoulders of those who prayed in front of them. Grace was touched by the fact that their faith needed no church nor pulpit, no pews nor priest. They carried God with them, along with the pots and pans and grinding stones, the bedding, rifles, children, dogs, and chickens.

While the women prepared the evening meal Grace walked away from camp. She had stuffed her skirt, blouse, and patent-leather shoes into a hempen bag of the sort the rebel soldiers carried. At night she used it as a pillow.

The khaki shirt, trousers, and straw sandals she now had on made riding Moses easier, and also this daily pilgrimage. The night's storm clouds were gathering in the north, but she started out anyway. At each new campsite she climbed to the highest point she could reach, in hopes of seeing the roofs of Cuernavaca somewhere in the distance.

Here, as from her other perches, all she saw were ranks of mountains one behind another. The setting sun told her where west was, but she didn't know her position in relation to it. Was she to the west of Cuernavaca or east of it, to the north or the south? She searched for the glint of sunlight on the iron rails of train tracks. She tried to find puffs of smoke from the engine's stack, but only saw wisps of clouds curling around the outcrops.

Grace had admired the distant, misty majesty of these mountains from her balcony. Up close, they were a sky-high heap of jagged, wind-whipped boulders interlaced with a labyrinth of chasms, clefts, and narrow passages skirting sheer canyon walls a mile deep.

Could she and the band of rebels have left Morelos altogether? That was possible. Ancient volcanic upheavals had formed the mountains called Sierra Madre Occidental. Northward they stretched to the border with the United States. South of Morelos they blended into the Sierra Madre del Sur.

The two ranges formed a towering rampart a hundred miles wide and fifteen hundred miles long. Grace shouldn't have been surprised that she was lost in the middle of it. She felt lost in other ways, too. At twilight the longing for home and for Rico became so intense that she wanted to start crying and not stop.

A murmur of voices and muted laughter from below caused the hair at the nape of her neck to stir. In the past three weeks on the run she had come to realize that this war consisted of skirmishes between army patrols and roving bands like Lieutenant Angel's. It was a metal-cold minuet of advance and retreat, bow and dissemble, snipe and run.

So, who was trying to sneak up on them? Grace lay on her stomach at the edge of the overlook and peered down at the tangle of bushes along the river below. On the ground the thicket looked impenetrable, but from her aerie Grace could see a clearing in the center of it and a striped blanket spread out there. In the pale light of day's end she saw Antonio lying on his back with Angel half on top of him, right arm thrown across him, right cheek resting on his chest. The second blanket was draped so carelessly over them that Grace could see they were naked.

She wriggled back from the edge, stood up, and brushed the dirt off her. She was surprised, but not shocked. She had stumbled over unconventional pairings in the dark back hallways and cluttered dressing rooms of London's theaters. But even though three weeks ago she had glimpsed Antonio and Angel kissing, she couldn't believe José's son would engage in buggery.

Angel did have something of the feminine about him, but not Antonio. He was tall and broad-shouldered, with features that looked as though they had been chiseled from the reddish-brown rock of these mountains. His penetrating black eyes brought the word "inscrutable" to mind.

Grace had decided back then that she must have been mistaken about the kissing thing. Now it appeared that she wasn't. Come to think of it, she had never seen Angel or Antonio flirt with any of the young women in camp.

She wondered if José knew about it, then realized she hadn't seen José for a day or two. She would ask Serafina where he had gone, but she didn't expect a reliable answer.

Usually Rico and Juan set their canvas camp chairs on the rim of a cloud-shrouded cliff not far from the army's adobe barracks at Tres Marías. Other than the spectacular view of Cuernavaca's valley, they couldn't have said why they liked to lounge on the lip of the abyss. Maybe they did it to provoke fate, as if fate hadn't enough tricks up its sleeves. But today was different. Today Juan sat and Rico paced along the edge of the cliff.

Juan poured a drink from one of the five bottles of Marqués de Riscals claret standing like an attentive honor guard next to his chair. He held the glass up so the first rays of the morning sun shone through it, scattering into flashes of ruby, amethyst, and gold. He would have been glad to see Rico even if he hadn't brought a case of fine wine from the port city of Veracruz, but he was worried about his friend. Rico was a warrior, not a pacer.

When Rico reached the northern end of his circuit he paused for several minutes to stare at the train tracks snaking down from the high pass. Then he resumed ranging along the edge of the precipice. He avoided looking at the valley below for two reasons. The burned cane fields, sugar refineries, and hacienda houses left ragged black holes in the tapestry of the countryside.

Cuernavaca's distant rooftops glowed golden in the dawn's light. The conflict had not touched them, but the sight of them compounded Rico's misery. Grace should have been sleeping under one of those roofs. He should have been able to ride Grullo down the mountain, across the valley floor, and along the broad highway from the train station into the heart of the city where the Colonial stood, solid, ancient, elegant, and welcoming. He should have been dancing with Grace to ragtime on the gramophone. He should have been laughing with her, making love with her. Not knowing where she was or what was happening to her was driving him to the brink of insanity.

The night's rainstorm had passed. The sleek needles of the pines were freshly washed and glistening. Juan glanced at the flame-colored clouds outlining the mountain peaks. The air smelled like incense.

"The sun has just awakened, my brother. The train isn't scheduled to arrive for four more hours. Wearing a ditch into the ground with your big feet won't cause it to get here any earlier."

"That damned engineer is probably dallying with one of his women."

"Even if Hanibal foreswears love and leaves the capital on time, we still have to wait four hours."

Rico wanted to saddle Grullo and ride off by himself in search of the rebels. When he asked Rubio for command of a company of men to hunt them he had forgotten how bureaucracies worked, or didn't. Two interminable weeks and a blizzard of telegrams passed before Rico received his orders and the recruits he needed. When the men finally assembled, Rico learned they had nothing to load into their rifles. Now he was waiting for ammunition to arrive on the train from Mexico City.

"Maybe bullets are cached in Cuernavaca and Rubio didn't mention them," said Juan.

"Why would he do that?"

"To make success more difficult for you." Juan held out the bottle of claret, one quarter full. Rico returned it empty

"Rubio doesn't like you." Juan opened another bottle.

"Rubio doesn't like anyone. Except Grace." Rico ventured a glance at Cuernavaca's red-tiled roofs. The sharp pain of angst in his chest made him regret it immediately. "Everyone likes Grace."

"Rubio hates you in particular."

This was news to Rico. "Why?"

"You're everything he's not. You're passably good-looking, although not as handsome as I. You're rich, fearless, rich, fairly intelligent. Did I mention that you're rich? And worst of all . . ." Juan paused for a swig of claret. ". . . you don't have to pay women to have sex with you."

"My grandfather is rich. I'm not."

"For a peasant like Rubio that is a distinction too fine to detect with *mira-lejos,* binoculars." Juan patted the wooden arm of the canvas chair next to him. "Sit, my brother. Take a siesta. You haven't slept more than an hour or two a night for the past two weeks. I'll wake you when I see the train's smoke."

"I don't trust you to wake me. You once slept through an earthquake."

But Rico sat. When he did, his eyelids felt as heavy as twenty-*peso* pieces.

"Why this one?" Juan sounded to Rico as if he were speaking under water.

"Which one?" Rico's lips and tongue felt swollen and sluggish as he tried to form the words.

"La Inglesa."

"I love her."

"You've loved many women."

"Not like this."

"How can you tell this love from the other kind?"

Rico was too exhausted to hear the wistfulness in Juan's voice. He might not have recognized it if he had. Wistfulness had never been part of Juan's nature.

Rico started to say true love meant being willing to die for the other

person, but that sounded too melodramatic. Besides, he knew for a certainty that Juan would lay down his life for him. Caring about his welfare, however, was another matter. If Juan were concerned about Rico's
well-being he wouldn't have taken advantage of his friend's distraction
to win a month's pay at whist. Rico didn't blame him though. Death
was serious. Cards were a lark. Rico would have done the same.

So, well-being was the key concept here. His words came out slurred,
as though he were drunk on exhaustion.

"When you care about a woman's happiness more than your own,
that is true love."

Rico fell asleep so quickly that if Juan had anything more to say on
the subject, he didn't hear it.

He woke with a start when Juan shook him. He jumped up so fast he
overturned the canvas chair. Juan grabbed a handful of his tunic to keep
him from pitching over the edge of the cliff and hauled him to safety.

"Has the train come?" Rico righted the chair and looked toward the
station below.

"Not yet, but this fellow claims to have information."

The peasant standing at attention wore a khaki uniform tunic, but
that didn't identify him as friend or foe. Federal soldiers and rebels alike
put on whatever clothing they could buy from the living or scavenge
from the dead.

"My name is Ambrozio Nuñez, esteemed sirs. I can tell you where a
notorious band of rebels has camped."

"If this is a trick . . ." Juan was all amiability and menace ". . . we
will tie you down, cut you open, and invite the wild beasts to feast on
your intestines."

"It is not a trick, I swear on the beard of St. Jude. The band that fol-
lows Lieutenant Angel is camped at the head of a canyon not far from
here." With a stick he drew them a map in the dirt, pointing out the
visible landmarks. "They plan to stay there for at least two more days."

"Why are you telling us?" asked Juan.

"At the train station they say the fair-haired captain is looking for
that same band of rebels. They also say he has money to spare. I am in
need of ten *pesos* to pay the *curandero* to heal my sainted mother." He

began the account of his mother's maladies, rehearsed and obviously bogus.

Rico held up a hand to stop him. "Do these rebels have a foreign woman with them?"

Ambrozio paused, choosing his words. A slip of the tongue could get him skewered on the end of the captain's sword like a chunk of mutton. "I have heard that they did."

"What do you mean, 'They did'?" For a heartbeat Rico allowed himself to believe they had released her.

Ambrozio put on a sorrowful face. "Alas, Captain, I heard that when the men had finished with her, if you know what I mean, they cut her throat and threw her off a cliff. Such a pity. They're brutes, those men."

Rico was known for his temper, but never a fury like this. Blood swelled the veins in his eyes until a red haze veiled his world. Feral rage roared in his head. Ambrozio threw an arm up as a shield, certain the captain would take a swing at him or worse.

Rico wanted to do more than hit him. He wanted to kill someone, and the messenger was as good a someone as any. But he had no time to waste for that, nor for grief either. He would grieve later. He started at a run for the station with Juan close behind.

Neither of them saw Ambrozio smile. He hadn't received the ten *pesos* he had requested, but he had not come for his thirty pieces of silver. Captain Grandee would give him something more valuable, revenge on the *perra* who called herself Lieutenant Angel.

Ambrozio pulled one of the canvas chairs back from the brink. He was surprised by how light it was. If he took it with him he doubted the captain would notice its absence. The captain owed him at least that much for his valuable information.

He settled into it. It was as comfortable as a hammock. He would definitely steal it. He picked up the empty claret bottles Juan had left behind, upended each of them, and drank the dregs.

31

EVIL AT THE WATER

If anyone had asked Angel what her people needed, she would not have thought to include "witch" on the list. Having a witch along, however, proved a boon at laundry time. Washing clothes that were mostly holes and patches might have seemed wasted effort to *los correctos,* but Angel knew clean rags were better for morale than dirty ones. Running water and a fragrant soap made from pounded *amole* roots cost nothing, but they gave even the most destitute members of the band a sense of dignity and pride.

Before the *gringa* arrived, laundry day caused considerable anxiety. The more superstitious folk, and that included almost everyone, feared *los aires.* The airs were malevolent spirits that lurked in rivers and springs. If the nearest body of water had a reputation for being infested with them, clothes and the bodies inside them stayed dirty.

Soon after *Inglesa* arrived, word spread that she could speak to the dead, but no one had had the nerve to ask her to have a heart-to-heart with *los aires.* Enlisting the aid of a homegrown witch was perilous enough. They had no way of knowing what powers a foreigner might possess, nor what devilish detritus might slough off onto them.

Serafina Perez convinced a small delegation of women to come with her when she asked *Mamacita* to chase off *los aires.* That way the favor would not be for any one individual, but for the good of everyone. Any residual evil would be diluted and distributed in smaller doses among them.

The *gringa* agreed to give it a try. From then on, her first task at every campsite was to clear the supernatural varmints from the water supply. Angel had to admit that she seemed to take the job seriously.

Angel, Antonio, and the men halted their horses at the canyon's rim and looked down at the women and children lined up a cautious fifteen or twenty feet from the river's edge. The *gringa* was working her magic again. She waded into the cold water, raised her arms, and shouted her incantations. She waved her hands as if to shoo the spirits away. Then she stood stock-still for several long minutes, maybe for effect, maybe waiting to see if they really had gone. Finally she turned, smiled, and beckoned.

The children stripped naked and ran shouting into the water. The women who had rifles leaned them against each other in proper military style and draped their cartridge belts over them. Laughing and talking they stepped out of their clothes at the river's edge and added them to the bundles of laundry. All except *Inglesa*. She must have suspected the men were watching from above. She put on her sombrero and sat with her mule while he grazed in the scanty shade of a gnarled pine tree.

Angel stared down at the hat and the long legs, demurely crossed, projecting from under it. She had to admit that *Inglesa* was tougher than she looked. She didn't complain or demand special treatment. She helped with the cooking and the chores. When rations were shorter than usual, Angel had seen her pass her small portion of parched corn to whichever child looked hungriest.

Inglesa's broad-brimmed straw hat hid the thick braid that reached the middle of her back. Angel couldn't see her face either, but she knew that when the *gringa* laughed, her teeth dazzled in her tanned face. In three weeks, hunger and hard work had begun sculpting the planes of her face into aristocratic angles that belied the rags she wore. She was taller than all of the women, and in the ragged khaki trousers, uniform shirt, and leather sandals she resembled a rebel soldier.

She insisted on saddling her mule herself, which amused everyone, the mule most of all. He would suck in air and expand his midsection. When she mounted, he exhaled, collapsing his sides inward and loosening the cinch. The saddle would slide off and dump her onto the ground while Moses lifted his muzzle for a good laugh.

Then José taught her how to get the better of him. Now the *gringa* walked her hands up Mose's lead line until she could stroke him and murmur insults in Nahautl. In mid-caress she braced her hands on his side, cocked her leg, and kneed him in the stomach. The blow knocked the breath out of him with a satisfying "whoof." Before he could inhale again she yanked the cinch tight with both hands and buckled it.

Besides learning to outwit the mule, the *gringa* could now clean and load rifles. She could ignite tinder with a fire drill. She could hone a knife blade and pat out tortillas that were edible if not symmetrical. But although she was tanned, calloused, and trouser-clad, *Inglesa* still stuck out like a long-stemmed rose among the hardy cactus flowers of the women's camp.

Angel had heard of gringos by the dozens joining Pancho Villa's army in Mexico's northern states, but this *gringa* would never be a Zapatista. Heaven had other plans for her. Angel decided that when she came back from this foray, she would do whatever was necessary to return *Mamacita* to Cuauhnáhuac. The band would miss her singing and her skill at exorcism, but she had earned the right to go home.

Angel and Antonio reined their horses around and headed for the trail, but the men were slow to leave the view at the river.

"Vámanos, muchachos." Angel rode back and circled them, as if herding sheep. "We're going to pay a visit to some *correctos*."

Like Angel, her commanding officer, Colonel Contreras, came from a middling upper class family himself. He wouldn't approve of her plan to rob a hacienda, but her people were starving and she had no alternative. *Federales* soldiers and their camp followers had so despoiled the villages that they had little to share. And what could he do to her other than scold?

As they rode away Angel turned around for one more look at the river and the high rock walls rising from its banks. This was the safest campsite she had found since joining General Zapata's forces more than six months ago. At the end of the box canyon the water rushed toward a cleft in the face of the cliff. It led to an escape route not likely to be noticed by enemies.

Angel had assigned sentry duty to the Gonzales boy because she intended to visit the hacienda where he had worked in the stables since he was barely old enough to shovel horse manure with a small spade. He was a loyal lad, and maybe some of that loyalty to his former employers still clung to him like a cocklebur. She did not want to strain his limited mental resources with such a conflict.

Besides, this campsite was so hidden that guarding it would not require much judgment. Everyone knew that common sense for the Gonzales boy was a rare commodity, but he was eager to please and not smart enough to fear anything. All he had to do was keep watch and shout a warning to the women and children should interlopers appear.

His sentry post was a ledge near the top of the cliff on the other side of the river. He had rolled up his baggy white trousers leaving his brown legs to dangle from a perch so narrow it would have given a buzzard second thoughts. He balanced his ancient rifle across his thighs, rolled a cigarillo, and smoked it as casually as if he were sitting on a bench in the plaza.

Angel spurred the mare after the men. She did not see the Gonzales boy leave his post soon after to take off in pursuit of a plump iguana longer than his arm. She did not see his eyes light up at the prospect of a steaming bowl of lizard soup.

Grace heard the hoofbeats fade as Angel and the men rode away. Soon after, the Gonzales boy left his ledge on the opposite side of the river. With the men gone Serafina waved to Grace to join her in the water. While the children splashed and shouted, the other women scrubbed themselves and their hair along with the clothes.

Grace walked to the water's edge with Moses trailing her as if he happened to be going that way, too. She kicked off her sandals and waded in ankle deep. She held out her hand so Serafina could put a scoop of the gelatinous *amole* root onto her palm. For a fraction of an instant its fragrance worked the magic that only the sense of smell possesses. It transported Grace to the high-ceilinged room behind the Colonial's kitchen where the maids gathered before work each morning.

The evocative powers of the *amole*'s aroma were so intense that

Grace could see the colorful tile on the walls. She could feel the heat radiating from the big bread ovens on the other side of the wall. She could hear the women's soft voices exchanging amenities that, spoken in Nahuatl, had always sounded deeply mysterious to her.

In that flash of memory she saw the maids tying on their aprons. She watched them pull their hair back and rebraid it, taut and shiny as patent leather. This fragrant gel that looked, to be honest, like a palmful of snot, was what they used to wash their hair.

The scene vanished as abruptly as it had appeared, and Grace thought about the parrots that roosted in the banana tree in the Colonial's court-yard. They came and went each day, unmindful of the bustle and fuss of the humans below. If she were a parrot she could fly home and all this would become a nightmare.

She amended that. The past three weeks had been frightening, cold, hungry, and exhausting, but not a nightmare. She had come to like people she never would have met among the Colonial's clientele. She had learned skills that she would never need again when she returned to her own life. And she didn't doubt that she would return to Rico and to her life. José had promised it, and José kept his promises.

She was about to take off her sombrero and loosen her braid so she could wash her hair when one of the children cried one word. *"Mamá."* He pitched forward and floated face down. Blood stained the water in expanding eddies around him. Bullets began spattering like hail into the water. Mothers snatched up their wailing children and what few clothes they could carry. They splashed toward the narrow cleft, black as a vein of coal in the granite wall at the head of the canyon.

The other women grabbed their rifles and cartridge belts. They took cover under the trees and struggled into their clothes as they tried to re-turn fire. It was like shooting from the bottom of a well. From their po-sitions on the opposite rim of the canyon the soldiers had clear aim at their prey while they themselves could keep mostly out of sight.

Maybe some of those men making target practice of women and children were the same gallant, rambunctious young officers who had stayed at the Colonial. In the past three weeks Grace had acquired a stone-cold dread of the Federal Army. The thought never occurred to her to wave her hat at them and shout that she was Grace Knight.

Bullets sent up geysers of sand all around her as she bolted toward Moses. She leaped for his broad, bare back as she had seen Lieutenant Angel do. She scrambled into a sitting position and shouted for Serafina. While Moses was in motion she pulled her friend up to sit behind her.

She grabbed the lead line on his halter, but he didn't require guidance. He galloped along the sandy shoreline toward the opening in the wall. Grace wondered if he would fit through it.

Between screams and rifle fire Grace heard the sound of men's laughter overhead.

32

FATE FULL

Rico couldn't have predicted that a lizard would alter the course of his life. If his men had not found the dusty *indio* trying to pull the iguana out of a crevice in the rock, they would not have stopped to take him prisoner.

Rico had galloped most of the way here with his company doing their best to keep up. Had he not been delayed by this pair of rebel feet and legs he would have arrived at the *Zapatista* campsite before the other units did. He might have been able to prevent what happened there.

When Rico's men found the rebel, he was lying on his stomach with his head and shoulders out of sight in the fissure, but they didn't have to see his face to identify him as the enemy. His straw sombrero lay nearby. Fastened to its crown was a medal embossed with a crude likeness of the Virgin of Guadelupe, the saint favored by Zapata's fighters.

If the rebel heard the clatter of rifle bolts and Rico's order to surrender, the filthy, calloused soles of his feet gave no indication of it. Rico couldn't see his face, but he could guess what was going on in his mind. A peasant would not let go of a meal no matter what the consequences.

When this one finally wriggled out of the crevice he dragged the iguana tail-first with him. The lizard was as stubborn about clinging to the rocks with all twenty, scythe-shaped toenails as the boy was about giving him up. The sergeant had to put a pistol to his head to make him surrender his prize to a grinning private.

Rico recognized the captive. For years the Gonzales boy had worked for his family until he disappeared six months ago. Rico wasn't surprised that the lad seemed more upset about the loss of his supper than his own fate. He hadn't the intellect to realize that before the sun set he would be hanging by the neck from a tree limb.

Rico also knew that when the boy felt the noose around his neck he would beg Captain Martín, the grandson of his former *patrón,* to save him. Rico liked the Gonzales boy, but the probability that he had participated in the assault on Grace and in her murder would make executing him not easy, but possible.

Rico spent most of every day fending off thoughts of what had happened to Grace. Now he faced the sullen, slack-jawed gaze of someone who at the very least had witnessed it. Rage, horror, and grief churned in his stomach and left the taste of bile in the back of his throat. While his men tied up the rebel and the reptile, Rico walked away to vomit into the crevice where the iguana had sought refuge. He had just rinsed his mouth with water from his canteen when the sound of distant gunfire reminded him of what had brought him here.

Vengeance.

Rico stood amid the laundry strewn along the riverbank and counted. Four women and five children. Some floated in the water. Some lay half on shore and half submerged. One woman sprawled on the sand, a hand outstretched as though begging for help.

Rico's company arrived after the other soldiers had ransacked the rebels' abandoned campsite, but they hadn't considered shovels and mattocks worth stealing. Rico ordered some of his men to use them to dig one large grave. He did not know if the children belonged to the women, but he thought perhaps they could comfort each other.

He assigned another detail to retrieve the bodies, most of which were naked.

"Treat them as you would your mothers and children," he said. "If anyone says or does anything lewd or insulting, I will shoot him."

As the men laid the bodies in rows Rico covered them with the wet clothes. One of the women and two of the children were still alive. He wrapped them in blankets, carried them to the copse of trees, and laid them gently in the shade. Juan found him there, cleaning and bandaging their wounds.

"The colonel left for Tres Marías," Juan said. "He plans to hang the *indio* there where more people will see him."

Rico felt a sudden stab of remorse about the Gonzales boy. He knew that even if he had tried to save the lad he almost certainly wouldn't have succeeded. That was far less consolation that he would have expected.

"I would bet he's also in a hurry to send a telegram to General Rubio," Rico said, "telling him how many rebels his soldiers killed here today."

Juan rolled his eyes. Lying about success in battle was a tradition with most of the officers in the Federal Army.

"Rubio is also impatient to hunt down the one called Angel. He said to tell you to leave the corpses for the buzzards, and follow him with your men."

One of the children moaned and Rico hunkered next to him and took his hand.

"He said to leave the wounded for the buzzards, too," added Juan.

Holding that small hand, Rico came to a decision he realized he should have made as soon as he heard about President Madero's assassination. He probably would have made it then, had Grace not existed.

He stood up and shouted at the men who were standing around watching their comrades dig. "The rest of you gather rocks to pile on top of the graves." He didn't have to tell them the rocks would keep feral dogs and wild pigs from digging up the bodies. They all knew about feral dogs and wild pigs.

He used his sword to hack branches into twelve sticks as long as his arm. He walked to the river and sorted through what was left of the laundry until he found a skirt. He ripped it into strips and began lashing the sticks together two by two at right angles. Juan picked up two of the sticks and began helping him make crosses for the graves.

Juan loved Rico as a brother. After countless hours sitting across from him at gaming tables, he could read his face like a lottery ticket.

He could see that Rico had no intention of reporting to the colonel. Not today. Not ever.

"They will shoot you for desertion," he said.

"They will have to catch me."

Juan lowered his voice. "It's Carranza then."

It was not a question. Juan would have been astonished if Rico had deserted the army to join Zapata's ragtag mob or throw in with that brute of a cattle thief, Villa. But Venustiano Carranza was another matter. He was of Rico's class and an educated man. He was also almost the only politician with the *cojones* to defy Huerta.

After the murder of President Madero, Carranza met with leaders of the Revolution. The resulting *Plan de Guadalupe* named him First Chief of the Constitutional Army. He was recruiting and arming men to overthrow President Huerta.

Rico turned to look Juan in the eyes. "Did you join the army to make war on women and children?"

"Of course not." Juan's smile had little mirth in it. "I have been waiting for you to decide to leave, *amigo*. We will ride north together."

"I have to go to Cuernavaca first. Take my men with you to Tres Marías. I'll meet you there in three days."

"What will I tell the colonel?"

"Tell him I went to the local village to ask about Lieutenant Angel. Tell him I speak their language and I can get more information going alone. Tell him I'll return soon. Act surprised when I don't arrive."

Juan chuckled. "My friend, I have had more than enough practice lying for you, and acting surprised, too."

Juan left at the head of Rico's company and his own. Rico planted the six crosses and said a prayer for the souls of the bodies lying under them.

The wounded woman and two children were well enough to ride. Rico helped them onto Grullo and led the horse out of the canyon and along the precipitous trail to the nearest village. He had no doubt that someone would take them in, nurse them, and see that they were reunited with their families if their families were alive. The train also stopped there, if flagged down.

He was sure the villagers would know something about Lieutenant

Angel's whereabouts, but he had no intention of asking them. The sight of the dead women and children at the river had drained him of hatred.

He remembered what Grace once had said. "Hating is like taking poison and hoping that your enemy dies." Rico was done hating. Hatred and arrogance were what had brought them all to this sorry situation.

The message he needed to deliver to the Colonial was not one that should arrive in a telegram. He would go there one last time to tell Lyda that her dearest friend was dead. Grace's life had ended, but his country still suffered. He would ride north with Juan and join Carranza's forces. He would live to see Mexico free of tyrants, or he would die trying.

He knew he should thank God for the short time he had had with Grace, but he could not find gratitude within him. He stopped just short of cursing the Almighty who was, if the priests were correct, responsible for everything.

He had learned one lesson since that traitorous wretch Ambrozio Nuñez told him Grace's body lay at the bottom of some crevasse. He now knew that his heart was not cold enough to keep vengeance from wilting. God's, however, was. The All Merciful could take care of retribution from now on.

Cosas a Dios dejadas son bien vengadas, the peasants said. Things left to God are well avenged.

33

DOWN A HOLY RABBIT HOLE

La Sierra Madre. The Mother Range. If Grace had had any energy left for irony she would have noted that there was nothing motherly about these jagged peaks and treacherous chasms. She and the women and children followed the steepest, narrowest trails until they reached the altitude where clouds wrapped like shawls around them.

Grace didn't have to ask Serafina if they were lost. Of course they were lost. None of these women had traveled farther from their villages than the nearest market town. No one had any idea where they were. They could only hope that *el gobierno*'s assassins didn't know where they were either.

They had spent the night cupped together for warmth on the bare, wet ground. They had started out again as soon as the gray sky lightened enough to see the rock falls and tree trunks in their path. The relentless rain and rocky terrain were tribulation enough. To make matters worse, the women, without forming a committee, holding a meeting, or calling for a show of hands, had elected Grace their leader.

Maybe they did it because the former dictator, Porfirio Díaz, had convinced even these poorest of the poor that everything foreign was superior. Maybe they did it because they had seen Grace chase those pesky *aires* away from springs and rivers. Maybe they did it bcause Moses, the only transportation available, trailed after her like a cantankerous, overgrown mutt.

Grace was used to taking charge. She accepted the responsibility without protest, but she saw herself as an imposter. A leader must be strong and Grace felt weaker than any of the women toiling along barefoot behind her, many of them carrying their children and what few belongings they had been able to grab as they fled. True, they were used to walking in mountainous terrain, but Grace had England's honor to uphold.

Pride alone would not allow her to ride while the others walked, but neither would pity. She led Moses with four small children and one very pregnant woman perched on his back. Grace had bandaged the leg wound on one of the boys, but another bullet had made him an orphan. Grace noticed that he kept looking back, as though to see if his mother were hurrying along to rejoin the group.

Adversity revealed a streak of gallantry in Moses. He placed each hoof as delicately as a cat walking on wet grass, doing his best to make the ride as smooth as possible for his small passengers. That was a courtesy he never had accorded Grace.

As Grace struggled up the steep path she waited for the shock to wear off her companions. She listened for the women to begin sobbing and wailing with grief, but they didn't. If Grace had had to abandon Lyda's or Annie's dead body at the river she would have been inconsolable, yet the women put one foot ahead of the other with stoicism that the ancient Spartans would have envied.

Grace hadn't seen the sun all day, but a chill in the air signaled that it had gone down behind the mountains. Night would arrive soon and heaven gave no indication that it had finished with weeping.

At least, she thought, we shall not die of thirst.

She shielded her eyes from the rain and scanned the heights for snipers and for a black blotch that might signal the opening to a cave.

Serafina grabbed her arm. "Look!" She pointed up.

"¿El gobierno?" Grace had a sudden surge of panic. Would the sharpshooters open fire again?

"A village," said Serafina.

"Where?"

"There."

Several houses clung like lichens to the side of the mountain above them. They were made of the same buff-colored limestone as their surroundings. If Serafina hadn't pointed them out, Grace would not have seen them. She and Fina found the trail leading to them and started up it. As they approached the outskirts of the village, Grace prayed they wouldn't find death and devastation.

The stone houses and their thatched roofs remained intact, but not a soul stirred in the muddy streets. Grace, Serafina, and Moses led the procession across the deserted plaza to the small stone church that had a low rambling building attached to the back of it. An ancient sacristan had just locked the church door for the night. He tried to wave them away, but Serafina fell to her knees on the lowest of the stone steps.

In Nahuatl she told him of being ambushed by *federales*. She reminded him that they were children of God. She pointed out the obvious, that they were cold, hungry, exhausted, and frightened. She implored him, in God's mercy, to grant them shelter for the night.

He muttered to himself as he fumbled the iron key into the big padlock. Grace tied Moses's lead line to a tree and helped the children and the mother-to-be dismount. She carried the wounded boy up the church steps and followed the aroma of incense inside. Soaked, shivering, their stomachs growling, they all crowded through the doorway and fanned out across the narthex, the vestibule at the rear of the nave. Such a filthy, bedraggled, hollow-eyed, wretched-looking lot they were. Grace, still holding the boy in her arms, thought her heart would burst with pity for all of them.

One of the children coughed. The sound startled a solitary nun praying at an altar enclosed in the glow of fifty or more candles. When she stood up, the rustle of her long robes echoed in the empty church.

Over her shoulders she wore a scapular, a wide, russet red band of cloth that reached to the hem. A black veil projected like a shawl out over her forehead. A close-fitting white coif framed her face. It covered her chin, forehead, and half of her cheeks. The shadow of the veil hid her eyes and Grace could not see whatever sign of hope or disappointment they might contain.

She stood at least a head-and-a-half shorter than Grace. She had a pert beak of a nose. Her patched and threadbare brown wool tunic increased her resemblance to a sparrow. Her thin, bare toes beneath her robe's frayed hem looked suitable for gripping a twig.

Serafina recognized the distinctive habit. "She is a Carmelite," she whispered. "She is *enclaustrada.*"

Grace didn't know what *enclaustrada* meant, but she was about to find out.

The nun glanced toward the small side chapel and Grace feared she would bolt for it and disappear like the white rabbit down his hole in *Alice's Adventures in Wonderland.* Instead of fleeing, the woman rose and pulled her veil across the lower half of her face. She stared at them for what seemed an eternity. Grace realized that the nun might think she was a man. She took off her hat and shook out her braid.

The sacristan elbowed his way through the crowd. "Forgive me, Holy Mother," he stammered. "They are in desperate need. I could not turn them away."

When the nun realized that the sacristan was the only adult male present she lowered the veil and beckoned.

Serafina leaned close to whisper to Grace, "She is *la priora.*" Grace looked blank. She had never had occasion to learn the word for prioress.

"La madre superior," Serafina said. "The mother superior."

The nun led them through a rear door so low Grace ducked her head to clear the frame. Still carrying the child, she entered a maze of dimly lit, low-ceilinged hallways that resonated with the chime of iron bells. Shadowy portraits of saints lined the walls.

As Grace passed open doorways she glimpsed closet-sized rooms beyond. Each contained a crucifix on the whitewashed wall, a neatly folded blanket with a small clay bowl on it, and a woman kneeling on the dirt floor. They all wore the same black veils, white coifs, brown robes, and rust-colored scapulars as the prioress.

Serafina had called them *enclaustrada.* Now Grace could guess what it meant. Cloistered. Shut away from the world.

So many rooms and so many women. Grace counted eighteen, and there may have been more in other corridors. With heads bowed and hands clasped they prayed in hushed voices, each separate from the others, yet joining in a single chorus.

The susurrus of prayer filled the hall like a sanctified fog. It clung to Grace's skin. When she breathed, it flowed into her lungs along with the censed air. She had never seen or experienced anything that remotely resembled the existence of contemplatives. She felt as if, like Alice, she had fallen down a rabbit hole and into an alien world.

The boy Grace was carrying did not complain, but his stomach did. Grace realized that she did not smell any odors of cooking. She whispered to Serafina, "Do you think they have any food to spare?"

"I doubt it," Serafina murmured. "The Carmelites take a vow of poverty. They trust God to provide for their needs."

Grace remembered the village's deserted streets and shuttered houses. She imagined God's voice echoing, unheard through it, asking for volunteers to feed the nuns.

At the far end of the hallway the prioress ushered them into the convent's reception room. It had a flagstone floor and straight-backed chairs around a long wooden table the same glossy, red-mahogany color as Grace's hair. Religious paintings hung on the walls. Best of all, a fire burned in the large adobe hearth in a corner. The women and children rushed to warm themselves at it.

Serafina knelt and clasped her hands in thanks. The nun leaned over to speak to her in whispers, but at the sound of a bell ringing outside she made a sign of the cross that included everyone and hurried to the front door. She slid open a square wooden panel in the door to expose an opening covered outside by an iron grate. She held a murmured conversation, interrupted by sobs from whomever was on the other side.

Serafina listened intently, then whispered to Grace. "The prioress's name is Mother Merced. She is comforting a woman whose daughter has entered the novitiate. The rest of the family is hiding with the other villagers in the mountains."

"Is that why so many nuns live here?"

"Yes. People leave their daughters to keep them safe, but when the door closes behind them their relatives can see them only once a year for two hours."

"Why?"

"The nuns who enter this order leave the world behind. They speak only with God and each other. But these are terrible times and Mother Merced has made an exception. She says we may sleep here. One of the sisters has nursing skills. She will see to the boy's wound."

Mother Merced opened the door and retrieved the large pottery bowl the woman had left. She set it on the table and the aroma of warm beans and corn tortillas wafted through the room. Everyone left the fire to gather around the table and stare at the bowl.

As if summoned by the smell three novices arrived. Two of them carried armloads of blankets. The third brought another bowl.

Sister Merced distributed the blankets among the refugees, which meant, Grace assumed, that the sisters would sleep on the bare floors of their cells. Then she divided the food between the two bowls. The nuns left with the smaller one, but Grace could tell that the portions would be very small for everyone. Whoever brought the food to the door didn't know that Mother Merced had added nineteen more appetites.

Grace and her companions made short work of the food. Then they set out on the nightly challenge of finding somewhere to relieve themselves before settling down for the night. If the convent had a privy it no doubt was reserved for the nuns' use. The old sacristan guarded the front door while the women and children scattered out into the darkness. Grace's companions seemed to think nothing of using all of nature as a privy, but Grace could never get used to it.

When everyone returned, they rolled up in their blankets as close to the fire as they could get. Their usual soft conversations were shorter tonight and soon Grace heard the long sighs of their breathing. The rain started again and the thrum of it on the tile roof was a lullabye.

Grace expected to fall asleep immediately, but maybe she had traveled beyond exhaustion. She lay on her back and stared at the hand-hewn beams overhead. She realized that the rebels might never let her leave their company. She had made the mistake of proving herself useful, even indispensible where *los aires* were concerned. But she could remedy that. If she passed her sham supernatural powers on to Serafina, the band would no longer have to rely on her.

In the morning she would begin teaching her friend the verse from 1 Samuel that she used in her conversations with the supernatural. It seemed as appropriate here as anywhere else in this poor, abused country. "I am a woman of sorrowful spirit."

Serafina stirred in her blanket. She turned to face Grace and whispered, "I know where we are now."

"You do?"

"Yes. The Carmelites are famous. This place is not far from Tres Marías. Mother Merced can tell us how to get there. You can go home."

"But you can't go to Tres Marías, Fina. The soldiers will shoot you."

"Macano xitequipacho," Serafina said.

It was one of the few Nahuatl phrases Grace knew well. She had heard Lieutenant Angel use it often.

It meant, "Don't worry."

34

Even here in this tiny village without a train depot, the local women and their wares swarmed around Rico and Grullo like enterprising flies. The Baldwin engine arrived on time. Rico took that as a good omen, although for what, he could not have said.

The Baldwin was almost as old as Rico's grandfather and almost as loud and irrascible. As it chuffed and clanged to a stop, its wreath of steam reminded Rico of the Old Man's luxuriant crop of white hair.

Everyone in Morelos was proud of this railroad. Foreigners had built rail lines in other states to transport Mexico's oil, minerals, and sugar out of the country efficiently so the rich gringo capitalists could get richer faster. This one served the same purpose, but at least it was the only railroad built and operated by Mexicans.

The iron rails and spikes came from England, but the passenger cars were made from the wood of local trees. The line cost six million *pesos* and at the peak of construction three thousand men worked on it. For all that, on any given day its timely arrival depended on love, or at least sex. The sex life of Hanibal the engineer to be exact.

Rico bribed a worker to let him load Grullo into the boxcar instead of the stock car. If the colonel was still at Tres Marías when the train pulled in he wouldn't likely check on the cargo and discover the handsome Andalusian stallion among the crates and sacks.

For the same reason, Rico passed the first and second-class coaches.

He strode through the fog of steam hissing from the drive wheels, swung up into the cab of the locomotive, and breathed in the bracing bouquet of oil and hot metal.

He had been acquainted with Hanibal, the engineer, for many years, but he knew that he and his Mauser would be welcome as protection in any case. He nodded to the fireman, who raised a hand in half salute and went back to staring at his dials. The cheery glow and low grumble beyond the open door of the boiler seemed to Rico the aura of an amiable genie willing to grant the gift of speed if asked properly.

Rico guessed that Hanibal was crowding fifty. His face was constructed of thick bones covered with well-oiled skin that thwarted the sun's attempts to age him. His hair would have been streaked with gray if he hadn't combed black shoe polish into it and slicked it back.

"Good day, Captain. Are you riding my elephant over the alps today?"

"I am."

Hanibal nodded at the cord hanging diagonally overhead and Rico reached up and pulled it. The shriek from the steam whistle signaled the brakeman to unlock the brakes on the cars. Hanibal eased the throttle forward.

Twenty tons of iron shuddered around Rico, then stirred under him. The vibrations coursed up from the soles of his feet as the locomotive gathered speed. If Rico had occupied a stained, velvet seat in the first-class coach he would not have felt the brute power pulsing through him. Nor could the view from a coach window compare to standing here, high above the awe-inspiring scenery and surrounded by dials, red-painted valve handles, and shiny black gears.

Hanibal was an affable man, but he stared at the rails ahead as though he were the cab's only occupant. Rico took no offense at being ignored. He, too, was on the lookout for the wink of sunlight on a rifle barrel among the rocks. Tunnels and long curves made him particularly wary. Rebels and bandits preferred to leave their surprises on the tracks out of sight beyond tunnels and long curves.

A sniper's bullet had plowed a narrow furrow along the side of Hanibal's skull, leaving an errant part in his hair. Another ball of lead ricocheting around the cab had left the little finger of his right hand numb. He held it stiffly extended when he operated the throttle, like an English squire sipping tea.

Like Grace sipping tea.

Rico wondered if ever a day would come when some subtle detail did not remind him of her. He doubted it.

To distract himself he asked, "Is it true that you built this engine?"

"No, *señor*. My *elefante* came from California." Hanibal said the word "California" with the tone reserved for Eden, Elysium, and Goshen, that biblical utopia fertile and free of the plague of war. "They could not drive her onto the ship so they took her apart. They dipped each rod and bolt in oil. They wrapped them all in straw and packed them in wooden boxes. I found them stacked on the dock at Acapulco. A mountain of boxes. A *cordillera* of boxes. We loaded them onto mules and hauled them here."

"Had you ever assembled a locomotive before?"

Hanibal gave him a sardonic glance. "*Don* Federico, I tell you the truth when I say that I did not know what a locomotive looked like."

"Then why did they hire you for the job?"

Hanibal's answer included English words for the gringo technology that under Díaz's thirty-year regime had barged into Mexico like a fat drunk into a cantina.

"When I worked in the mines I learned how to repair engines, boilers, riveters, torsion spring hammers, gang saws, circular saws. I can bring back to life anything that operates with God's breath." Hanibal always referred to steam as *el súspiro de Dios*.

As they approached the station at Tres Marías, Rico saw the gnarled *huizache* known as the hanging tree. General Rubio had selected it for executions because it stood at the crest of the ridge. Trains coming from north and south had to slow while the engine labored up the steep slope. Passengers and crew had time to take long, instructional looks.

The Gonzales boy was hanging from one of its horizontal branches. He was silhouetted against the sunset sky, his chin resting on his chest as if bowed in prayer. Soon the parched mountain air would dry his corpse like a slice of mango. He would hang there until another miscreant replaced him.

Rico remembered the boy's smile, how hard he worked, and his eagerness to please. The sight of him added to Rico's sorrows and regrets. His biggest regret was that he had been so full of hatred when the boy was captured that he wouldn't have saved him if he could.

As the tile roof of Cuernavaca's depot came into sight, Rico moved against the back wall, out of sight of the cab window. Hanibal and the fireman glanced at him and then at each other, but they said nothing. They preserved their health and livelihoods by not poking their noses into *el gobierno*'s business.

As Hanibal had observed more than once when an army officer was not within hearing, "My policy is to stand back and let the scorpions sting each other to death."

Rico wasn't surprised to find the Colonial's lobby deserted. Grace had always given her hotel its life and vivacity. He would have been distressed to find everyone carrying on as usual.

His boots echoed when he crossed the ballroom to where Grace's piano stood, the top lowered, the keyboard covered. He ran his fingers across the lid and they left a gleaming track in the dust. That saddened him more than the echoing corridors. Rico had never seen dust on the piano.

He went to the front desk and called out. "Lyda! Annie!"

The answer was not what he expected. A scream came from the kitchen and he headed there at a run. He found the maids and the kitchen staff huddled next to the big table in the middle of the room. Wing Ang stirred a pot at the huge adobe stove as if none of this concerned him, but the weeping women clustered around Rico. Some caught his sleeve. Others knelt, their palms together in supplication. All of them begged him, for the love of God, to save Socorro.

"José's daughter?"

"Yes."

"Where is she?"

"The brute took her." They pointed to the back stairs that the servants used.

"Rubio?"

"Yes, Rubio."

Rico ran up the stairs two at a time. Socorro's screams became louder. Rubio hadn't bothered to close the door. His trousers already encircled his knees. He had thrown the girl onto the bed and pinned her there. He covered her mouth and nose with one hand and clawed at her skirt with the other.

Rico crossed the room in three strides. With both hands he grabbed the back of Rubio's sweat-stained uniform jacket. He had thought he was done with hatred, but now he was given the strength of two men by a loathing whose intensity surprised even him. He lifted Rubio and heaved him off the bed like a sack of cornmeal thrown from the back of a wagon. Socorro slid past them and ran for the door.

"*¡Hijo de la madre de todas las putas!*" Brandy slurred Rubio's speech. His beady eyes were glazed, and his breath smelled like plums rotting in a barrel.

He swung a roundhouse right and missed. The momentum spun him like a top, winding him up in the pants still crumpled around his knees. He toppled forward reaching for Rico as he fell. Rico had seen Rubio drunk more often than sober. He knew how clumsy and cowardly he was, but he forgot that cowards can be cunning.

Rubio yanked on the cord hidden next to the bed. The other end was attached to a bell in the guards' quarters off the back courtyard.

Rubio pulled up his trousers then lunged at Rico, who circled him like a matador. Rico could have left, but he wanted to give Socorro time to escape. He assumed the army would dock him for this, but he rarely bothered to collect his pay anyway. The possibility of a court-martial didn't worry him. His grandfather's influence among the ruling elite had always gotten him out of scrapes before.

Then he remembered. None of that mattered. By the day after tomorrow he and Juan would be on their way to join the army that Venustiano Carranza was raising.

A sergeant and two privates formed a clot in the doorway. From where they stood the general and the captain appeared to be engaged in an odd sort of dance.

"What's happening here, my General?" the sergeant asked.

"Shoot the son of a bitch," Rubio screamed.

Rico half-turned so he could look at them and keep an eye on Rubio, too. He held his hands away from his sides to show he had no intention of drawing his pistol.

"Pay no attention to the general. He's drunk."

"Don't shoot him." Rubio had a change of mind, if not of heart. "Arrest him."

The soldiers took Rico's Colt pistols and marched him out of the Colonial's front door and down the street. Rubio waddled behind them to the massive stone building that served as a prison. Wood smoke and the aroma of roasting meat drifted out of it. The authorities provided no food or clothing for the men and women jailed here, so they depended on their families for life's necessities.

A parallel economy had evolved as a result. The inner courtyard looked like any market in the city, except that when the sun set, the vendors would return to their cells and not their homes.

Prisoners and visitors alike bargained for goods in the stalls. Rows of women cooked the evening meal on small charcoal fires. People parted to make way for Rico, Rubio, his soldiers, and two jail guards as they headed for the wing that housed the military detainees.

Rico walked down a long, dimly lit hall and into a windowless cell that smelled like an open sewer. The rats that scurried for cover looked as big as the hairless dogs from the state of Chihuahua. Cockroaches swarmed on the dank, bloodstained walls. Old feces and dried vomit formed crusts on the dirt floor. A pile of filthy straw occupied one corner and a battered tin bucket stood in the other. The bucket's function was evident from the feces that crusted it.

The door clanged shut behind him. Rubio grasped the bars as if he wished they were Rico's throat. Rico walked away and faced the rear of the cell. He stuck his hands in his pockets and cocked one ankle as casually as if admiring art on a gallery wall.

Rubio shouted at his back, spraying the bars with spittle.

"I shall see you executed at sunup, you smug, coddled, worthless, dog-shit bastard son of an Indian whore." He turned to the prison guards. "No food. No water. No visitors. Anyone who agrees to carry a message for him will hang beside him."

Rubio reeled away. The two jailers sauntered off to continue their card game in the guardroom. Rico prowled the cell's perimeter, looking for some way to escape. He found none.

He had been in jail before in his misspent youth, usually on drunk and disorderly charges. He leaned one shoulder against the wall, crossed his ankles again, and folded his arms on his chest. One skill a soldier learned early was how to sleep standing up. This would be a long night, but he would not dirty his uniform nor bruise his dignity by lying in the filthy heap of straw.

He didn't think Fatso would carry out the execution order. Not even Rubio was stupid enough to hang the scion of the Martín clan. Unless, of course, he was still drunk. Rico did not care much either way.

Grace was dead. What reason had he to live?

35

KEYS TO THE KINGDOM

Angel, Antonio, and their forty-six men rode two-by-two up the mile-long carriage path to *Hacienda Las Delicias*, the Delights. The eucalyptus trees lining the road formed a fragrant tunnel of dense shade, but a medallion of sunlight glowed at the far end of it. The golden aura looked like the entrance to heaven, or at least Felipe Trinidad's description of it.

Felipe was a new recruit from this very estate. In his short time with them they all had heard the story of how he had fallen off a roof and died. No matter how many times he told it, his comrades listened raptly. He had seen with his own eyes what the priests and the pope himself could only imagine.

He was telling the story again as they rode along.

"After I died I walked down a long, dark tunnel, although my feet did not touch the ground. At the end of the passageway shone a light so bright I could not look straight at it." He put a hand up to shield his eyes against the dazzle of eternity. "That light, my brothers, was Heaven. I had almost reached its gates when a voice said, 'Felipe Trinidad, your time had not yet come to be with Me. You must go back.'"

The men asked what the voice sounded like. They always asked what it sounded like. Who would not want to know the timbre, the inflection, the volume of God's voice, in case He came calling?

"It was like the tolling of church bells," Felipe said. "Like a waterfall ten thousand feet high. Like a thousand drums played in unison." His eyes, the color of pools of tar, resembled even more than usual the despair of a hurt dog. "Such sorrow washed over me when God told me I must return to earth. I swam in sorrow vast as an ocean. I thought I would drown in it."

Angel rolled her eyes in Antonio's direction, but she gave Felipe credit for creativity. He found new embellishments for the account of his death and resurrection each time he told it. So far, none of his flourishes had included the sharp, insistent aroma of eucalyptus leaves that Angel was breathing in now.

The neat ranks of these ancient trees disoriented her. She had forgotten what tranquility, order, and privilege looked like. They made her uneasy, as a dog who has experienced cruelty will shy away from kindness.

A fist-sized padlock and a heavy chain hung on the spiked palings of the wrought-iron gate in the fifteen-foot-high adobe wall. Angel turned in the saddle and called to Jesus the jailer. The men made way for him and his swaybacked old mule. He rode to the head of the column holding aloft his heavy ring of keys like a trophy.

When he joined Angel's troop, Jesus had mentioned that his cousin was the only locksmith in all of Morelos. He also had confided that his cousin was lazy. Most of his customers did not know that he had changed his template only a few times in the past twenty-five years. The five or six keys that opened the cell doors in all the jails also gave access to most of the houses and gates in the state. Jesus's cousin had given him copies of them.

This gate opened with the third key on Jesus's ring. Behind it lay an immense courtyard. At the courtyard's far end was a roofed veranda bigger than most of the houses in which Angel's men lived. It had a high raftered ceiling and a floor of polished stone. Sofas, upholstered chairs, persian rugs, and tables were grouped for conversation.

"We are not bandits," Angel told her men. "We take only food and weapons. And be quick about it." But Angel had no intention of inspecting their pouches and saddlebags when they left. If some of *los correctos'* finery and trinkets fell into them it was no concern of hers. God alone knew how much grandees like *Don* Bonifacio had stolen from *los indios,* the rightful possessors of all this land.

Some of the troops scattered down the main house's arched open corridors. Others headed for the stables, barn, summer kitchen, store-houses, and servants' quarters.

The hacienda looked as if its occupants had gone off for the afternoon and would return soon. Its serenity made Angel more suspicious. She turned in place, surveying the second floor galleries. So many open, half-walled balconies, huge old trees, curtains of vines and high walls where snipers could hide.

"Felipe," she called out. "Are you sure no one is here?"

"Yes, Lieutenant. I saw them leave a week ago—the servants, the spin-ster aunts, the nieces, nephews, cousins, and their battalion of brats. A regular parade of carriages and wagons piled with baggage left here with *Don* Bonifacio leading them on his fine horse. Such weeping and wail-ing."

"Where did they go?"

"They have a mansion in the capital, my Lieutenant. I suppose they are there. Or maybe they have gone to El Norte, the United States. They spoke of it."

Felipe saluted and headed off to see what he could find in the kitchen. Angel knew she should follow him and supervise the men's foraging, but the stillness at *Las Delicias* still bothered her. She and Antonio walked down an open corridor, pausing along the way to use Jesus's keys to open doors.

Angel stood stock-still in the doorway of the main parlor, stunned by the accumlated extravagance of things. Objects of all sizes and descrip-tions. Felipe had said *los correctos* fled with as many boxes and crates in each wagon as four mules could pull, and yet so much remained. The dusty, musty smell of it all made her sneeze.

"Why haven't bandits stolen all this?"

"Los chinitos," said Antonio.

"Chinamen?"

"I heard they used to be soldiers in the army in Japan."

"How many are there?"

"Don Bonifacio hired six of them as guards."

"Only six?"

"Yes, but there are stories."

"What kind of stories?"

"The local people say *los chinitos* have supernatural powers."

"Sorcery?"

Antonio nodded. "Not the usual sort though. They have warriors' witchery. People say they can make themselves invisible. They can sneak into an enemy's house while he sleeps and kill him with the touch of a finger. They can shoot arrows behind them and hit a man between the eyes, even if he's standing a mile away. Their swords can cut through steel. I heard that in their homeland, their king gave them permission to behead anyone they met on the road, just to test the edge on their blades."

"So, where are they?"

Antonio chuckled. "My father said that as soon as Old Man Martín left *Las Delicias,* all the *hacendados* for many miles around flocked here like buzzards to bid for the *chinitos'* services. They packed up their magic and went with the highest offer. Felipe suggested we come here before bandits realize they're not guarding the Old Man's hacienda anymore. But I think the local people believe *los chinitos* left traps behind, magic spells that will curse anyone who comes here."

"Superstitious foolishness," said Angel. But suddenly the suffocating, fusty odor in the room seemed sinister. The hair stirred on her arms and she stared around her, on the lookout for signs of *chinito* witchcraft.

She spotted a familiar face among the dozens of hand-tinted photographs on a tall oak chest. He was wearing an army tunic with captain's bars on the collar. She picked it up and stared at it. Antonio looked over her shoulder.

"That's *Don* Bonifacio's grandson, Federico Martín."

"I saw him at Tres Marías." She put the picture frame back, lining it up precisely in the clean strip it had left in the layer of dust. "He led the company of men who ambushed us when we attacked the train."

"He is *Mamacita's* fiancé."

"Is he." It wasn't a question.

Angel turned on her heel and marched out with Antonio behind her. She had begun to like the *gringa*, just a little bit. But the *gringa*'s lover was a federal officer. Now she had a new reason to detest the English-woman.

36

CONDEMNED TO LIVE

Rico's grandfather was berating him, which was odd. *Don* Bonifacio rarely scolded him, not because Rico was a well-behaved child—he wasn't—but because a look from the Old Man served as reprimand enough. Odder still, for once Rico couldn't think of anything he'd done to deserve a scolding, yet the tirade went on.

He opened his eyes and rubbed his elbow and arm, numb from the weight of his body leaning on his shoulder. His heartbeat marked the passing of several seconds while he tried to get his bearings in the darkness. He squinted at the bars silhouetted in the languid light of the candle stubs guttering in niches in the hall and remembered where he was.

The angry voice that he had woven into his dream came from the guardroom. Maybe Rubio had become drunk enough to decide not to wait for daylight. Maybe the thought had occurred to him that murder was most wisely done in the dark.

Footsteps approached in the hall. Rico took a position at the center of the cell's back wall. He rolled up his sleeves and bounced lightly on the balls of his feet like a boxer. He sucked in a lungful of the fetid air that expanded, solid as armor plate, inside his chest.

He figured if he put up enough of a fight they would shoot him now and spare him the humiliation of a hanging. He smiled at how angry that would make Rubio. If Rubio knew that by murdering Rico he was sending him to meet his beloved he would be even more furious.

Rico was still smiling at the prospect of a good brawl when four shadowy figures gathered outside the door. One of them rattled an iron key, big as a jaguar's femur, into the lock. The door swung open. The man who walked through it wore a peasant's hat whose cantilevered brim threw an opaque shadow across his face.

"Captain, come quickly," said the hat.

"Who are you?"

"José Perez."

"Socorro's father?"

"Yes."

Even though Rubio had attacked José's daughter, the soft-spoken, mild-eyed potter was the last person Rico expected to see here in the lion's den.

"We must hurry, Captain."

José held a torch high, and Rico hurried after him through the maze of corridors that led deeper into the prison. As Rico passed a cell at the rear of the building he saw two guards inside. They were tied up, gagged, naked, and unhappy.

José used one of the keys to open a side door and Rico breathed in the night air, perfumed with the flowers that filled Cuernavaca in every season. The three other men each grasped José's hand, arm, and shoulder in a quick embrace, then hurried off around a corner and out of sight.

A small figure waited in the shadows with a pale horse and a grizzled mule. The horse and the boy's white cotton trousers and shirt gave off a ghostly glow in the moonlight. José and Rico followed him down a side street lit by a single, sputtering street light. When the boy handed Rico the horse's reins he recognized her face under the hat.

"Socorro!"

"May God, the Holy Virgin, and all the saints bless you, Captain."

Rico looked at the white horse. The street lamp's dim light outlined the hammock-curve of his spine under the clumsy wooden burlesque of a saddle. This was not an animal he would ride if his life depended on it.

José was apologetic. "They will not look for you on this creature."

Rico did not say, "They will not find me on this creature," but he thought it.

"I thank you, *maestro,* but my horse is in the Colonial's stable."

"Maybe he is there. Maybe he is not."

"Rubio?" The thought of Rubio in possession of Grullo made him angrier than the general throwing him into jail and plotting his execution.

"Tonight he was bragging in his favorite whorehouse that he had acquired *Don* Bonifacio's famous gray."

Rico did not ask how José knew what Rubio said in a bordello this evening. José was no fool. He had almost certainly kept track of General Fatso's whereabouts so he would know when it was safest to come to the jail.

José gave him a satchel made of supple leather. "The general left your pistols in the guardroom strongbox. Before the guards and I had our difference of opinion, they told me he intends to kill you with one of your own guns before sunrise."

"Even Rubio isn't stupid enough to think he can get away with murder."

"Not murder, Captain. Suicide."

Rico could feel the slender barrels of the Navy Colts inside the sack. He felt the grips, worn to fit not only his hands, but his father's, grandfather's, and great grandfather's. He buckled on the gun belt and returned the Colts to their holster. Now he felt dressed.

"Thank you, *Maestro* Perez."

"We tied the guards up tightly. With luck no one will discover them until sunrise. That gives you a five-hour advantage."

Socorro held out a cotton feed sack. "These are farmer's clothes, Captain. They are old, but clean and mended."

Rico started to say he would not need a disguise, then thought better of it. Her eyes pleaded with him to allow her to help him, to pay him back in some small measure, for what he had done for her. He took them with a bow.

He knew that the longer José and his daughter stayed here with him, the more the danger to them.

"And now I shall say good night and pray that God watches over you."

José took a big key off the ring of them and gave it to Rico. "This will open the side door of the Colonial's stable."

"The same key that opened my cell?"

"Yes." José glanced toward heaven. "God arranges everything." He held out the reins again. "Take the horse, Captain."

Rico started to refuse, and José raised a diffident hand ever so slightly, to stop his protest. "If your gray is in the stable, you can leave this one in his place. Imagine the look on Fatso's face when he finds him there tomorrow."

Rico chuckled at the image and accepted the reins. As he led the old horse off into the night, Socorro whispered to her father, "Why didn't you tell him you know where *Señora* Knight is?"

"Even if General Fatso is mad at him, Captain Martín is still *el gobierno*, my daughter. He is still the enemy. I could not take him back to Angel's camp with us, could I?"

"No, *Papi*." But tears glistened in Socorro's moonlit eyes.

Socorro did not speak much in her months working at the Colonial, but she saw a great deal. She knew as well as anyone how much the handsome captain and *Señora* Knight loved each other.

"What will become of him?" she asked.

"Do not worry about Captain Martín. His grandfather will use his influence to resolve everything for him."

Just as he always has, José thought.

José knew that Cuernavaca was as dangerous for his daughter and himself as it was for Captain Martín. The two of them mounted the mule and headed out of town. José knew a cave where they could sleep for the rest of the night. At first light tomorrow they would ride to the canyon where José's wife and the others were camped.

"When you see *Mamacita*, do not tell her about what happened at the Colonial. Do not tell her we saw her captain."

"Why not?"

"We have meddled enough with fate tonight. When God wills it, if God wills it, they will find each other."

37

LOAVES AND DRESSES

Angel hooked a leg over her saddle's pommel and struck a friction-match on the edge of her boot sole. She held the flame to one of Don Bonifacio Martín's slender cigars, and sucked on it until the tip glowed like a cat's eye in firelight. She scowled through the fragrant cloud of its smoke while Antonio rang the bell hanging above the iron grate in the convent door.

The day was almost half over and the men were impatient to return to camp. Angel was, too. The Martín hacienda lay farther away than they had thought. She worried about leaving the women and children alone for three days. And maybe putting the Gonzales boy in charge hadn't been a good decision.

She was also annoyed by Antonio's misguided generosity. She was willing to share their loot with hardworking farmers and laborers. Her men had plenty of it, piled on two pack mules and stuffed into saddlebags. But she was not happy about giving precious food to women who did nothing but pray and loaf around all day. Antonio, however, insisted on it.

"*'Haz bien, y no acates a quien,'*" he said, "*'Do good and mind not to whom.'*"

"'Light in the street shouldn't mean darkness in the house,'" she muttered. "'Charity begins at home.'"

After a few minutes the wooden panel behind the grate slid open and a woman's voice said, "Praise be to Jesus."

Antonio set three sacks by the door. He crossed himself, took off his hat, and held it respectfully to his chest. "We bring provisions for the sisters."

"God will bless you."

"Holy Mother, may we water our horses at the well?"

"Of course, my son." A hand reached out and pulled the sacks inside.

"Antonio?" Serafina's voice came from somewhere behind the door. "*¿Mamá?*"

The door again opened a crack and Serafina edged through it. The others followed her, blinking in the glare of sunlight. *La gringa* brought up the rear.

Before Angel could ask why the women and children were here, the mother of the Gonzales boy ran toward her shouting, "Lieutenant, where is my son?"

"I told him to keep watch at the river." Angel's uneasiness hardened into dread. She did a quick head count and realized that some of her people were missing. "Isn't he with you?"

"*¡Ay Dios!* They have killed him."

The boy's mother began to wail. She pounded on her chest with her fists, as if to end her torment by stopping the drumbeat of her own heart. Her cries set off three women related to those killed at the river. The din made conversation impossible.

Angel was relieved when *Inglesa* put an arm around Mrs. Gonzales and walked her, still howling, into the church. The other mourners followed as if in a funeral procession that lacked corpse and coffin. The big door shut behind them and muted the women's grief enough for Serafina to give an account of the attack at the river.

Angel glanced at Antonio. *Señora* Gonzales's instincts about her son were probably right. He might be wandering somewhere on his own, but that was unlikely.

When she had given him his orders, Antonio had raised one eyebrow to signal that he didn't agree with her decision. Any other man would now have leaped at the chance to say "I told you so," but he gave no hint of reproach.

Since childhood she had always known that Antonio was like no

other member of his gender. Two months ago Colonel Contreras had
offered him a lieutenant's bars and his own company of men. He had
declined the honor, choosing instead to keep his sergeant's stripes. He
said he preferred to stay with his father, with Angel, and with his comrades, the fellow workers on her father's estate.

Angel turned her thoughts to how *los federales* had found her campsite. Had someone betrayed them? As if he could read her mind Antonio muttered one word, "Nuñez."

Of course. Nuñez.

Zapata and his officers might destroy the haciendas and mills that
provided employment, but they did not not compel anyone to join their
forces. Men came and went in the rebel army. Angel hadn't thought
much about Ambrozio Nuñez's disappearance, but she thought about it
now.

Today they would make camp on the plaza. They would distribute
chunks of brown sugar to the children. They would feast on the food
they had brought from old man Martín's storerooms. The women would
smile when they saw the dresses, shoes, and ruffled scarves, the aromatic
lotions and the tortoiseshell combs their men brought for them.

Looting was like drinking tequila. Once Angel's men started de-
spoiling the hacienda they found it hard to stop. As with the unpleasant afteraffects of tequila, Angel might regret the thievery the next
morning, but not for long. After all, she and her comrades were helping
Don Bonifacio accumulate goodwill in heaven. When had that old
reprobate ever made so many poor people as happy as he was about to
do now?

Angel decided that tomorrow she would put on some of the stolen
finery stowed in her saddlebag. She would go to Tres Marías to learn
where Rubio's men were and what they intended. She would also try to
find out if Nuñez had betrayed them.

While she was at it, she might as well take the *gringa* with her. The
woman's hocus-pocus was useful at bathing and laundry time, but Angel could tell she would never shoot an enemy or share a blanket with an
ally. Women who followed the rebel army had to be willing to do one or

the other or both. Getting rid of *Inglesa* would mean one less mouth to feed.

Grace would have preferred to sleep another night in the convent, but now that the men had returned, that wasn't possible. She could have asked Mother Merced to let her spread her blanket in the parlor again, but that would mean deserting Serafina and the others. She could not bring herself to do it.

Only the Gonzales boy's mother still grieved, and she had wandered off among the surrounding trees and boulders to do it. The rest of the band set up camp on the plaza where families laid out their blankets to claim very small territories. The children gathered firewood and carried water from the village fountain. Some of the women built hearths of stones while others mixed water with the confiscated cornmeal and patted out tortillas.

Serafina held up a sack of white flour. "*Mamacita,* how do we do make souls of this?"

Grace knew what she meant by that. The Colonial's kitchen maids referred to leavened loaves of wheat flour as *almas,* souls. The name had always amused Grace, but it was apt. Rising dough did seem possessed of a living spirit that transformed a heavy, gummy mass into something light, perfectly formed, moist, and delicious.

She assumed yeast was available even in an abandoned village. It was a byproduct of beer's fermentation process, and homemade beer was ubiquitous in Mexico. Goat's milk gone sour, however, was easier to find on short notice. While the other women looked on, Grace showed Serafina how to mix the milk into the flour, knead the dough, cover it with a cloth, and let it rise.

The aroma of the flat loaves baking on hot stones brought back the Colonial's kitchen in every vivid detail. The longing for home, friends, and most of all, Rico, became unbearable. Grace found a wrought-iron bench in the darkest corner of the plaza and sat down for a long, hard cry.

When she had no tears left, she thought about tomorrow. Serafina said that Tres Marías was not far away. If no one offered to take her there, Grace decided to strike out on her own. She could savor everything about this night with *los indios* because, one way or another, it would be her last.

She wiped her eyes and blew her nose on one of the big handkerchiefs that were part of Lieutenant Angel's booty. She had accepted it with misgivings, but she had refused the dress that Angel offered her. She drew the line at wearing stolen clothes. Besides, she had come to prefer the freedom of trousers. The other women were enjoying their new finery though.

As the day's light faded, Angel's band built up the fires and wedged torches in the forks of trees. From Grace's bench in the darkness the bustle in the light of the campfires seemed like theater. She knew her experiences of the past two weeks would make entertaining stories, but she doubted she would tell anyone except Lyda and Annie. She certainly couldn't tell the officers quartered at the Colonial. And most of her guests would not appreciate the courage, resilience, and poignancy of Lieutenant Angel's *indios*. Grace leaned against the curved iron back of the bench and enjoyed the show.

While the women tried on their new finery, the men smoked and played cards, using cartridges as ante. Between hands they swallowed pinches of gunpowder for a taste like salt, and washed them down with the *hacendado*'s tequila. A few musicians struck up "Valentina" on guitars and a violin. Two or three couples got up to dance.

The villagers must have heard that forty heavily armed rebels now occupied the plaza. As night fell they arrived by twos and threes, carrying their meager belongings bundled in bandanas and shawls. Grace wasn't surprised that Lieutenant Angel invited them to share the bounty. Nor was she surprised when they added their own contributions to the feast. Food often had a way of appearing when Grace would have sworn all the larders were empty.

Five men wearing the torn and faded uniforms of the Federal Army walked slowly onto the plaza. They held their Mausers high and horizontal over their heads to show they intended to surrender. Like most of the army's northern conscripts they looked hungry. They had no shoes and their rifles were dirty and rusty. Before long they were drinking tequila, playing cards, wagering cartridges, and singing with the rest.

Grace wondered if they had been among the soldiers shooting at her and the others at the river, but no one else seemed bothered by that possibility.

El gobierno's foot soldiers, with their woebegone black eyes and coffee-with-only-a-hint-of-cream complexions would become indistinguishable from the rebels. In the weeks to come they would acquire sombreros, colorful vests, striped serapes, bandanas, sashes, and the other paraphenalia that made each rebel's clothes far from uniform.

The past two wakeful nights finally caught up with Grace. She set her sandals side-by-side under the bench. She spread her nun's blanket on the seat, lay down, and pulled the top half over her. She enjoyed a brief look at the moon and stars twinkling in a cloudless sky beyond the canopy of trees. Then she was aware of nothing more until several raps on the soles of her feet awakened her.

38

"HOME! HOME! HOME!"

"*¡Guate!*" Grace growled. "Dog shit."

She drew her knees up, rolled over on her side, and almost fell off the wrought-iron bench. She felt another blow on her foot.

"I said bugger off!"

Whoever had it in for her feet hit them again; quick, light blows that stung nonetheless.

"Get up, English, or you'll miss the train."

Train? What train? Exhaustion and predawn darkness conspired to confuse Grace about where she was and what language she was hearing. She could think of only one person with the nerve to come into her room and wake her.

"Sod off, Lyda."

Her bones creaked when she shifted on the iron seat. The pain in her joints was the first hint that she wasn't in her bed in the Colonial. She jacked one eye open and tried to focus on her torturer. That only deepened her confusion. The face and voice were familiar but not the outfit.

Lieutenant Angel wore a long, white cotton skirt, freshly laundered and starched, but with creases from where it had been folded. A wide flounce decorated the bottom of it. Its clean, crisp condition was enough to identify it as part of the new loot. The lieutenant had folded a large scarf in half diagonally and tied it at a rakish angle at his waist. A shawl covered his short, touseled hair. The cords that gathered the open neck of his calico blouse were loosely tied, exposing an inch of cleft between two small breasts.

Grace sat up and stared. The lieutenant had breasts.

"Angel?"

"Some call me Angel. Some call me a devil." Angel rapped the sole of Grace's foot again with his riding crop. Her riding crop?

"Hurry up."

Grace put on her sandals, got to her feet, and folded her blanket as automatically as if still asleep. She clasped the blanket to her chest and swayed like a sapling in a wind while Serafina saddled Moses. Fina put several tamales wrapped in banana leaves into the flour sack and tied it to the pommel.

Grace finally woke up enough to realize she was going home.

"Please return this to the nuns." She handed Serafina the blanket. "Do you remember the incantation against *los aires*?"

"Yes, *Mamacita,* I remember."

Grace turned to Angel who, she had to admit, made a very beautiful woman. She supposed she would find out the lieutenant's story on the ride to Tres Marías.

"I have taught *Señora* Perez the words to chase away evil spirits. She can make the water safe wherever you camp."

"Bueno." The lieutenant hiked up her skirt, swung into the saddle, and reined the mare into a tight turn. When she said *"Vámanos"* she was already heading away.

Grace should have been elated about leaving, but she realized she might never see Serafina again. She put her arms around her and the two held each other as if to defy fate to separate them.

"Ma xipatinemi," Grace said. "May you be well."

"And may you also be well, *Mamacita,"* she added in a lower voice. "And may you find your handsome captain."

Grace mounted Moses and rode after Angel as the camp's early risers began to stir. She dozed in the saddle for the first few miles. When the sun rose, she woke up enough to take deep breaths, inhaling the fragrance of the stand of tall cedar trees all around her. The birds seemed giddy with joy at the prospect of a sunny morning in the rainy season. Grace understood how they felt.

When she and Angel left the forest, she saw that the dome of the dawn sky blazed with oranges and purples, crimson and golds. In the distance the valley's ring of lavender mountains floated on a sea of mist. Her countrymen might go on, and on, about the beauty of the English countryside, but it could not compare with Mexico.

Grace decided the time had come to ask some questions. She glanced over at the slender, long-legged young woman who rode astride with her skirt hiked above her knees.

"Who are you?"

"My name is Angela. I am the daughter of Petra Cordero and Miguel Sanchez y Solís."

Grace chuckled. This explained her glimpse of Lieutenant Angel entwined, naked, with Antonio.

Angel glared at her. "Is my name a joke?"

"No, of course not." But Grace kept smiling. Even in the midst of war, love could find a way. She wondered if love would find a way for her and Rico. "Why do you dress as a man?"

"Why do you?"

"You know why I wear trousers, but I don't know why you do."

Angel didn't answer and Grace thought maybe she had asked one too many questions. She expected the answer to this one to be the Spanish equivalent of "None of your business."

Finally, Angel spoke. "General Rubio's dog-shit soldiers burned our house. They murdered my father's workers in the field. They threw their bodies into a ditch. I saw them do it. Only Antonio lived. Plinio and the others arrived after the soldiers left."

"When did that happen?" Grace didn't want to hear that Rico had been one of those soldiers, but neither could she bear not knowing.

"Six or seven months ago."

"December? November?"

"Near the end of November."

Grace released the breath she had been holding. She remembered with crystal clarity the date and almost the exact time when he first held her hand lightly in his palm and kissed her fingers. And from that night on he had entertained the topers in the Colonial's bar every night. Grace realized, with a start, that he must have been trying to get her attention with all that silliness.

Grace returned to the task of unraveling the mystery of Lieutenant Angel. "Where are your parents?"

"They fled. Colonel Contreras told me that my father rides with Pancho Villa in the north. He's a general now."

"Don't you want to see him?"

"Villa is a good general, but a bad man. I would rather pledge my loyalty to General Zapata. Zapata is a true revolutionary. He's the only general who cares for the people."

Grace had to admit Angel was probably right.

"And your mother"

"I pray she is with my father. Or with God."

Grace silently seconded that. A peasant woman's alternatives to being safe or being dead were too terrible to contemplate.

"I am not a religious person," said Angel. "I do not go to church to whine to God and beg for favors. I do not try to bribe Him with candles and *centavos* in the poor box. But I tell you this, English, I pray to Him every day that General Fatso waddles into my gun sights.

"I want to hold my pistol this close to his face . . ." She held her hands a foot or so apart ". . . and pull the trigger so his brains spray out the back of his head. If God disapproves of that plan, then I will stroll contentedly into hell. I will greet with *abrazos* the friends who arrived before me."

They stopped at a village and left the mare and Moses with a family Angel seemed to know well. Angel dug into her saddlebag and held out a dress for Grace, but she refused again. The two of them walked to the main road and Angel pointed down it.

"Tres Marías is a mile or two away."

Grace assumed the lieutenant would send her off with a wave and an airy *"Hasta la vista."* Instead, Angel set out on foot at her side. She did not hesitate when the tile roofs of the army's adobe barracks came into view.

"Are you crazy, Angela?"

"Without doubt." Angel grinned at her.

"*El gobierno* will hang you if they catch you. Or worse."

"And you, do you plan to live forever, English?"

"I don't go looking for trouble."

"Weren't you looking for trouble when you went to San Miguel that day?"

"I was looking for vases."

"To sell to your gringo tourists with their skin like fish bellies."

Grace let that pass. "Will you take the train to Cuernavaca?"

"No. We orphans will ride into Cuauhnáhuac soon enough. Today I'll stir myself in with *el gobierno*'s whores like a jalapeño into weasel stew and see what I can learn."

Angel strolled toward the station as casually as she claimed she would enter hell. The thought occurred to Grace that Angel had planned from the start to use her as cover. Who would suspect a young woman traveling with *Señora* Knight, proprietor of the Hotel Colonial, friend of martyred Francisco Madero, and acquaintance of President Huerta and General Rubio?

That should have annoyed Grace instead of amusing her. She felt a rush of affection for the brash young rascal she had known as Lieutenant Angel.

"Take care of Moses, *Señorita* Sanchez."

"I will." Angel raised a hand in good-bye. "May you be well."

Grace watched her stride, slender hips swaying, toward the sprawling encampment of the federal army's women.

Grace removed her torn, sweat-stained straw sombrero and shied it off the edge of the cliff. It sailed away like a condor on a thermal. She untied the straw cord that held her braid. She shook her hair to set it loose, then ran her fingers through it to restore some order. She laughed and heard an echo of her laughter from the canyon below.

"I am going home!" she shouted.

"Home," the canyon answered.

"Home, home, home," added the echo.

39

RIDING IN THE ZULU CAR

"*Señora* Knight!"

Grace turned to see Rico's friend Juan hurrying toward her. After weeks of wandering lost in the mountains, the familiarity of Tres María's shabby train station disoriented her. She was too distracted to notice the look of astonishment that flashed across Juan's face, or the glint of guile that replaced it.

Juan bowed, then snapped erect and clicked the glossy heels of his boots. He grasped her elbow and steered her toward the train platform, talking all the while in his haphazard mix of Spanish and English.

When he paused to take a breath Grace asked, "Where is Captain Martín?"

"He go Cuernavaca. Three, *quizás* four day past."

Grace's heart did a little quick-step bounce with a whirl and a dip thrown in. Rico was in Cuernavaca. In a few hours she would feel his arms around her. She would dance with him to the music of the phonograph he had given her in what seemed another lifetime.

She hoped Juan hadn't noticed how red her cheeks were at the thought of what she and Rico would do in the welcoming darkness of her rooms.

"What is today?" she asked.

"*Sábado.*"

"What day of the month?"

"Thirty *Mayo.*"

May thirtieth. Grace had spent more time on the run with Lieutenant Angel's rebels than she realized.

"Are the trains still running?"

"Yes, *Mamacita*. You have *suerte*. See! Now it comes." He pointed to a puff of smoke in the distance.

He excused himself with another bow and rushed off to the ticket counter. He shoved to the head of the line and hustled back waving the rectangle of pasteboard that would carry her home. Such a beautiful bit of pasteboard it was, the color of old ivory embellished with crimson curlicues. Her destination, Cuernavaca, was stamped in bold red letters across the center of it.

"I have no money with me, Captain, but I can pay you later."

He dismissed such an insignificant debt with a wave of the hand. "*Me alegre* to do for you."

As the train slowed, Lyda and Annie leaned out a window of the first-class coach. They screamed so loudly they drowned out the engine's steam whistle. They pelted down the steps before the car came to a complete stop. They danced Grace around the platform, then Lyda grabbed her in what she always referred to as a bear hug.

"Thank God," she sobbed. "We thought those *brutos indios* had killed and barbecued you."

The three of them stayed locked in each other's arms until the conductor shouted "All aboard." As Grace followed Lyda and Annie to the steps to the coach she noticed the four guards sitting in a roofless box car with slits cut in the sides for their rifles. From the wood smoke floating through the slits they must have been cooking breakfast. Grace wondered if her friends would be attacking the train today.

She climbed the steps and did not glance back. She did not see the look of relief on Juan's face as the train pulled away. She did not see the dark silhouette of the Gonzales boy against the pale gray sky, his body swinging gently in the wind.

Nor did she remember what Angel had said.

"We orphans will ride into Cuauhnáhuac soon enough."

. . .

The first-class coach, with its shabby, broken seats, sagging luggage racks, and the lavatory closet containing one overflowing thundermug, looked mighty good to Grace. More passengers came aboard at Tres Marías creating an superabundance of baggage and humanity.

Lyda stood in the doorway and muttered, "A Zulu car. That's what this is."

Grace thought that if she asked Lyda questions, she could delay Lyda asking them of her. "What's a Zulu car?"

"It's a name people give to the westbound immigrant trains in the States. Entire families set up housekeeping in those cars. Babies are born there, and old people sometimes depart this mortal coil in them."

Grace made her way among the colorful clusters of *indios* camped in the aisle and on the seats. The smell of roasted meat made the stale, soot-laden air almost aromatic. Besides cooking on their small braziers, they slept, drank, gossiped, smoked cigars, played cards, and sang lullabyes to their babies. They looked, in fact, very much like Angel's band in camp. Grace felt at ease among them.

She had to acknowledge that the *indios'* reasoning was more logical than an Englishman's. They would agree with Spinoza that nature abhors a vacuum. If a dearth of first-class passengers left seats empty, then the third-class passengers had the right to fill them.

Lyda arrived at the four seats she had reserved, and paid the boy she had hired to guard the belongings sitting on them. She and Annie cleared away some of the sacks and packages to make room for Grace to sit.

As soon as Grace sank into the seat facing them, they leaned forward, elbows on knees in that undignified American way. They looked ready to light off questions like strings of firecrackers.

Grace held up both hands to stop them. "First tell me this, is Rico in Cuernavaca?"

"No, Gracie." When Lyda shook her head her blond curls bounced around her neck. Grace realized that she hadn't seen yellow hair in over a month. "Rico went looking for you, then he disappeared, too. We haven't seen hide nor hair of him for two weeks or more."

"Juan said he went to Cuernavaca three or four days ago."

"Well, I expect he's there then. We've been shopping in Mex City since Monday, and the rebs cut the phone lines again."

"And the Colonial?"

"So few guests have come, I had to let most of the staff go."

"María and Socrates? Socorro?"

"I kept them on, along with the gardner, Leobardo, a few of the maids, and the Chinaman, but they haven't been paid. To tell you the truth, Gracie, I was going to shut the place down when Annie and I got back."

Grace was horrified. "Shut it down?"

Tears welled up in Lyda's eyes. "We thought you were dead, darlin'."

Annie couldn't contain her curiosity any longer. "Did you stay with the rebels, Auntie Grace?" she asked. "Did you meet General Zapata? Did you fight in any battles? Did you get those clothes off a dead man?"

Grace should have known that people would ask her these sorts of questions, but she wasn't prepared for them. At least the first ones to interrogate her were her dearest friends. How would she respond when General Rubio demanded answers? And what if something she said now made its way back to him? She couldn't bear the thought of her own careless words causing *el gobierno* to find Lieutenant Angel's people and murder them.

She knew she was not capable of lying to Lyda and Annie, but she couldn't tell them the whole truth either. She closed her eyes and pretended to fall asleep while Lyda kept up a stream of gossip about the goings-on in the capital and Cuernavaca in her absence.

Actually, Grace didn't have to pretend to sleep. Exhaustion sat as stone-heavy as gargoyles on her brow. The car swayed and rattled. The walls creaked like arthritic knee joints.

In the past, the swaying and noise had bothered Grace, but now they were the rocking of a cradle and a lullabye. She fell asleep to them, and to the sound of Lyda's voice. The crooning of a mother nursing her baby in the aisle nearby was a sweet and familiar comfort.

40

THE TRUTH AND ANYTHING
BUT THE TRUTH

Juan crossed his arms and lounged against the wall of the ticket booth until the caboose vanished around the first curve. He lit a cigar and puffed on it while he watched the fluffy burps from the smokestack getting smaller, like Indian signals indicating that the coast was clear. He did not leave the station until he was sure the *gringa* had truly gone. Gone but not, as Ambrozio Nuñez had led him and Rico to believe, departed.

He knew the train might stop and back up. It had happened before when Hanibal the engineer had forgotten to remind his Tres Marías sweetheart that she was his true love. Hanibal had a true love at every depot, which was one of many reasons the train arrived late so often.

Juan didn't feel guilty about letting *Mamacita* Knight think Rico was waiting for her in Cuernavaca. But then, guilt rarely bothered Juan. "Consciences . . . ," he said, when alcohol made him philosophical, ". . . are for people who don't know how to enjoy the lives God gave them."

Nor would he hesitate to keep his friend in the dark about the fact that the rebels had not thrown *Inglesa* off a cliff. The woman had caused Rico trouble enough already. If he knew she had returned to the Colonial the fool would waltz right back into Rubio's snake pit after her. Not that he was much safer anywhere else.

A friend like Federico Martín was a rare find. Juan had been drawn to him because of his charm, his pranks, his powerful family, and his money. But when tested in combat Rico proved to be much more than the spoiled, womanizing only grandson of Old Man Martín. Beyond that, Juan had come to think of himself as a better man because Rico thought he was.

Juan had read Rubio's cable as it came in last night. The telegraph key had transmuted its rat-a-tat-tat into a death sentence for Juan's dearest friend, maybe the only person in the world he truly loved. The telegram ordered every man in Rubio's command to forget their other assignments and hunt for Captain Federico Martín. It warned that Martín was a violent criminal who had attacked a superior officer without provocation. It advised anyone who encountered him to shoot on sight.

Rubio also must have lumbered straight from Rico's empty jail cell to the printer's shop. A messenger had arrived this morning with hundreds of handbills to distribute among the locals. They offered a substantial reward to anyone who brought in the fugitive, dead or alive. They included a drawing of Rico and a description of his horse. One of them had been posted in plain sight on the depot's wall. Juan had hustled *Señora* Knight past it, talking all the while to distract her.

Juan knew Rubio would not stop until someone, preferably Rubio himself, brought in Rico's corpse draped across the back of a horse, donkey, burro, or dung cart. Rubio thrived on grudges the way mules relished thistles. Juan imagined how purple Fatso's face must have turned when he found out Rico not only had escaped the noose, but had taken his grandfather's prized Andalusian with him.

Now Rico had the best, or worst, possible reason to join Venustiano Carranza's army. He was a walking dead man in Morelos. Juan was packed and ready to go with him.

It would be a long ride. Carranza's home state of Coahuila lay over five hundred miles to the north. Maybe when they left Morelos they could take the train.

Juan had emerged from the barracks this morning to find an urchin waiting for him with a note. He recognized the handwriting, which was helpful since the unsigned message contained only two words. "Goat hut."

He threw some of his clothes into his saddlebag and set out for the abandoned goat herders' shack in a shallow canyon not far above the train station. It sat in the middle of a high meadow surrounded by juniper and piñon trees. When Juan arrived he found Grullo tearing at rangy tufts of grass. He tethered his own horse nearby. Grullo seemed glad for the company.

The hovel's plank door hung askew on its leather hinges. Rico sat on an upturned wooden bucket in the doorway and leaned a shoulder against the frame. His hair was tousled and the stubble of a beard made his face look haggard. His eyes were closed, either in sleep or to block out the midday sunlight.

"You look terrible, brother," said Juan.

Rico stood up and the two friends clasped each other's arms, then embraced.

"*Carajo, niño.*" Juan stepped back and wrinkled his nose. "You stink of the calaboose. Rubio only has to follow his nose."

"You heard what happened?"

"Everyone in Morelos has heard what happened. Or at least Fatso's version of it."

Rico laid into the food Juan brought like a starving wolf feasting on a fresh sheep carcass. When he had licked the last of the pork grease off his fingers Juan handed him a bundle of clothes held together with a tooled leather belt. Rico recognized the silver buckle on the belt. Juan considered it his lucky charm.

He held it up. "Thank you, brother."

Juan started off to retrieve his horse. He called back over his shoulder. "I'll return at sunset and we can ride north."

"I'm going to *Las Delicias* first."

Juan did an about-face. "Rico, it is not safe for you in Morelos. Rubio has put a bounty on your head."

"I won't go to Carranza empty-handed, like a *pelado,* a pauper. We need money and supplies and men. I know at least twenty of our workers who would agree to come north with us."

"*Las Delicias* will be the first place Fatso looks."

"Rubio fears my grandfather."

"God fears your grandfather." Juan crossed himself to neutralize any celestial offense his irreverence might have caused.

It wasn't a bad plan though. Rico's grandfather might even sympathize with his grandson for perhaps the first time ever. The Old Man considered a coarse, low-class brute like Huerta useful as a general, but he hated him as president. Venustiano Carranza, on the other hand, oozed gentility. His skin, pale as any Swede's, raised him high in the Old Man's estimation.

"I'll come with you."

"It would be better if you stayed here, Juancito. We need to know what Rubio is up to."

Rico didn't mention that there was no sense in both of them getting killed if they were sighted. Nor did he remind Juan that his grandfather would not be happy to see him. The Old Man considered Juan of common birth and would almost certainly insult him.

Juan amused himself pitching *centavos* while Rico bathed in the spring bubbling up among rocks nearby. When he finished he put on Juan's clothes—tight leather pants, a white linen shirt, short wool jacket, and a *vaquero*'s felt hat with a jaunty brim. Juan's striker had polished the black half-boots until he could see his reflection in them.

The two men rode together as far as the first fork in the trail.

"I will meet you at Rosa's cantina in three days," Rico said. "If I have not returned by the fourth day, ride north without me."

They leaned across from their saddles and clasped arms again. Without looking back, Rico rode away. Juan dismounted, tied the reins to a tree, and climbed to an outcrop. From there he could see the trail snake downhill for a mile or more before it lost itself in a disorder of rocks and brush.

He drew his sword and stood on the highest point of the ledge. He grasped the tip of the blade in both hands and held it straight up with arms fully extended. The blade, hilt, and handguard formed a slender cross. It was an ancient Crusader's salute given by warriors who believed they would not see their comrade again. At least not alive.

41

HOMECOMING

The quantity of Lyda's Mexico City purchases and the fact that she didn't trust them to ride in the baggage car should have given Grace a clue. More must be amiss than a temporary decrease in the Colonial's room reservations. But she fell asleep too quickly to wonder about the sacks and boxes stuffed onto the luggage rack overhead, stashed under all four seats, and stacked on the floor and on the empty seat next to her. She awoke only when the train pulled into Cuernavaca's station and the usual uproar started.

Before the engine came to a stop the local touts swarmed aboard. Each one tried to outshout the others in praise of whatever hotel, restaurant, or hackney driver had hired them. Lyda bellowed above the din and enlisted three of them as porters. The *muchachos,* as she called them, passed her boxes and sacks through the window to compatriots on the platform. Lyda leaned out of a nearby window with her derringer cocked and made sure none of the goods vanished.

As Grace tried to descend the steps without getting knocked down by the mob of passengers pushing to board, she heard Lyda swearing behind her. Americans, Grace thought, swore with such conviction and original-ity. She admired that about them. Grace could imagine her and Lieu-tenant Angel getting along splendidly. Yanks, after all, were old hands at rebellion.

Grace had become so used to wearing khaki trousers and shirt with rope sandals that she didn't notice the stares from the two hundred or so foreigners and *correctos* milling about on the platform. Their lace-trimmed parasols and plumes, their buttoned spats, straw boaters, baggy golf pants, and matching luggage gave the place a festive air, as if they were all headed off on holiday.

Grace dodged among handcarts heaped with steamer trunks, satchels, and carpet bags. She soon realized that the mood in the station was frantic, not festive. The owners of the baggage wrangled with porters who knew to a *centavo* the price of desperation. Hats in hands they smiled like deacons and demanded highwaymen's fees.

Hiring the two horse-drawn victorias proved easy. More people were coming to the station than were leaving it. Lyda supervised the loading of the baggage, leaving Grace nothing to do but sink back into the tufted leather seat and enjoy the ride. Four of Lyda's *muchachos* stood on the running boards of the second taxi.

Trees lined the busy boulevard leading from the station to the center of town. Two things told Grace she was home—the smell of flowers and the music of cascading water. Along the way, each blue army uniform caused Grace's heart to race until the carriage came close enough to see that Rico was not wearing it.

The victorias pulled up to the Colonial. As the *muchachos* unloaded Lyda's purchases, Grace pushed on the gate. It pushed back. The sun would not set for an hour and Grace had never locked the gate in the daytime.

Leobardo swung it open when she knocked. Leobardo had the quality most desireable in a gatekeeper, imperturbability. He took off his hat and greeted Grace as if she had just returned from an errand or a stroll on the plaza. However, besides his rifle he now carried a machete and a pistol.

Annie dodged around him and ran to look for Socorro. Leobardo kept a wary eye on the *muchachos* as they stacked Lyda's purchases in the courtyard.

"Why is the door locked?" asked Grace.

"Thievery," he said.

"Thievery?"

"People are hungry, *Mamacita.*"

Grace looked at Lyda for an explanation.

"Darlin', when I saw you on that railroad platform in Tres Marías you looked like you'd been dunked in a river, beaten on a rock, and run through a wringer. I didn't want to give you all the bad news at once."

"What bad news?"

"Rubio ordered barricades set up on the roads in the countryside. I reckon his plan is to capture any *Zapatistas* stupid enough to blunder into them. But his men assume that everyone is a rebel and they are terrorizing the *indios.* The villagers can't bring produce to market. If it weren't for the train we would be in a bad way for supplies."

Grace decided to worry about that tomorrow. She had a more urgent concern.

"Is Captain Martín here, *Señor* Leobardo?"

"No, *Mamacita.*"

Annie came running from the kitchen. "Socorro is gone!"

María and the maids followed and clustered around her, all talking at once in Nahuatl and Spanish. Socrates arrived still holding the chamois cloth he had been using to buff the lacquer on the Pierce.

"Where is Socorro?" Grace asked.

"God alone knows, *Señora* Knight." Socrates told her about Colonel Rubio's attempt to ravish Socorro, the fight with Captain Martín, and the captain's escape from jail. He neglected to mention that José was the one who had helped him escape.

"Does anyone know where Captain Martín went?"

"No, *señora,*" said Leobardo, "but the general has offered a reward of five hundred *pesos* to anyone who shoots him." Leobardo was blunt as well as imperturbable.

"That son of a bitch." Grace headed for the front gate.

"Where are you going?" asked Lyda.

"To the Governor's Palace."

"General Rubio is not there, *señora,*" said Socrates. "He marched his men away three days ago with a great waving of flags and tooting of horns."

"Their strumpets and brats followed them," María added.

"The general said he would return bringing a wagonload of the rebels' heads, with General Zapata's on top," added Leobardo.

All Grace heard was that a five-hundred-*peso* bounty had been set on Rico. That was more than the average laborer could earn in a year. Grace kept walking even though her knees wobbled and she feared she would faint.

Lyda grabbed her arm in the doorway. "Wait, Gracie."

"Someone at the palace will know where Rubio is."

"They will ask you where you've been. They might think you're in sympathy with the rebels."

"Rubio intends to kill him."

"Rico's smarter than Rubio and all that unshod rabble Fatso calls an army."

Grace tried to pull free, but Lyda was strong. With her free hand she pointed toward the stairs and made the motion of opening a spigot. One of the maids hurried off to turn on the water heater and start the bath running in Grace's apartment.

"It's Saturday night, Gracie, and the boss is away. His underlings will all be tipling in the cantinas. Some of them might even come here to get drunk."

"I have to do something." Grace started to cry.

"Take a hot soak. Get a night's sleep. When you wake up, put on something that doesn't make you look like a *Zapatista*." She surveyed Grace's soiled outfit and wrinkled her nose. "Tomorrow we'll burn those clothes and think of a plan."

Lyda and Annie went home. Grace started up the stairs, but stopped when Socrates cleared his throat.

She turned to look at him. "Yes?"

"Captain Martín's grandfather was a famous judge. He knows many important people who can help the captain."

"Where is his grandfather?" Grace realized that although Rico had mentioned his parents dying when he was young, he rarely spoke of his family.

"I think maybe he's in Mexico City."

"Thank you."

Grace climbed the stairs. She walked down the corridor to her room as if in a dream, or a nightmare. She didn't expect to sleep. She knew the sort of man Rubio was. What he lacked in intelligence he made up for in spite, bulldoggedness, and brutality.

Already she was thinking of people who might help her. At the top of the list was her old acquaintance, President Huerta. Maybe she could convince him to pardon Rico and call off his beast of a general. And she would look for Rico's grandfather.

Gunfire woke Grace. Still more than half asleep, she threw back the covers and tried to bolt. She flailed for balance when her feet hit air instead of the ground. She landed on the floor with a thud. She lay in the dark trying to remember where she was. She groped with her hand until she touched the bed, the first clue.

She was in her flat in the Colonial. She was not wrapped up in a flea-infested blanket in a dank cave. She wanted to weep with joy. Then she remembered the rest.

Hotel guests were few and fewer. People were shooting guns in Cuernavaca again, something that hadn't happened since the rebels thought they had won their war two years ago and installed Francisco Madero as president. And the worst, Rico was in the mountains somewhere, with a price on his head.

Grace lit a candle, put on her kimono, and went downstairs for a predawn prowl through the premises. She needed to reassure herself that she really had come home. She checked the back courtyard, the kitchen, and the stable where the gleaming, red Pierce motorcar slept. She looked in on Leobardo, who slept in his hammock slung in the shed by the front gate. She put her head against the wall in the corridor where she could listen to the comforting hum of the electrical switching station outside.

She returned to the lobby and sank into the huge leather easy chair. It was positioned with a view of the courtyard through the arches of the open corridor. She fell asleep curled up in it.

She woke up at dawn. She yawned, stretched, and saw María waiting patiently, her white apron as pristinely white and starched as usual. Come war, famine, or pestilence, María would face them well laundered.

"*Señora*," she said. "*El chinito* has gone."

Grace couldn't blame Wing Ang for leaving. According to Lyda, no one, including herself, had been paid for two weeks. The chef's departure meant one less mouth to feed. These days there was no call for his roast beef, kidney pies, trifles, or yorkshire puddings anyway. Wing Ang was a cypher to Grace, but he was honest and hardworking, and she hoped he had found somewhere safe to go.

"If you and Socrates want to leave, María, I understand."

"We will stay, *Mamacita*. I will cook."

Grace went upstairs to dress for her sortie to army headquarters in the Governor's Palace on the far side of the main plaza. Now she had another mission, to find a source of funds. If no one at the palace would rescind the execution order, she would go to Mexico City and make her case to President Huerta. While she was in the capital she could hock her jewelry at the Bank of Pity. In the meantime she had something else of value to sell and she knew at least two people who would like to buy it.

After hours of waiting on hardback chairs in one smoke-choked government office after another, she returned to the Colonial. Her clothes and hair smelled so strongly of cigars she wanted to go straight upstairs and take a bath. But Lyda and Annie were waiting for her. The rest of the household gathered to hear the news. They all could tell from Grace's face that she had had no success.

"Don't let those petty functionaries get you down, Gracie. President Huerta will help you. He likes you. How many people can make that claim?"

"How many people would want to." Grace carried a cotton sack slung over one shoulder. It clinked when she hefted it with both hands onto the front desk. "They played cat-and-mouse with me at the palace, but at least I can pay your wages."

Grace opened the sack and poured silver coins out across the lacquered mahogany desktop.

For once Lyda needed several seconds before she could say anything.

"Where did you get that? And what possessed you to carry it through the streets? Someone could have killed you for it."

"I sold the Pierce."

When Annie translated, Socrates gave a small cry and turned away. Grace had expected he would mourn the loss of the Pierce. She called him back.

"The gentleman who bought it offered to hire you as driver and mechanic. He says he will pay you well."

Socrates shook his head. "I will stay here with you, *Mamacita.*"

Everyone went back to their chores. Lyda put the money in the doghouse-sized cast-iron safe in Grace's office. She came back out and leaned her elbows on the front desk. Grace sat in the big leather chair and she and Lyda both watched the hummingbirds dart among the flowering vines covering the courtyard wall.

"Lyda, what causes men to wage this malarial warfare?"

"You mean why do they snatch defeat time and again from the jaws of victory?"

"Too right."

"They remind me of a story." Lyda had an endless supply of those. "One of Abraham Lincoln's neighbors saw him striding past her house with two of his sons. Both of the boys were wailing like they had their toes in a mousetrap. The neighbor asked, 'Why, Mr. Lincoln, what ails the lads?' Lincoln replied, 'Just what's the matter with the whole world. I have three walnuts and each wants two.'"

Grace laughed. It felt good.

42

DESTINY'S DESTINATION

Rico wanted to believe that the black clouds hanging over *Las Delicias* meant a gentle evening rain, but he knew better. He urged Grullo into a gallop down the carriage drive. The shreds of smoke were small ones. Maybe he could chase away whomever had started the fire. Maybe he could put out the flames before they did much damage. That the blaze might have started accidentally didn't occur to him. Fires rarely started by accident these days.

He was so intent on what he would find beyond the open gate he didn't notice the handbill nailed to it. The house looked intact, but the ruins of the sugar refinery beyond it still smoldered. Only the mill's stone chimney remained, like a forefinger pointing in reproach toward heaven.

When Rico went inside the house he saw that its stone walls formed a shell around chaos. Looters had taken almost everything, yet still managed to leave it littered with trash they didn't consider worth stealing. They had set a fire at the back of the house. Rico could tell from the streaks of soot on the walls that the flames had licked upward and ignited the beams. A portion of the roof had collapsed, leaving a pile of broken tiles on the floor.

Rico put a hand on the ashes and felt the warmth from them. He waded through the ankle-deep rubbish in the maze of rooms, dim in the day's fading light. He called out as he went in case anyone lay hurt, or trapped under a fallen beam. He didn't bother to search for anything the thieves might have left. Nothing had remained here for him even before the looters came. He stood ankle-deep in the debris of his childhood and gave several heartbeats' thought to his situation.

His beloved was dead. His past was in ashes. His future was smoke on the wind.

The extent of the destruction didn't surprise Rico. He didn't have to be a mind reader to know that although the local villagers recognized his grandfather's authority, they did not like him. Rico had spent his entire life trying to be the kind of man his grandfather was not.

He could imagine the scene here, with the local villagers swarming through these rooms. It must have looked like Mexico City's sprawling Thieves' Market on bargain day. He wondered how many of his family's treasures would end up in the Thieves' Market or in the Bank of Pity, the national pawnshop.

He discarded his plan to recruit men for Carranza's army. He had no way of knowing which of the locals had participated in this. He didn't want to go to the nearest village and see his family's furniture, knickknacks, and paintings in the houses of people he had known all his life. In any case, everyone would assume he had come to punish the culprits. He could imagine them shuffling their feet, shifting their eyes from his gaze, and mumbling to avoid answering his questions.

He would volunteer his services to Carranza. He would fight to overthrow the likes of Huerta and Rubio. He would do his best to make up for the injustices inflicted on the laborers who made the extravagance of his family's lives possible.

When he left the house, the sun had advanced too far toward the horizon for Rico to travel. As he unsaddled Grullo he noticed the paper nailed to the front gate. In the pale light he could barely read it. The drawing hardly approximated him, but the handbill gave a good description of Grullo. He realized that would be a problem in the days to come. He could disguise himself, but he couldn't disguise his horse.

He brushed Grullo and led him to the stream running helter-skelter over rocks at the far end of the lawn. He lay on his stomach and took a long drink, too. He hobbled the horse on the lawn where the family had played tennis, croquette, and squash. The familiar sound of him

munching on the succulent grass was a comfort. Rico wished his own
hunger could be as easily appeased.

He spread his blanket on the thick moss in the triangular niche between two of an ancient fig tree's enormous roots. A dense curtain of
vines covered the tree. It had started as a vine itself, twining up around
the hapless trunk of another tree long gone now. The fig had grown,
drawing nourishment from its host. It had expanded and hardened until it stood on its own.

Its radiating system of roots took the shape and curve of a cathedral's flying buttresses. As a child Rico had imagined they were his cas-
tle, his fortress, his Spanish galleon, his hideaway. He lay with his head
against the trunk and looked up at the canopy of leaves. A shepherd
moon watched over the flock of stars grazing among the branches.

Rico was partial to irony. He drifted toward sleep with a smile on his
face and his hand resting on the sleek, rounded top of the fig tree's
root. Whoever had looted the house had not been able to steal the only
material thing from his past for which he really cared and that now cradled him.

The market town of Mazatl was the heart of the district. The Carmelite
convent was the soul of Mazatl. Rico's family had donated to its support
since its founding. For the first time in a hundred years there would be
no donation. Before Rico left Morelos he felt obliged to explain and
apologize, two things his grandfather never did.

Mother Merced probably knew what had happened at *Las Delicias*,
and why Rico's grandfather had not arrived with the quarterly alms. She
might have been cloistered, but she was not in the dark. The grate in the
door was like the window on a confessional. People came here from all
over to tell her their troubles. Very little happened in the district that
Mother Merced didn't know about.

He rode down streets empty except for old people. Weeds and vines
had begun to overrun the kitchen gardens. When he came to the plaza
with its palms, fountain, and Victorian bandstand he was relieved to see
the sacristan sweeping the flagstones.

"Thanks be to God!" The old man dropped to one knee and crushed his battered hat to his chest. "He has answered our prayers. We knew you would come to our aid, *Don* Federico."

Rico dismounted. As he helped the old man to his feet he saw his grandfather's stick pin holding the faded bandana around the sacristan's withered neck. A silversmith had adorned the pin with a horse's head engraved in such detail that the individual hairs in his mane were visible. The horse was Grullo's sire and the pin was one of a kind. *Don* Bonifacio wore it only on formal occasions.

Rico said nothing about it. Better the sacristan have it than some bargain hunter at the Thieves' Market. This meant that Mother Merced must know who had ransacked and burned his family's estate. Rico didn't intend to ask her. Even if he did, she was unlikely to tell him. Mother Merced did not repeat the confidences whispered through the iron grate.

Rico tied Grullo to a tree, walked across the stone paving of the outer reception area, and rang the bell on the door. From infancy until he boarded the steamer for Boston, his grandfather had brought him here every three months. After they delivered the family's gift of money, they attended mass in the church next to the convent.

As a boy Rico had been fascinated by the sweet soprano chants echoing in the darkness beyond the grate or from behind the screen in the nun's chapel. He listened intently now, but he heard no singing. Nor did he hear footsteps because Mother Merced did not wear shoes, but he did hear the rustle of her robes amplified by the walls of the narrow corridor.

He expected the panel behind the grate to slide open as usual. When the door itself swung wide he jumped back in surprise. He almost bowled over the sacristan hovering behind him.

Mother Merced stood like a plaster statue in the doorway. Her tight-fitting coif framed the stricken look on her face. Her eyes were red and her cheeks streaked with tears. The tears started again when she saw Rico.

"What happened, Holy Mother?"

She spoke in a choked whisper. "The *federales* came."

"When?"

"Yesterday." Mother Merced swayed and Rico reached out to catch her should she faint. "They took the sisters, the young ones. Only we old women are left."

"Where did they take them?"

"I heard someone say Veracruz."

"I am riding north. If I can find them I will punish the ones who took them."

"Retribution is for God, my son. But if you find them, please make sure they come home."

"I will." He hesitated to ask her for a favor, but he could not leave without doing it. He knelt and bowed his head. "Will you say a *novena* for someone?"

"For whom, my child?"

"Her name is Grace Knight."

"The tall Englishwoman with hair like old copper?"

Rico thought he would faint and fall nose-first onto the paving. Not the sort of thing for an officer and a gentleman to do.

"You know of her?"

"She slept here three nights ago." The arrival of a champion and holy work to do seemed to revive Mother Merced. "Why do you ask us to pray her through purgatory?"

Rico collected his wits. Crying was also not appropriate for an officer and a gentleman.

"I heard the rebels had killed her."

"If so, her ghost is quite substantial. She came here with the women who travel with Lieutenant Angel."

Rico was so stunned he did not feel the grind of the flagstones on his knees. His beloved had returned from the grave. He felt as if he himself had been raised from the dead. He could not believe that he, who had sinned so much, could receive such a gift.

He finally registered the rest of the information. Lieutenant Angel was the one Ambrozio Nuñez said had killed Grace. And Angel's miscreants were the ones who harrassed the train on a regular basis. Rico would have bet that Angel's men were the ones who had looted *Las Delicias,* but as Grace would say, it mattered not a fig now.

"Where are they headed?"

"Angel said they were going to meet Zapata's army in Ayala."

Rico gave her the only objects of value he had, his pocket watch and Juan's silver belt buckle. She blessed him and promised to pray for him on his journey. He mounted Grullo in a daze.

Destiny. Destination. *Destino* and *destinación* had the same meaning in Spanish. Destiny had given Rico a new destination.

Ayala.

43

Rico met a mule driver who was heading in the direction of Rosa's cantina. He gave him his second-to-last *peso* to deliver a message to Juan, telling him to start north without him. That was just as well. Looking prosperous was unhealthy these days, and Juan would not be happy to see what Rico did to the clothes he gave him.

He tore the ruffles off the white linen shirt. He ripped the sleeves from the embroidered jacket, then turned it inside out so only the brown wool lining showed. He waded through brambles in the leather trousers, then soaked them in a stream and beat them with rocks to age them. He packed his boots into a saddlebag and wore rope sandals he found discarded by the side of the road.

He had left his rifle in Juan's keeping. Now he stuck his knife under his waistband at the small his back. He cut a slit in the middle of his blanket so he could wear it as a serape and hide his pistols, knife, and cartidge belt under it. The only things he didn't have to alter were the ancient straw hat the sacristan gave him and the mud that had splattered all over him and his horse.

He knew the main route to Ayala, but he couldn't risk running into a barricade or patrol. He intended to follow mountain trails etched into the rocky soil by centuries of burros' hooves and the soles of peasants' feet. The problem was the Martíns had never been the sort to travel back roads.

He hadn't ridden far into the mountains before he realized how difficult finding and following those trails would be. All he could do was keep the sun on his left and pray that rain clouds didn't cover it. Whenever he met the occasional muleteer or peasant on a burro he asked directions. Asking for help was also a new experience for him.

He needed money, but he couldn't bring himself to sell Grullo, his only asset. Fortunately for Rico, plenty of people wanted to steal the horse. Even more fortunately, the first band of cutthroats to accost him numbered only three.

Rico breathed a thanks to God for sending them. Most *renegados* traveled in larger packs. What gave them away as criminals were the cigars. From the aroma of the smoke wafting toward him on the breeze Rico knew they were imported.

The old saying was right. *Pobre con puro es ladrón, seguro.* A poor man with a cigar is a thief for sure.

The leader had an extortionist's eyes and pendulous jowls that gave him a greasily prosperous look. He stroked his large paunch as if it were a pet pig snoozing in his lap. He probably considered his hammock-backed, gray-muzzled plow horse to be figuratively as well as literally beneath him, but even if he didn't, Rico's Andalusian would be worth the taking.

The second man perched on the rump of a stout burro. The view of him was obscured by two bulging hemp sacks lashed across the animal's back. A rusty shovel was tied on top of them. The third malefactor sat on a heavily laden, ladder-ribbed mule that wheezed like a windlass with a case of the glanders. The man was grinning like a cheerful death's head, probably in anticipation of trading up to the plow horse when Jowls took possession of this handsome silver-gray stallion.

Jowls waved his rusty, pepperbox pistol in Rico's general direction, as if that were all the attention such a shabby chump required. Rico tried not to smile. The gun had been new when his grandfather was in diapers.

A smarter man would have taken one look at Grullo and suspected that his rider wasn't whom he seemed, but Jowls probably assumed Rico had come by the stallion dishonestly.

"We will relieve you of the responsibility of such a fine steed, *compadre.*"

Rico raised his hands high in hasty surrender. "Take him with God's blessing, but please don't shoot me."

He fell out of the saddle as though in a panic, and landed on Grullo's far side. He knew the bandits would kill him without blinking, but they would hesitate to harm the fine horse serving as his shield. He pulled both Colts from under his blanket and extended them around each side of Grullo's neck. Grullo didn't so much as twitch. Rico sighted across the horse's whithers to take aim at the leader.

"Throw your weapons into the arroyo." He used the parade-ground voice that always snapped the rowdiest troops to attention. "Knives, too."

Jowls's partners patted themselves down. They produced hardware from holsters, hats, serapes, shoes, and shirts and lobbed them over the side of the cliff. Jowls hesitated and Rico shot off his new sombrero to chivvy him along. Jowls muttered a rendition of Rico's lineage to the counterpoint of his rifle, pistols, and cutlery clanging against the side of the cliff.

Rico knew he shouldn't waste time. Another gang of *sin verguenzas,* shameless ones, could round the bend at any time.

"Put the sacks there and pile your clothes next to them."

"Shoes, too, *señor?*" asked one of the cronies.

"Shoes, too."

Crony Number Two surveyed the rocks and thorns that carpeted hundreds of square miles. "For the love of God, *señor,* not the shoes."

Rico smiled like a wolf at a plump deer. "You may throw your shoes over the cliff empty or I will throw them over with your feet inside them."

With a pistol still pointed at Jowls, Rico walked out from behind Grullo and hefted the gunny sacks. The bandits had reaped a rich harvest from some haciendas. When threatened with disaster, the well-to-do's first impulse was to bury their valuables. The flaw in that plan was that most bandits were peasants, and if peasants knew anything, it was how to dig.

Rico upended the sacks and spilled out the bounty. The silver candlesticks, Greek statues, porcelain shepherdesses, and mirrors framed in gilded plaster cherubs looked familiar. These were at least three of the looters who had plundered his family's home. He gave them a wolfish grin. God did have a sense of humor after all.

With a pistol trained on the bandits, he bundled their clothes with his other hand and flung them into the abyss. Then he kicked the booty after them. He couldn't say why doing it gave him such joy. Maybe it was because they represented afternoons spent sweltering in a starched collar in parlors that were burlesques of London drawing rooms. The stench of camphor and the jumble of useless gewgaws had always given him a headache.

The bandits groaned as their treasure rattled to the bottom a thousand feet away. Rico imagined some farmer in the canyon, standing bewildered in his rocky field while riches fell around him.

He mounted Grullo and rode off leading the mule by a rope. The plow horse and burro followed. He would have bet all the loot lying at the bottom of the canyon that Lieutenant Angel could find a use for the extra mounts.

Angel put great faith in the apocryphal belief that, like lightning, the federal army would not strike twice in the same place. So her company returned to the caves in the high cliff below San Miguel. The men slept in the largest cave and the women and children in the smaller ones. They were hard to reach and easy to defend and Angel's people felt safer than they had in a long time.

Angel and Antonio sat on a ledge and watched the swallows dart in and out of the spray and mist where the hundred-foot-high waterfall hit the river. They leaned back against the limestone wall with their legs dangling, and enjoyed two of *Don* Bonifacio Martín's *habano puro* cigars, imported from Cuba.

Everyone knew that Cubans made the best cigars. The word *cuba* itself meant casks of the sort that contained tobacco. Angel preferred *habanos puros* for their symbolism as much as for the euphoria their smoke caused. Cubans believed that slaves could produce sugarcane, but only free men cultivated tobacco.

In a little while the band would leave for General Zapata's headquarters in Ayala, but Angel was enjoying this early morning respite on the ledge. For a few minutes she could pretend that life was always like this, with rare June sunshine, waterfalls, and the finest of cigars. Then small stones rattled down the slope. With regret, Angel and Antonio tossed the *puros* into the river and drew their pistols.

Socorro lost her footing and slid the last few yards down the steep path. Antonio caught her before she pitched over the edge. Her hair was in tangles, her clothes torn. Her bare feet left bloody prints on the pale limestone rock. She was out of breath.

" 'Tonio, they took *Papi*."

"Fatso's dogs?"

"Yes. We avoided the barricades, but a patrol caught us. *Papi* shot at them so I could escape. They had a lot of men tied together."

Angel knew the federal army's routine. *El gobierno* rarely kept prisoners for long in Morelos for fear their comrades would free them. They loaded them onto trains and transported them far away.

The rendezvous in Ayala would have to wait. Angel had a chore to do first. This time she would make sure the train never carried any of her people into exile again.

44

T H E   L A S T   T R A I N

Grace packed a single valise. She only intended to stay in Mexico City long enough to visit President Huerta and, if necessary, find *Señor* Bonifacio Martín. She dreaded seeing Huerta. He obviously had not mellowed since the days he quartered at the Colonial. She hoped he would be sober, but she wasn't counting on it. From what she had heard about Rico's grandfather, she wasn't eager to meet him either.

Her late husband's family had provided most of the information concerning *Don* Bonifacio. Workers had braved sniper fire to restore the telegraph wires and Grace had exchanged a flurry of cables with her former in-laws. They insisted that she stay with them while in the capital.

Messengers also delivered telegrams from several of the Colonial's frequent guests from Mexico City. They said they had heard that Cuernavaca was peaceful and they planned to arrive on Friday's train. Lyda was ecstatic. Grace ventured cautious optimism, but remembered what María often said: *"La confianza mata al hombre."* Confidence kills the man.

To the casual visitor, Cuernavaca did seem its normal, carefree self. Thanks to the promise General Huerta made to Grace two years ago, a military band gave a concert every night in the kiosk just across the tram tracks from the Colonial's front door. Cuernavacans attended stage plays and dances. They "oohed" and "aahed" at the moving pictures shown in the new theater. Families and lovers strolled through Borda Gardens and rowed boats among the waterlilies on its lake.

Grace took a horse-drawn cab to the depot. She arrived early, only to learn that some mechanical problem would delay departure by at least two hours. She had brought a copy of *Ben Hur* to read on the train and she headed for the big waiting room to lose herself in the story. She stopped when the station master's office door opened and two soldiers hauled a familiar figure along between them. Their prisoner sagged in their grip. A starched-and-pressed colonel followed.

"*Señor* Perez," Grace called out.

As the soldiers hustled José away he turned to look at her, though his eyes were almost swollen shut. He spoke through bruised lips.

"Good morning, *Señora* Knight. May God keep you in His care."

Grace walked alongside the colonel and chose her Spanish words carefully. Irritating or insulting him would not help José.

"Where is Mr. Perez going?"

"To Quintana Roo, to the jungle where such wild animals belong. They'll leave with the troop train tonight."

"He's an honest man, Colonel. He's one of my employees. Let him come with me and I will be responsible for him."

"I must follow General Rubio's orders."

The crowd of waiting passengers made way for the armed soldiers, but not for Grace. As they closed in behind José she lost sight of him. She hurried down the steps at the end of the platform and strode through the steam and cinders in search of him.

She found soldiers loading him and seventy-five or eighty other prisoners into a cattle car on a siding. The guards prodded their charges with bayonets, but none of the men resisted. They didn't plead or protest. Silent and stoic in their white cotton trousers and shirts, they looked like the impoverished farmers they were.

Their women, some with small children slung in the blue *rebozos* at their backs, climbed the rungs bolted onto the side of the car. Others handed their toddlers to those already on top. They settled in up there with satchels and baskets, hands of bananas, birds in cages, live chickens, and blanket rolls. Grace looked for Serafina, but did not see her or Socorro.

She tried to reason with the colonel.

"You mustn't crowd those men like that. They can't even sit down. They will starve or smother or be trampled to death."

"If it is God's wish that some of them die, that will leave more room for the others. So you see you have no need to concern yourself, *señora*."

Grace stood on tiptoe, put her face to an opening between the slats that made up the sides, and called out.

"José."

He made his way to her and crouched to be at her level. Grace didn't know what to say. She could promise to try to convince Rubio to free him, but she and José both knew he would never do it. Socrates had finally told her that José had helped Rico escape from jail. Grace wondered if that was why the soldiers had taken him prisoner.

"Where are Fina and Cora?" she asked.

"They're safe, *señora*."

"What do you need most? What can I bring you and the others?"

He shook his head. "Do not trouble yourself, *Mamacita*. God will care for us."

Grace wanted to point out that if God cared for them they wouldn't be in this stock car.

"Helping you is no trouble, José. I can never repay you for saving Captain Martín's life."

"He saved my daughter's honor. I owe him more than my life." He put his face close to the slats so the guards would not hear. "You and *Señora* Lyda and her daughter must take the morning train to Mexico City. Do not take this evening train."

She nodded. "I came here to take the early train."

"Good."

The guard noticed them whispering. *"¡Váyase!"* He waved his rifle at Grace to shoo her off. *"Vaya."*

He was young and excitable, and Grace backed away with her hands up, palms out to show she was not passing anything to the prisoners.

She hurried to the telegraph office and composed a cable. She paid extra to have it delivered to the Colonial as fast as possible. She dared not mention José in the message, but she asked Lyda to collect all the blankets not in use and have Socrates bring them to the train station right away.

She left the depot and crossed the street to the local market. The flies swarmed as thickly as ever. Blue-jacketed soldiers were more numerous than ever. The place wasn't empty, but the goods looked as picked over as if it were late afternoon.

Grace bought every chicken, bundle of tortillas, and sack of corn-meal and beans she could find. She added serapes and shirts, jars of water, and whatever small items she thought might be useful for such a long journey. Hiring a man with a barrow to bring the goods back across the street lightened Grace's purse even more.

Lyda, Annie, and Socrates were unloading blankets from a station cab as Grace arrived with the supplies. The sight of Annie disconcerted her. The child mustn't find out about José and the cattle car, but how to explain the need for all those blankets?

"Gracie, have you been to the market alone?" Lyda asked

"It was safe. The place teems with soldiers."

Lyda made a face.

"What?"

"Rubio has ordered them to patrol the markets and prevent food from leaving Cuernavaca. He intends to starve out the villagers."

Starve out the villagers. Grace was appalled. And as usual with Rubio's tactics, it was having unplanned-for consequences. His current scheme had apparently affected the supply of food coming into the city as well as going out. Grace knew Rubio's lack of intellect well enough not to ask herself why that had not occurred to him.

Hardly able to see over the stacks of blankets, Grace, Lyda, and Socrates marched down the platform. Lyda glanced back at the barrow rolling along behind them.

"Why do you need blankets and all this truck?"

"They've taken Mr. Perez prisoner."

"Has something happened to Cora's father?" Annie looked distraught.

"They've captured José?" asked Lyda. "What did he do?"

"I don't know. None of them looks like an insurgent."

"None of them? How many are there, Gracie?"

"Seventy-five, maybe a hundred."

"Oh, dear lord."

Annie ran on ahead, down the platform stairs, and onto the gravel right-of-way. The brakemen had attached the stock car to the rear of the troop train waiting on the siding for the train's evening departure. When Grace and Lyda arrived, Annie was standing on the narrow ledge where the car's floor projected beyond the slatted sides. She had hooked her arm between two of the horizonal boards.

Annie looked at them with tears streaming down her cheeks. "Don't let them take Socorro's *papi* away."

"There's nothing we can do, Annie."

Annie hiked up her skirts and charged past before Lyda could grab her. With both fists she pounded on the chest of the nearest guard.

"¡Bruto! Chinga tu madre."

She accompanied the beating with an impressive assortment of slurs in English, Spanish, and Nahuatl. When she ran short in one language, she switched to another.

Grace stood frozen in horror, expecting the guard to knock the child senseless or skewer her with his bayonet. But he looked embarrassed and almost sad as he held up his arms to take the blows. Lyda grabbed Annie around the waist and pulled her away. Grace helped Lyda hold her as she kicked and wriggled.

"They're going to hang them all at Tres Marías," Annie wailed. "Don't let them kill Cora's *papi*."

"They're not going to kill him. They're taking him to another state."

The thought of the army executing José hadn't occurred to Grace. She had a stomach-churning image of returning from Mexico City and seeing him hanging among the bandits and rebels in the gnarled old tree near the crossroads.

Lyda distracted her daughter with a task. "Annie, your Injun talk is better than ours. Help distribute the beans and fixin's to the women up top there." She nodded at the families camped on the roof of the car. "They'll be cooking for the men."

Annie pulled the back hem of her skirt between her legs and knotted it to her belt in front to create trousers of a sort. She scrambled up the ladder to oversee the distribution of the supplies.

Lyda shoved the blankets and clothing through the openings between the slats while Grace kept the guards at bay with the last of the coins in her purse. Then she went back to bid José farewell.

He put a hand through the slats and grabbed her wrist. That he would touch her indicated the urgency of what he had to say. Grace thought, not for the first time, that José had the saddest, most luminous eyes in creation.

"*Mamacita,* promise me you will take the early train today."

"I will."

"Tell the *Americana* that she and her daughter must go also."

"I'll tell them."

The truth was, Grace had no money left for a ticket on the early train, much less for three tickets. She would have to postpone the trip until tomorrow, but she would not add to José's distress by telling him so.

Grace held on to José's hand. "God go with you, my friend."

"And with you, *Mamacita.*"

"Good-bye, *Papi.*" Annie clung to the slats so fiercely that Lyda and Grace had to pry her fingers off and pull her down from the car.

As Grace and Lyda led Annie away, Grace did not see Angel and Antonio climb up the rungs on the opposite side of the stock car. Nor did they see her.

The federal uniform Antonio wore and the army-issue Mauser he carried made him look the part of a soldier ordered to guard the women. Angel, dressed in skirt and blouse, handed up what appeared to be a baby wrapped in a shawl. She adjusted the large bundle slung across her back and climbed after him. She settled down to wait for evening and the troop train's departure.

Angel was counting on the government soldiers to be on guard against an attack from the ground, but not from above. If Angel's scheme worked, this would be the last train to leave Cuernavaca.

June 1913

The army of the South is entirely anarchistic in their ideas, confiscatory in their methods, and extremely arbitrary in their dealings.

—A. Bell

We were just poor people fighting for our stomachs. The talk of flag-waving and brotherhood came later from our suffering.

—Manuela Oaxaca Quinn (mother of Anthony Quinn)

45

K A - B O O M !

As the evening troop train left Cuernavaca, the women and children camped on top of the stock car sought relief from the late afternoon sun. They huddled under scraps of canvas, burlap feed sacks, articles of clothing, and palm fronds. A lucky few had umbrellas. They sat on their sleeping mats, but still they felt the heat of the corrugated steel roof under them.

By sunset the steel felt hot enough to toast tortillas, but Angel was grateful for a clear sky. Rain would have made blowing up the train more difficult, but blow it up she would.

The train made its usual slow progress across the valley and into the foothills. A full moon rose as darkness fell. Its orbit brought it as close to earth tonight as it ever came. It looked unnaturally large, as if it had defied the laws of the universe and left its usual orbit. It was so bright that its light cast shadows. Angel could see the pinks, purples, reds, and oranges of the bouganvillea flowers along the railbed.

The devout ones on the roof saw the moonlight as a sign that God was with them on this mission. Angel knew better. The Devil might approve, but she did not expect God to condone what she was about to do. She would have much to confess, if she ever met up with a priest again.

Angel had wrapped three eight-inch-long sticks of dynamite in oil-cloth before folding a shawl around them to make them look like a swaddled infant. She wore her blouse loose to hide the thirty-two-caliber Smith and Wesson revolver stuck into the back of her belt. She put the sticks of dynamite under her belt next to the pistol. Over her shoulder she slung a pouch containing a pair of homemade grenades. She draped another shawl around her to cover everything.

She crossed herself and grinned at Antonio. "If I miscalculate . . ."

"Ka-boom!" Antonio had learned the word when he worked for the American Mining Company.

The Americans laughed when they said "Ka-boom," but then, they weren't the ones setting the sticks and lighting the fuses down in the tunnels. Antonio had stolen this dynamite from that same mine, so the laugh, he said, was on the gringos.

Angel took a liking to the word "ka-boom" and it became a joke between them when they made bombs or deployed them. Now it didn't seem funny. If Angel's arsenal detonated too soon it would kill everyone on top of the stock car.

Behind the engine and wood tender came the first-class passenger car with the officers. Behind that were three freight cars filled with conscripts who had set up their own camp inside. The mail car rattled along between the last freight car and the stock car that held José and the other prisoners. This train had no caboose.

Before leaving the station Angel had sold tamales to the two soldiers assigned to guard the mail car. She had passed the time of day with them as they sat smoking in the open doorway. Behind them she could see the weapons and ammunition stored with the sacks of mail.

Those same two men were now sitting on top of the car. More soldiers should have been keeping watch up there, but the train was climbing up into the mountains now. No one wanted to be picked off by rebel snipers hiding in the heights. Under orders, guards would climb up top, then sneak back down through the trapdoors in the roofs as soon as their commanding officer settled into his first-class seat.

The men on top of the mail car were there in hopes of seeing the tamale seller named Angelina again. Angel guessed they were deciding which of them would be the first to invite Angelina into the mail car so he could enjoy her. She would have bet that they were also discussing how much they should pay her, and whether they need pay her at all.

Antonio kissed her. "Be careful, *mi Angelita*."

Angel kissed him back. "*De la muerte y de la suerte, no hay quien se escape.* There's no escaping death and fate."

Angel put a box of matches and a couple cigars in the pocket her friend Berta had sewed into her skirt. The folk of Berta's village had also agreed to let Angel's people pasture their horses and mules there. They would retrieve them when they finished this job.

Angel started for the front end of the car, stepping around the women and children. She could have tucked up her skirt, taken a running start, and leaped across to the mail car, but that would've alerted the guards that they might be getting more than they were preparing to bargain for.

She climbed down the rungs on the end of the stock car. Grasping the brakeman's handholds, she stepped across the gap with the tracks roaring past in a blur under her feet. Once on top of the mail car, she shrugged her shawl off the shoulder without the pouch of grenades and cocked a hip at a come-hither angle.

In the distance she saw the bulge of rock projecting like a parrot's head and beak. Beyond it was a railroad trestle spanning one of the many deep ravines. If Angel did not time everything perfectly they all would die, and the next charge she led would be through the gates of hell.

She took a deep breath and exhaled slowly. Her vision narrowed like a camera's aperture, but what she saw had a preternatural clarity. This was how she felt every time she raised her unit's flag and galloped into a battle.

As the two soldiers approached, Angel arched her back as though to relieve an ache. She had seen the women do it often to show off the breasts with which God had blessed and cursed them. In the process she put a hand on the rubber grip of her pistol, just for reassurance.

She would not use the revolver unless she had to. A gunshot wasn't like other sounds. The troops would hear it over the rumble, clatter, and creak of the train. They would come swarming up here.

Angel bantered with the two while she waited for the curve with a drop-off on one side. As it neared, she pulled one of the men close as though to kiss him. She pretended to lose her balance and shouldered him toward the abyss. He fell with his head and chest hanging over the edge of the roof.

When his friend bent to help him, Angel pushed him. She put her bare foot on the first man's backside and shoved as the train went into the curve. The centrifugal force of the turn sent both men flying over the edge of the cliff.

Antonio jumped the gap to join her while Serafina, Socorro, and nine other women and older girls lined up at the near end of the stock car. Angel slid back the trapdoor in the mail car's roof and peered in to make sure no one else occupied it. She lowered herself through it and handed Mauser rifles, full cartridge belts, and bandoleers of stripper-clips up to Antonio. He gave them to Serafina and the others, who buckled on the belts, slung the bandoleers over their shoulders, and passed the rifles to the rest of the women to hold.

Angel's first plan had been to detach the mail car, too. Antonio pointed out that the weight of two cars moving backward downhill might cause them to overshoot the level ground they were aiming for. There would be nothing to stop them from rolling back down into the valley.

When Angel had passed as many rifles, pistols, and cartridge belts through the trapdoor as everyone could carry, Antonio grasped her hands and hauled her out. He left her there and returned to the rear of the mail car to wait for her signal to climb down and separate the two cars.

Angel ran shoeless and light-footed along the roofs until she reached the front of the first-class car. Up ahead loomed the rock shaped like a parrot's head. It marked the site of the next part of her plan and it was speeding toward her.

Angel had thrown a lot of homemade bombs, but she had never handled dynamite. She did not know that what she was about to do was foolish to the point of suicidal. If she had known, she would have done it anyway. As her father's old *mayordomo*, Plinio, always said, no one lives forever.

She did know that each of the three slow fuses allowed a different time before ignition—ten seconds, twenty seconds, thirty seconds. She had to pitch them accurately and in the proper sequence. Accuracy was not a problem for Angel, and Antonio had tied one, two, or three pieces of string around each stick to indicate the order in which to throw them.

Angel struck a match. Turning to one side and hunching her shoulders to shield it from the wind, she lit a cigar. She enjoyed the first few puffs, flexing her knees and rocking in rhythm with the train.

She signaled Antonio to get ready to uncouple the stock car. As the train slowed down on its approach to the longest of the trestle bridges, Angel sucked on the cigar until the tip glowed a deep red. Her first target was the big, mushroom-shaped smokestack. If she missed it, she would have two more chances. Landing the explosive in the stack was the key to the enterprise.

The first stick with the slowest fuse made a perfect arc. It tumbled end over end in tight revolutions, and flew straight and vertical into the stack like sugarcane down a chute. From there it should be able to blow open the boiler.

As the train clattered onto the boards of the trestle Angel lobbed the second stick between the wood tender and the first-class passenger car. It should land on the trestle and go off as the freight cars passed over it. The third one she heaved over the engine and onto the tracks ahead.

She sprinted back along the train's roofs, pausing to light the fuses on the two grenades and drop them into the mail car. Enough ammunition remained down there to make a first-rate show, and she didn't want a front row seat.

She leaped onto the stock car as Antonio uncoupled it. Angel knew the topography of the railbed like the workings of her rifle. The stock car rolled backward down a gentle slope and around a curve. It came to a stop on level ground while three explosions knocked rocks loose to roll down the sides of the canyon. The ground shook, rattling the badly riveted sleepers that held the rails in place. The rails bucked and the stock car vibrated.

"Ka-boom," Angel murmured. She stood awestruck by a fireworks display like none she had ever witnessed.

Flames shot thirty feet above the outcrop between the train on the trestle and the runaway car. The blasts launched body parts, chunks of metal, splintered logs, and hot water from the boiler. Several drops of blood, blown by the wind, landed on Angel's arm. She wiped them onto her skirt.

She refused to give in to the weakness of remorse. The men who had belonged to those detached arms and legs and heads would have done the same to her. And they would have done it after they had waited patiently in line to rape her.

Antonio jimmied the lock on the stock car door with a crowbar. The women dumped out the dirt and grass and pieces of wood they had stuffed into their satchels and tied up into their shawls to make them look full of personal possessions. They replaced the bogus goods with the small arms and pouches of ammunition. They all buckled on as many cartridge belts and bandoliers as they could carry.

Angel led the exodus off the roof. She and Antonio, José, the prisoners, and their families shouldered the federal army's rifles and ran for cover among the trees and boulders. From there they would walk the three miles to the village where they had left their belongings and animals.

46

IN HOT WATER

Rico bore little resemblance to the cavalry officer he once had been. He was dirty and bearded. His clothes were torn and filthy. He wore his cartridge belt slung bandolier-style across his chest like any rebel or bandit. The brilliant light of the full moon didn't improve Rico's appearance, but it made Grullo's silver-gray coat glow until he looked supernatural.

The direct route to Ayala took Rico dangerously close to Tres Marías, but he was in no mood to waste time with a detour. With the moon this bright he could travel the winding sometimes-cobblestone road at night. Once he was south of Cuernavaca he would be in Zapata's home district. Running into Rubio's troops there would be even less likely than meeting a night patrol here. The *federales* conscripted so many *indios* as cannon fodder that they gave Rico at least one advantage. The *indios* firmly believed that witches, ghosts, shape-takers, and demons held dominion over the night, even one as brightly lit as this one.

At first Rico thought the distant explosions were thunder, but the moon still shimmered in a clear sky. Rico had heard many explosions in his year of patrolling the rails, but this was bigger than any of them. He assumed the blasts came from the train tracks. Nothing else in these mountains merited blowing up.

He headed for a vantage point where he could see the tracks. Soon he could follow the glow in the sky. By the time he found an overlook, soldiers from the barracks were searching for survivors in the wreckage of the last freight car that had advanced only halfway out onto the trestle. Judging from the blanket-shrouded bodies laid out in a line in the moonlight, they weren't recovering many. Rico figured most of the casualties were conscripts. The dead among them all would be dumped into a hastily dug trench. The Army did not consider rank-and-file corpses worth the bother of identifying.

The *indios* probably had been transported from the northern states. Their faraway loved ones might never know what had become of them. Rico took off his hat and prayed for their souls.

From this height he could see the extent of the damage. The trestle ended in splinters about a third of the way across the canyon. What remained was on fire. The engine and wood tender had run off into the abyss and lay on their sides among the boulders in the river eight hundred feet down. The passenger and freight cars were stove in, burning, and hanging cantilevered out into thin air. The wind carried the smell of charred wood, blood, and cordite.

Rico wondered if Hanibal, the engineer, had been in the engine's cab tonight. If so, he almost certainly lay at the bottom of the canyon with his beloved *elefante,* the locomotive.

The rebels' homemade explosives could not have caused this much destruction. They must have used dynamite. He wondered who had done it. The usual suspects would include Lieutenant Angel's men, but Mother Merced said they were on their way to Ayala. With Grace.

Rico wanted to help the wounded, but if he went down there the soldiers would open fire. All of them would want to collect the five-hundred-*peso* reward that Rubio had offered. Hell, any wounded survivors able to pick up a gun would try to shoot him.

His reasoning eased the conscience that knew the truth. He was relieved to have an excuse to continue on toward Ayala.

Rico had a long way to ride, but at dawn he could not pass up the hot spring bubbling up in a natural pool among the rocks. He didn't know if he would have another chance to make himself a bit more presentable for his reunion with Grace.

He turned Grullo loose to graze on the grass, lush and hip-high from the summer's rains. He leaned his rifle against the trunk of a nearby cedar and laid his gun belt and Colts on the rock rim of the spring. He undressed and climbed into the hot water.

He rinsed out his shirt, socks, and underwear and spread them to dry on the rocks. He laid his head against the rim, closed his eyes, and let the sun warm his face. It glowed behind the translucent lids of his eyes and filled his head with light. The warmth of the water took him back to Grace's rooms and the times they had shared the big bathtub there.

The clatter and slam of a rifle bolt jerked him out of his revery. He grabbed his Colts, but saw more than one muzzle glinting among the boulders above him. All of them pointed in his direction.

"Do not be stupid, friend." A woman sat astride a big mule. The butt of her Remington rested on her thigh. The rifle barrels withdrew and a few minutes later twenty-three more women rode up behind her.

Rico didn't have to be introduced to know who she was. People in this district called her *La Gata,* The Cat. When fighters in the rebel forces were killed, their women usually set up housekeeping with other men. Some widows, however, chose to become combatants themselves. *La Gata* and her followers had decided to avenge their men.

Their definition of revenge included stealing from the rich whenever they had the chance. For the most part they dressed in the same khaki pants and shirts as the men, but each one accessorized in her own way. A few of them carried parasols. Others wore skimmers, boaters, and merry widow hats adorned with plumes and enough flowers for an arboretum.

They had on an assortment of army boots and patent-leather shoes, silk scarves, and at least one feather boa. All of that was topped with bandoliers and cartridge belts. The variety of their weapons went from *La Gata's* rolling block rifle with a pistol grip stock to a flintlock pistol that must have belonged to someone's great-great-grandfather.

Still sitting in the water, Rico reached for his trousers. A bullet from *La Gata's* Remington richocheted off the pool's rim.

"We like you better as God created you." She stood in the stirrups to assess his equipment.

The women debated whether to shoot him or make a slave of him, but all of them agreed that they would take his money.

"I have no money," he said.

"You have a fine horse, *cabrón*."

"You can't take him."

La Gata laughed so hard her breasts jounced on either side of her bandoliers like children at piñata party. "And who will stop me?"

"I will." The voice was accompanied by a breech bolt slamming home.

The young man sat on a ledge with his legs dangling, his sombrero pushed back on his head. His Winchester rested on his thigh as though he knew he could shoot *La Gata* without the effort of lifting it.

"He belongs to us, Angel," shouted *La Gata*.

"General Zapata would not approve of wasting a healthy young fellow hauling wood and servicing a flock of whores."

More men appeared and stood on the outcrops around Angel.

La Gata hadn't survived this long by giving in easily. "Maybe Zapata prefers to have us beauties fight alongside him than a gang of smelly *pendejos* like you."

"We will take him."

"And may he bring you bad luck." *La Gata* also knew when she was bested. "We've no use for his little thing anyway. It's the size of a rooster's."

Rico opened his mouth to dispute that, thought better of it, and closed it again.

La Gata spat in Rico's direction, then reined her horse around and rode away with her women following.

Rico's shirt was only damp now. He used it to dry off before he pulled on his leather trousers.

"I would say his thing is bigger than a rooster's," Angel observed to his men. "It's at least as big as a goose's."

Rico put on his shirt and vest and picked up his weapons. Nothing Angel said could bother him. He was a happy man.

He had found Lieutenant Angel, or to be exact, Lieutenant Angel had found him. Grace must be camped with the women of the band somewhere close by.

Rico held on to Grullo's reins and waited for the rebels to converge on him in a shower of gravel. Angel hooked a khaki-clad leg over the saddle's pommel and pointed the Winchester in his general direction.

"I recognize you," Angel said. "You're one of Fatso's bastards."

"Fatso would rather hang me than you."

"That's right," Angel said. "I hear Fatso is offering a reward."

Rico wasn't worried much. He doubted that Angel would ride to Rubio's headquarters and demand the five hundred *pesos*.

"I'm looking for an Englishwoman," he said. "Her name is Grace Knight. People say she rides with you."

"We know nothing of an Englishwoman." Angel turned to his partners in crime. "Shall we hang him or let him go free to search for his *gringa?*"

They gathered for a conference. The jury did not deliberate long.

Angel turned back to Rico. "They vote to hang you."

47

CIRCLING THE WAGONS

Grace worried too much about José to sleep much. She heard the bell on the front door jangle just after dawn. Whoever wanted in was insistent.

Tradesmen went to the back door and the hour was too early for train arrivals. Grace herself wouldn't leave for the station for two hours to go to Mexico City to see President Huerta. She dressed quickly and hurried downstairs.

Leobardo looked worried. "They say they are policemen and they have a warrant to search for contraband."

He stood aside so Grace could peer through the barred window in the door. The five men standing outside did have on the blue jackets and khaki trousers of Cuernavaca's police force, but something about them looked amiss. The city's policemen took great pride in their appearance. Their uniforms were always starched, pressed, and tailored. Their white gloves were pristine.

These men's trousers had horizontal creases above the knees where they had hung drying over a line. The men's smiles fit them as badly as the jackets. Grace suspected they had snagged the clothes from a laundress. The police didn't hang their service pistols out to dry, which made them less accessible. These men were trying to hide their machetes behind their backs.

One of them held up a smudged paper with a red wax seal in the lower left-hand corner.

"*¿Qué pasa?*" Socrates joined Grace and Leobardo.

"They say they have an order to search the Colonial."

"*Banditos.*" Socrates sized them up with a glance. "*Asesinos. Sinvergüenzas.* Assassins. Shameless ones."

What irked Grace most was that the thieves thought her stupid enough to fall for their ruse.

When the doors didn't swing open, the leader of the gang shouted threats. Grace knew a woman's voice would carry little authority for the likes of them. She turned to ask Socrates to tell them to go away, but he had disappeared. Muttering a few expletives of her own, she started off to look for him. Halfway across the courtyard she saw him trotting toward her with her shotgun in his hand.

"You can't shoot them." Grace did not want corpses piled up at the door and a mob of real policemen clogging the lobby. She imagined reams of official forms to fill out. "You might hit an innocent passerby."

"Don't worry, *Mamacita.*"

When the men heard Socrates pump the shotgun they started backing away. He poked the muzzle between the window's bars, aimed slightly over their heads, and fired. The blast would have riffled their hair if it hadn't been plastered down with handfuls of grease. They skulked off shouting promises to return with the army.

"I doubt that," Grace muttered. What was left of the federal army in Cuernavaca rarely left their barracks.

"Shall I open the doors, *Mamacita?*" Leobardo put a hand on the rope that lifted the big beam from across the massive gates.

Leobardo's first official act each morning was to open the doors wide. Masses of crimson bougainvillea framed the doorway and the splashing fountain and luxuriant greenery in the cool courtyard beyond the entryway. The open doors were more than a ploy to lure in travelers. Grace considered them her contribution to the beauty of Cuernavaca.

She had a subtler reason for wanting them open. She never lost hope that Rico would find his way back to her, in spite of all Rubio's threats. She feared if he did return and found the doors closed, he would assume she had left the city, and would turn away.

Grace looked through the barred window. The area was clear except

for the men sweeping the plaza with their big push brooms. She nodded to Leobardo to raise the beam and open the doors. Lyda, Annie,
and Jake McGuire were the first to walk through them.

Annie's eyes were still red from crying over José. Lyda looked ashen.
Grace wondered what news could possibly be worse than Rico threatened with execution and José sent into exile.

"What's happened?"

Jake took off his Stetson, ran his long, knobby fingers through his
hair. "Zapata's rabble has blown up the troop train."

"Was anyone hurt?" asked Grace.

"I don't know. The lines are all down. I just heard it from someone
who rode down from Tres Marías last night."

"They've killed Socorro's *papi* and the other poor prisoners," sobbed
Annie. "They've blown them up."

Lyda tried to reassure her. "We don't know that."

"The rebels have damaged the tracks before," said Grace.

"Not like this. I hear the main trestle's destroyed. I'm putting together
a convoy to take the company's executives and their families to Em Cee.
We have horses, mules, a truck, and a Gatling gun. You and Lyda and the
young 'un can come with us."

"I thank you for the offer, Mr. McGuire, but I cannot leave the
Colonial."

"Miss Grace, I'm all for loyalty and commerce. But the time has
come to pack your possibles, kick out the cook fire, and decamp."

"I won't leave my staff."

"Hell, they'll be the ones sacking the place as soon as your heels clear
the lintel."

"They will not!"

Jake was a good fellow at heart and a droll one, but he had that per-
nicious American sense of superiority over Mexicans, and everyone else
for that matter.

Grace had to admit that she didn't have complete confidence in the
people of her adopted country either. She assumed that if she abandoned the Colonial, the local folk would swarm in. They would smash

what they could not steal and set fire to the rest. The fact that her staff believed the same thing didn't make her feel any less hypocritical.

Grace didn't expect Jake to understand her reluctance to leave. He was a wildcatter for the oil company. He moved from place to place and felt beholden to nowhere. His job was to destroy the landscape, and he did it with matter-of-fact efficiency. But Grace tried to explain herself anyway.

"We have guests staying here," she said. "And army officers."

"If the guests are smart they'll come with us. The soldiers can fend for themselves."

"My mind is made up, Mr. McGuire. Thank you all the same."

"Well then, Lyda May, pack your things and Annie's. I'll meet you at the house in an hour. You two can ride Duke."

Annie crossed her arms and planted her feet. "I won't leave without Aunt Grace."

Lyda tucked her wild blond hair behind her ears, stood behind her daughter, and put her arms around her. "We'll stay here a while longer."

Jake blew out his breath in exasperation. "I have to get those starched collars to Em Cee. As soon as they're safely stowed, I'll come back and help you circle the wagons and hold off the hostiles."

Grace smiled at him. He was gallant in his own thorny, Texas way.

"What do you ladies have in the way of firepower?" he asked.

Grace retrieved the Winchester Ninety-Seven pump shotgun and boxes of ammunition. She had had the gunsmith cut the barrel down to her specifications. Antonio Perez had told her that if she didn't mind ruining the plaster on the wall, this was the best weapon to keep under the bed. "Just point it in the general direction and squeeze the trigger."

Jake hefted it, inspected it, then nodded and gave it back. "Will you use this should the occasion arise, Mrs. Knight?"

"I will."

Jake gave Lyda a quick kiss on the forehead and patted Annie on the head.

His bashfulness about kissing in public amused Grace. For all his bravado, she suspected Jake McGuire had a streak of shyness where women were concerned. Lyda agreed. She once had observed to Grace that cowboys only feared two things: being set afoot, and a good woman.

Jake put three fingertips to the brim of his Stetson and gave them a flick that was part salute, part wave. He swiveled on the tall heels of his cowboy boots and left. Grace and Lyda stood in the doorway and watched him walk across the zócalo. They both liked to watch long, lanky Jake walk. Annie said he looked like he had a pair of stilts in the legs of his dungarees.

Annie headed for the kitchen to see what María had prepared for breakfast.

When she was out of hearing, Grace said, "You and Annie should go with him, Lyda."

"The Colonial weathered the 1910 uprising. We can wait this one out."

"This is different."

"What do you mean?"

"Zapata has vowed to keep on fighting, no matter what."

"Maybe Zapata could be president."

Grace shook her head. "Too many men with ambition and no conscience are arrayed against him. He will always be an ignorant *indio* to those in power."

Annie returned peeling a banana and Grace changed the subject.

"Jake does have a point," Grace said. "Maybe the time has come to circle the wagons, as they say in the moving pictures. You and Annie should stay here. Goodness knows, we have room."

"What about Duke?"

"Bring your horse, too. He can keep the hotel mule company."

Annie and Lyda exchanged looks.

"He'll be safe," said Grace. "Socrates sleeps in the stable."

"Duke won't come down," said Annie.

"Down from where?"

"My bedroom." Annie rushed to assure Grace that they hadn't put Duke in solitary confinement. "The landlady loaned us her goat to keep him company."

"We think they're in love," said Lyda.

"Annie, your bedroom is on the second floor. What's he doing up there?"

"We didn't want anyone to eat him. We don't want anyone to eat the goat either."

48

A HIGH HORSE

Lyda's old horse, Duke, proved that what goes up does not necessarily come down. Annie led him to the top of the stairs at the end of the corridor outside her bedroom. There, he planted his front hooves and rocked back on his haunches.

He weighed almost three times as much as Annie, Lydia, Grace, and Socrates combined, so hauling on his lead line and shoving on his caboose proved futile. All of their reassurances, bribes, and cajolery couldn't persuade him to risk plummeting headfirst to the flagstones of the courtyard. He also refused to back down them.

The house that Lyda rented was a modest one made of the local volcanic stone with terra-cotta tiles on the roof. It was built in a square around a small, weed-grown courtyard. The exterior stairway leading from the courtyard to the second-floor corridor was wide but steep.

Grace assumed that if Duke had been born with two legs, he would have become a philosopher. He stood at the top of the stairs and gazed down at Lyda and Grace in that thoughtful way of his. Lyda called up to Annie.

"Send his girlfriend down. Maybe he'll follow her."

Annie ran inside and reappeared leading the goat. Lyda waved an ear of corn at her and the goat almost fell head over hooves in her hurry to reach it. Duke looked stricken by her betrayal.

He threw his muzzle into the air and neighed as if his heart were breaking. He shifted his soulful gaze to Lyda, rolled back his lips, and whinnied so long and loudly that passersby looked in at the open gate to see what the commotion was about.

"Try putting a towel over his eyes," suggested Lyda.

Annie shook her head. "He might fall and break a leg if he can't see."

"Miserable damned cayuse." Lyda planted her fists on her hips and glared up at him. "Hammer-headed, cat-hammed plug."

"I thought you knew about horses, Lyda, you being a cowgirl from Texas."

Lyda swiveled her gaze to Grace, then resumed her stare down with Duke. "We don't stable them in the attic in Texas, Gracie."

"I have an idea."

"Then have at it, because I'm plumb out of ideas."

"Plums have something to do with it. Annie, come down here, please."

Annie scampered down the stairs, took the handful of dried plums, and listened while Grace whispered in her ear. With food so scarce, even fruit was precious, but not so valuable as Duke.

Annie went back to the second floor to confabulate with her love. He pricked his ears forward and listened intently. Annie held a plum out over the outer half wall of the stairwell. Duke's muzzle followed until he was standing sideways on the landing and no longer looking straight down. She gave him the plum, moved down a step, and held out another, still over the edge of the wall. Duke sidestepped to put one hoof on the first step, then the other, and craned to reach the treat.

Annie moved backward and lured him down another step so that his rear hooves had to follow. Crab-stepping sideways, with his neck still over the wall, he and Annie reached the courtyard. Annie hugged him.

"What made you think of that, Gracie?" asked Lyda.

"The back stairs of the theater where my parents worked were steep and dark. When I was a very young girl I imagined hellfire and Old Scratch waiting for me at the bottom. The only way I could descend was to hold on to the rail, step sideways, and not look down."

As Annie led Duke out into the street, Grace scanned the neighborhood. She noticed that a few other horses and mules were looking out of second-floor windows. She wondered how their owners intended to get them back down to earth.

Socrates tied Duke's lead to the back of the hired victoria cab and loaded his tack and sacks of feed into the boot. He helped Grace, Lyda, and Annie up the steps, then climbed in next to the driver. He braced the shotgun on his knee with the muzzle in the air, clearly visible to anyone with evil intentions.

Three samples of the skulking sort formed a clot on a corner and watched them pass. The wide brims of their hats shaded their eyes, but Grace could tell they were deciding how best to attack the taxi. The sight of them saddened more than alarmed her.

Grace had always felt safe in Cuernavaca, except for a brief time at the beginning of the rebel army's occupation of the city in 1911. And then she only had to go to Zapata's headquarters in the Governor's Palace and protest the rowdy behavior of some of his men toward her chambermaids. The problems ceased.

From time to time, in the back courtyard, Socrates still told the story of when *Mamacita* pushed her way past Zapata's heavily armed guards and demanded an audience. Socrates had gone with her. He said he had been sure they both would end up shot, skewed on bayonets, and carved into little pieces by machetes.

Grace wished that a word in some official's ear would make things right these days. Besides waylaying cars and carriages, the usual methods for today's thieves were armed break-ins, kidnapping, and snatch-and-run. Sometimes they took their victims' money, jewelry, and clothes and let them go, but now and then the rays of the rising sun fell across dead bodies in the bottoms of the ravines.

Lyda pointed her derringer at these banditti and gave them the look she called "arsenic and chained lightning." They ducked into an alleyway.

Lyda watched them go. "Why is it that the bad eggs tarry after the decent folk exit?"

" 'Opportunity makes a thief.' "

Annie looked ready to throw rocks at them. "Thieves aren't getting Duke!"

Lyda put an arm around her, maybe to comfort her, maybe to keep her from yelling at the men and irritating them. "You know what President Lincoln once said."

"What did he say?"

"When he heard that Confederates had captured a brigadier-general and a number of horses, he said, 'Well, I'm sorry for the horses.' The Secretary of War exclaimed, 'Sorry for the horses, Mr. President!' 'Yes,' said Lincoln. 'I can make a brigadier-general in five minutes, but it is not easy to replace a hundred and ten horses.'"

Now that Duke was safe, Annie settled back against the seat. She had heard that the prisoners had escaped when the troop train blew up. Now that Socorro's father was safe and her horse could stay at the Colonial with her, Annie was happy.

Lyda went on chatting as though war and disaster weren't breathing down their necks, but Grace didn't relax until she saw the graceful roof of the bandstand among the greenery of the zócalo. The zócalo meant home. It was an oasis of tranquility, a remnant of gentility.

She dismissed Jake's dire predictions about the train no longer running. Mexicans would take their time about it, but they could repair anything. She wondered how long the rail crews would require to fix this latest damage.

The worst part of it was the cruel murder of so many people. She was glad that José and the others had escaped, but she had a feeling that Angel was the cause of those deaths.

In the rebel camp, Grace had seen Angel gambling, smoking cigars, swearing, and washing down dashes of gunpowder with tequila. But that wasn't her parting image of her. Grace hoped she was wrong, but she feared she wasn't. She wondered how that sweet-faced young woman could have commited such a heartless act.

49

The men of Angel's company had gathered in a big circle for a spirited game of dice. At stake were Rico's boots and horse, his saddle, rifle, and Navy five-shooters. They were so intent on the outcome that they seemed to have forgotten their primary chore for the day.

Rico's own troops relished hangings, so he was not surprised that the rebels did, too. What did surprise him was how heavily the noose dragged on his neck. The rope was thick enough to anchor a ship. His captors were taking no chances that it would break.

Rico wanted to scratch where the coarse hemp itched, but his hands were tied behind his back. Astride his horse, he scanned the surrounding peaks for the glint of a rifle barrel or the flash of a signal mirror. This would be a good time for Juan to arrive with a troop of cavalry. But by now Juan was probably in a cantina in Coahuila, drinking tequila and winning money from a whole new crop of second lieutenants.

Rico even would have welcomed Rubio. Fatso would be easier to outwit than the rebels.

One of the men tied a knot in the other end of the rope as weight. When he threw it, the knot arced over a limb and hit the horse's nose on its way down. Grullo half-reared, then crow-hopped. The rebels had taken Rico's saddle, tack, and weapons, so he had no stirrups. He tightened his knees to keep from pitching off backward and ending the show before it started.

Lieutenant Angel sauntered over. "If you join us, *muchacho,* you will live . . ." Angel shrugged. ". . . or at least we will not be the ones to kill you."

"No one lives forever."

Even though the lieutenant had called a vote to decide Rico's fate, he had the feeling that Angel wasn't in favor of hanging a possible recruit. Rico could empathize. Leading was often a case of being pushed from behind.

He tried one more time to find out where Grace was. The information would be of no use to him now, but he did not want to die without knowing she was safe.

"Mother Merced told me the Englishwoman rode with you."

"Do you see her here, *cabrón?*"

"I think you know where she is."

"You should save your breath to beg God to forgive you for your sins, Captain." Angel stalked off to sit on a rock, smoke a cigar, and stare out at the valley below.

With the disposition of Rico's worldly goods decided, the rebels returned to the task at hand. He ignored their taunts and jokes as they cut switches to whip his horse out from under him. Several of them hauled on the rope, pulling the noose taut under his chin and cutting off air to his windpipe. He gripped more tightly with his knees and raised up to create enough slack to breathe.

A couple of the men lashed at the horse. Grullo fidgeted and sidestepped but he refused to run. Muttering an oath, one of them pulled his old forty-five from a tooled holster worn low, gunslinger style.

Grullo's new owner stepped in front of him. "*Pendejo,* don't kill my horse!"

The first man fired just behind Grullo's head. The bullet tore a chunk from his ear and he bolted. The horse, the earth, and everything solid and dependable shot out from under Rico. Lights exploded like pinwheel fireworks at a festival.

As the brilliance blinked out, blackness engulfed him. Pain radiated from his cowlick to his calluses. Maybe he should have used the last fraction of a second of his life to rehearse what he would say to his Maker, or to the Devil, but only one regret resonated.

He would never hold Grace in his arms again.

Rico couldn't convince his eyes to open, but the fingers pressing against his neck must belong to Grace. Who else would dare lay hands on him?

"My dove," Rico murmured, "I've searched for you."

"I lack the equipment for flying, *Capitán*. Lucky for you I didn't arrive a blink of an eye later."

The voice arrived echoing and distorted, as if shouted down a mine shaft.

Rico assumed he lay at the bottom of that shaft. He opened his eyelids a slit, then closed them again. The sun shone too intensely for a mine, and the leaves of the gallows tree shimmered in a kaleidoscope of green and gold.

José hunkered next to him, his arm half extended from checking for a pulse in Rico's bruised and bloody neck. Rico sat up. When the landscape stopped spinning he brought José into focus. Antonio, Serafina, and Socorro stood behind him.

"Am I dead, *amigo*?"

"Do I look like St. Peter, *Capitán*?"

Rico laid his fingers on the long, curved abrasion the noose had left on his neck. He gave a jerk of his chin toward Angel's sullen, disheveled pack of ne'er-do-wells lounging in the shade and picking their teeth with their big knives.

"One look at those devils made me think I'd died and gone to the hotter place."

Rico levered his aching body onto its feet as if just learning the knack of it. He put a hand on Grullo's back to steady himself. He must have been unconscious for quite a while. Someone had curried him until he gleamed in the sunshine.

They also had replaced his saddle and bridle. Rico unwound the reins from the pommel and stuck a boot into the stirrup. He tried to swing onto his horse but blacked out again. José and Antonio caught him as he pitched backward.

He awoke propped up in a sitting position and leaning against the front wall of a cave. Lieutenant Angel, Antonio, and José sat eating nearby. Angel was defending the decision to hang him.

"I recognized him, José. He led the charge out of the cattle car when we attacked the train last year. His men almost killed us. And I have seen him among the soldiers at Tres Marías."

"He's the man who saved my daughter from Rubio."

Angel shrugged. "I didn't know that."

Serafina handed Rico a tortilla with a few beans rolled up in it. Rico couldn't remember his last meal. He ate it in two bites.

He started to ask for another, then looked around. He saw no sacks of corn nor beans. The men and women were thin. The children had the potbellied, bright-eyed, brittle-haired look of malnutrition.

"*Señora* King is safe in Mexico City, *Capitán,*" José said. "I spoke to her the day she left on the train."

If Grace was in Mexico City, then Cuernavaca no longer concerned Rico. He wanted to ask José if she was well when he spoke to her. He wanted to ask if she had mentioned him.

"Where will you go now?" asked José.

"The capital."

"Permit me to speak frankly, *Capitán.*"

Rico nodded.

"Huerta's informants are everywhere, and Rubio has posted a reward for your death. If word reaches them that you are with *Señora* Knight, they might imprison her as an accomplice." José didn't have to add what would happen to Grace in jail.

"You're a *guacho,* an orphan like us." Angel waved a hand at the men playing cards and napping. "Huerta has screwed all of us poor people and now he's screwing rich ones like you, *Don* Rico."

Rico ignored him. He led Grullo upstream from where the women were bathing and washing clothes. He took a wooden box from the bottom of his saddlebag and turned Grullo loose to graze.

The box contained a pen, an ink bottle that was not quite empty, and Grace's last letter to him. He sat in the shade of an overhanging cypress. Using the box as a desk, he wrote on the reverse side of the Grace's letter. He wrote a lot, but it all came down to a simple message. He told her he loved her. He folded it and put it back into the envelope in which it had arrived.

If he was killed on the way to Mexico City, maybe this would reach her. All he had to do was live long enough to find a muleteer or charcoal seller, a *pulque* dealer or market-bound farmer to deliver it.

"*Capitán Martín.*"

An old mule approached with Serafina and Socorro on his back. José and Antonio walked alongside. Serafina dismounted and held out a banana leaf with a handful of salve on it.

"This is for the mark of the rope."

"Thank you."

Socorro gave him a bright red bandana. It had been freshly laundered and had that new-cut grass smell about it from the soap they had used. The aroma always reminded him of his Zapotec nurse.

Rico tied the bandana around his neck. It would come in handy. The red mark of a noose was a badge of honor in some places, but in others it could get him hanged all over again.

"Are you well, Socorro?" he asked.

"Yes, sir."

Rico had never grown a beard before. It felt like a thicket had sprouted on his face. He had developed a recent habit of rubbing its wiry nap whenever he pondered something.

He rubbed his jaw now and surveyed the mule. The beast was spindle-hipped, sway backed, and bucktoothed, but his eyes had the wily glint of a partner-in-crime. That appealed to Rico.

"José, I want to exchange Grullo for the mule."

"We are poor people, *Capitán*. We cannot accept such a gift."

"Then consider him a loan."

Socorro handed Rico the mule's reins. "We call him Moses."

Moses. A good name. A good omen.

Angel approached as if she just happened along. "You understand why we were going to hang you, don't you, *guacho,* foundling?"

"I'm the enemy."

"Enemy no more." Angel held out a hand and after a moment's hesitation, Rico shook it.

It was a remarkably small hand. It reminded Rico that wars were started by the old, but fought by the young. The lieutenant didn't appear to be more than seventeen.

"You look familiar. When were you at Tres Marías?"

Angel took off the wide-brimmed hat. Her hair reached almost to her shoulders. She laughed at the surprise on Rico's face.

"You sold candy on the train platform," he said.

"Your friend Juan claimed he was crazy with love for me."

"He spoke half the truth. He is crazy."

Angel threw her head back and laughed.

It was such a melodic, carefree laugh that Rico wondered how he could have mistaken her for a man. As a rule, most people saw what they wanted to see, but Rico didn't like to think of himself as most people.

"I have a proposition for you." Angel stuffed her hair back under her hat. "Come with us and we'll help you find your *Inglesa.*" She held up a hand before Rico could refuse. "Fatso's men are thick as fleas, and he's put a lot of money on your head." She grinned. "I'm tempted to turn you in myself."

"Answer this. Did your people blow up the troop train?"

"I blew up the train." She pointed a finger at the tip of her own nose. "It was carrying José and a hundred other men to die of starvation and hard labor in the jungle."

"Innocent civilians died. Women and maybe children."

"War is war. If they rode on a troop train they were not innocent."

Rico knew there was no effective rebuttal for that. When fat, pampered leaders bragged of victories, of villages occupied, of enemies killed or taken prisoner, they left out the most important statistic. How many young souls had been hardened by the brutality of it all? And more important, would they be able to regain their humanity when this was all over?

"I will not shoot my former comrades-in-arms," he said.

"To hell with you then, *cabrón.*" But she kept smiling.

"If God and the Devil wish it." Rico remembered something Grace used to say. "Heaven for the scenery. Hell for the company."

The railroad had put a lot of mule drivers out of business, but not all of them. Rico heard the familiar jingle of a bell mare from around a bend in the high, narrow trail. Maybe he could persuade them to deliver the letter to Grace. He urged Moses into a faster walk.

The five mules and three drivers ambled along the windswept height as if it were a broad thoroughfare. As Rico caught up with them he heard the creak of hempen ropes and leather packs over the song and banter of the men. The muleteers wore wide-brimmed leather hats, rawhide leggings, thorn-torn serapes, and dusty sandals.

They listened to Rico's request to deliver the letter and the offer of his last two *pesos*.

"Is this for a woman?" they asked.

"It is."

"Then put away your money. We will do it in the name of love."

Rico mounted Moses and rode on ahead of the pack train. When they had dropped back out of hearing range, Rico felt the urge to sing. He would serenade Grace with a ballad when he saw her, but what came to mind now was something totally different.

He belted out his alma mater's fight song at full volume. A choir of mountain echoes accompanied him.

" 'Ten thousand men of Harvard want victory today.' "

50

THE BANK OF PITY

Rico had always viewed the outskirts of Mexico City from a train window. He knew the streets were a maze, but he had never navigated them on foot, much less on the back of a shambling, talkative mule. He stopped to ask directions at a small general store in a tree-shaded village that the expanding metropolis would swallow any day now and spit out in unrecognizable form.

The store owner, with his long, thin nose, stiff bristle of hair, and skinny legs, reminded Rico of an amiable rooster. When Rico asked if he would like to buy a mule his eyes lit up.

"God has sent you." He looked as if he would leap the counter and plant a kiss on Rico's bearded cheek. "My mule has just died."

He assured Rico that Moses would only be required to pull a delivery cart. "And not many deliveries at that," he said sadly. "The people suffer, but what cannot be remedied must be endured."

Rico guessed that what they endured was President Huerta. *"Por cada cochino gordo llega su Sábado,"* he said. "Every fat pig ends up as a main course on Saturday."

Rico unsaddled Moses and turned him loose in the pasture next to the store. Moses wasn't interested in tender farewells. He lost no time getting down to the business of grazing.

As Rico left he glanced at his reflection in the store's front window. He stared into the deep-set eyes of a filthy, bearded stranger wearing a

beggar's clothes. He resolved not to appear at the Mendozas' door looking like Lazarus the leper.

The sale of Moses brought enough money for cab fare with a little
left over, and Rico decided to treat himself. He let the horse-drawn
cabs pass him by and hailed a traffic-scarred Ford Model T touring car
with FOR HIRE painted in black letters on the passenger-side wind-
screen. He was surprised when the driver yanked and pressed the lever
and pedal to brake the car and put it in neutral. If Rico had been at the
wheel he wouldn't have stopped for anyone who looked like him. He
climbed into the backseat and relaxed for the first time in longer than
he could remember. He had three stops to make before he could see
Grace.

"Take me to Uncle's."

"*Sí, señor.*"

Rico didn't doubt the driver would know what he meant. The official name of the national pawnshop was *El Monte de Piedad,* the Bank
of Pity, but everyone called it "Uncle."

The prospect of seeing Grace preoccupied Rico, and he hardly heard
the blare of car horns and the clang of trolley bells. Wheeled traffic increased and the buildings loomed four and five stories high. He had
become a stranger in a familiar land, out of place among the brown
suits, starched collars, glossy shoes, and derby hats. The Ford chugged
past the elegant restaurants and cantinas where Rico used to meet his
friends. Posh was what Grace had called them.

He stepped down from the taxi's running board at the northwest corner of the main plaza. In front of him stood the majestic stone building
that housed the Bank of Pity. Spanish monks had founded it in 1775 to
help the poor, but it lent money to anyone with something to leave as
collateral. The well-to-do and the middling classes came here, too. Rico
and his army comrades had often gone to Uncle's for cash to cover gambling debts.

The Bank's employees made swift appraisals of every sort of object
imaginable, then handed over cash for thirty percent of the value. If
the goods weren't redeemed at a low rate of interest within a month they

went up for sale. Tens of thousands of items, from diamonds to cellos to grindstones, filled the cavernous building.

Rico went straight to the far corner of the mezzanine where firearms were displayed, and pawned the only things of value remaining. When he left Uncle's he felt odd without the weight of his tooled leather belt and the Colts in their holsters.

He would have to do his shopping in the sprawling cacophony known as the Thieves' Market. No one there would question a bedraggled beggar with cash in his pocket. Not everything for sale in the Thieves' Market had been stolen, but a lot of it had. Even pilfered crosses, chalices, and church vestments turned up there.

Its apparel section encompassed several city blocks. Tiers of garments hung from lines stretched overhead, like a grove of clothes in a season of abundant rains. Rico hurried through the ranks of army uniforms, dangling in ranks as if on gravity-defying parade. Rust-colored patches of dried blood stained many of them.

They reminded Rico of a story he had heard. Late in 1910, then-President Porifiro Díaz received a box from one of the Revolution's generals. The box contained a dozen federal army uniforms, tattered and bloody, but neatly folded. The note that came with it said, "We are returning the husks. Send us more tamales."

Beyond the uniforms hung clusters of twills, tweeds, and herringbones. Rico stopped to admire a handsome white linen Palm Beach suit. On the counter below, the shopkeeper had laid out a pale blue cambric shirt, red silk four-in-hand tie, crisp white funnel collar, silk socks, patent leather shoes, and a jaunty fedora.

They tempted him, but he remembered how Grace once had described the New World's mania for Old World fashions. "Why do Mexican gents dress like whifling Brit stiffs when they cut such a smashing dash in their own duds?" She had surveyed him in his dark blue army tunic, then kissed him. "But a uniform, my love," she had added in her for-Rico-only voice, "a uniform is honey to ants in any language."

Rico couldn't wear a captain's uniform, but he could cut a smashing dash in the next best thing.

. . .

Rico left the public bath clean, beardless, and with well-scrubbed teeth.
Over a white cotton shirt and red cumberbund he wore a waist-length
deerskin jacket with silver buttons. His tight leather trousers were open
from knee to ankle at the side of each leg. Their rawhide laces exposed
the loose white cotton pants underneath. The flared hems broke grace-
fully across the sheen of his half-boots. As for the silver buttons that
marched in military order up each side of the pants, he had polished
them until he could see his freshly shaven chin reflected in them. His
flat-brimmed black felt hat was the sort matadors wore.

He walked to the Mendozas' white stucco mansion, but when he
pulled the cord on the brass bell at the front gate his heart pounded as if
he had run all the way. The *mayordomo* opened the door, went goggle-
eyed, crossed himself, and looked about to faint with terror. Rico had to
convince the old man he was not a ghost before he would usher him into
the high-ceilinged parlor with its red velvet draperies and European art
on the walls. Rico didn't have to wait long for the family to gather.

Grace's former father-in-law was short and tightly packed. When he
embraced Rico the top of his head easily fit under Rico's chin. He had
been one of Díaz's *científicos,* and with the survival instincts of an alley
cat, here he was, still alive and prospering. But then, so was General
Huerta.

Mendoza held Rico at arm's length to get a good look at him, then
embraced him again. "We heard that the rebels had hanged you. General Rubio and President Huerta certainly think so. They've called off
the search for you."

"Where is Grace?"

"In Cuernavaca."

"Cuernavaca!" Rico wondered how many disappointments and ob-
structions fate planned to inflict on him and Grace. "I was told she came
here."

"We begged her to leave her hotel in the hands of God and come to
the capital, but stubborn as three mules, she refused." Mendoza gave
him a telegram. "Before Zapata's criminals cut the wires she sent this."

The cable had been sent a week ago. Rico imagined Grace in Cuernavaca's telegraph office dictating the message: "I am in God's hands Stop The hotel is in mine Stop."

Rico read it over and over. He looked so forlorn that Mendoza waved a hand, urging Rico to keep it. Rico folded it and put it into the inner pocket of his vest. It proved she existed. At times in the past weeks he had wondered if he had dreamed her.

"Are the telegraph lines still down?" he asked.

"Worse." Mendoza mopped his glistening brow with a big silk bandana. "Zapata's rabble has laid siege to Tres Marías. We believe they intend to take Cuernavaca."

"Why doesn't Huerta send reinforcements?"

"He did. Most of them deserted to the rebels."

"Lend me your best horse."

"You can't reach Cuernavaca, Captain Martín."

"Yes, I can."

Señor Mendoza smacked his forehead with the flat of his hand. "How could I forget? Actually, we thought you might come here."

"Why?"

"Some mule drivers left a letter from Grace this morning, but it's addressed to you."

Mendoza held out an envelope with Rico's address in Grace's handwriting. The envelope had part of a mule's hoofprint on one corner, but otherwise it was intact. It was the note Rico had written on the back of Grace's letter. It had arrived before he did.

Rico put it in the inner pocket of his vest. Surely fate had no more jokes to play on him, sending him here, there and, back again. Surely God would allow him to deliver this letter to Grace.

5I

EATING EDEN

Two hours before dawn the nightly summer rain stopped on cue, as if God had assigned a member of His staff to turn off the celestial spigot. Grace stood on her balcony and looked out at the raindrops sparkling like jewels in the light of the gibbous moon. Then she dressed and went to the kitchen.

While she waited for the kettle to boil on the big, brightly tiled stove, she wet the tip of her finger so that the last flecks of tea leaves would stick to it. Now the tin of Sir Lipton's oolong was truly empty. When the tea finished steeping, Grace carried the steaming cup through the rear courtyard, out a side door, and into her own little Eden.

Four years ago, this garden had been a vacant lot hip-deep in garbage. Grace had hired a small army of men to haul the trash away and bring in wagonloads of rich dirt. Socrates had installed a door in the wall to give entry from the rear courtyard. Grace's gardener had abracadabra'd the bare lot into a jungle of fruit trees and green bounty.

Because of the garden, the Colonial enjoyed a reputation for fresh fruits and vegetables that diners could eat with no intestinal regrets. Foreigners journeyed from Mexico City and beyond to enjoy what the garden produced. In those prosperous days Grace had never imagined that her household's survival would depend on it.

Hunger had become so widespread in Cuernavaca that people stole in order to eat. Now, not only fine horses gazed out of second-story windows, but mules and nags. Tomatoes, squash, and beans, mangoes, avocadoes, oranges, and plums were not safe. To discourage thieves, the gardener had had to cement broken beer bottles along the top of the wall, with their jagged ends up.

The broken bottles meant that iguanas could no longer lounge on top of it. Grace missed them, basking in the sun with their eyes half-closed. They had accepted chunks of mango from Grace's fingers as graciously as if they were doing her a favor. She was charmed by how they cocked their heads, like birds, and inspected her before they took the fruit.

She observed that when they rested, their closed eyelids met at the middle, but when sound asleep the lower lid covered the entire eye. She also learned to recognize the "Glare," when they turned their heads to focus one eye in a stare meant to intimidate.

Lyda advised against naming the "gonners," as she called the iguanas. "Don't make pets of them," she said, but Grace did it anyway. Lyda had been right. The broken bottles on the wall allowed Grace to imagine that the gonners had found somewhere else to nap, but she knew better, or worse. Foraging Cuernavacans had almost certainly turned them into soup.

As Grace stood in the moonlight, sadness swept over her. She wanted to weep for the iguanas, for the starving folk who ate them, and for this Eden of a land. Huerta and Rubio possessed an extraordinarily destructive talent to cause famine in Morelos. The Mexicans had a knack for agriculture, but even if they hadn't, flowers flourished like weeds here. Crops sprouted so fast Grace could almost see them increasing in height by the hour.

To lay waste to a country this bountiful, inhabited by people so artistic, resourceful, hardworking, and faithful, was a crime against humanity. A few days ago Jake McGuire had asked Grace if she would pull the triggers on her shotgun. She had said "Yes." In truth, she would shoot over the head of an intruder, but should she find the *generalísimos* in her sights, she would aim lower.

Grace felt among the leaves for new sprouts, but the members of her household had picked the garden almost bare. That was why Grace was awake so early. Still holding her cup of tea she headed for the front gate.

Leobardo and Socrates waited for her with Duke and the hotel mule.

The mule was affable enough, but he lacked Moses's roguish charm. The shotgun's saddle scabbard was fastened in what Jake McGuire called the northwest position. Jake had taught Socrates to buckle it so it rode horizontally, with the shotgun's butt pointing forward to make it easy to draw. Grace had the feeling that Socrates imagined himself a cowboy or an outlaw whenever he mounted the mule with the shotgun holstered in that position. She made a mental note to ask Jake, the next time she saw him, where she could buy a Stetson for Socrates.

Grace swayed sleepily, squinting in the fretful flare of the torch in Leobardo's hand. She held the chipped porcelain cup under her nose so she could breath in the aroma. It was the last of it she would smell for the foreseeable future.

"Must we leave so early?" English was difficult enough for Grace at this hour. She concentrated on making sense in Spanish. "The market stalls will be empty anyway."

Socrates handed her Duke's reins and the riding crop. Grace understood that the crop was more for discouraging ruffians than encouraging Duke.

"If anything is for sale," said Socrates, "it will be snatched up before the sun wipes the sleep from his eyes."

Since traveling with Lieutenant Angel's rebels, Grace considered riding sidesaddle too effete. She wore what looked like a skirt that reached a few inches above her ankles and just below the tops of her high, lace-up shoes. Full pleats in front and back hid the fact that the garment was a pair of wide-legged trousers.

Grace followed Socrates through the gate and heard Leobardo slide the big bolt home. The winch creaked as he lowered the oak beam into its iron cradle with a thud like a fortress's portcullis locking. Or a cell door.

One advantage of leaving this early was that the scores of refugees camped on the two plazas were still asleep. Grace did not have to ride past the children and sorrowful women pleading for the gift of a *centavito,* a little penny. She did not have to see the hunger in their eyes.

The rain had stopped, but torrents of water rushed past, forming plump wakes behind Duke's ankles, and the mule's. The flood, with its crust of garbage and debris, tumbled down the steep street and plunged over the rim of the brush-choked gorge. In another hour the edges of the remaining puddles would shrink and dry in the morning sun.

As usual, vendors had spent the night sleeping on mats next to their stalls. Now they were awake and hoping for customers. The market lacked the former throngs of people, dogs, livestock, produce, and poultry, but one thing remained plentiful. Grace wrinkled her nose. Even with so little food for sale it smelled as bad as always.

She dismounted and led Duke down the first side street. Today she got lucky early. A black hen, tethered by a string, pecked at the litter of garbage. An old woman sat nearby, presiding at her makeshift stall of old boards and torn canvas like a judge on his bench. Grace started toward her, but Socrates made a small hissing sound.

"What's the matter?"

He turned away so the woman could not see his face. He lowered his voice to a murmur.

"The hen is there for a reason, *Mamacita*. Do not buy her."

"Why not?"

"She is black."

"What difference does that make?"

"A healer rubs his patients with a live black chicken to absorb the illness. That hen probably carries someone's sickness inside it."

Grace knew better than to scoff at a superstition powerful enough to make a reasonable man like Socrates reject food in a famine.

"Can the black chicken be cleansed of the sickness?"

Socrates hesitated. "Maybe."

"Do you know how?"

"It must be smoked over a fire made of palm leaves, *copal* resin, and bay leaves that have been blessed by a priest."

Grace was relieved. As exorcism rituals went this was a simple one.

"Palms are everywhere and we can buy *copal* and bay leaves here in the market."

"And a priest for the blessing?"

"I'll think of something."

Socrates looked dubious and for good reason. Priests were scarcer in

Cuernavaca these days than Yorkshire pudding. But Grace found two
more black chickens and a small sack of dried beans before giving up.
Tied by their feet to the pommel, the chickens seemed resigned to their
fate, but Socrates eyed them as though they harbored all the plagues of
Egypt.

On the way home Grace stopped at a small church on a narrow back
street. It was called the Church of Jesus of Nazareth. She had passed
it often, but she had never ventured inside. Several blocks away, the
cathedral was more impressive, but Grace had always preferred the sim-
plicity of this one. She dismounted and climbed the broad steps to the
church while Socrates waited below with Duke and the mule.

The carved plaster entryway was an orange-red, but showing white
where the paint had chipped and fallen away. A plaque on the wall read
in Spanish, "Lord, make me an instrument of Thy peace."

Where there is hatred, let me sow love;
Where there is injury, pardon;
Where there is doubt, faith;
Where there is despair, hope;
Where there is darkness, light;
And where there is sadness, joy.

Grace touched it lightly with the tips of her fingers. She stood that
way for a minute or more, as if to give the words entrance to her heart.

The weathered oak doors stood open and Grace walked into the cool
twilight beyond them. Inside, the walls were of whitewashed plaster
with a stripe of faded red trim around the base of the ceiling dome. The
morning light from one small stained-glass window splashed in colorful
patterns across the altar's marble top. No pews stood between the door
and the altar, nor hid the vivid patterns of the majolica tiles on the floor.

Grace expected the church to be empty, but a hundred or more devout
filled the nave. Shawls hid the faces of the women. The men kneeled on
the wide brims of their straw hats. Except for the occasional cough, the
low murmur of prayer, and the clicking of rosary beads, a stillness per-
vaded the place.

Grace fed coins into the slot in the poor box and picked up six candles and a handful of the pale, fragrant chunks of *copal* from a basket. Brightly painted saints stood in niches in the white plaster walls, but Grace was interested in only one. She stood in front of Saint Jude Tadeo, the patron of desperate causes. She lit the candles and set them among the scores of others flickering at the statue's feet.

She had little use for religion. She rather agreed with Lieutenant Angel, who said, "Don't expect much from priests or cats." But Grace considered faith as something separate from religion, and faith had a powerful presence here.

She asked for St. Jude's blessing on the leaves and the incense so she could feed the people she considered family. While she was at it, she asked him to help the widowed, the orphaned, the hungry, the ill, the frightened, and the homeless. When she finished, she had one last request.

"Please, do not let them kill Federico Martín."

52

ALMOST DOG FOOD

Artillery speaks its own language and a soldier quickly learns it. Angel had heard the cries of wounded men and the agonies of dying horses. She was familiar with the pop-pop-pop of rifles and the bone-vibrating pulse of machine guns.

She knew the crack of breaking bones and the sucking sound an abdomen made when sliced open by a machete. She was used to the keening of widows and orphans, and to the abrupt racket of grenades followed by the sigh of falling sand and the rattle of airborne rocks and debris. The only noise that could unnerve her was the screech of an artillery shell headed straight at her.

A shell posted to her most current address had a different volume and pitch than one destined to land on one side of her or the other. By the sound, Angel could gauge how far and in which direction she had to run to avoid it.

As this one whistled toward her she waved her men to scatter and spurred her horse toward a boulder. She leaned along the mare's neck and pulled her serape over her own head and the horse's. The mare flinched as the shell exploded, and Angel murmured in her ear to calm her.

When the blanket had absorbed the thump of the last falling rock, Angel spurred the mare into the open and surveyed the rock-strewn landscape for signs of her command.

"*Vengan, muchachos,*" she shouted. "Come out, boys."

Plinio rode toward her, but the others must have had their doubts.

She could see the straw-colored peaks of sombreros here and there among the rocks and trees and the occasional horse's rump, but no one left whatever cover they had found.

"The boys are not used to artillery." Plinio had a wry way with the obvious.

"Soon those guns will be ours."

Angel looked back toward the distant roofs of Berta's village. It had become Zapata's headquarters for this assault on *el gobierno*'s barracks at Tres Marías, and the sixty pack mules of the government's supply train milled about in a corral there. Their escort of federal soldiers had handed them over to Zapata and reined their own mounts in among his men. At least half of the mules had carried ammunition.

"The *federales* must be almost out of bullets," Angel said.

Plinio shrugged. "Almost out of bullets is not the same as out of bullets."

Angel cupped her hands around her mouth. *"El gobierno no tiene bolas,"* she shouted. "The government has no balls."

Laughter bounced among the rocks as the rebel troop emerged, their horses' hoofs clattering on the stony ground. Once her company had assembled Angel looked for Antonio. Her own men's welfare came first, but she did not feel at ease unless she knew where he was.

Another lieutenant had been killed this morning and Antonio had accepted command of his company. Now he rode along the rim of the deep ravine that separated him from her, but no matter. He and Angel shared the rare gift of being together in spirit even when they were apart.

A wave would be seen by their men as a signal to charge, so Antonio touched the brim of his hat with two fingers. Angel returned the salute. She braced the staff of her company's guidon on her thigh, held the reins lightly in her other hand, and waited for her men to assemble behind her.

The rattle of their spurs and rifles and the creak of their saddles as they shifted their weight for the charge were music to her. When she raised the flag the wind caught it. Fluttering and snapping, it came alive like a horse eager to start a race he knew he could win. She turned to stare at Zapata sitting astride his white horse on a rise overlooking the mountainous terrain.

His arm swept forward in the signal to charge. Angel raised the flag as high as her arm would reach.

"Adelante, mis guachos," she shouted. "Forward, my orphans."

With a cry of "Land and liberty," she spurred the mare into a gallop. All she heard was the thunder of hooves and her own voice, but she knew her men were shouting, too. The charge became a series of skirmishes. Angel fired as she rode, chasing the *federales* through thorny underbrush, into canyons, and among rock falls.

The thrill of it intoxicated her. By midafternoon the government soldiers had fled helter-skelter toward Cuernavaca. Coated with dust, bleeding from cuts and scratches, soaked in sweat, and grinning, Angel rounded up as many of her men as she could find. Together they rode back to Tres Marías. The barracks, the train station, and the village were theirs.

She watered and rubbed down her mare and tethered her in a patch of grass. Then she went to the makeshift hospital under a canvas awning. She found all three of her missing men there, and after she made sure that their wounds weren't serious, she sauntered to the camp to compare stories with Antonio.

She didn't find him. She didn't find him in the thatched shelter that served as a kitchen, or in the market near the train station. He wasn't tending to the horses. He wasn't at the periphery of the officers in conference with General Zapata. By late afternoon all of Antonio's men had returned and no one had seen him. When his horse walked in, reins dragging, Angel tried not to panic.

She stuffed bandages into her knapsack and filled one canteen with water and another with tequila. She found José and the two of them separated so they could cover more area in the search for him. She rode slowly over the broken ground, calling his name.

She saw plenty of corpses. Almost all of them wore government uniforms, but her breath caught in her throat anyway until she made sure none of them was Antonio. She hadn't time for prayers, but she made the sign of the cross over each one, barely slowing her mare before moving on.

She cursed the sun as it slid closer to the western peaks, gathering its light to take with it. She cursed herself for not having thought to bring a torch. By the time the rocks loomed like ghosts in the deepening twilight, she had strayed several miles from Tres Marías. Every hundred yards or so she reined the mare to a stop, cupped her hands around her mouth, and called Antonio's name

When his reply came, Angel thought it might be a bird or animal. She froze, listening as if her own life depended on it. The cry came again and this time she recognized the voice.

"Mierda."

She laughed. *"¿'Tonio, donde estás?"*

All she heard was, *"Malditos perros."* Damned dogs. And she barely heard that.

She walked to the edge of the ravine and saw him lying half covered by rocks at the bottom. A fallen boulder stopped just short of crushing him, but it had wedged over his chest, making movement impossible. A pack of gaunt dogs with a lot of wolf in them were eyeing him from about ten yards away. Angel pitched rocks at them, but that didn't impress them. They continued staring at Antonio.

Angel wished she could lob a grenade in among them, but that might have harmed Antonio. Besides, she had used her last grenade to blow up a machine gun emplacement. Firing her last two rounds finally convinced the dogs to leave the larder.

She shouted for José, then walked along the rim until she found a slope gradual enough for her mare. The two of them slid down it in a riot of gravel and dust. Climbing back up would be difficult, but as Antonio often observed about her, she would blow up that bridge when she came to it.

Rocks covered Antonio's legs. He must have dislodged them when he fell off his horse and slid down the side of the ravine. Blood from a gash on his temple ran down his cheek and soaked his collar. His face was ashen, probably from loss of blood, but he managed to wink at her.

Angel wanted to sob with relief. Instead, she put her hands on her hips and shook her head as though the sad state of his uniform had failed an inspection. The disappointed wolves-in-dogs'-clothing howled not far away.

"Now you have a new nickname, Ugly."

"What, Brat?" His voice was barely a whisper.

"Dog Food."

She started pulling off the rocks and pitching them. Most of them weren't much bigger than a loaf of bread, but they made quite a heap. Another hour or two and they would have been his cairn. If Angel hadn't found him before nightfall he would not have lived to see the sun rise.

José appeared at the rim of the ravine. "I wondered who was making so much racket."

He helped Angel roll the boulder off Antonio and down a slight slope. It scattered the dogs who went off in search of easier pickings. They would find plenty to eat today.

Angel allowed herself a few tears as she poured tequila on the gash on his face. It was a deep one that just missed his eye. She bound it with strips of cloth from the bottom of some *soldadera*'s skirt, and then helped José clear away the last of the rocks.

José probed along his son's legs and feet. "I think the ankle is broken."

Angel sat behind Antonio and pulled him into a half-sitting position so his back rested against her chest. She gave him a long drink of tequila from the canteen, then took one herself before pushing the cork back into it. She put her arms around him, laid her cheek against his, and held him while José pulled on his foot to straighten the ankle bone.

She kept holding him while José cut a branch from a pine tree, shaved it flat with his machete, divided it in two, and shaped it into splints. Angel folded rags to cushion the leg and José bound the splints tightly in place. They helped him stand and mount the mare.

Angel had plenty of time to think in the corpse-strewn darkness as she led the mare back to camp with Antonio lying along the horse's neck. She thought about how panicked she had been when he didn't return today. She felt the icy wind that commenced howling around her heart every time she imagined burying his lifeless body. She tried not to think about how unbearable life would be without him.

At the army's sprawling encampment at Tres Marías she wrapped her serape around her and sat by his mat while he tossed and moaned in his sleep. She murmured reassurances and covered him when his blanket slipped off. She gave him sips of water when he woke up. She laid wet cloths on his forehead to ease his fever. She dozed a little, but most of the night she stared into his face, pale in the moonlight.

The sun had been up an hour when Antonio awoke. Only after he attempted a smile and asked for breakfast would Angel believe the exhausted *medico* when he said Antonio would survive. She shared her tortillas, beans, and roast pork with him.

"You look like you'll live, Ugly."

"I'm ready to ride."

"That's good, because General Zapata says we'll be galloping into Cuernavaca soon."

53

BEER AND BANANAS

Leobardo rolled his belongings into his canvas hammock and tied it onto his back with one of his wife's shawls. He opened the back gate, his last official act as the Colonial's doorman. Socrates stood ready to close the gate behind him and the last two chambermaids.

Leobardo held his sombrero against his chest and waited for the weeping maids to make their farewells to Grace, Lyda, Annie, and the Colonial.

The maids had their own name for the hotel. "May God take care of you, *Mamacita,* and the Big House, too."

"You know you are welcome to stay here at the Big House," said Grace.

The maids looked at Leobardo, but he shook his head. Grace only recently had learned they were his nieces.

"We have relatives in a village held by the *Zapatistas,*" he said. "We can find food there."

Socrates muttered too low for Leobardo or the maids to hear, "The Zapatistas are starving, too."

Grace was grateful to be relieved of responsibility for three people, but she was sad to see them go. Leobardo's stories of misadventures with witches amused her. And she would miss the maid's laughter and the patter of their bare feet running on the tile floors.

She couldn't bear to watch them walk off down the narrow side street in a forlorn little procession. Lyda waved good-bye to them, but Grace headed inside. Lyda called her back.

"Gracie, looks like the Hoffmans have decided to vamoose."

Grace and Lyda watched the landau carriage stop at the gate. Three wagons pulled up in a line behind it. Each wagon held a mountain of canvas-covered possessions. Herr Gustav Hoffman's brewery workers perched on narrow board benches along the sides. They carried rifles instead of the usual big wooden stir paddles.

With his incorrigible yellow hair and rosy cheeks and nose, Herr Hoffman looked like Bacchus in green suspenders and short leather breeches. He wrapped the reins around the brake lever and stepped down from the carriage to supervise the unloading. His men stowed their machetes, slid their rifles around to their backs, and jumped down. They unlashed the tarpaulins and lowered the wagons' tailgates. They put planks in place and trundled three oak barrels down the ramps.

After they rolled the beer into a shed in the back courtyard, they carried in a dozen sacks of grain. Grace wasn't sure how useful the beer would be, but she almost wept with relief at the gift of grain. She had faced the necessity of selling Duke and the mule or watching them starve.

"This is very generous of you, Herr Hoffman."

"My dear lady, better you and your people enjoy my beer than it vanish into the mouths of rabble."

"We cannot begin to thank you."

"I do not want to boast, Mrs. Knight, but this is *bock* beer."

While his wife signaled impatiently to him from the carriage, the imperturbable brewer made sure Grace understood what she was getting.

"In Germany we call bock beer 'liquid bread.' In old times, the monks they brew this beer to . . ." he searched for the words in English ". . . to bear them up while fasting."

"We surely are fasting," said Grace.

"Bread in a bottle must've made piety more palatable for the *padres*," added Lyda.

"This beer, he is good with food, too, like roasted beef, *yah*. Is good even with Mexican food."

Frau Hoffman gave up trying to hurry her husband along and stood up in the carriage. Herr Hoffman translated her invitation.

"They say the road to Acapulco is safe, Mrs. Knight. Better you all come with."

"We thank you for the kind offer, but we have seen bad times before. This storm will pass." Grace turned to Lyda. "You and Annie should go with them though."

"Jake said he would come back for us. We'll wait for him."

Lyda put an arm around Grace in a show of solidarity, but as the two of them waved good-bye to the Hoffmans, she muttered, "Roast beef. I've forgotten what that tastes like."

"Now, Lyda, he said it's also good with Mexican food."

"When he said Mexican food, I doubt he meant bananas."

The Colonial's larder held perhaps two weeks' supply of dried beans and rice if the five of them shared a very small portion for one meal a day. They supplemented that with bananas from the trees in the two courtyards. María served the bananas fried, boiled, grilled, poached, baked, roasted, stewed and a few other ways Grace couldn't identify.

The evening the Hoffmans left, Annie ventured across the street to hear the nightly concert in the zócalo. She returned in tears at the misery she saw there. After that neither Annie, Grace, nor Lyda went outside the Colonial's front gate unless necessary.

They could not bear to watch people search trash heaps for anything edible or dig weeds in the plazas to make into broth. In the days that followed, starving Cuernavacans stripped the fruit trees bare. Litter on the street consisted mostly of sugarcane stalks chewed into fringe. Finally, even the nightly concerts ceased.

Keeping bodies alive in a famine was one thing. Keeping spirits up was another. Herr Hoffman's liquid bread helped Grace do both. It even earned a little income.

With few choices for evening entertainment, *los correctos* and the remaining foreigner residents gravitated to the Colonial to drink Herr Hoffman's beer and the Colonial's wine, and play cards. Annie cranked up the phonograph for those who wanted to dance in the ballroom. When Annie's arm grew tired, Grace played the piano.

The explosion came during a chorus of "Jarabe Tapátio." The shock wave vibrated the piano stool. The lights rattled in their sockets, flickered, and died. Everyone froze, waiting to see if they would come back on. They didn't.

Grace lit candles and showed the guests out. On her way back she heard Annie and Lyda call from upstairs. She joined them on the second-floor balcony. Flames from the electrical plant on the outskirts of town danced above the rooftops. They made Grace uneasy, but the plant had come under attack before when Madero's rebel forces prevailed against Díaz's army in 1910.

The glow in the nighttime sky in the mountains to the north was a different matter. The fire must be an inferno to reflect so much light off the underside of the cloud cover. Then the distant rumble of cannon fire reached them.

"Do you think the rebels have taken Tres Marías?" asked Lyda.

"Dear God, I hope not."

Annie hung out over the rail, fascinated by the show. The girl was amiable and polite, yet Grace could imagine her riding off with Angel's band of rebels. She had a tough core, a quick intellect, and a bold spirit. She was also lovely to look at and almost fourteen years old. A chill went through Grace at the thought of what could happen to her if war entered Cuernavaca.

The nightly rain drove them back inside. No one wanted to be trapped on the second floor should a mob storm the hotel, so Lyda, Annie, and María went to bed in the rooms opening off the rear courtyard. Duke and the mule shared another room there, and Socrates took up sentry duty at the back gate.

As she did every night, Grace sat in the big leather chair under one of the arches along the open corridor. It gave her a view of the rain splattering on the paving stones of the front courtyard, the covered entryway, and the main gate. She held the big hotel guest book on her lap and leaned the loaded shotgun against the tiled column.

She kept the shotgun close at hand these days. María had told her about the rumor in town. People claimed that the Englishwoman stored tens of thousands of *pesos* in a chest under her bed. María said that lately, *Mamacita*'s treasure had grown in the collective imagination to millions of *pesos*. Why else, people asked each other, would a foreign woman stay here unless her treasure was too heavy to move?

She turned up the wick in the oil lamp and opened the leather-bound guest book. Each signature summoned up a face and a personality, but Grace's favorite entry was the first one, written by Lyda. Lyda had come bursting through the doors as soon as Grace pushed them open. She had spied the book on the front desk and had written in Spanish, "May you have love, health, money, and time to enjoy them."

Grace came to the end of the guests' remarks and turned one more page, though she couldn't have said why. She drew a sharp breath at the bold script. She could picture Rico writing it with his left hand curled over the top of the page. He said he learned to write that way so his teachers wouldn't punish him when his letters slanted in the opposite direction from the other children's.

"I will find you, if not on earth then in heaven." He had written it in English and in Spanish, but why? Did he think she was dead? Did he think he would die before he saw her again?

It was dated May 29. Grace guessed he had made the entry in the book after he escaped from jail. Socrates said Rico had sneaked into the stable at dawn and exchanged an old swaybacked farm horse for his grandfather's gray Andalusian. He said when General Fatso discovered the switch he had gone into the worst rage any of them had ever seen.

Grace smiled. Even under a death sentence, Rico would play his pranks. She fell asleep with her hand resting on his words.

The clock in the lobby had just chimed two when the sound of rifle fire and running footsteps jerked Grace awake. With heart pounding, she put the book on the floor. She grabbed the shotgun, thumbed the hammer back, and leveled it at the front gate.

"Death to the Spaniards," someone shouted. Then he passed on by, his footsteps fading in the distance.

Grace lowered the hammer to half-cock and leaned the gun against the pillar. Lyda arrived, yawning, and Grace moved over to make room for her and her derringer. She opened the guest book to the last page and turned up the wick on the oil lamp so Lyda could read it.

"What did he mean, he'll find me in heaven?" Grace started to cry. "Do you think he's dead?"

"No, Gracie. He's not dead. I'm sure of it."

"And neither is Jake." Grace pushed the corn-tassel-blond hair back from Lyda's face and kissed her on the foreheard. "He'll find a way to return to you and Annie. He'll make sure no harm comes to either of you."

With their arms around each other the two of them cried each other to sleep while the sky wept, too.

The sun had been up an hour and already the buzz of flies from the zócalo sounded like a distant sawmill at peak operation. The wounded soldiers lying in ranks around the bandstand were not suffering in silence. They cried for their mothers and pleaded for water.

The larger plaza just to the south filled up, too, as more soldiers and civilians streamed into the city. The able-bodied had carried their wounded comrades twenty mountainous miles from Tres Marías. They slept, exhausted, in the midst of scattered equipment, swarms of flies, and the perpetual screaming.

The *soldaderas* did their best to wave away the flies, staunch the bleeding, and bind up the broken bones. They had torn so many bandages from the bottoms of their skirts that they were close to half naked. When Grace gave them the bundles of strips ripped from the Colonial's bedsheets, they murmured thanks.

Grace and Lyda walked up and down the lines with their buckets. They lifted each man's head and held a gourd of water to his lips. Annie had a bucket, too, but she had filled it with beer. "The men might be hungry as well as thirsty," she said. "And Herr Hoffman said his beer was good for body and soul."

"*¡Mamacita!*"

Grace hung the curved handle of the gourd on the rim of the bucket and stood up. "Colonel Rodriguez! What happened?"

"The *Zapatistas* outnumbered us four to one. They have our artillery now. They have the weapons and supplies that were meant for us."

"The rebels stole them?"

Rodriguez avoided her eyes. "The supply train's escort deserted. And some officers have gone over to the rebels and taken their men with them."

Only a week ago the colonel had come to the Colonial to tell Grace not to worry. His men would protect the city. Now here he stood with his arm in a sling. His head was bound by a bloody strip of flowered calico that probably has served as a ruffle in its previous life.

Before he went back to the task of moving the wounded to the old monastery, he said, "We will make a stand here in the city. We will not desert you."

Lyda put an arm around Grace's waist and asked the question her friend could not. "Do you know where Captain Martín is?"

"Dead." The colonel studied the ground. "The rebels hanged him."

Grace heard the words, but her brain declined to process them.

"The rebels?" Lyda asked. "Not General Rubio?"

"They say Lieutenant Angel's mob did it."

Grace screamed and swayed. Annie came running and she and Lyda supported her to keep her from falling.

"Lo siento, Mamacita," Rodriguez said. "I'm sorry. *Lo siento.*"

He kept saying it as Lyda and Annie led Grace across the street and through the Colonial's front gates. They sat her in the big leather-upholstered chair. Lyda gave her several handkerchiefs, but they lay unnoticed in Grace's lap. María brought her a rare treat, a bowl of chicken-foot broth, with the foot still floating in it. Annie tried to coax her to drink some water. Grace shook her head. She sat, silent and dry-eyed, the rest of the afternoon.

As dusk gathered, Lyda laid out straw mats and blankets in the corridor near Grace's chair. Before she and Annie lay down to sleep, Lyda sneaked the shotgun and pistol away from Grace. She figured if her friend could make it through the night alive, there was hope for tomorrow.

54

GIFTS FROM GOD

To an outside observer, the hundreds of cookfires and acres of trash would have looked like open sores on the stump-studded slopes around Tres Marías. To Angel and Antonio the encampment resembled heaven. Eight thousand men and their women had gathered here. Artillery carriages and ammunition caissons sat in ranks.

The government's barracks lay in charred ruins. The federal army was in disarray. With this force, Zapata's Southern Army of Liberation would take Cuernavaca, the state of Morelos, and, ultimately, the country.

José grinned as he led the big, steel-dust stallion toward Angel. The reprobate mule, Moses, ambled along behind. No one knew how Moses had found his way back to the Perez family. They had discovered him one morning with his coat covered in burs, grazing with the rest of the stock as if he had never left. Some people in Angel's band said his return was a miracle. Others claimed it was a curse.

José held aloft the new company flag his wife and daughter had just finished sewing. It fluttered in the breeze as he walked. It had a new motif—a red field with an angel in a white robe brandishing a sword. Across the top Socorro had appliquéd "Land and Liberty" in green outline in black.

José held out the flag's staff and Grullo's reins. Angel took the staff, but she refused the reins, although it pained her to do it.

"He's your horse, *Maestro* José."

"My daughter, when you lead us into battle we have to make a good show. We cannot shame Colonel Contreras in front of Carranza's flock of peacocks." José waved the flag toward the men setting up tents not far away.

The tents were so white they stood out like flares in the general disorder of the camp. One of Venustiano Carranza's battalions had arrived this afternoon from the northern state of Coahuila. Angel and her people were glad for the reinforcements, but they envied Carranza's men the abundance of supplies. They also resented the newcomers' air of superiority, as if they had come to save the day from a bunch of bumblers.

Ever the optimist, Antonio said, "Maybe they'll share their ammunition with us."

"I doubt it," muttered Angel.

As if on cue, Rico Martín's old comrade, Juan, strolled up. A major's insignia decorated the starched collar of his new uniform. He stared at Angel, probably trying to decide where he had seen her before. She didn't let on that he had flirted with her when she sold tamarind candy on the Tres Marías train platform.

That a federal officer had joined Carranza's forces didn't surprise Angel. Every day more gray uniforms of the rural police and *el gobierno*'s dark blue ones mingled with Zapata's men.

Juan didn't waste time with pleasantries. "Where did you get that horse?"

"A federal officer traded him," said Antonio.

"For that mule." Angel nodded toward Moses whose sly expression gave the impression he had a scheme to pick their pockets.

"A mule?" Juan looked skeptical, and who could blame him? Rico trading Grullo for a mule? Not likely. "Was the officer's name Federico Martín?"

"It was," said Angel. "He rode with us for a time."

"If you've harmed him, I will kill you, here and now."

"We intended to hang him," said Angel. "But he pleaded so pathetically for his life we let him go."

Juan knew that Rico would never plead for his life. He may not have recognized Angel, but he knew when he was being needled. He addressed his question to Antonio. "Where is he now?"

"The last time we saw him he was heading for the capital to find the Englishwoman."

"On the mule," added Angel.

"I'll buy Captain Martín's horse from you."

"You can't afford him," said Angel.

"I will give you two cases of cartridges and my sorrel."

Angel remembered Juan's reputation at Tres Marías. The soldiers said he could obtain hard-to-find supplies in a hurry. The impossible ones took a little longer. She pulled Antonio and José aside for a conference.

The major's big sorrel gelding could not compare with Grullo, but he was a cavalry officer's mount and better than average. They had shot a lot of bullets at *el gobierno*'s fleeing army. They all agreed that they needed the ammunition. José made the deciding argument. "God has sent us this gift. We cannot refuse it."

Angel turned to Juan. "Show us what you have."

He led them to a stone building and slipped the guards some money. Inside, wooden crates of weapons and ammunition were stacked to the ceiling with narrow aisles among them. Angel had never seen so much ammunition.

Juan pried the lid off a crate in the rear. Inside nestled seven-by-fifty-seven Mauser cartridges loaded into stripper clips.

"How many rounds?" asked Angel.

"Five rounds in a clip, a hundred and sixty clips per box."

As a child Angel had avoided school, but she had learned addition, subtraction, multiplication, and division by counting out ammunition to share among her eighty men. Not all of them carried Mausers, but even so, this would only give each of them about four clips, or twenty cartridges.

"Not enough."

"Three crates."

"Not enough."

Antonio started to say something, but José elbowed him and he closed his mouth.

"We can't chance two trips." Juan looked exasperated. Maybe he had expected the rustics to be an easier sell. "There are three of you. That's one crate each."

"You can carry the fourth box."

"Oh, no." Juan backed away as if to dissociate himself from them here and now. "I've taken a big risk already."

"*Ahoga en poco agua*. He drowns in little water," Angel muttered as she turned on her heel and headed for the door.

She had come to the conclusion that he would let her leave when he called her back.

"Three crates and a box of thirty-caliber centerfires for your Winchester."

"How many rounds in a box?"

"Two hundred. I'll bring them to your camp tonight."

Angela calculated. Nine of her men carried the same 1894-model Winchester. One box meant only twenty cartridges for her and each of them. "Two boxes of centerfires."

"Are you crazy?"

"Good, day, Major." She continued toward the door.

"*Bueno, pués*. It's a deal."

Angel, Antonio, and José carried the crates back to their camp. Juan came at dusk to deliver the sorrel gelding and the Winchester cartridges, which were disguised in a feed sack.

Saying good-bye to Grullo was more difficult than Angel had expected. She would not likely have the chance to ride such a horse ever again. As Juan started to lead him away, Angel asked one more question.

"Do you know General Miguel Sanchez?"

"He commands artillery for General Villa in Sonora." Juan stared at her. "Do I know you, Lieutenant?"

"No sir." Angel saluted.

As Juan left with the stallion, she muttered, "You don't know me at all."

. . .

The women's dresses hung on them in more shreds than the average, but their shawls were what caught Angel's attention. One was made of the usual blue cotton. The rest were of frayed and faded black wool. They all wore them pulled forward to hide their faces. The one in blue was obviously with child.

The thirteen women had arrived with the men from Coahuila, but they did not act like *soldaderas*. They huddled around a cookfire near the Carranzista campsite, but they did not flirt with the men. The soldiers, in turn, left them alone, which was also unusual.

Angel filled a pot with beans, picked up a stack of tortillas, and walked over for a closer look. When she approached, the women recoiled and covered their faces completely.

"I brought food, little mothers." A better look at the black shawls revealed who they were. Or had been. "Are you the holy sisters from the convent?"

"Yes." The oldest one spoke for them. "We will return there tomorrow."

"I'm Lieutenant Angel." Angel took off her hat and shook out her hair. "Mother Merced gave us shelter when *el gobierno* was trying to kill us."

"Angela?" The woman in the blue shawl let it drop onto her shoulders. "My daughter, Angela?"

"*¡Mamá!*"

Petra Sanchez stood up, though her watermelon belly made it difficult. Angel threw her arms around her. She did not ask where her mother had been or what had happened to her. If Petra Sanchez chose to tell her, she would listen, but she would not ask. Not ever.

Petra pushed the hair out of her daughter's eyes. It was a familiar gesture that Angel had missed more than she had realized. The nuns moved over to make room for both of them. Angel took her mother's hand in both of hers. It felt smaller than she remembered it.

"You look thin, child."

"I am well, Mother. Many of our men are here with me—Plinio, Antonio, and the others."

"And your father?"

"He's with Villa's army. When General Zapata's forces have taken Cuernavaca I will come for you at the convent. We can go north to find him."

"No, my daughter." Petra Sanchez put her other hand on her swollen belly, as if to protect it. "I will stay with the nuns."

Angel imagined how her father would react when he saw that his wife was carrying another man's child. Staying with Mother Merced and the Carmelites was probably the best plan.

"Will Mother Merced let the child stay?" she asked.

Petra's voice was barely audible. "All of us are with child."

Angel returned to her own camp long enough to retrieve her mat and blanket. She also took a trenching shovel and the largest tarpaulin. When her men protested, she only glared at them. Antonio insisted on hobbling along on his homemade crutches to help her erect a lean-to for the nuns. Angel dug a ditch around it to keep out water from the night's rain. By doubling up on the mats, all the nuns could fit under the shelter.

For a long time Angel lay on her side with her head cradled in the crook of her elbow and listened to her mother's quiet breathing.

55

GIFTS BY COINCIDENCE

Dictionaries define despair as the absence of hope.

Grace had known sorrow in her life, but she probably never had used the word "despair" in a sentence. Even when she learned that General Rubio had issued an execution order for Rico she had had the consolation of hope.

Now despair engulfed her. It stung her eyes like bees. It echoed in her skull like the tolling of funeral bells. It turned breath to hot tar in her lungs.

The tough, fist-sized muscle that was her heart ached from wrestling with it. Despair seeped into her bones and replaced them the way minerals transformed logs into stone. Like petrified wood, she looked the same, but the news of Rico's death had fundamentally and forever changed her.

The hard rain turned to a drizzle then stopped. The waning moon ventured out from behind the clouds. Water glittered like diamonds in the banana trees in the courtyard. Distant rifle fire started up again.

Grace heard singing, in English. And it was headed her way.

I may die out on the ocean,
Or be shot in a gambling house brawl;
But if you follow to the end of my story,
You'll find a blond was the cause of it all.

Lyda sat bolt upright on her mat like a newly revived Lazarus with places to go. "Gracie, Annie, wake up. Jake's come back."

Everyone slept in their clothes these days. Lyda tried to straighten out hers as she ran, barefoot, toward the front gates. Annie pelted along behind her.

"Be careful," Grace called after them. "The paving stones are slippery."

The sound of her own voice startled her into stirring. She followed slowly on legs that felt as if she had borrowed them from an invalid.

Lyda and Annie heaved the oak beam out of its iron brackets and pushed open the heavy doors. The moonlit rectangle framed four pack mules and Jake on horseback. He ducked so the crown of his Stetson cleared the door frame and rode inside leading the mules.

He dismounted, picked Annie and Lyda up in turn, and whirled them each around. For once he dismissed decorum. He kissed Lyda long and longingly before he set her down. She surveyed the empty street outside the Colonial's gates.

"Did you come alone?"

"Yes, darlin'. One uprising. One Ranger." He saw Grace and touched the brim of his hat in greeting. "Mornin', Miz Knight."

"Good to see you, Mr. McGuire." The demands of courtesy returned Grace to the here and now, at least for the time being. Blessed are the amenities, she thought. They grease the wheels of life.

Odd to think that commonplace civilities could revive Grace when sympathy couldn't. But then, Jake didn't know that condolences were on the agenda. Food topped his list.

"I could eat a plate of horseshoes smothered in María's green chili sauce."

"We have beer," said Annie. "The Hoffmans brought it."

"Beer sounds mighty fine."

Annie ran to fetch it. Socrates arrived with his pistol and machete in hand. Jake handed him the lines for the horse and mules and he led the animals away.

"Is beer all you have?" asked Jake.

"No," said Lyda. "We have bananas, too."

Jake nodded toward the drag mule's hindquarters sashaying down the corridor toward the rear courtyard. "That critter carries a load of vittles. We can have some for breakfast, but we'll need the rest on the trail."

"What trail?" asked Lyda. "The rebels control the road to Tres Marías."

Jake turned to Grace. "I thought maybe you could make a deal with Zapata's apostates, Miz Knight. Seein' as how you're chummy with Lieutenant Angel's crowd."

Lyda saw distress flare in her friend's eyes. "Angel's mob hanged Rico Martín."

Jake took off his hat and bowed to Grace. "I'm sorry to hear that, ma'am. Cap'n Martín was the best sort of fella, true-blue and four-square."

Here come the condolences, Grace thought. She took cover behind amenities.

"How did you get through, Mr. McGuire?"

"I came from Toluca, west of Em Cee. The Toluca road ain't as infested with hooligans yet. On the way here I met a lot of people heading north on it. Looks like your whole town is skedaddling. Come sunup we'll pack your possibles on the mules."

"I'm not leaving," said Grace.

"With all due respect, ma'am, you might as well come along peaceable-like. I will hog-tie you and throw you onto the back of a mule if need be."

Grace believed him. Lyda had shared with her Jake's rule about relations with the fair sex. It went, "Never bluff when you're dealing with a woman."

With a nod of thanks, Jake accepted a pint-sized mug of warm beer from Annie. He glanced at Lyda's mat and rumpled coverlet. "I'll bed down here in case trouble comes knocking. I suggest you ladies get some shut-eye. Tomorrow will be a long day."

Grace started for the stairs, but stopped when she reached the deep shadow at their base. She sat on the bottom step and fought back tears. She was surprised that her heart went on beating and her lungs kept filling with air. If life was determined to go on she needed to consider her options.

She could try to hire men to guard the Colonial in her absence, but she could think of no one trustworthy. She could ask Colonel Rodriguez for protection, but he had more important duties. Or she could refuse to go tomorrow and hold Jake off with her shotgun when he tried to carry out his threat to hog-tie her.

Grace did not believe in the existence of an all-powerful God. She accepted coincidence and randomness as the ruling forces in the universe. God had not caused this war. God had not taken Rico from her. Neither had God sent Jake McGuire, whose snores now echoed along the corridor. Coincidence accounted for the fact that he had arrived to help her and Lyda when they most needed it.

Grace finally admitted to herself that dying in the attempt to protect her hotel would accomplish nothing. Coincidence had sent her the gift of Jake and his mules. She should accept it graciously.

Grace meant to go to her room under the eaves, but her feet carried her to the ballroom instead. She sat on the piano bench and folded back the lid from the keys. She did not have to see them, which was just as well. Darkness and tears made sight impossible.

She played and sang much more slowly, softly, and sadly than either Mr. Gilbert or Mr. Sullivan had intended.

> *A pallid and thin young man,*
> *A haggard and lank young man,*
> *A greenery-yallery, Grosvenor Gallery,*
> *Foot-in-the-grave young man.*

Grace tried to carry on calmly, as if her beloved city weren't exploding into flames around her. After the fourth artillery salvo from the hill just outside town, she only flinched when the big guns went off. Even so, she found it hard to pack for a journey into uncertainty with the racket of battle growing louder by the hour. What finally caused her to panic was not gunpowder, but a sheet of paper.

She and Lyda sat in her apartment stitching paper *pesos* into the hems of their riding skirts. While she was at it, Grace made a drawstring bag she could hang inside her skirt to hold her most cherished belongings. Now that existence had narrowed to a dash for life, she was struck by how few possessions really mattered.

She included the deed to the Colonial, the daguerreotype of her parents, and a photograph of Rico in his dress uniform. She always wore the locket he had given her, but she put it in the bag to keep it out of sight. Then she realized that her favorite letter was not with the others in the rosewood box on her bureau. She searched frantically through her drawers, sobbing as she threw clothes on the floor.

Lyda tried to calm her. "Gracie, what are you looking for?"

"The letter." She looked under the bed and ransacked the sheets and coverlet.

"What letter?"

"This one." Grace found it under her pillow. She sank to the floor amidst the heap of bed linens and held the paper to her heart. "I thought I had lost it."

"The maids don't miss much, and you know how superstitious they are." Lyda sat next to her and put an arm around her shoulders. "I reckon they noticed that particular letter was important to you and they put it there to make your dreams happy ones. What does it say?"

Grace unfolded it, but she didn't have to read it. She had memorized the poem that Rico recited whenever he returned from duty. One of his British poets had written it.

Thou art my life, my love, my heart,
The very eyes of me;
And hast command of every part,
To live and die for thee.

She got as far as "To live" when a weary bullet wobbled through the open doorway from the balcony. It hit the floor and rolled to a stop at their feet. They both drew their knees up to make themselves as small as possible.

"Shake a leg, ladies," Jake shouted from the bottom of the stairs. "We have a lot to do before sundown."

Grace, Lyda, and Annie packed their valises. María and Socrates stowed silver, china, and other valuables in a crawl space hidden under the eaves. Then Socrates filled jugs from the roof cistern.

Jake trimmed the hooves of the mules and horses and made sure the saddle cinches were sound. He assembled medical supplies and sacks of grain. With this many people needing mounts only two of the mules would be available as pack animals. As members of the household piled their baggage in the lobby he warned Grace and Lyda that forage for the animals took priority. Most of their belongings would have to stay here.

By afternoon the *Zapatistas* ringed the city and a shroud of black smoke draped it. Bullets landing in the courtyard forced Jake to tether the two horses and five mules in the corridors. Annie occupied herself shoveling up what they deposited and cutting armloads of grass from the small park outside the back gate. She and Jake bundled the grass as fodder for the journey.

Socrates offered to hide the cantina's supply of beer, wine, brandy, and champagne, but Grace had a better idea. At twilight, ignoring the distant noise of fighting, she walked outside where *indio* refugees huddled against the buildings surrounding the zócalo. They were preparing to spend another perilous, rainy night in the open with their meager bundles of worldly goods.

The men pulled the broad brims of their hats down to shield their faces. The women wrapped themselves and their babies in their shawls. Their older children slept curled up between them.

Grace invited them all inside. They followed her in a shabby parade and gathered, stoic, sloe-eyed, and silent, in the candle-lit cantina. They accepted the glasses of spirits with such gentle dignity that Grace wondered how they could have come from the same stock as the men slaughtering each other not far away.

Grace asked Annie to tell them they were welcome to spend the night under her roof. As the alcohol took effect they settled down around the walls of the bar and corridor and talked softly among themselves. Someone began to sing a haunting ballad and others joined in.

Jake was not charmed. "Miz Knight, if you allow them to bunk down here they will steal everything."

"No, they will not."

"Do as you wish." Jake shrugged. "We'll be leaving at sunup anyway."

"I've decided to wait one more day." Grace held up a hand to ward off his objections. "Cuernavaca's ravines form a natural entrenchment. Colonel Rodriguez told me his men can easily defend the few roads leading into the city."

A series of explosions left a ringing in Grace's ears, and set the candle flames to dancing. The *indios* glanced up, then went back to singing and making camp for the night. From the big balcony on the second floor, Grace, Lyda, Annie, and Jake saw flames engulfing the area near the army barracks.

"They've blown up the arsenals," said Jake.

"The rebels?"

"The blue-jackets would be my guess, so the rebs can't get their hands on the weapons and ammo. That's what an army does just before hightailing it."

Jake leveled at Grace the azure-steel stare he reserved for wild mustangs, striking oil-field workers, and strong men whom rye whiskey has made contrary. It was a compliment, a recognition that she was tough enough to take it.

"Now do you agree to leave with us at first light, Miz Knight?"

Grace locked cool blue looks with him for several heartbeats.

"I should look the proper fool if I didn't, now wouldn't I, Mr. McGuire?"

"I take it that's Brit for 'yes.'"

"Yes, it is."

56

LOST AND FOUND

Rico knew better than to ride into the middle of what probably would be the biggest battle the state of Morelos had ever hosted. He could not risk traveling the main road to Cuernavaca, but the roundabout route the Mendozas mapped out took much longer than he expected. He also could have made his way along the main road after dark, even in the rain, but not this one. He would be of no use to Grace if he were lying dead at the bottom of a ravine, so he lost more precious time huddled all night in a shallow cave.

As the second day dawned, then the third and the fourth, Rico came to dread every meander and switchback. He cursed each rockfall and downed tree that blocked the way between him and Grace.

The isolation of the back country also made the war seem so remote Rico could almost dare to hope that peace had broken out. Then the high limestone walls of the defile ended abruptly. The world opened up in front of him. He looked out at a soaring dome of blue sky, a scarred valley ringed by pale purple mountains, and hundreds of vultures circling over Cuernavaca in flames. He spurred Mendoza's horse down the slope and into a trot across the valley floor.

The road led straight into the worst of the inferno consuming the ramshackle houses on the outskirts of town. He turned aside and rode in search of a clear route. He found an area untouched by fire, but even there the heat was intense. He waded into a public fountain to soak his clothes and scooped up water in his hat to wet down the horse.

He guided his skittish mount toward the heart of the city, making his way around corpses and piles of rubble. Judging by the damage to almost every building, the artillery fire must have been intense. What disturbed Rico was that, other than sporadic rifle fire and the crackling of flames, the city was eerily quiet. The battle for Cuernavaca must have ended and he had little doubt as to who had won.

Where was Grace?

He found Colonel Rodriguez's body near the Governor's Palace. His lifeless hand still grasped his sword and half a dozen rebels lay dead around him. Rico made the sign of the cross as he passed his old comrade.

He was elated to see that the Colonial looked unharmed and the front gates were closed. As he rode toward them a shot ricocheted off the cobblestones in front of his horse. Judging from its directon and angle it must have come from atop the hotel. He shaded his eyes to look up at the uniformed figure standing on the edge of the roof with his rifle aimed at him.

"Juan!" He took off his hat so his friend could see his face.

"Rico?"

When Juan opened the gates he held a champagne bottle in one hand and his rifle cradled on the other arm. Rico looked beyond the entryway and saw Grullo pulling at banana leaves in the courtyard. When Rico embraced Juan he smelled the alcohol on his breath.

Rico didn't have to ask how Juan had gotten in. All the young officers had used a thick fig vine to climb to a rear balcony after Leobardo locked the Colonial's doors for the night.

"I decided to keep looters away until you arrived." Juan waved the champagne. "Judging by the empty bottles in the cantina, the Colonial's guests must have had a magnificent going-away party."

"How did you know I would come here?"

"Your old friend, Lieutenant Angel, told me you went to the capital in search of your sweetheart. I knew when you discovered that *Señora* Knight was in Cuernavaca, you'd come back. People always come back to the Colonial." He glanced at Grullo. "I persuaded Angel to sell your horse so I could return him to you. Angel drives a hard bargain."

"Thank you." Rico wondered if Juan knew that he himself had

proposed marriage to Lieutenant Angel at Tres Marías more than once. However, now was not the time to discuss it.

"Of course, I will expect half of whatever he earns racing," said Juan. "Where is Grace?"

"I don't know." Juan waved the bottle at the deserted corridors. "Maybe she's gone with the others."

"Where did the others go?"

"What's left of the army and Cuernavaca's citizens are on their way to Toluca."

"Where are the *Zapatistas*?" Rico began to get an excoriating sense that fate wasn't through harassing him yet.

"They've ridden into the mountains to ambush the army and the citizens. You know how exposed the Toluca road is to ambushes. Shooting people there will be like swatting flies on a mule's rump."

Grace felt exposed riding across the valley floor and vulnerable to attack. The burnt sugarcane and refineries, the destroyed haciendas, and abandoned villages added to her melancholy. At least the mountains provided cover and places to hide. She gave a sigh of relief when she reached the far edge of the fields. The terrain became more broken. Trees closed in around her.

Jake rode at the head of the little caravan and he must not have shared her optimism. He loosened his Sharps hunting rifle in its saddle boot and set his pistols at half-cock. Lyda followed Jake, with Annie in front of her on Duke. Grace and María were each mounted on one of Jake's mules ahead of the two pack animals. Socrates and the shotgun brought up the rear on the Colonial's mule.

Many of the families who had spent the night in the Colonial followed Grace's convoy through Cuernavaca's deserted streets before dawn this morning. Maybe they noticed that the army had decamped and so had most of the city's inhabitants. Maybe they thought the gringos' guns and special status would protect them. They traveled on foot, though, and fell farther and farther behind.

The road snaked sharply upward, but at the first wide place with a view, Grace reined the mule around. She stood in the stirrups and looked back across the valley. Cuernavaca continued to burn.

When the rain started, Grace hoped that it would move across the sunny valley and quench the fires, but it formed a visible wall, gray on one side, bright on the other, between her and the city. The squall line seemed content to stay where it was, drenching all of them and making the ground even more treacherous. Grace pulled her hat lower to keep it off her face.

She was about to continue on when she saw two bands of horsemen converge on the ragged line of refugees. They rounded them up like cattle and began driving them back toward the city.

"Lyda, Jake," Grace shouted. "Look what they're doing."

"Bound to happen," said Jake.

"We have to help them."

"There's nothing we can do for them, Gracie." Lyda flipped the reins to get Duke moving forward again. "If they intended to kill them they would have shot them where they stood."

Grace didn't find that consoling.

The road grew steeper and more slippery. The cobblestones in the paved stretches were missing or loose as often as not. Grace concentrated on letting the mule find his own way, but the temptation to pull on his reins and steer him away from the brink was almost more than she could resist. She had learned to trust Moses's instincts on such trails, but although this animal seemed sure-footed, he wasn't Moses.

The angles of the switchbacks grew more acute, and as Grace rounded each turn she could see others fleeing on the road above and ahead of her. Even a wagon bumped along, although its axles came dangerously close to the edge.

The surrounding ledges, outcrops, and overhangs provided perfect places for snipers to hide, but the overcast sky and steady drizzle made it impossible to spot the flash of rifle barrels. Grace ducked reflexively when a shot echoed through the canyon. One of the people toiling along two switchbacks above her fell. Grace watched, as with arms and legs outspread, he went over the edge. His anguished cry grew fainter as he plummeted out of sight.

The next shot hit Jake. He slumped forward to lie along his horse's neck with his arms dangling. Lyda screamed. She slid off Duke and ran to him. Grace was relieved to see him rouse enough to put an arm around her neck. With one hand Lyda helped him stay in the saddle while with the other she grasped the horse's halter to guide him. Annie rode into the lead position to keep an eye out for rock falls or cave-ins.

Grace would not have chosen this place to die, though she wondered what difference it would make if she did. No one and nothing waited for her at the end of this road. She could not bear the thought of her friends dying though.

She was glad to see the surface ahead broaden into a shelf fifty feet wide that ran along the base of a gentle upgrade covered with evergreens. There, the road had room to swerve away from the cliff's edge and everyone speeded their pace to reach it.

The overloaded wagon was already trundling along it when several shots rang out from the slope above. Bullets kicked up the gravel under the hooves of the two mules pulling it. They reared and bolted. The top-heavy cargo shifted, tilting the wagon until it was balanced on the two left wheels. The passenger leaped to safety as the saturated ground gave way under it. The driver was not so lucky.

The wagon rolled onto its side, teetered on the rim of the chasm, then slowly slid off, dragging the mules, secured in their harnesses, with it. The driver slid off the seat, which was now at a ninety-degree angle, and kept falling. Grace was so intent on watching the horrifying acrobatics of the wagon and mule team that she didn't notice the passenger.

Bullets continued to raise geysers around him as he put his head down and charged toward Annie and Duke. Annie screamed when he grabbed Duke's bridle and Grace realized that the man was General Rubio.

She kicked the mule into a trot that shook her hat off, and pulled up alongside Rubio. Socrates had been about to shoot Rubio, but now Grace was in the way.

Shouting at him to let Annie go, Grace beat him with her riding crop. She kept hitting him until he drew his service pistol and pointed it right between her eyes.

"Move away from him, Grace!"

Grace froze. That was Rico's voice.

Ignoring the gun, she turned her head and saw Rico's big gray stallion sliding almost on his rump down the slope above her. Time slowed as she tried to get a grip on this new reality.

Rico was leaning back in the saddle to keep from pitching forward over Grullo's head. He held his rifle in one hand and waved it, gesturing for her to move aside.

She turned back and saw the muzzle of Rubio's pistol inches from her face. Then it swiveled in Rico's direction.

Without conscious thought, Grace slid down from the mule's off-side and hit him on the rump as hard as she could with the riding crop. He bolted forward, knocking Rubio's gun aside. Grace didn't hear the shot that killed Rubio, but she saw the look on his greasy, porcine face as he fell sideways into the mud. A large chunk of wet clay broke off and slid down the face of the cliff. It took Rubio with it.

Rico leaped off Grullo before the horse slid to a stop, and hit the ground running. He lifted Grace and swung her around to safer ground. Oblivious to the steady rain, Grace put her arms around him, leaned against his shoulder, and sobbed. He laid his cheek against her hair and held her so close that they could not have detected where one stopped and the other started.

"I'm here, my heaven. Nothing will part us again."

Neither of them were willing to separate long enough to look up. If they had, they would have seen Angel, Antonio, and José lift their rifles in salute. Antonio's was still warm from the shots he had fired to make Rubio dance, and then the one that killed him. The three of them reined their horses around and vanished over the ridgeline. Their men wheeled and followed. They had a long way to ride to join Lieutenant Angel's father, a general in Pancho Villa's army far to the north.

Two very real women, Rosa King and Angelina Jimenez, inspired the characters of Grace Knight and Angela Sanchez.

In 1905, newly widowed Englishwoman Rosa King came to Cuernavaca from Mexico City to open a tea shop catering to the city's foreign community. The governor convinced her to buy and restore the almost-four-centuries-old ruin of a hacienda's manor house in the heart of the city. Rosa named her hotel the Bella Vista. After the Revolution's decade of warfare, she wrote *Tempest over Mexico,* a compelling memoir of her experiences before, during, and after the fall of Cuernavaca. Little, Brown and Company published her book in 1935.

Angelina Jimenez, who became known as Lieutenant Angel, tells her story in a book called *Those Years of the Revolution: 1910–1920.* It's a collection, in English and in Spanish, of the memories of the Revolution's veterans who fled to California toward the end of the war. Edited by Esther R. Perez and James and Nina Kallas, the book was published in 1974. It contains a photograph of Lieutenant Angel at about age seventy-five.

Rosa King refused to leave her hotel until General Zapata's troops were storming the city. Her descriptions of the Cuernavacans' flight through the mountains are harrowing. She wrote that eight thousand people started out, but only two thousand made it to safety.

Rosa waited out the war as a refugee in Veracruz. She returned to Cuernavaca after hostilities ended with the eventual assassinations of many of the Revolution's leaders. She found her beloved hotel in ruins. She tried to make a new start, but conditions in the devastated city were so dire that even she, as determined as she was, could not manage it.

Lieutenant Angel's experiences were more amazing than Rosa's. After stealing weapons, blowing up a train, and rescuing comrades imprisoned on it, she rode north to join her father. She, her father, and other officers were captured, imprisoned, and sentenced to death when a former ally betrayed them. Angel's account of her perilous escape and flight to safety across the border to El Norte is also a page-turner.

Students of Mexican history may notice that in *Last Train from Cuernavaca* I have engineered the fall of Cuernavaca a year before it happened on August 13, 1914. The city did come under siege and attack by the rebel forces in the summer of 1913, but managed to revive and survive for another year.

Sadly, while dictators Porfirio Díaz and Victoriano Huerta lived in exile, revolutionary leaders Emiliano Zapata, Pancho Villa, and Francisco Madero were murdered. Venustiano Carranza was killed in 1920 by followers of General Álvaro Obregón, who was subsequently elected president. Obregón was a pragmatist who said, "The days of revolutionary banditry have ended because I have brought all the bandits with me to the capital to keep them out of trouble."

Today Cuernavaca is a bustling city built on top of and around those deep, lush ravines known as *barrancas*. A city bus route passes the concrete bridge and steep path to the village of San Anton, the inspiration for San Miguel. Now a suburb of Cuernavaca, San Anton is known to this day for the ancient style of pottery that Rosa King and Grace Knight bought there almost a hundred years ago. The village overlooks two spectacular waterfalls in the gorge below it and the openings to caves are visible in the face of the cliff.

The railroad station, built in 1899 during the regime of Porfirio Díaz, remains standing across the street from the depot where buses arrive from Mexico City, which lies about thirty miles across the ten-thousand-foot-high mountain range. The two volcanoes, Popocatepetl and Iztaccihuatl, keep watch over the valley.

The building that was Rosa King's Bella Vista Hotel still exists across the street from the city's main plaza. It now houses small businesses and doctors' offices, but the courtyard and wide corridors with their elegant arches are in place. The Victorian bandstand graces the zócalo and a band plays concerts there on Sundays.

Cuernavaca has two nicknames: the City of Eternal Spring and the City of Flowers. Even today it is easy to see why Rosa King and Grace Knight loved it.